SLIGHTLY WICKED

"Sympathetic characters and scalding sexual tension make the second installment in [the Slightly series] a truly engrossing read.... Balogh's surefooted story possesses an abundance of character and class."
—*Publishers Weekly*

SLIGHTLY MARRIED

"Intriguing ... [A] whimsical Regency-era romance ... [filled] with homespun humor."
—*Publishers Weekly*

"[A Perfect Ten] ... *Slightly Married* is a masterpiece! Mary Balogh has an unparalleled gift for creating complex, compelling characters who come alive on the pages."
—*Romance Reviews Today*

A SUMMER TO REMEMBER

"Balogh outdoes herself with this romantic romp, crafting a truly seamless plot and peopling it with well-rounded, winning characters."
—*Publishers Weekly*

"The most sensuous romance of the year."
—*Booklist*

"This one will rise to the top."
—*Library Journal*

The Secret Pearl

MARY BALOGH

A DELL BOOK

THE SECRET PEARL
A Dell Book / December 2005

Published by
Bantam Dell
A Division of Random House, Inc.
New York, New York

Dell is a registered trademark of Random House, Inc., and the colophon
is a trademark of Random House, Inc.

ISBN 978-0-440-24297-0

Printed in the United States of America
Published simultaneously in Canada

www.bantamdell.com

OPM 10 9 8 7 6 5 4

For Rita Latham, Mary Balogh, and Erma Gallagher,
my sisters-in-law, with love

Dear Reader,

A large number of you, especially those who have discovered me only recently with the Bedwyn series (the *Slightly* books), have written to ask me when my backlist is going to be available again. I am as delighted as any of you may be that it is happening now with this republication of *The Secret Pearl*. The book has a gorgeous new cover but no changes to either the title or the contents—I know that is important to many of you.

The Secret Pearl is often listed by readers as one of their favorites among my books. I think they are drawn to the wounded hero, who is trapped in a world of barren honor, and to the fugitive heroine, who hides deep wounds of her own. They meet under unhappy circumstances, but despite almost overwhelming odds, passion grows between them as they discover healing in each other—until they find themselves confronted with a classic dilemma, the choice between honor and love. Can they have both—and happiness and each other too? Well, this *is* a love story, and we all know that romance writers will settle for nothing less than happy endings. . . .

For those of you reading this earlier book of mine for the first time, I do hope you will enjoy the story and return for the republication of the *Web* trilogy sometime soon. And for those of you who are reading this for a second or third or twenty-third time, I hope you will like it just as well or even better in this new and lovely packaging.

Happy reading!

Mary Balogh

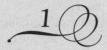

1

THE CROWD OUTSIDE THE DRURY LANE THEATER had dispersed for the night. The last carriage, with its two occupants, was disappearing down the street. Those few theatergoers who had come on foot had long ago set out on their way.

It appeared that only one gentleman was left, a tall man in a dark cloak and hat. He had refused a ride in the last carriage to leave, preferring, he had told his friends, to walk home.

And yet he was not the sole remaining occupant of the street, either. His eyes, as he looked about him, were caught by a figure standing quietly against the building, her cloak a shade lighter than the night shadows—a street prostitute who had been left behind by her more fortunate or alluring peers and who seemed now to have lost all chance of a fashionable customer for the night.

She did not move, and it was impossible to tell in the darkness if she was looking at him. She might have swaggered toward him. She might have moved out of the shadows and smiled at him. She might have hailed him, offered herself in words. She might have hurried away to find a more promising location.

She did none of those things.

And he stood looking at her, wondering whether to begin

the solitary walk home he had planned or whether to engage in an unplanned night of sport. He could not see the woman clearly. He did not know if she was young, enticing, pretty, clean—any of those qualities that might make it worth his while to change his plans.

But there was her quiet stillness, intriguing in itself.

She was looking at him, he saw as he strolled toward her, with eyes that were dark in the shadows. She wore a cloak but no bonnet. Her hair was dressed neatly at the back of her head. It was impossible to tell how old she was or how pretty. She said nothing and did not move. She displayed no wiles, spoke no words of enticement.

He stopped a few feet in front of her. He noted that her head reached to his shoulder—she was slightly above average height—and that she was of slim build.

"You wish for a night's employment?" he asked her.

She nodded almost imperceptibly.

"And your price?"

She hesitated and named a sum. He regarded her in silence for a few moments.

"And the place is close by?"

"I have no place," she said. Her voice was soft, devoid of either the harshness or the cockney accent that he had expected.

He looked at her out of narrowed eyes. He should begin his walk home, make a companion of his own thoughts as he had planned to do. It had never been his way to copulate with a street whore in a shop doorway.

"There is an inn on the next street," he said, and he turned to walk in its direction.

She fell into step beside him. They did not exchange a word. She made no move to take his arm. He did not offer it.

She followed him into the crowded and rowdy taproom of the Bull and Horn and stood quietly at his shoulder as he engaged a room abovestairs for the night and paid for it in advance. She followed him up the stairs, her feet light on the treads so that he half-turned his head before reaching the top to make sure that she was there.

He allowed her to precede him into the room and closed and bolted the door behind him. He set the single candle he had brought up with him in a wall sconce. The noise from the taproom was hardly diminished by distance.

The prostitute was standing in the middle of the room, looking at him. She was young, he saw, though not a girl. She must have been pretty at one time, but now her face was thin and pale, her lips dry and cracked, her brown eyes ringed by dark shadows. Her hair, a dull red in color, was without luster or body. She wore it in a simple knot at the back of her head.

The gentleman removed his top hat and cloak and saw her eyes move over his face and along the ugly scar that began at the corner of his left eye, slashed across his cheek to the corner of his mouth and on down to his chin. He felt all his ugliness, with his near-black unruly hair, his dark eyes, his great aquiline nose. And it angered him to feel ugly in the eyes of a common whore.

He strode across the room, unbuttoned her pale gray cloak, which she had made no move to take off herself, and threw it aside.

Surprisingly, she wore a blue silk dress beneath it, long-sleeved, modestly low at the bosom, high-waisted, unadorned. But the dress, though clean, was limp and creased. A gift from a satisfied customer some weeks before and worn nightly ever since, he guessed.

Her chin lifted an inch. She watched him steadily.

"Take your clothes off," he said, unnerved by her quietness, by her differentness from all the whores he had known in his youth and during his years in the army. He seated himself on a hard-backed chair beside the empty fireplace and watched her with narrowed eyes.

She did not move for a few moments, but then she began to undress, folding each garment as she removed it and setting it on the floor beside her. She was no longer watching him, but kept her eyes on what she was doing. Only when she came to her chemise, her last remaining garment, did she hesitate, her eyes on the floor at her feet. But she removed that too, drawing it up over her head, folding it as she had done her other garments, and dropping it to the top of the pile.

She set her arms loosely at her sides and looked at him again, her eyes steady and expressionless, as they had been before.

She was too thin. Far too thin. And yet there was something about the long slimness of her legs, about the shape of her hips and the too-small waist, about the high firm breasts that stirred the gentleman who watched her. For the first time he was glad of his decision to engage her services. It had been a long time.

"Unpin your hair," he told her.

And she lifted thin arms to do so and bent to set the pins carefully beside the pile of her clothes. Her hair fell over her shoulders and about her face and halfway down her back when she straightened again. Clean, lifeless hair, not red, not blond. She lifted a hand to remove one strand from her mouth, her eyes steady on his.

He felt a surging of lust.

"Lie down on the bed," he told her as he got to his feet and began to undress himself.

She folded the bedclothes back neatly and lay on one side of the bed, her legs together, her arms at her sides, her palms against the mattress. She did not cover herself. She turned her head to one side and watched him.

He undressed completely. He scorned to try to hide himself from a whore, to try to hide the purple and disfiguring marks of the wounds on his left side and left leg, which even in a mirror made him grimace with distaste, and which must repel any stranger not expecting them. Her eyes moved down to them and then returned calmly to his face.

She had courage, this whore. Or perhaps she could not afford to lose even the most repulsive of customers before she had earned her pay.

He was angry. Angry with himself for returning to whoring, something he had given up years before. Angry that he felt self-conscious and ashamed with a prostitute. And angry with her for being so much in control of her feelings that she would not even show her revulsion at his appearance. If she had done so, he could have used her accordingly.

And the thought revolted him and angered him further.

He leaned across her and took her by the upper arms, moving her so that she lay across the bed instead of along it. He grasped her hips and drew her forward until her knees bent over the side of the bed and her feet rested on the floor.

He slid his palms between her thighs and spread her legs wide. He pushed them wider with his knees, bending his legs so that they rested against the side of the bed. And he spread his fingers across the tops of her legs and opened her with his thumbs.

Her eyes were lowered, watching what he did.

He positioned himself and mounted her with one sharp deep thrust.

He heard the sound of shock deep in her throat and watched her bite down on both lips at once and shut her eyes very tightly. He felt all her muscles tense in self-defense. And he waited, standing above her, buried deep in her, watching her with hooded eyes, until the breath came vibrating out of her and she imposed relaxation on her muscles. Her eyes were fixed on his.

He slid his hands beneath her, holding her steady above the mattress as he leaned over her and took the pleasure for which he had employed her. She remained still and relaxed as he moved swiftly and deeply in her, her arms spread across the bed at her sides, her eyes wandering over his facial scar and looking back up into his. Once she looked down to watch what he did to her. Her hair was spread across the mattress to one side of her, where he had moved her across the bed.

He closed his eyes as he released into her, and bowed his head over her until he could feel her breath against his hair. And along with the blessed relaxation he felt the stabbing of a nameless regret.

He straightened up and disengaged himself from her body. He turned away to the washstand opposite the foot of the bed and poured cold water from the pitcher into the cracked bowl, dipped the rag of a cloth into it, squeezed out the excess water, and returned to the bed.

"Here," he said, holding out the cloth to her. She had not moved beyond bringing her legs together. Her feet still rested on the floor. Her eyes were still open. "Clean yourself with this." He glanced down to her bloodstained thighs.

She raised one hand to take the cloth, but it was shaking so out of control that she lowered it to the bed again and turned her head to one side, closing her eyes. He took her hand in his, turned it palm-up, and placed the cloth in it.

"You may dress when you have finished," he said, and he turned his back on her in order to dress himself.

The quiet rustlings behind him told him that she had brought herself under control and was doing as she had been told. And yet when he turned at last, it was to find her trying to do up the three buttons of her cloak with hands that were trembling too badly to accomplish the task. He took the few steps toward her, brushed her hands aside, and did the buttons up for her.

The sheet at the edge of the bed, he could see over her shoulder, was liberally stained with blood. He had ripped her quite effectively.

"When did you last eat?" he asked her.

She straightened her cloak, looking down at it.

"When I ask a question, I expect an answer," he said curtly.

"Two days ago," she said.

"And what did you eat then?"

"Some bread."

"Was it only today you decided to turn to the profession of whore?" he asked.

"No," she said. "Yesterday. But no one wanted me."

"I am not surprised," he said. "You have no idea how to sell yourself."

He took up his hat, unbolted the door, and left the room. She followed him. He paused at the foot of the stairs and looked about the noisy taproom. There was an empty table in a far corner. He turned, took the girl by the elbow, and crossed the room toward it. Any customer who was in his path took one look at him, at his fashionable clothes and harsh, scarred face, and instantly moved to one side.

He seated the girl with her back to the room and took the seat opposite her. He instructed the barmaid, who had followed them to the table and was bobbing curtsies to him, to bring a plate of food and two tankards of ale.

"I am not hungry," the girl said.

"You will eat," he said.

She did not speak again. The barmaid brought a plate on which were a large and steaming meat pie and two thick slices of bread and butter, and he gestured to her to set it before the prostitute.

The gentleman watched the girl eat. It was very obvious that she was ravenous, though she made an effort to eat slowly. She looked about her when her fingers, which still trembled, were covered with crumbs of meat and pastry, but of course it was a common inn and there were no napkins. He handed her a linen handkerchief from his pocket, and she took it after a moment's hesitation and wiped her fingers.

"Thank you," she said.

"What is your name?" he asked.

She finished chewing the bread she had in her mouth. "Fleur," she said eventually.

"Just Fleur?" He was drumming his fingers slowly on the top of the table. He held his tankard of ale in his other hand.

"Just Fleur," she said quietly.

He watched her silently until she had eaten the last crumb on her plate.

"You want more?" he asked her.

"No." She looked up at him hastily. "No, thank you."

"You don't want to finish your ale?"

"No, thank you," she said.

He paid the bill and they left the inn together.

"You said you had no place in which to ply your trade," he said. "Do you have no home?"

"Yes," she said. "I have a room."

"I will escort you there," he said.

"No." She hung back in the doorway of the Bull and Horn.

"How far away do you live?" he asked.

"Not far," she said. "About a mile."

"I will take you three-quarters of a mile, then," he said. "You are an innocent. You do not know what can happen to a woman alone on the streets."

She gave a harsh little laugh. And she hurried along the street, her head down. He walked beside her, experiencing for the first time in his life, though only at second hand, all the despair of poverty, knowing that his own problems, his own reasons for unhappiness, were laughable in comparison with those of this girl, London's newest whore.

"Please do not come any farther," she said at last, stopping at a corner outside a dingy shop that advertised itself as an employment agency.

"You cannot find employment?" he asked her.

"No," she said.

"You have tried?"

She looked up at him with that little laugh again. "Do you think that this is anything but a very last resort?" she said. "It is hard to persuade oneself to starve to death when there is one last thing to sell."

She turned and would have hurried away. His voice stopped her.

"Have you not forgotten something?" he asked.

She looked back at him.

"I have not paid you," he said.

"You bought me a meal," she said.

"A meat pie, two slices of bread, and half a tankard of ale in exchange for your virginity," he said. "Was it a fair bargain?"

She said nothing.

"A word of advice," he said, taking her hand in his and closing her fingers about some coins. "Don't undersell yourself. The price you asked would invite only contempt and rough treatment. The treatment I gave you, by the way, was not rough. Your price should be triple what you asked. The higher your price, the more respect you will command."

She looked down at her closed hand, turned, and walked away without another word.

The gentleman stood and looked broodingly after her before turning and striding toward more fashionable and more familiar streets.

ISABELLA FLEUR BRADSHAW DID NOT leave her room the next day. Indeed, she did not even leave her bed for much of it, but lay staring listlessly up at the water-stained ceiling or at the dull brown walls from which age-old paint gave evidence of its existence only in a few dirty flakes. She wore only her chemise. Her silk dress, her only dress, was draped carefully over the broken back of the lone chair in the room.

For the first time in her life that day she touched despair and did not have either the will or the energy to pull herself free of it. She had been close before during the past month, but by sheer willpower she had clung to hope, to a dogged determination to survive.

Sally, the seamstress's assistant who lived upstairs, knocked on her door at midday, as she often did. But Fleur did not answer. The girl would want to talk, and she would want to share her own meager meal. Fleur did not want either the company or the kind charity.

She had survived. She would survive—perhaps. But she had discovered that survival after all was not necessarily a triumphant thing, but could take one into the frightening depths of despair.

She bled intermittently through the day. She was so sore that sometimes she squirmed against the sharp pain of her torn virginity.

And that was not the end. It was merely the beginning. Her first customer had paid her handsomely—three times the sum she had asked for in addition to the meal. The money would pay her overdue rent and keep her in food for a few days besides. But then she would have to go out again to pursue her new profession.

She was a whore. She shut out the sight of the ceiling, closing her eyes wearily. No longer was she contemplating becoming one with horror and the fading hope that she might somehow avoid the inevitable, believing in her heart of hearts that something would come along to save her.

She was a whore. She had agreed to be hired by a gentleman, walked to an inn with him, removed all her clothes at his command while he watched, lain naked on the bed at his bidding, watched him strip away all his clothes, and then allowed him to open her up and take his masculine pleasure in the most secret depths of her body. She had given her body for his use and taken his money in payment.

She quite ruthlessly enumerated in her mind all the stages by which she had entered the profession that would be hers until she was too old and ugly and diseased to attract even the meanest customer. Or until something even worse happened.

She was a member of a profession the very thought of which had always horrified and disgusted her.

She was a whore. A prostitute. A streetwalker.

She swallowed repeatedly and determinedly until the urge to vomit receded.

Soon, within a week, she would be standing outside the theater again, hoping to attract another customer, dreading success.

He had not been rough with her, the dark and frightening gentleman who had been her first customer had told her the night before. Heaven help her if any man ever did subject her to rough treatment. She felt hot and clammy with terror again at the memory of his hands—long-fingered, well-manicured, beautiful hands—pushing her thighs apart, of his knees pinning them wide, of his thumbs touching her *there*, spreading her, and of the sight and feel of that other part of him huge and hard against the tender inner flesh and then ripping swiftly and deeply into her so that she had thought she would die of the shock and the pain—and had hoped she would.

The mental images came, unbidden and unwelcome: the terrible scarred and discolored and puckered wounds on his side and leg; the terrifyingly powerful muscles of his chest and shoulders and arms, the triangle of dark hair across the expanse of his chest and tapering to below his navel; his angular hawkish face with the direct and fierce dark eyes, the prominent nose, and the disfiguring scar; his hands, touching her, cupping her buttocks, holding her steady so that she could not shrink from the full force and depth of his thrusts.

She did not have either the energy or the will to shake off the memories. And there was no point anyway in trying to relegate them to memory. It was to be her profession to allow such men the use of her body in exchange for the means of survival. She must deliberately remember, accustom herself to the memories, learn to accept the same and perhaps worse—if there could be worse—from other men.

It was a fair exchange, was it not? For it was not just the choice between survival and death that she must make, but the choice between survival and a slow and painful death through starvation. Never, even during this day of blackest despair, had she considered suicide as an escape from her predicament.

It was no choice, then, that she had to make. She had to feed herself in the only way that was left to her. There was no other employment to be had. She had no experience and no references. Miss Fleming at the employment agency had told her that on numerous occasions. One did not need either in order to become a whore, only a reasonably young and well-formed woman's body. And a strong stomach.

She was a whore. She had sold her body once and would continue to do so over and over again until there were no more buyers. She must accustom herself to both the thought and the deed.

And indeed she must count herself happy if she was allowed to live out her life as a whore. There was always the chance of something even worse and more terrifying if she were found. She had changed her name, and her earlier and constant terror had paled in comparison with the very real fear of a life lived in totally unfamiliar surroundings and on the brink of starvation. But she must not become complacent. There was always the chance of being found, especially if she must stand outside the Drury Lane Theater every night and be seen by all the fashionable people of London.

What if Matthew had come to London? And Cousin Caroline and Amelia had come there even before she came.

When Sally knocked on her door later in the evening and called her name through the lock, Fleur stared at the ceiling and made no reply.

• • •

ADAM KENT, DUKE OF RIDGEWAY, leaned one elbow on the marble mantel in the study of his town house on Hanover Square and tapped his teeth with one knuckle.

"Well?" His dark eyes narrowed on his secretary, who had just entered both the house and the room.

The man shook his head. "No luck, I'm afraid, your grace," he said. "It is too little to go on, to know just a girl's first name."

"But it is an unusual name, Houghton," the duke said. "You knocked on every door?"

"Along three streets and around three courts," Peter Houghton said, making an effort to hide his exasperation. "Perhaps she gave you a false name, anyway, your grace."

"Perhaps," the duke agreed. He frowned in thought. Would she be outside the theater again that night? That employment agency—did she ever go there looking for work? And would she look for other work now that she had chosen and entered a new profession? Perhaps she did not live in that part of London at all. And perhaps she *had* given a false name. She had not answered his question immediately.

"Life will be less arduous for you during the next few days," he said with sudden decision. "You are going to hire a new servant for me. In any capacity you think suitable, Houghton. Perhaps as a governess. Yes, I think as a governess if you find her capable of filling the post. I have the feeling she might be suitable. There is an agency close to the streets you were combing today."

"As a governess?" The secretary frowned at him.

"For my daughter," the duke said. "She is five years old. It is time she had more than a nurse despite her grace's reluctance to have her begin her schooling."

Peter Houghton coughed. "Pardon me, your grace," he said, "but I understood that the girl is a whore. Should she be allowed within ten miles of Lady Pamela?"

The duke did not reply, and the secretary, who understood the look on his employer's face very well, was reminded that he was merely a lowly employee in the service of one of the richest noblemen of the realm.

"You will sit at the agency for the next few days," the duke said, "until I tell you you need no longer do so. In the meanwhile, I shall become a regular theatergoer."

Houghton bowed and the duke pushed himself abruptly away from the mantel and left the room without another word. He took the stairs to his private apartments two at a time.

"Every whore was a virgin once." The poet William Blake had written that somewhere, or words to that effect. There was no reason to feel any special guilt over being the deflowerer. Someone had to do it once the girl had chosen her course. If he had been her second customer instead of the first, he would not have known the difference and would have forgotten about her by that morning. She had had no skill, no allure, nothing that would make him wish to find her again.

He had not realized that a woman would bleed so much. And he had seen and felt her pain as he tore through her virginity.

If he had known, he could have done it differently. He could have readied her, gentled her, entered her slowly and carefully, nudging through the painful barrier. As it was, he had been angry with both her and himself. He had wanted to degrade them both, he supposed, standing over her, imposing his mastery on her.

But then, he owed her no consideration. She had been quite freely selling, he buying. She had been paid three times what she had asked. He had been left quite dissatisfied beyond the momentary relief that had come with the release of his seed. He had no reason to feel guilt.

Yet all night and all day he had been unable to shake his mind free of the girl—her thin body, her pale complexion, her dark-circled eyes and cracked lips, her calm courage. He had been unable to rid himself of the knowledge that poverty and desperation had driven her to the life of the commonest of street prostitutes.

He could not help feeling responsible. He could not forget the calm acceptance, the blood.

He wondered if he would ever find her again. And he wondered for how long he would keep trying, the Duke of Ridgeway in search of a street whore with large calm eyes and refined manners and voice.

Fleur. Just Fleur, she had said.

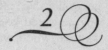

*M*ISS FLEMING, WHO OWNED AND RAN THE EM- ployment agency close to where Fleur lived, had always treated Fleur with an air of hauteur and condescension. Her nasal voice had always drawled as if with boredom. What proof could Miss Hamilton give, she had always asked, that she would make a competent lady's companion or shopgirl or scullery maid or anything else? Without someone to recommend her there was really no way Miss Fleming could be expected to put her own reputation on the line by sending her to be interviewed by a prospective employer.

"But how can I gain a recommendation until I have had some experience?" Fleur had asked her once. "And how can I gain experience unless someone will take a chance on me?"

"Do you know a physician who could speak for you?" Miss Fleming had asked. "A solicitor? A clergyman?"

Fleur had thought of Daniel and felt a stab of pain. Daniel would give her a recommendation. He had been willing for her to open a village school with his sister. He had been willing to marry her. But he was far away in Wiltshire. Besides, he would no longer be willing either to marry her or to employ her or recommend her for employment, not after what had happened there and after she had fled.

"No," she had said.

It was only her despair that drove her back to the agency five days after she had become a whore. She felt no real hope as she opened the door and stepped inside. But she knew that that night she was going to have to return to the Drury Lane Theater or somewhere else where fashionable gentlemen congregated and would be in search of a night's pleasure. Her money was gone.

The bleeding had stopped and the soreness had healed. But her disgust and terror at what had been done to her body had grown by leaps and bounds so that she felt almost constantly nauseated. She wondered if she would ever become accustomed to the life of a whore, if she would ever be able to treat her work as simply that. Probably, she thought, it would have been better if she had gone out the very night after that first, soreness and all, and not given the terror a chance to impose its grip on her.

"Do you have any employment suitable for me, ma'am?" she asked Miss Fleming, her voice quiet, her eyes steady and calm—she had trained herself through a difficult childhood and girlhood never to show any of the pain or degradation she might be feeling.

Miss Fleming looked up at her impatiently and seemed about to make the usual retort. But her eyes sharpened and she frowned. Then she adjusted her spectacles on her nose and smiled condescendingly. "Well, there is a gentleman in the next room, Miss Hamilton, conducting interviews for the post of governess to his employer's daughter. Perhaps he will be willing to ask you a few questions, even though you are a young lady who has no letters of recommendation and who knows no one with any influence. Wait here, if you please."

Fleur found herself clasping her hands painfully together, her nails digging into her palms. She felt breathless, as if she had run for a whole mile. A governess. Oh, no. She must not even begin to hope. The man would probably not consent even to see her.

"Step this way, if you please, Miss Hamilton," Miss Fleming said briskly from the doorway of the adjoining room. "Mr. Houghton will see you."

Fleur was very aware of her wrinkled silk dress and drab cloak and the absence of a bonnet. She was dressed in the clothes she had been wearing more than a month before when she had run away. She was aware of the plain style of her hair, of the shadows below her eyes, of her cracked lips. She swallowed and stepped through the door. Miss Fleming closed it quietly behind her, remaining on the other side of it.

"Miss Fleur Hamilton?" The man who was seated behind a large table examined her slowly and keenly from head to foot.

Fleur stood still and looked back. He was young, bald-headed, thin. If her appearance was unacceptable, then let him tell her so now before her hopes soared despite herself.

"Yes, sir," she said.

He gestured to a chair, and she sat, her back straight, her chin high.

"I am interviewing for the post of governess," he said. "My employer is Mr. Kent of Dorsetshire. His daughter is five years old. Do you consider yourself in any way qualified for the job?"

"Yes," she said. "I was educated at home until I was eleven and then at Broadridge School in Oxfordshire. I was proficient in all my lessons. I speak French and Italian tolerably well, I play the pianoforte and have some skill with watercolors. I have always been particularly interested in literature and history and the classics. I have some skill with a needle."

She answered his questions as clearly and as honestly as she could, the blood hammering through her temples, her hands clasped into fists in her lap, the fingers of both hands crossed out of his sight.

Please, God, she prayed silently. *Oh, please, dear God.*

"If I were to communicate with your former school, the headmistress would confirm what you have told me?" he asked.

"Yes, sir," she said. "I am sure of it." *But please don't. They would not recognize the name. They would deny that I was ever there.*

"Would you tell me something of your family and background, Miss Hamilton?" Mr. Houghton asked her at last.

She stared at him and swallowed. "My father was a gentleman," she said. "He died in debt. I was forced to come to London in search of employment."

Forgive me, Papa, she begged her dead father silently.

"What?" she said.

"How long ago?" he repeated. "How long ago did you come to London?"

"A little over a month ago," she said.

"What employment have you had since?" he asked.

She was silent for a while, staring at him. "I had enough money to last until now," she said.

She sat still while his eyes moved over the unsuitable silk dress beneath her cloak. He knew. He must know. How could she have lived through all the pain and degradation of the past week and keep it all invisible to the eyes of strangers? He must know that she lied. He must know that she was a whore.

"Recommendations?" he asked. "Do you have any letters with you?"

She had known it was cruel, this hope. She had not really hoped at all. "I have none, sir," she said. "I have never been employed. I have lived as a gentleman's daughter." And she waited quietly for dismissal.

But hope had been cruelly kindled. *Please, God,* she prayed. *Please, dear God. Oh, please.*

And she wished she had not come. She wished there had not been this illusory hope.

"What?" she said again.

"The post is yours if you wish for it," he repeated.

She stared at him. "Will Mr. Kent not wish to speak with me first?" she asked.

"He trusts my judgment," Mr. Houghton said.

"And Mrs. Kent?" she asked. "Will she not wish to interview me?"

"Mrs. Kent is in Dorsetshire with the child," the man said. "Do you want the post, Miss Hamilton?"

"Yes," she said, one fingernail finally cutting through the flesh of her palm. "Oh, yes. Please."

"I will need your full name and address," he said, drawing paper toward him, picking up a quill pen and dipping it in the inkwell, his manner brisk and businesslike. "I will deliver to you within the next few days a ticket for the stage into Dorsetshire and will arrange to have you met at the town of Wollaston and taken to Willoughby Hall, Mr. Kent's home. In the meanwhile, I have been empowered to pay you some money in advance so that you may purchase clothes suitable for a governess." His eyes lifted and ran over her again.

She sat numbly listening to the impossible, the unbelievable. She was going to be a governess. She was to live in the country and have charge of the education of a five-year-old child. She was being handed enough money to buy herself some decent dresses and bonnets and shoes. She was to live with a respectable family in a respectable home.

What would Mr. Houghton say, she wondered, how would he look at her, if he knew the truth about her? What would happen if he ever did find out? Or if Mr. and Mrs. Kent ever found out? How would they feel if they knew that their man of business was employing a whore to teach their child?

"No," she said, rising from her chair as Mr. Houghton stood at his side of the table, "I have no questions, sir."

"I shall bring your stagecoach ticket within the next few days, then, Miss Hamilton," he said, inclining his head dismissively to her. "Good day to you, ma'am."

She left the room and the agency in a daze, hardly noticing Miss Fleming, who nodded to her graciously as she passed.

Inside the inner room, Peter Houghton pursed his lips and

stared at the closed door through which his master's ladybird had just passed.

He could not see the attraction. The girl was thin and pale, with unremarkable features and reddish hair that lacked luster. When she had some weight on her, perhaps she would have a pretty-enough figure. But when all was said and done, she was but a whore whom his master had picked up outside the Drury Lane a few nights before.

He had never known his employer to house a mistress even in London. And yet this girl was not to be set up discreetly in a town house of her own, where she could be visited and enjoyed at the duke's leisure. She was to be sent to Willoughby, housed under the same roof as the duke's wife and daughter. She was to be the daughter's governess.

His grace was a strange man. Peter Houghton respected his master and valued the employment, but still there was something strange about the man. The duchess was ten times lovelier than the ladybird.

Wife and mistress under the same roof. Life could turn interesting. Presumably his grace would soon decide that a return to the country and domestic bliss would be in order.

Peter Houghton smiled slightly and shook his head. One thing was certain, anyway. He would be delighted to be free of this room and Miss Fleming's simpering and flirtatious smiles after four whole days of waiting for thin, red-haired Fleur to put in an appearance.

FLEUR LEFT LONDON ON the stage six days later, having had one more brief meeting with Mr. Houghton. She took with her a trunk of modest size in which were folded neatly her blue silk dress and gray cloak as well as several plain but serviceable new clothes and accessories.

It was a long and an uncomfortable journey, in which more often than not she was squashed between large and irritable and unwashed passengers. But she would not complain, even in the privacy of her own mind. The alternatives were all too real to her.

If she were not on this journey, she would be living in her little hole of a room by day and plying her trade as a whore by night. By now she would have experienced several different customers, and perhaps she would have discovered the truth of what her first had told her. Perhaps it would have been possible for other men to treat her more roughly. And perhaps they would have paid her less, so that she would have been forced to work every night.

No, she would not complain. If only Mr. and Mrs. Kent did not discover the truth about her. But how could they? Only one man on earth knew the truth, and she would never see him again, though he would live in her nightmares for the rest of her life.

Of course, there was another truth for Mr. and Mrs. Kent to discover too. And once London and its terrors were left behind, she was reminded more strongly of it again and found herself looking nervously about her for she knew not what.

She saw Hobson's dead face more often in her mind once she was back in open countryside, the eyes staring, the jaw dropped open, the face ashen and surprised. She was amazed it had not haunted her dreams more than it had during the past seven weeks. But of course there had been the even greater terror of surviving in the slums of London.

It haunted her waking dreams now.

She had killed him. As well as a whore, she was a murderer. What would these people in the stage do or say if they knew who she was or what she was? There was something almost hilarious in the thought. Horrifyingly hilarious.

"What's the joke, ducks?" a buxom woman carrying a basket almost as large as herself asked from the seat opposite.

Fleur sobered instantly. "I was just thinking how we might

all be bounced to a jelly by the time we cross this particular stretch of road," she said, and smiled.

It was a fortunate answer. All the inside passengers brightened as they aired their grievances against the parish responsible for the repair of that stretch of the highway over which they were passing.

No, she was not a murderer. She must not put that label on herself. She had pushed him and he had fallen and caught his head on the corner of the hearth and been killed. It had been an accident. She had been defending herself. He had been going to hold her at Matthew's signal. She had been struggling to free herself.

Matthew had used the word "murder" after examining the body. It was that word and the shock of seeing the chalky dead face that had sent her fleeing blindly instead of continuing with the plans she had made.

She tried not to think of it. Perhaps there had never been any pursuit. Perhaps, after all, Matthew had explained it as an accident. And even if there had been pursuit, perhaps it had been called off by now. Or perhaps she would never be found. It had all happened seven weeks before. But she had felt safer in London.

She half-smiled again. Safer!

She tried to picture little Miss Kent in her mind, and the child's mama and papa. She placed them mentally in a cozy manor, a close-knit family group held together by love—rather like her own parents and herself as a young child. She tried to picture herself being drawn into the group, being treated almost as one of the family.

She would make up to them for the great deception she was perpetrating against them. She had not answered Mr. Houghton's question honestly. When he had asked how she had been employed since her arrival in London, she had pretended that she had had enough money with which to keep herself. She had not told him of the only employment she had found.

But she would put it behind her. No one need ever know. The only person she would ever feel obliged to tell was a future husband, and she did not imagine that she would ever wish to marry. Not now. She thought briefly of Daniel, but pushed the image of his kindly smile and blond hair and clerical garb from her mind. If circumstances had been different, she might have married Daniel and been happy with him for the rest of her life. She had loved him.

But circumstances were not different. There could be no going back to him now, even if she could suddenly hear that Matthew had not called that death murder. There could be no going back. For now she was a fallen woman. She closed her eyes with brief regret and opened them in order to study the scenery that was bouncing past the windows of the carriage— or past which they were bouncing, to express the matter more accurately.

She was beginning a new life, and she must be forever grateful that it had been made possible for her, that she had called at Miss Fleming's agency during the precise hour when Mr. Houghton was there to conduct interviews. She could wish and wish that he had appeared there just five days earlier, but he had not, and that was that. She would not be ungrateful for the gift of a new life and a fresh start. She would show her gratitude by being the very best governess that a family had ever had.

MATTHEW BRADSHAW, LORD BROCKLEHURST, had taken bachelor rooms on St. James's Street during his stay in London, preferring not to take up residence with his mother and sister during all the bustle of a London Season, though he did call on them with the news, which did not surprise her in the least, his mother had said arctically. She had always known that Isabella would come to no good.

He did not at first anticipate that his stay would be a long one. Isabella had thoroughly frightened herself and disappeared from the neighborhood of their home in Wiltshire. She had not even run to the Reverend Booth, he had discovered when he had pursued her to the parsonage. She must have come to London. It was the only possible destination she could have chosen. She would have thrown herself on the mercy of his mother or of some acquaintance, though she could not have many in town. She had not been from home a great deal during her life except for the five years when his mother had insisted on sending her away to school to be rid of her.

He had found no trace of her, though he had searched for more than a month and made endless inquiries. And of course she had not run to his mother. It was stupid of him to have expected it.

Finally he had been driven to desperate measures. The stocky, red-faced man standing feet astride in his parlor two mornings after Fleur left London, his cravat none too clean, his greasy-looking hat turning and turning in his hands, was a member of the Bow Street Runners. The two of them had been talking for some time.

"That's what will have happened, sir, mark my words," Mr. Henry Snedburg assured him. He had refused to be seated, explaining that his time was a valuable commodity. "She will be hiding in the poorer quarters and looking for employment."

"The search will be hopeless, then," Lord Brocklehurst said. "The proverbial needle in a haystack."

"No, no." The Runner raised a hand to scratch the back of a large red neck. "I would not say that, sir. There are agencies. As a lady, she would have thought to try one or more of those. All I need is a list, which I daresay I have filed away somewhere, and off I go. Wanted for murder, you say, sir?"

"And attempted theft," Lord Brocklehurst said. "She tried to run off with the family jewels."

"Ah," Mr. Snedburg said, "a nasty piece of work she is, then, sir. I will begin my search without any delay at all and with all caution. She will be a desperate young lady. We will have her in a twinkling, you may be sure. What names might she assume, may I ask?"

Lord Brocklehurst frowned. "You think she will have changed her name?" he asked.

"If she has a modicum of sense, she will, sir," Mr. Snedburg said. "But I find that people rarely fabricate a wholly new name. You give me her full name, sir, and her mother's name, and the names of some of the servants at your home and those of some of the young lady's friends and acquaintances."

Lord Brocklehurst frowned in thought. "Her full name is Isabella Fleur Bradshaw," he said. "Her mother's name was Laura Maxwell, her personal maid's, Annie Rowe, her closest friend's, Miriam Booth."

"Your housekeeper's, sir?"

"Phyllis Matheson."

"The girl's grandmothers?"

Lord Brocklehurst thought. "Hamilton on the father's side," he said. "Lenora, I believe. I don't know about the mother's side."

"Your butler?"

"Chapman."

"I'll try these, sir," Mr. Snedburg said finally. "I'll come up with something. I don't doubt. Now, I need a description of the young lady."

"Somewhat above average height," Lord Brocklehurst said. "Slender. Brown eyes. Red-gold hair."

"Her crowning glory, would you say, sir?" the Runner asked, eyeing his client closely.

"Yes." Lord Brocklehurst gazed sightlessly across the room.

"Her crowning glory. Like the sunshine and the sunset all tangled up together."

Mr. Snedburg coughed. "Exactly, sir," he said. "A beauty, then, you would say?"

"Oh, yes." The other looked back to him. "A beauty, indeed. I want her found."

"As a justice of the peace, I understand, sir," the Runner said. "Because, despite the fact that she is your cousin, she must stand trial for the murder of your personal servant."

"Yes, for that reason," Lord Brocklehurst said, his hands opening and closing at his sides. "Find her."

Mr. Snedburg executed an inelegant bow and strode from the room without further ado.

"MISS HAMILTON?"

Fleur turned in some surprise to the young man in smart blue livery who questioned her as she descended from the stage in Wollaston. "Yes," she said.

"Ned Driscoll, ma'am," he said, "come to fetch you to the Hall. Which are your trunks, ma'am?"

"Just that one," Fleur said, pointing.

The young man was dressed very smartly indeed. And he hoisted her trunk to his shoulder as if it weighed no more than a feather and strode across the cobbled yard of the inn where the stage had stopped toward a closed carriage with a coat of arms painted on the side panel.

A cozy manor? A small family group?

"You are Mr. Kent's servant?" she asked the groom, following him. "This is his carriage?"

He turned to grin at her in some amusement. "Mr. Kent?" he said. "He had better not hear you call him that, ma'am. He's 'his grace' to the likes of you and me."

"His grace?" Fleur felt rather as if her knees were turning to jelly beneath her.

"His grace, the Duke of Ridgeway," the groom said, looking at her curiously. "Didn't you know?" He strapped her trunk securely to the back of the carriage.

"The Duke of Ridgeway? There must be some mistake. I was hired as governess to the daughter of a Mr. and Mrs. Kent," Fleur said.

"Lady Pamela Kent, ma'am," the groom said, extending a hand to help her into the carriage. "Mr. Houghton was it who hired you? His grace's personal secretary. He must have been having a joke with you."

A joke. Fleur sat in the carriage while the groom climbed to the box, and closed her eyes briefly. Her employer was the Duke of Ridgeway? She had heard of him. He was reputed to be one of the wealthiest peers of the land. Matthew had known his half-brother, Lord Thomas Kent. Kent! She had not even noticed that it was the same name.

She should have done. She should have been very much more on her guard. Matthew knew her employer's brother! But she had never met the man herself. And he would not recognize her or know her name now that she had changed it. She must not start jumping at shadows.

Willoughby Hall. Mr. Houghton had given that name as the home of her employer. But the mind is a strange thing. She had conceived such a strong and early mental impression of the Kent family that she had instantly visualized a modest manor. But she knew of Willoughby. It was one of the largest estates in England and was reputed to have one of the most magnificent mansions and parks in the country, besides.

And then, long before her mind had adjusted itself to the new facts of her existence, the carriage was traveling past a high park wall dotted with mosses and lichens and overhung with ivy, and turning to pass between massive stone gateposts onto a winding avenue lined with lime trees.

She could see rolling lawns dotted with oak and chestnut trees to either side. She even had a momentary glimpse of a group of grazing deer. Then the carriage rumbled over a bridge and she spotted rushing cascades passing below it. But even as she turned her head to get a better look, her attention was distracted.

The lime trees did not stretch beyond the bridge. Open and rolling lawns did nothing to obstruct the view of a mansion whose magnificence made the breath catch in Fleur's throat.

The house had a long front, its low wings extending to either side of a high pedimented central section, its columns of exquisite fluted Corinthian design. A great central lantern and dome rose behind the pediment. The parapets were lined with stone statues, busts, vases, and urns.

A great marble fountain before the house played among clipped hedges and terraces of flowers and greenery.

She had thought Heron House, her own home—Matthew's home—quite splendid. It would seem little more than a rustic cottage if set against this.

So much for her cozy manor and small, close-knit family group, Fleur thought, resting her head briefly against the cushions behind her as the carriage drew up before the marble horseshoe steps leading up to the main doors and the *piano nobile*, the main floor.

But it was the double doors below the steps that opened to admit her, the doors leading to the servants' quarters. Mrs. Laycock, the housekeeper, would be pleased to receive Miss Hamilton in her private sitting room, a servant informed her with a half-bow before turning to lead the way.

Mrs. Laycock looked rather like a duchess herself, Fleur thought, her slim figure clad simply yet elegantly in black, her silver hair dressed smartly on top of her head. Only the bunch of keys at her waist proclaimed her status as a servant.

"Miss Hamilton?" she said, extending a hand to Fleur. "Welcome to Willoughby Hall. It must have been a long and tedious journey all the way from London. Mr. Houghton informed us that you would be arriving today. I am pleased that his grace has seen fit to employ a governess for Lady Pamela. It is time she had more stimulation for the mind and more activity than an elderly nurse can provide."

Fleur set her hand in the housekeeper's and received a firm handshake. "Thank you, ma'am," she said. "I shall do my best to teach the child well."

"It will not be easy," Mrs. Laycock said, motioning Fleur to a chair. "May I pour you some tea, Miss Hamilton? I can see you are weary. You will have the duchess to contend with."

Fleur looked her inquiry.

"Armitage, her grace's personal maid, has confided to me that the duchess is not pleased with his grace's sending a governess without even consulting her," the housekeeper said, pouring a cup of tea and handing it to Fleur.

"Oh, dear," Fleur said.

"But you are not to worry," Mrs. Laycock said. "It is the duke who is master here, and his grace has seen fit to look to the future of his daughter. Now, Miss Hamilton, tell me something about yourself. You and I will get along well together, I believe."

3

PETER HOUGHTON, SORTING THROUGH THE DUKE of Ridgeway's post and setting aside invitations that he thought his master might wish to accept, knew that the duke was in a bad mood as soon as he entered the house and even before he came into the study. There was a certain tone to his voice, even when one could not hear the exact words, that betrayed his mood.

And his grace was limping slightly, the secretary saw, getting to his feet as the duke entered the room and sinking back into his chair again when the latter waved an impatient hand. Normally his grace went to great pains not to limp.

"Anything of importance?" he asked, nodding in the direction of the pile of mail.

"An invitation to dine with his majesty," Houghton said.

"Prinny? Make my excuses," the duke said.

"It is a royal summons to dinner and cards," the secretary said with a cough.

"Yes, I understand," the duke said. "Make my excuses. Is there anything from my wife?"

"Nothing, your grace," Houghton said, looking down at the pile.

"We will be leaving for Willoughby," his grace said curtly. "Let me see. I have promised to accompany the Denningtons to the opera tomorrow evening in order to escort their niece. There is nothing else that cannot be canceled, is there? We will leave the day after tomorrow."

"Yes, your grace." Peter Houghton smiled to himself as his employer strode from the room. It was two weeks to the day since the ladybird had been sent on her way by the stage. The duke had shown great fortitude in waiting that long before finding an excuse to go in pursuit.

The Duke of Ridgeway took the stairs two at a time, as he usually did, despite the fact that his leg and side were aching. He rubbed absently at his left eye and cheek. It was the damp weather. The old wounds always acted up when the weather turned for the worse.

Confound Sybil! She had consistently refused to accompany him to London since the time four years before when he had been forced to confront her and put an end to the wildest of her indiscretions. And yet it seemed that almost every time he had settled in London alone for a few months of peace, she had decided to organize a large country party, inviting every disreputable member of the *ton*, male and female, who could be persuaded to leave London for Dorsetshire.

Very rarely did she think it necessary to inform him of her plans. He was left to find out—if he found out at all—by accident. On one occasion two years before he had not known until he returned home to find that all the guests had been and left again except for one straggler. And that straggler had been kind enough to do the chambermaids a favor by vacating his own guest bedchamber in order to share that of the duchess.

The duke had sent that particular gentleman on his way within an hour of his return, and the man seemed to have taken to heart the advice not to show his face either at Willoughby or in London for at least the next ten years.

And he had given his duchess a tongue-lashing about propriety before the servants and those dependent upon them that had finally turned her pale and reduced her to tears. Sybil always looked more beautiful than usual when in tears. And she had accused him of hard-heartedness, neglect, tyranny— all the old charges.

This time his grace had learned of Sybil's party from Sir Hector Chesterton at White's. The man had seemed pleased by his invitation as he creaked inside his stays and wheezed for breath.

"There's nothing much to do in town these days, old chap," he had said, "except ogle the young things. And their mamas cling to them like leeches so that all one can do is ogle. Decent of Sybil to invite me."

"Yes." The duke had smiled arctically. "She likes to surround herself with company."

And so he must return to Willoughby himself, many weeks before he had planned to do so. He pulled the bell rope in his dressing room and shrugged out of his coat while he waited for his valet to arrive. For the sake of his servants and for Pamela's sake, he must return. It would not be fair to allow them all to be witnesses to the debaucheries of Sybil and her friends.

God! He pulled at his neckcloth and tossed it aside. He had loved her. Once upon a time, an eternity ago, he had loved her. Sweet, fragile, blond and beautiful Sybil. He had dreamed of her, ached for her all the time he was in Belgium waiting for the battle that had become the Battle of Waterloo. He had lived on the memory of her bright smiles, her sweet protestations of love, her shy acceptance of his marriage proposal, her warm maiden's kisses.

God! He pulled at the top button of his shirt and watched it sail across the room and tinkle against the china bowl on the washstand.

"Get someone to sew these infernal buttons on firmly," he barked at his valet, who had the misfortune to come through the door at that moment.

But his valet had been with him from boyhood, and accompanied him to war and been his personal servant in Spain and in Belgium. He was made of stern stuff.

"The leg and side are aching, are they, sir?" he said cheerfully. "I thought they would in this weather. Lie down and let me massage them."

"How will that keep the buttons on my shirts, confound you?" the duke said.

"It will, sir, take my word on it," the valet said. "Lie down, now."

"I want my riding clothes," the duke said. "I am going for a gallop in the park."

"After I massage you," his man said like a nurse talking to a child. "Going back to Willoughby, are we, sir?"

"Houghton has been spreading the glad tidings, has he?" his grace said, stretching out obediently on a couch in the dressing room and allowing his valet to remove his clothing and set to work with his strong and expert hands, which never failed to ease the aching. "Will you be glad to be home, Sidney?"

"That I will," his man said firmly. "And you too, sir, if you will but admit it. Willoughby was always your favorite place in the whole world."

Yes. It had been. He had grown up with a conscious awareness that it would all be his one day. And his love for Willoughby was deeply ingrained in him. It had stayed with him during his years at school and university and during his years in the army. He had insisted on buying his commission in an infantry regiment despite the fact that he was the elder son and heir and despite the opposition of his father and just about everyone who knew him.

But Willoughby had remained in his blood. It was what he had fought for—Willoughby, his home, England in miniature.

And yet now he hated to go back there. Because Sybil was there. Because life could never be what he had grown up dreaming that it would be.

And yet he must go. And something deep in him was perversely glad that he must. Willoughby in the late spring and summertime—he closed his eyes and felt that deep surge of longing that he always felt for his home when he was away from it and allowed himself to think of it.

And there was Pamela. Sybil did not care a great deal for her despite her protective attitude, despite the fact that she hated to allow him near the child. She spent almost no time with their daughter. Pamela needed him. She needed more than a nurse.

She had more than a nurse. She had a governess.

Fleur.

He had put her from his mind after salving his conscience by finding her employment. And Houghton had assured him that she seemed qualified to be a governess. Houghton would have interviewed the girl thoroughly.

He did not want to think of her. He did not want to see her again. He did not want to be reminded. He had only ever been unfaithful to Sybil that once, though there was precious little to be unfaithful to.

Why had he had Fleur sent to Willoughby? He had other properties. He could have sent her to one of them in some servant's capacity.

Why Willoughby? To be in the same house as his wife. As himself. To teach his daughter.

A whore teaching Pamela.

"That's enough, confound it," he said, opening his eyes. "Are you trying to put me to sleep?"

"That I was, sir," Sidney said, smiling cheerfully. "There is less of your temper to contend with when you are asleep, sir."

"Damn your impudence," the duke said, sitting up and rubbing at his eye again. "Fetch my riding clothes."

FLEUR DID NOT MEET either her new charge or the duchess during the day of her arrival at Willoughby Hall. They had apparently gone visiting during the afternoon, taking the child's nurse with them.

"Mrs. Clement was her grace's own childhood nurse," Mrs. Laycock explained. "They are very close. I am afraid she will resent you as much as the duchess will, Miss Hamilton. You must just keep in mind that it is his grace who pays your salary." She spoke briskly, so that Fleur got the impression that she was not the only servant who must keep such a fact in mind.

His grace was, apparently, from home. It was likely that he was in London for the Season if the Mr. Houghton who had interviewed her was his personal secretary. Mrs. Laycock did not know when he was to be expected home.

"Though he will be here, no doubt, if he gets wind of the fact that her grace is planning another party," that lady said, "and a grand ball." Her tone was disapproving, though she said no more on the topic. She would take advantage of the absence of her grace, she said, to show Fleur something of the house abovestairs.

It was so magnificent and built on such a massive scale that Fleur could only trail along behind Mrs. Laycock, gazing in awe and saying almost nothing. All of the state and family and business apartments were on the *piano nobile*, the schoolroom and the nursery and the servants' quarters in the smaller rooms above. Fleur had already seen her own room, small and square and light and airy, next to the schoolroom. It overlooked back lawns and trees. It looked rather like heaven in comparison with her room in London.

The tour of the house began in the great domed hall at the front of the house with its clerestory lantern high, just below the dome, flooding the room with light, and the dome itself painted with soaring angels. A gallery ran the circle below the lantern.

"An orchestra sits up there on grand occasions," the housekeeper explained. "When there is a ball, the doors to the long gallery and saloon are kept open to make one grand ballroom and promenade. You will see it if it rains the day of her grace's ball. It is to be outdoors by the lake, and we will be invited, Miss Hamilton, it being an outdoor affair. But it will be moved indoors if the weather is inclement, of course."

Fleur looked up and tried to imagine an orchestra sitting up there and music echoing around the circular pillared hall. She imagined crowds of people dressed in their evening finery, bright and laughing and dancing. And she smiled. Oh, she was going to be very happy. Despite what Mrs. Laycock had hinted about the duchess and Lady Pamela's nurse, she was going to be happy. How could she not be? She had had a glimpse of hell and had survived it.

The long gallery ran the whole length of one of the wings, along the front of the house, one side of it consisting entirely of long windows and ancient Roman busts set in niches. The coved plasterwork frieze and ceiling gave an impression of great height and splendor. The long wall opposite the windows was hung with portraits in gilded frames.

"His grace's family from generations back," Mrs. Laycock said. "You would need the master himself to explain it all to you, Miss Hamilton. There is nothing about Willoughby that he does not know."

Fleur identified a Holbein, a Van Dyck, a Reynolds. It must be wonderful, she thought, to have such a line of ancestors to picture in one's mind. The Duke of Ridgeway, Mrs. Laycock told her, was the eighth duke of his line.

"We are all waiting for an heir," she said, her voice turning a little stiff. "But so far there has been only Lady Pamela."

The offices and most of the guest rooms were behind the long gallery, Fleur was told, though she was not taken there.

The great saloon was on the central axis behind the hall, two stories high, its wall hangings of crimson Utrecht velvet, the heavy furniture arranged neatly around the perimeter of the room upholstered in the same material. The great pedimented doorcases and the cornice and mantel were gilded, the ceiling painted with a scene from some mythological battle that Mrs. Laycock could not identify. Large landscape paintings in heavy frames hung on the walls.

The dining room, the drawing room, the library, other rooms, and the private family apartments were in the other wing, the one that balanced the gallery wing.

Fleur was awed by it all. She had grown up in a grand house. Indeed her father had been its owner until his death in an inn fire with her mother when Fleur was eight years old. Both the house and his title had passed to his cousin, Matthew's father, and she had become a mere ward of the master, kindly though carelessly treated by him, unwanted and resented by his wife and daughter, ignored by Matthew until recent years.

But Heron House was not one of the great showpieces of England. Willoughby Hall evidently was. And despite her regret over the lost dream of a cozy manor and a small family group, she felt excited. She was to live in this magnificent mansion. She was to be a part of its busy life, responsible for the education of the duke and duchess's young daughter.

Good fortune was to be with her, after all, it seemed. Perhaps she was to have a small glimpse of heaven to balance her other recent experiences.

"I would take you walking in the park," the housekeeper said, "but I can see that you are weary, Miss Hamilton. You must go upstairs and rest for a while. Perhaps her grace will wish to speak with you later and perhaps you will be expected to become acquainted with Lady Pamela."

Fleur retired gratefully to her room. She was feeling somewhat overwhelmed by it all—by the events of the past two months, by the great good fortune of finding such a post when she had not been to that employment agency for a week, by the unexpected discovery that the post was no ordinary one at all. The journey had been long and exhausting.

And she had just that morning had one of her great fears put to rest—she was not with child.

Altogether, she thought, sitting by the window of her room, enjoying the peaceful scene outside and the gentle breeze that lifted the curtains and fanned her cheeks, she was far more well blessed than she could have expected to be just two months before.

She might have hanged. She might still hang. But she would not think of it. Today her new life had begun, and she was going to be happier than she had been at any other time in her life—since the age of eight.

She removed her dress, folded it neatly over the back of a chair, and lay down on top of the bedcovers in her chemise. How different from her room in London, she thought again, looking up to a silk-covered canopy over the bed, and looking about at neatness and cleanliness and hearing nothing but silence about her, except for the distant chirping of birds.

She closed her eyes to float on blissful drowsiness. And saw him again—his face dark and angular and harsh, the scar a livid slash across it from the corner of his eye to his chin. Bending over her, his dark cold eyes looking directly into hers.

His hands on her, first between her thighs and at the most secret place and then beneath her. And that other part of him searing its red-hot and relentless path into her very depths. She could feel it tearing her apart.

"Whore," he said to her. "Don't think ever again to escape that label. You are a whore now and will be for the rest of your life, no matter how far or fast you run."

"No." She shook her head from side to side on the bed, braced her feet more firmly on the floor, tried to pull back against his powerful hands so that he would not push so deeply into her. "No."

"This is not rape," he said. "You have sold yourself to me of your own free will. You are going to take my money."

"Because I am starving," she said, pleading with him. "Because I have not eaten for two days. Because I must survive."

"Whore," he said softly. "It is because you enjoy it. You are enjoying it, aren't you?"

"No." She squirmed to release herself from the strong hands that held her while he worked his pleasure in her. "No."

No. No. There was nothing of herself left. No dignity. No privacy. No identity. Deprived of her clothes. Held wide by his knees and the powerful muscles of his thighs. Invaded to the very core of her being. No.

"No. No. *No!*"

She was sitting up on the bed, sweating, shaking. The familiar dream. The dream that was haunting her nightly. One would have thought that it would be Hobson's dead face that would come to her as soon as she released her hold on consciousness, she thought, but it was not. It was that of the gentleman with the ugly scar who had hovered over her, taking the very last possession that had been hers to give—or sell.

Fleur got up wearily from the bed and stood before the window to cool her face. Would she never forget him? The sight of him? The feel of him?

Had he really said those words to her? She could no longer remember. But his face and his body had said them even if he had not uttered them aloud.

There surely could not be an uglier, more evil man in the world, she thought. And yet, memory reminded her, he had bought her food and insisted that she eat it. And he had paid her three times what she had asked for outside the theater. He had not done anything to her that she had not freely consented to.

And he had brought her a cold cloth with which to cleanse away the blood and soothe herself.

She rested her face in her hands. She must forget. She must accept this gift of a new life that some benevolent power had granted her.

• • •

"THAT IS PRETTY, DARLING," the Duchess of Ridgeway said, bending down to kiss her daughter on the cheek and glancing smilingly at the painting the child held up for her inspection. "I will certainly see her, Nanny. It must be made clear to her that she is to be subordinate to you and that she must not force Pamela into doing anything she does not wish to do."

"She is expecting to meet her charge this morning, my lady," the nurse said. "I have explained to her that Lady Pamela likes to be quiet in the nursery during the mornings."

"Must I meet my new governess today, Mama?" the child asked petulantly. "Did Papa send her?"

"He did it to provoke me, did he not?" the duchess said to her nurse. "He must have heard of my plans and thought to have his revenge by sending a prosing schoolmistress for my darling. But I have a right to company, don't I? Just as much as he does. He is enjoying the Season in London. Does he think I can live here all alone and be dull? Does he think I do not need company too to dispel this endless boredom?" She coughed dryly and reached for a handkerchief.

"I told you to wear a pelisse yesterday, lovey," the nurse said. "It is still just spring, even if the sun does shine. You will never get rid of your chill if you don't take care of yourself."

"Don't fuss, Nanny," the duchess said crossly. "I have had this cough since winter, even though I always bundled up warmly then, as you told me to. Do you suppose he will come home if he hears?"

"I daresay he will, lovey," the nurse said. "He usually does."

"He does not like me to have any enjoyment or company," her grace said. "I hate him, Nanny. I really do."

"Hush," the nurse said. "Not in front of Lady Pamela, lovey."

The duchess looked at the child and touched one soft dark ringlet. "Send her down to my sitting room, then," she said, "this Miss Hamilton. Adam may have hired her, Nanny, but she must be made to see that she will be answerable to me. After all, Adam—"

"Hush, lovey," the nurse said firmly.

The duchess kissed her child's cheek again and swept from the room, her morning robe flowing out behind her.

Her daughter watched her go wistfully. "Do you think she liked my picture, Nanny?" she asked.

"I'm sure of it, lovey." The nurse bent to hug her. "Mama adores you and everything you do."

"And will Papa like it?" the child asked. "Is he coming home?"

"We will keep it carefully until he does," Mrs. Clement said.

WHEN FLEUR WAS USHERED into the duchess's sitting room a short time later, it was empty. She stood quietly inside the door and waited, her hands folded before her. It was a small room, but quite exquisite. It was oval, with a painted dome for a ceiling and slender gilded Corinthian columns supporting the entablature. Decorative panels on an ivory-colored ground in pale reds, greens, pinks, and gold leaf made the walls delicate and feminine.

She did not have a long wait. The door at the other end of the room opened to admit a small and dainty lady in a delicate blue muslin dress, her silver-blond hair piled in soft curls and ringlets on her head and about her face. The duchess was extremely beautiful and looked younger than her own twenty-three years, Fleur thought.

"Miss Hamilton?" the duchess asked.

Fleur curtsied. "Your grace."

She found herself being openly surveyed from head to foot by the duchess's light blue eyes.

"My husband has sent you here as governess to my daughter?" The voice was sweet and breathless.

Fleur inclined her head.

"Do you realize that at the age of five she is not yet in need of teaching?" her grace asked.

"But there is a great deal even so young a child can learn without actually sitting over a book all day long, your grace," Fleur said.

The duchess's chin came up. "Do you presume to disagree with me?" she asked, both her voice and her face pleasant and somewhat at variance with her words.

Fleur was silent.

"My husband sent you," the other said. "What was your relationship with him, pray?"

Fleur flushed. "I have not met his grace," she said. "I was interviewed at an employment agency by Mr. Houghton."

The duchess looked her up and down once more. "As you will have gathered," she said, "I am in disagreement with my husband on my daughter's need of tuition. She is a young and delicate child who needs only her mother's love and her nurse's care. You will not tax her brain with useless knowledge, Miss Hamilton, and you will take your orders from Mrs. Clement, Lady Pamela's nurse. You will consider yourself one of the servants of this house and keep to your own room or the servants' hall when your presence is not needed in the schoolroom. I do not expect to see you on this floor of the house unless expressly summoned by me. Do you understand me?"

All was spoken in a light, friendly voice while large blue eyes regarded her from a fragile, beautiful face. An adoring mother afraid of releasing her child from babyhood, Fleur thought with some sympathy despite the imperious nature of the words themselves.

"Yes, your grace," she said.

"You may leave now and spend half an hour with my daughter under the supervision of Mrs. Clement," her grace said.

But as Fleur turned to leave, her grace spoke again.

"Miss Hamilton," she said, "I approve of the way you are

clothed this morning and of the way you have dressed your hair. I trust that your manner of dress will always meet with my approval."

Fleur inclined her head again and left the room. And since she was dressed in a severe gray cotton dress, one of her new purchases, with a small white lace collar, and had her hair combed entirely back from her face and confined in a heavy bun at her neck, she thought she understood the duchess perfectly.

Was the duke the type of man to harass his younger servants, then? Was that why her grace had asked about her relationship with him in London? She hoped fervently that he would keep himself there for a long time to come.

Well, she thought, thinking back, with a slight chill, to the duchess's words and manner, she had been warned that neither her grace nor Mrs. Clement would be pleased to see her. And she must not complain. Neither of them had been openly hostile to her. They would come around, surely, when they realized that she had no intention of standing over Lady Pamela with a stick all day long in a stuffy schoolroom.

MR. SNEDBURG WAS AT the end of a long day's work. He had unbent enough to take a seat in the parlor on St. James's Street and even to accept a glass of port.

"Much obliged, sir," he said, taking the glass from the hand of his host. "The feet get sore from so much walking and the pipes dry from asking so many questions. Yes, indeed, Miss Fleur Hamilton. Too much of a coincidence not to be the same young lady, would you not say? And she fits the description."

Mr. Snedburg did not add that both his informants, Miss Fleming and the young woman's landlady, had described Fleur Hamilton as a very ordinary-looking young lady with very ordinary-looking reddish hair. He understood that his client rather fancied his cousin even if she was a murderer and a jewel thief. And men in the throes of an infatuation were to be forgiven if they occasionally waxed poetic. Sunshine and sunset tangled all together, indeed. It was enough to make the Runner want to toss up his victuals.

"And?" Lord Brocklehurst was watching him keenly, his own glass of port halfway to his lips. It had taken the Runner well over a week to make his first report, despite his reputation.

"And she has been hired as governess to the daughter of a Mr. Kent of Dorsetshire. By"—the Runner paused for effect—"a gentleman who waited four whole days at the agency just for her, for a red-haired Fleur. She has left on her way already."

Lord Brocklehurst frowned. His glass was still stranded several inches from his mouth.

"There can't be that many Kents in Dorsetshire," Mr. Snedburg said. "I shall look into the matter and see if we can't nail our man to one single spot on the map, sir."

Lord Brocklehurst drank, deep in thought. "Kent?" he said. "Not the Ridgeway Kents, surely?"

"As in the Dook of Ridgeway?" the Runner asked, raising one hand to scratch the back of his neck. "Is he a Kent?"

"I knew his half brother," Lord Brocklehurst said. "They lived in Dorset. Willoughby Hall."

Mr. Snedburg dug into his ear with his little finger. "I'll see what I can find out for definite, sir," he said. "We will run her to ground in no time at all, take my word on it."

"Fleur," the other said, gazing into the swirling contents of his glass. "She used to have tantrums as a young child because my mother and father would not call her that. Apparently it was the name she went by until her parents died. I had forgotten."

"Yes, well, right you are, sir," Mr. Snedburg said, downing what remained in his glass in one gulp and getting to his feet. "I'll see what I can find out about this dook and his governess."

"I want her found soon," Lord Brocklehurst said.

"It will be soon, or sooner," the other said briskly. "My word on it, sir."

"Well," Lord Brocklehurst said, "you were recommended to me as the best. Though it has taken you precious long to find out this much."

The other chose not to comment on either the compliment or the criticism. He saluted in almost military manner and hurried smartly from the room.

4

*F*LEUR'S LIFE WAS BY NO MEANS ARDUOUS DURING
her first two weeks at Willoughby. She had been instructed to take her orders from Mrs. Clement, and Mrs.
Clement, it seemed, did not approve of schooling for her
young charge any more than the duchess did. The new governess was lucky if she was granted an hour morning and
afternoon with her pupil.

She was somewhat uneasy, perhaps a little worried that she
would be dismissed as a servant of little use or that the duke
and Mr. Houghton would come home and find that she was
not after all earning her keep. But she tried to take the advice
of Mrs. Laycock, who told her to relax and do her best, and
who assured her that when his grace finally arrived home—
and he would surely come when he heard about the party that
her grace had organized—all would be set to rights.

In the meanwhile Fleur became familiar with and comfortable in her new home. There were long hours of quiet and
peace in which to allow the old fears to die and the old wounds
to heal. Sometimes a whole day would pass without her feeling that old urge to look anxiously over her shoulder for a pur-
suer. And sometimes she could sleep for a whole stretch
without seeing that hawkish and scarred face bending over her
and telling her what she was while making her into just that.

She was eating well and had put back on some of the weight she had lost. Her hair seemed thicker again and shinier. The worst of the shadows had disappeared from beneath her eyes. There was color in her cheeks. There was energy in her muscles. She was beginning to feel young again.

Mrs. Laycock found the time over those two weeks to stroll over much of the vast park with her. And always Fleur found out more from the quiet conversation of the housekeeper about her new home and the family for whom she worked.

"It was laid out years ago to give the impression of natural beauty," Mrs. Laycock said of the park. "The lake was dug and the cascades created and every tree planted in order to give a pleasing prospect from almost every vantage point. A little silly, I call it, Miss Hamilton, when nature does very nicely on its own without the help of men to make their fortunes out of landscaping the gardens of the rich. I would prefer to see flat formal gardens with a good show of flowers myself. But that is only my opinion."

Fleur loved the park and its rolling and seemingly endless lawns and groves of trees. She loved the winding avenues and stone temples and other follies. She felt that she could wander there forever and never tire of the views or the sense of peace that it all brought her.

His grace, she discovered from Mrs. Laycock, had fought with the English army in Spain and at the Battle of Waterloo, even though he had always been the heir to the late duke, and had already succeeded to his title when he left for Belgium.

"He never shirked any duty," the housekeeper said. "There were those, of course, who said that his duty was to remain here safe and alive in order to take over his responsibilities. But he went."

"And he came back safely," Fleur said.

Mrs. Laycock sighed. "It was a dreadful time," she said. "He was so happy before he went back to fight again when that monster escaped from Elba. He had just become betrothed to her grace—the Honorable Miss Sybil Desford she was then—and was as happy as the day was long. They had been intended for each other for years before that, but it was only during those months that he really had stars in his eyes for her."

"But he came back to her," Fleur said. "All ended happily."

"We thought he was dead," Mrs. Laycock said. "News came that he had been killed in battle, and his man came home all broken up—he had been with his grace for years. I don't like to remember that time, Miss Hamilton. First the old duke and then our boy. Boy!" She chuckled. "Just listen to me. He is past his thirtieth birthday already."

They sat on a wrought-iron seat beside the path they were strolling along and looked down through trees to a crescent-shaped lake with an island and a domed pavilion in its center.

"Lord Thomas assumed the title," Mrs. Laycock continued. "His grace's half brother, that is. They look alike, but as different they are as chalk is from cheese. There are those who prefer Lord Thomas because of his sunny nature and his smiles. He betrothed himself to her grace—to Miss Desford."

"All so quickly?" Fleur asked. "But surely the mistake was discovered very soon?"

"It was a whole year," the housekeeper said with a sigh. "His grace was taken for dead and stripped on the battlefield. Those French, or those Belgians, behaved just like barbarians, Miss Hamilton. But one decent couple discovered that he was still breathing and took him to their cottage to nurse him back to health. He was dreadfully wounded." She shook her head.

"He was unconscious or in a fever for weeks," she continued. "And then he could not remember much. He did not know who he was for months, and then apparently he had trouble convincing anyone that he was who he said he was. He was naked, poor gentleman, when he was found."

"So for a whole year he was thought to be dead?" Fleur asked.

"I'll never forget the day he came home," Mrs. Laycock said.

"Still limping and sadly disfigured, poor gentleman. I'll never forget it."

"What happened to Lord Thomas?" Fleur asked when her companion stared quietly down to the lake.

"He left," Mrs. Laycock said. "Just disappeared about three months after his grace came home. There are those who said there was not room for the both of them in the one house and that his grace ordered him to leave. And there are those who say other things. I do not know the rights of it. But he has never come back."

"And the duchess married his grace after all," Fleur said. "The story has a happily-ever-after ending."

"Yes." Mrs. Laycock got to her feet and brushed at the folds of her black dress. "She married him. Though such a wailing she put up when she came here with her papa and discovered that Lord Thomas had gone, that I had a hard time of it to quiet the servants' talk, Miss Hamilton. And his grace so happy to be home only three months before that and catching her up in his arms and twirling her about when she stepped from her carriage for all the world to see."

They strolled on, each wrapped in private thought. It was strange that the duke spent so much time from home if he loved it so much, Fleur thought, and if he loved the duchess so much and had such a strong sense of responsibility.

But not all of Fleur's time was spare time, of course. She did have about two hours each day with her pupil, a small, thin, dark-haired child who might one day grow up to be handsome if her frequently petulant look did not become habitual. She did not resemble her mother in any way at all. She must be all her father.

The child was difficult. She did not want to look at books, she did not want to listen to stories, she did not want to pick up a needle, and when she painted she often did so carelessly, wasting both paper and paint and becoming mulish when Fleur insisted that she clear away the mess she had made.

Fleur tried to be patient. Lady Pamela was, after all, little more than a baby, and she must know, as children usually did, that her mother and her nurse were on her side. Fleur tried to entice the child into wanting to learn.

There was an old harpsichord in the schoolroom. Fleur sat at it and played one afternoon when Lady Pamela had refused to cooperate in any of the planned activities, and she continued to play when she was aware of the child standing still to one side of the stool.

"I want to play," Lady Pamela demanded when Fleur's fingers finally fell still.

Fleur smiled. "Have you had any instruction?" she asked.

"No," Lady Pamela said. "I want to play. Get up."

"Please," Fleur said.

"Get up!" the child said. "I want to play."

"Please," Fleur said again.

"You are a servant," Lady Pamela said haughtily. "Get up or I will tell Nanny."

"I will gladly get up," Fleur said, "if you will ask me rather than tell me."

The child flounced off in order to scold and slap a shabby doll she had brought to the schoolroom with her.

Fleur sighed inwardly and resumed her quiet playing. It all reminded her of so much. Cousin Caroline and Amelia, haughty and imperious because they were suddenly Lady Brocklehurst of Heron House and the Honorable Miss Amelia Bradshaw after the death of her parents.

And they had treated her just so because they were obliged to offer her a home in the house where she had always lived. Amelia had taken her lovely Chinese bedchamber and relegated her to a plainer room at the back of the house.

She had a few good days with her pupil. Lady Pamela had been excited one morning because her mother was to take her visiting in the afternoon, but word came to the nursery at luncheon time that her grace was feverish and had been told by the doctor to rest during the afternoon.

Fleur, who was taking her luncheon upstairs, saw the look of intense disappointment on her pupil's face and the tears that formed in her eyes and her trembling, pouting lip. The child saw far too little of her mother. But Fleur knew that the chief disappointment would be in not seeing the Chamberlain children and their dogs after all. Lady Pamela also saw very little of other children.

"Would it be possible for me to take Lady Pamela to visit the children?" she asked Mrs. Clement when the child could not hear her.

She expected a rebuff, but the nurse looked at her consideringly and said she would consult her grace. Within half an hour Fleur had the pleasure of seeing the child's face light up so that she had looked almost pretty. She jumped up and down on the spot, cheering until her nurse cupped her face in her hands and told her not to get overexcited.

She had done one thing at last, Fleur thought, that had won her pupil's approval.

They set out as soon as they were ready and the carriage had been brought around. And Fleur smiled as she watched Lady Pamela sit forward in her seat, looking at the scenery pass the window, waving at the gatekeeper's wife, and chattering intermittently about the Chamberlains' dogs.

"Mama will not allow me to have a dog," she said, "or a cat. Or a rabbit," she added a moment later.

For almost the first time in their acquaintance, Fleur felt, her pupil looked like a child.

Mr. Chamberlain was a widower of about forty years, who lived with his sister and his three children in an elegant manor that looked remarkably like the cozy manor of her dreams when she had been traveling into Dorsetshire, Fleur thought.

She explained to Miss Chamberlain, an elegant lady in her mid-thirties, who wore a lace cap on her smoothly parted dark hair, that her grace was indisposed and that Lady Pamela had been disappointed at the prospect of losing the treat of playing with the children. She asked to be allowed to sit in the servants' quarters for an hour.

"In the servants' quarters?" Miss Chamberlain said with a laugh. "I would not hear of any such thing, Miss Hamilton. You are Lady Pamela's new governess? We heard that there was one. You will take tea with Duncan and me, if you please, while the children play."

Fleur followed her hostess into the drawing room, where they were soon joined by Mr. Chamberlain, who bowed to her and showed no outward chagrin at being forced to take tea with a mere governess.

"Our conversation will doubtless be drowned out by barkings before long, Miss Hamilton," he said. "The poor dogs will be dragged inside to the nursery to be played with. It is always so when Lady Pamela is here. She does not have the chance to mingle with other children or with animals often enough, I believe."

"And she had been taught that horses are dangerous," Miss Chamberlain added, handing Fleur her cup and saucer.

Her brother smiled at her. "I suppose it would be easy to be overprotective of an only child," he said. "It is a pity Adam is not home more often. Have you heard if he is to return for the ball, Miss Hamilton?"

"I am afraid I do not know, sir," Fleur said.

"It will not be the same without him," he said. "But the Willoughby balls are always the most splendid of occasions. Opinion seems to be evenly divided in the neighborhood as to whether the indoor balls or the outdoor are the more so. Emily believes the outdoor ones far more romantic, don't you, my dear?"

"Oh, more romantic, yes, without a doubt," she said. "I am not sure that they are more splendid. There is nothing like a promenade along the long gallery, Miss Hamilton, with music wafting through from the great hall and candles lit in all the wall sconces and all the Ridgeway ancestors watching. Are you pleased with your place of employment?"

Fleur spent a pleasant hour conversing with brother and sister and walking in their flower arbor with them. They seemed quite unperturbed by the sounds of boisterous merriment coming from the upper part of the house.

"I employ a nurse to worry about broken bones and pulled hair and such," Mr. Chamberlain said when Fleur expressed her hope that Lady Pamela was behaving as she ought. "A little noise I can easily endure."

"By shutting yourself off into your books, Duncan," his sister said. "One could yell boo into his ear when he is reading, Miss Hamilton, and he would be oblivious."

For one hour Fleur felt like a real person again. Though perhaps even the word "again" was inappropriate, she thought as she led a reluctant Lady Pamela to the carriage for the return ride home. She had never been treated with a great deal of respect when she lived at Heron House.

"We will bring the children to the Hall for a return visit one afternoon," Mr. Chamberlain said, taking Fleur's hand to help her into the carriage. "Thank you for bringing the child, Miss Hamilton. I am sure the outing has done her good. And thank you for calling on us."

"I do not know what your working hours are," Emily Chamberlain said, "but I suppose you must have some time to yourself. Do call here at any time, Miss Hamilton. I would enjoy your company."

"One of the dogs bit Randall's bottom when he was climbing over a chair," Lady Pamela told Fleur as the carriage jerked into motion. "Their nurse said it was because we had made the dog overexcited." She giggled. "But it was ever so funny."

Fleur laughed with her but resisted the urge to hug the child. It was too early for that yet.

True to his promise, Mr. Chamberlain brought his sister and

his children to call several days later. While Miss Chamberlain sat drinking tea with the duchess, he brought his children upstairs, only to find that Lady Pamela was in the middle of an arithmetic lesson in the schoolroom.

"I do beg your pardon," he said when Fleur answered the door to his knock. "May I invite your eternal wrath, Miss Hamilton, and beg that Lady Pamela be released early from classes in order to play with my trio? I am sure she will work twice as hard tomorrow, won't you, Pamela?"

"Yes," she cried eagerly, jumping to her feet.

"She is also an accomplished little liar," he said quietly to Fleur with a smile, "as are all children. Can I persuade you to step outside so they may romp and shriek and argue without murdering our ears?"

"What a splendid idea," Fleur said, and led the way downstairs and out through a door at the back of the house to lawns that led back to a distant tree line. She hesitated when he offered his arm while they walked. The children had run on ahead with a ball, which one of the Chamberlain children had been clutching. Was it proper? She was a servant. He was a visitor.

She took his arm.

"If we stroll slowly enough," he said, "the children will get far enough ahead that we will not feel obliged to listen for naughty words or unkind insults. The very best way to deal with children, Miss Hamilton, as I have found from personal experience, is to become blind, deaf, and dumb. And, of course, to have a competent nurse and a long-suffering resident sister. Tell me about yourself. What has brought you here?"

Fleur felt guilty about the lies and half-truths she felt forced to tell.

"You will be at the ball?" he asked when taking his leave of her some time later and turning to summon his three children. "I hope to dance with you there, Miss Hamilton."

She hoped so too. As she led Pamela by the hand back upstairs to the nursery, and endured the icy glares of Mrs. Clement when she observed the child's flushed cheeks and somewhat disheveled hair, Fleur hoped so profoundly. She returned to the schoolroom to put away the books they had abandoned earlier, and twirled about, the arithmetic book clasped to her bosom.

It was so good to feel young and happy and full of hope again. And to have had an attractive gentleman ask her to dance with him at the ball.

Not that she would be seduced by expectations for the future, of course. Nothing but the very mildest of flirtations was at all possible for her. Certainly marriage was completely out of the question. But she would settle for a mild flirtation. It would be quite enough.

And finally, it seemed, his grace was to come home. Lady Pamela brought her the news one afternoon, rushing through the schoolroom door, when she usually dragged her feet and frequently looked sullen as well.

"Papa is coming home," she announced triumphantly. "Mama has just had a letter from him. He should be here any day. He should be here before any of Mama's guests arrive."

The duchess was expecting close to twenty guests within the week, the day before the ball.

Fleur smiled. "How lovely for you," she said. "You will be very happy to see your father."

"No, I won't," the girl said. "I shall be cross with him."

"Indeed?" Fleur said. "Why is that?"

"Because he has been gone forever," the child said. "And because he sent you."

Fleur smiled quietly to herself. She thought she had been making progress. But only outside the schoolroom, it seemed. Rome was not built in a day, she had to remind herself. "Shall we look at the alphabet book?" she suggested.

"I have a headache," Lady Pamela said. "I want to paint."

"A picture for your papa?" Fleur said. "A very good idea. But ten minutes of the book first."

Battle was engaged.

"I shall get Papa to send you away again," Lady Pamela said.

"Will you?" Fleur said, seating herself beside the girl and taking her gently by the arm when she would have got up from her place. "Do you remember this letter?"

"A for apple," Lady Pamela said without even looking. "That is easy. I don't remember the others. I have a headache."

Yes, Fleur thought, his grace might well dismiss her. She worked for no more than two hours a day, and even then, trying to teach Lady Pamela was rather like trying to pull a mule.

But she would not think of dismissal and all it would mean to her. She would not allow herself to be plunged into gloom again. It felt altogether too good to be happy and alive.

Houghton was a valuable employee. He had been in the Duke of Ridgeway's service for more than five years—almost since the duke's return from Belgium, in fact. And his grace had come to rely on him more and more to conduct the day-to-day business of his life. The man was sensible and hardworking and discreet.

One quality in Houghton the duke valued as much as any other, though, and that was his ability to sense his employer's mood and to adjust his own behavior accordingly. They took their meals together when in London and frequently conversed on a wide range of topics. But when the duke wished to be silent, his secretary seemed not to feel the necessity of keeping a conversation going.

Today as they neared Willoughby, Houghton sat quietly in the carriage, regarding the scenery through the window beside him, and held his peace.

His grace was grateful. That ache of love and nostalgia was in him again. They were driving beside the old park wall. Soon now they would be on the lime avenue and he would be home indeed. He wondered if all men felt about their homes as he did about his. It was like a part of his identity, a part of himself.

He thought in particular of that time six years before when he had returned after so long and so painful an absence. The porter's wife had had her apron to her eyes, crying at the sight of him—her wrinkled face was wreathed in smiles now as she bobbed him a curtsy. He raised one hand in greeting and smiled at her. All the servants had been out on the upper terrace to greet him—they had even cheered him—and he would swear that their happiness had not been feigned.

And Thomas. The memory lost some of its luster. He had not thought—foolishly he had not thought of what the year of his reported death had meant to Thomas. He had been the Duke of Ridgeway and was now merely Lord Thomas Kent again.

The duke had always thought Thomas was fond of him, although they had had their differences and although they were only half-brothers—Thomas was the son of his father's second wife. Perhaps he had been. Perhaps the blow of finding himself suddenly deprived of a title and property he had thought his had been just too much.

And Sybil later that same day. Sybil, about whom he had dreamed for weeks before that, ever since his memory had returned. Back in his arms again—for a brief moment. More beautiful than ever.

He would not think of it. He was coming home again now and there was excitement in him despite the fact that Sybil was there.

Mrs. Laycock and Jarvis, the butler, were standing at the top of the horseshoe steps before the massive double doors leading into the hall. Dearly familiar. Mrs. Laycock had been housekeeper at Willoughby for as long as his grace could recall, and Jarvis had been at the house all his life, rising through the ranks of the footmen to his current position, which he had assumed four years before.

Mrs. Laycock curtsied and Jarvis inclined his body into the bow that had stiffened noticeably the very day of his promotion. The duke smiled and greeted them.

Sybil had not come outside or even into the hall to meet him. She was in her sitting room, Mrs. Laycock informed him.

Almost an hour passed before he attended her there. Sybil would not appreciate being greeted by an eager husband dressed in the creased garments he had traveled in. He bathed and changed first.

His wife was reclining on the daybed in her sitting room. She did not rise at his entry.

"Adam," she said breathlessly, smiling at him. The same beautiful, fragile, wide-eyed Sybil he had fallen in love with once upon a time. "Did you have a comfortable journey?"

He bent over her to kiss her and she turned her cheek to his lips. "How are you, Sybil?" he asked. There was a high flush on her cheeks.

"Well," she said. "Bored. Sir Cecil Hayward held a dinner last evening and entertained the company with stories of his new hunter and praises of his hounds. I left early. I could not stop yawning."

"He is, I'm afraid, just a typical country gentleman," he said with a smile. "Have you recovered from your chill?"

She shrugged. "You are not going to fuss, are you?" she said. "Nanny does enough of that."

"I must remember to thank Nanny, then," he said. "How is Pamela?"

"Well," she said, "despite circumstances, the poor darling. You really must get rid of that governess, Adam. What whim was it that made you send her here?"

"Is she not doing a good job?" he asked.

"Pamela is too young to be spending hours in a schoolroom," she said. "And she dislikes her governess. I would like to know what she was to you, Adam."

"Houghton hired her," he said. "Whom have you invited here apart from Chesterton?"

"Just a few people," she said. "It was so dull here with you gone."

"You know that you could have come with me," he said. "I asked you. I would have taken you and Pamela both. We could have shown her London."

"But you know you would have been playing jealous husband as soon as I smiled at another gentleman," she said. "You always do, Adam. You hate to see me enjoy myself. Have you come home to spoil things for me again? Will you be scowling at all my guests?"

"Will I need to?" he asked.

"You are horrid to me," she said, her large blue eyes filling with tears. "Did you know about the ball?"

"Ball?" he said.

"I have arranged it for the night after everyone arrives," she said. "And I have invited everyone, Adam. You need not fear that anyone will feel slighted."

"You planned a ball without me here?" he asked. "Would that not have struck our neighbors as strange, Sybil?"

"Can I help it if you take yourself off to London at every opportunity in search of pleasure?" she said. "I would imagine everyone would sympathize with me. It is to be an outdoor ball. An orchestra has been hired to play in the pavilion. A dance floor is to be laid on the west side of the lake—in the usual place. And the lanterns have been arranged for and the refreshments. I hope it does not rain."

"This is all to take place in four days' time?" he said. "I am so glad you thought to mention it to me today, Sybil. I hate surprises."

"And I hate that tone of sarcasm," she said. "You used not to use it with me. You used to be kind to me. You used to love me." She started to cough, and drew a handkerchief from beside her.

"It is so hot in here," she said fretfully. "I think I ought to rest now. The doctor told me to rest more. You will be anxious to leave me and go about your own business anyway."

"Let me help you to your bed," he said, bending toward her. "I would have brought a physician with me from town if I had known you were still unwell. Obviously Hartley is not doing you much good."

"You never wrote to ask after my health," she said. "I shall be quite happy to rest here, thank you, Adam."

Don't touch me. She had not said the words, but her actions had said them for her. The slight shrinking from his outstretched hands. The refusal to be helped. The turning of her cheek for his kiss of greeting. The duke's jaw tightened as he stood outside her door a few moments later. The old familiar words, sometimes spoken, sometimes merely implied.

Would Pamela still be at her lessons? he wondered. Or in the nursery? He would go and see. He had missed her.

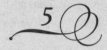

5

$\mathcal{F}$LEUR WAS READING A STORY TO LADY PAMELA, although she knew that the child was not listening. She had seen her father arrive more than an hour before from the nursery window, where she had been with Mrs. Clement. But her nurse had not allowed her to rush downstairs to greet him and had sent her to the schoolroom soon after.

The child was torn between an impatient eagerness for him to come and a stubborn insistence that she did not care, that she did not wish to see him anyway.

Sullen and petulant as her charge was much of the time, sometimes Fleur ached to take her into her arms, to hold her close, to assure her that she was loved, that she mattered, that she was not forgotten.

She knew what it was like. Oh, she knew, though she had not known at so young an age. And by the time it had happened she had been old enough to know that her parents were in no way to blame. She had always been able to comfort herself with the knowledge that they had loved her totally, that she had meant all the world to them.

Perhaps Lady Pamela's case was worse than hers after all. Her mother rarely visited her, though she showered her with love and endearments when she did. Her father had been away for many weeks.

But he did come at last. They heard a firm masculine tread in the corridor outside the schoolroom and a deep voice talking to Mrs. Clement. And Fleur breathed a sigh of relief for Lady Pamela, whose face brightened into that rare expression of pretty eagerness as her governess got quietly to her feet to cross the room and put the book away in order to leave father and daughter some privacy.

The door opened and she heard a childish shriek. She smiled and arranged the book carefully on its shelf with the others. She was nervous, if the truth were known. The Duke of Ridgeway! She had always thought of him as a very grand personage indeed.

"Papa, Papa!" Lady Pamela shrieked. "I have made you a picture, and I lost a tooth—see? What did you bring me?"

There was a deep masculine laugh, the sound of a smacking kiss.

"Cupboard love," his voice said. "I thought it was me you were happy to see, Pamela. What makes you think I have brought you anything?"

"What did you bring?" The child's voice was still a shriek.

"Later," he said. "You look lopsided without your tooth. Are you going to get a big one instead of it?"

"How much later?" she asked.

The Duke of Ridgeway laughed again.

Fleur turned, feeling foolish at her own nervousness. She was the daughter of a baron. She had lived in a baron's home, at Heron House, for most of her life. There was no reason to be awed by a duke. She held herself straight, folded her hands in front of her in what she hoped would look like a relaxed attitude, and raised her eyes.

He had his daughter up in his arms and was laughing as she hugged him tightly about the neck. The scarred half of his face was turned to Fleur.

She felt suddenly as if she were in a tunnel, a long and dark tunnel through which a cold wind rushed. She could hear the hum of it, though there was surely not air enough to breathe.

His eyes met hers across the room, and the coldness rushed into her nostrils and up into her head. The sound of the wind became a thick buzzing. Her hands felt cold and clammy and a million miles away from her head.

"Miss Hamilton?" The Duke of Ridgeway set his daughter down on the floor and took a few steps toward Fleur. He made her a slight bow. "Welcome to Willoughby Hall, ma'am."

She knew that if she could just breathe deeply and evenly for long enough, her vision would return and blood would flow to her head again. She thought only of her breathing. In. Out. Don't rush it. Don't fight it.

"I trust you have found everything to your satisfaction here," he said, indicating the schoolroom about them.

Breathe slowly. No, don't give in to panic. Don't faint. *Don't faint!*

"Papa." Lady Pamela was tugging at the leg of his pantaloons. "What did you bring me?"

Those intense dark eyes turned from her to look down at his daughter. He smiled, but the side of his mouth that Fleur could see, the scarred side, did not lift.

She felt a black terror, which had her gasping for air for a moment before she imposed control over her breathing again.

"We had better go down and see," he said, "or I am not going to have any peace, am I? Sidney grumbled about it all the way from London. I only hope you like it."

He held out a hand for his daughter's—a hand with long, well-manicured fingers.

Slowly. In. Out.

"Sidney is silly," was Lady Pamela's opinion.

"I shudder to think what Sidney would say if he were ever to hear you say that," he said.

"Sidney is silly, Sidney is silly," she chanted, giggling and taking his hand.

Those dark eyes were on her again, Fleur could feel, though she kept her own resolutely on Lady Pamela.

"Miss Hamilton will come down with us," he said, "and bring you back again before Nanny can send out a search party."

Fleur walked through the door ahead of him and along the corridor beside him to one of the twin staircases that flanked the great hall.

"Ma'am?" he said at the head of the stairs, extending his free arm to her.

But she heard an inarticulate sound come from her throat, and she shrank farther away from him so that her dress brushed against the wall as they descended. He turned to listen to Lady Pamela's chatter.

Fleur listened to the echo of their footsteps as they crossed the great hall, noted the smart way a footman sprang forward to open the double doors for them, felt fresh air and sunshine against her face, counted the marble steps as they descended them, and felt beneath her feet the cobbles of the winding avenue that led to the stable block.

She concentrated hard on immediate physical sensation. It was by far the best way to occupy her thoughts.

"Where are we going? What is it?" Lady Pamela tripped along at her father's side, still clinging to his hand.

"You will see soon enough," he said. "Poor Sidney."

"Silly Sidney," she said.

It was a puppy, a round, snub-nosed little Border collie with white fur about its nose and in a lopsided stripe over its head and about its neck. Two feet and its stomach were white. The rest was black.

It was protesting the fact that it had been placed in a makeshift pen with a pile of straw that it tripped on as it tried to walk. It was crying a loud protest, a demand for its mother.

"Ohhh!" Lady Pamela withdrew her hand from her father's and stood staring speechlessly until she went down on her knees beside the pen and lifted the little bundle into her arms. The puppy stopped its crying immediately and licked at her face so that she wrinkled her nose and turned aside, giggling.

"Sidney traveled from London with a clean face and nipped fingers," his grace said. "And frequently with wet breeches."

"Oh." Lady Pamela gazed in awe at her present. "He is mine, Papa? All mine?"

"Sidney certainly does not want it," her father said.

"I am going to take him to my room," she said. "I am going to sleep with him."

"He is a she," the duke said. "And your mother and Nanny might have something to say about a house pet."

But Lady Pamela was not listening. She was playing with her puppy and laughing as it caught at her fingers with its sharp little teeth.

Fleur kept her eyes on the child and the puppy, her shoulders back, her chin high, her hands clasped together as she felt him turn to her and his eyes pass over her.

"You did not suspect?" he asked her quietly.

She could not move. If she moved a muscle, she would come all to pieces.

"You did not suspect," he said, and knelt down beside his daughter.

It was arranged that the puppy would stay in the stables until it had been house-trained. Pamela could visit whenever she wanted as long as doing so did not interrupt either her lessons or her rest. After that she would be able to take her pet into the house, provided it was never allowed to stray down onto the *piano nobile* to give her mother a fit of the vapors or to send Sidney into a roaring rage.

The duke remained in the stables as Fleur took his daughter by the hand and led her back to the house, chattering without pause. The puppy was the sweetest little thing. The Chamberlain children were going to be ever so envious when they saw him—her. She was going to train it to sit up and beg and to walk at her heels. Wasn't her papa the most wonderful papa in the whole wide world?

Fleur took the child back the way they had come, up the steps, across the great hall, through the archway and up the stairs, along the corridor to the nursery, where Mrs. Clement was waiting. Lady Pamela's chatter increased in speed and volume for the benefit of her new audience.

"Classes are at an end for today, Miss Hamilton," the nurse said dismissively.

Fleur walked to her room without hesitation, closed the door behind her, and leaned back against it, her eyes closed, as if by doing so she could keep out the world.

And then she went rushing across the room to the closet, where she leaned over the closestool and retched and retched until her stomach was sore from dry heaves.

"HIS GRACE THE DOOK has left London," Mr. Snedburg reported to Lord Brocklehurst on a sweltering hot day in May. His face bore a distinct resemblance to a lobster. "Taking his secretary, Mr. Houghton, with him. That seems to settle the matter. He was the very man who hired Miss Fleur Hamilton, sir."

"It must be her and that must be her destination," his client said, watching with frowning disapproval as the Runner mopped at his face with a large handkerchief. "What excuse can I find for going there? You have not discovered the whereabouts of Lord Thomas Kent by any chance, have you?"

"I have not yet turned my inquiries his way," Mr. Snedburg said. "I can do so, but is it necessary, sir? If the young lady is wanted for murder, I can go down there posthaste with your say-so as a justice of the peace and a warrant for her arrest and haul her back. She will not escape from me, you may be sure. You can have her head in a noose and her feet swinging on air in no time at all, sir."

Lord Brocklehurst shuddered slightly. "Find Lord Thomas

Kent for me," he said, "or find me a way of appearing at that house without seeming to be a complete imbecile, and your job will be at an end. I'll do the bringing back."

"Then all you need to do, sir, is go down there and fetch her," Mr. Snedburg said, wiping the back of his neck and eyeing the decanters on the sideboard with a decidedly wistful air. "You don't need no excooses when the dook's governess is a murderer and a jewel thief."

"Thank you." Lord Brocklehurst fixed the Runner with a cold eye. "I shall do this in my own way. Bring me the information I want and I will settle with you."

"There is to be a party at Willoughby Hall," the Runner said, "by all accounts, sir. I shall get you a list of the guests and which of them are in London and have not left yet."

"As soon as possible, if you please," Lord Brocklehurst said, brightening. He rose dismissively.

"You may depend upon it, sir," Mr. Snedburg said. "And if Lord Thomas is in England, I shall ferret him out."

Lord Brocklehurst crossed the room to pour himself a drink when he was alone again, and stood with the decanter in his hands, staring frowningly at it.

She had to be Isabella. But working as governess to the Duke of Ridgeway? And hired by his secretary, who had sat at that agency for four days waiting just for her?

What the devil was going on? If Ridgeway or anyone else had laid a hand on her . . . His hand tightened on the decanter.

He was going to find her. She was going to see things his way if it was the last thing he ever accomplished. Now, of course, she would have little choice but to view things as he did. Not that he had ever wanted to threaten her. He had never thought it would be necessary.

Foolish woman. He had always been amazed by her stubbornness. He had not been able to understand her reasoning. Of course, women in love were never reasonable. And she had fancied herself in love with that milksop Daniel Booth.

Though what Isabella had seen in a clergyman who was still only a curate, it was impossible to say. Long limbs, blond curls, and blue eyes—he supposed they must be enough for a woman who did not know what was good for her.

He closed his eyes and thought of Isabella's sunset-gold hair, felt his fingers twined in its silkiness, smelled its fragrance.

Damnation, but he had her where he wanted her now, and she would be made to see it. If he had to start threatening, then he would do so. A dangling noose did not make a comfortable mental image. He would make it up to her later.

IT ANGERED THE DUKE of Ridgeway, standing on the upper terrace outside his house early on the morning after his arrival and looking out over the park that was almost everything of home to him, to know that it was all to be invaded in two days' time.

He loved to entertain at Willoughby. He loved to host concerts and grand balls when possible and to entertain his neighbors to dinner and cards or conversation. He even enjoyed having the occasional overnight guest. But he hated having a houseful of people who looked for nothing but gay and mindless entertainment—Sybil's type of people. And he had seen the guest list. This occasion was to be no exception to the general rule.

He loved the peace and quiet of his home almost more than anything else in his life. And that was to be shattered for goodness knew how long. Sybil's guests never knew quite when to leave once they had come.

He strolled across the terrace and along the side of the house to the lawns at the back and the kitchen garden and greenhouses.

What he would not give for his freedom, he thought in an unguarded moment, and immediately had a mental image of

Pamela and her excitement over her dog, which she had insisted on calling Tiny, though he had explained to her that the puppy would grow. And he thought of her sleepy face and tumbled hair when he had gone to her the night before, not realizing that she would be in bed already. He thought of her warm clinging arms and her wet kiss and her question.

"You won't go away again, Papa?"

"I will be here for a good long while," he had assured her.

"Promise?"

"I promise," he had said, hugging the slight little body and kissing her. "Go to sleep now. I will see you tomorrow."

No. A child had a right to a secure home and two parents even if they were not model parents by any stretch of the imagination. He had been wrong to leave her for so long merely for the sake of his own peace of mind.

He drew to a halt. There was a woman strolling past the massive flowerbeds, where the house flowers were grown.

She was not quite as he remembered her. In fact, when he had looked at her the afternoon before, his first impression had been that Houghton had made a mistake and engaged the wrong woman. But it was she, of course. He had seen that on a closer look.

Whenever he had thought of her in the past weeks, he had pictured her as thin and pale, not at all pretty, only marginally attractive. There had been those long, slim legs, of course, and the shapely hips and firm, high breasts. But a basically unattractive woman—a gentlewoman down on her luck, he had guessed, someone he had felt obliged to help for some unknown reason.

He had helped her.

She was not as he remembered her. She had put on enough weight that her figure was now alluring even through the barrier of her clothes. Her face had color and a healthy glow. It was no longer shadowed and haggard. And her hair, which he had remembered as a dull, tired red, now glowed fire-golden.

Miss Fleur Hamilton, he had discovered the day before with something less than pleased surprise, was a startlingly beautiful woman.

In one way only was she as he remembered her. She was like a marble statue: cool, remote, unresponsive. She had spoken scarcely a word to him during their first encounter, though she had watched him every moment while he took his pleasure of her, he recalled. She had spoken not a word the day before. She had not even curtsied to him.

She had only shrunk from him, naked terror and revulsion in her eyes, when he had offered her his arm to go down the stairs. Why would he have offered his arm to a servant, anyway?

Don't touch me. His lips thinned. She could probably teach Sybil a thing or two about cringing.

He continued his progress toward her, and he knew before he came up to her that she had become aware of his approach, though she gave no visible sign and did not look his way.

"Good morning, Miss Hamilton," he said quietly, stopping when he was still several feet away from her.

She looked back at him with that steady, direct look he remembered.

"Do you like the early morning too?" he asked. "I always find it the loveliest time to be outdoors."

"I will not be your mistress," she said in a steady, low voice.

"Won't you?" he said. "Pardon me, but did I ask?"

"It is so very clear," she said. "I understood perfectly as soon as I saw you yesterday. I will not be your mistress."

"I understood that you had been employed as my daughter's governess," he said. "I expect you to devote all your energies to that task, ma'am."

"It is disgusting," she said. "You are a married man. You have brought me here to live beneath the same roof as your wife and daughter. You expect me to spend several hours a day teaching your daughter. And you expect me also to be your whore here under such conditions. Is that why you paid me so well and fed me? So that I would be beholden to you? I will go back to the gutter where I belong, but I will not allow you to touch me again. You disgust me."

He was angry with the girl. Furious. How dared she? Accusing him of bringing her here to his ancestral home to teach Pamela so that he could sport with her among the groves and in the attics.

"Let me make one thing clear, Miss Hamilton," he said quietly, his hands clasped behind his back. "I instructed my secretary to employ you because you were desperately in need of employment other than that in which you had chosen to engage. I was satisfied from his report that you had been employed in a suitable capacity. You are my servant, ma'am, well paid and well looked after, I believe you will agree. I am not in the habit of consorting with my servants. I am certainly not in the habit of sleeping with them. When I need a whore, I employ one who offers her services for the purpose, and I pay her accordingly. Have I made myself clear?"

She flushed and said nothing.

His eyes narrowed. "I seem to recall having to tell you once before that when I ask a question I require an answer," he said. "Answer me."

"Yes," she whispered. She looked at him steadily, her chin up. "Yes, your grace."

He inclined his head to her. "You may continue your walk," he said. "Good day to you, ma'am."

He strode back the way he had come, the morning ruined by the heat of his temper and the turmoil of his feelings. But he was thankful for his years in the army, which had taught him the discipline of releasing his temper only through words.

He had wanted to take the woman by the arms and shake her until her head flopped on her neck. He had wanted to hurt her, to leave bruises.

He branched off from the terrace to cross a lawn that would take him to the lake. And he deliberately slowed both his steps and his mind. His experiences as an officer had taught him to do the latter, to think with icy logic rather than with white-hot fury.

If she had believed what she said—and she obviously had—then he must admit to himself that she had shown remarkable courage. He supposed that it would not be easy for a woman in a lowly and precarious situation to spit in the eye of a duke. And that was what she had done, figuratively speaking.

She had shown a moral outrage at what she thought he had planned. A whore with morals? But why not? There were any number of respectable women who entirely lacked them.

She had told him that he was disgusting. Was it just the behavior she had imagined him capable of? Or was it his person she had found repulsive?

He did not doubt that it was at least partly the latter. He had unclothed himself completely in front of her, something he had not done with any woman before—not since acquiring his wounds, anyway. And he had stood before her, fully visible to her all the time he had been coupling with her.

He had done it deliberately, he realized now, a release from all the pain and self-consciousness and degradation he had lived with for six years. He had wanted one woman to see him, a woman who could not afford to show revulsion or to refuse him.

And she had passed the test, courageous Fleur, whose eyes had not wavered from his despite the fact that for her it had been a far more momentous occasion than he had realized until it was too late.

Well, so she found him disgusting. Was it so surprising? And did it matter? She was his servant, one of countless many. He had given her employment because she needed it and would never have made a success of being a whore. He had done his part to atone both for his sin of infidelity and for his part in setting the girl on the road to degradation and ruin.

It did not matter. He had done his part and he would forget

about her. If she did not do well as Pamela's governess, then he would have her removed to one of his other estates as some other kind of servant.

He stood gazing down at the lake, willing his land, his home, to perform its old magic on his soul.

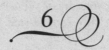

6

*L*ADY PAMELA BACKED UP A FEW YARDS FROM HER puppy and went down on her knees while it tried to run toward her. She laughed helplessly as it tripped on the long grass and rolled over before getting to its feet and resuming its chase.

She picked up the puppy and fell over onto her back. She held it close enough so that it could lick her face, and continued to giggle.

Fleur did not have the heart to remind her pupil that they had come outdoors to paint and that she had had to do some pleading with Mrs. Clement in order to be allowed to bring the child out-of-doors at all. They had been granted only an hour. Lady Pamela so rarely seemed to enjoy herself—except with the Chamberlain children and except on the previous afternoon, when her father came home.

Fleur shuddered.

"You see?" she said when the giggles had abated. "We can see the pavilion on the island and reflected in the lake and framed by trees. You were right. It will make a very pretty picture."

"Ouch!" Lady Pamela giggled again. "Don't bite, Tiny."

"Or perhaps for today you would like to paint Tiny rolling in the grass," Fleur suggested.

"Yes." The child looked at her, bright-eyed. "Is she not funny, Miss Hamilton? Isn't Papa wonderful?"

"Very definitely," a voice said from behind Fleur. "But what is this? A blank piece of paper and dry brushes? Grass in your hair, Pamela? And all over your dress? Whatever will Nanny say?"

"She will scold," Lady Pamela said. "Papa, come and feel Tiny's funny nose. It's all cold."

The Duke of Ridgeway passed Fleur and knelt down beside his daughter.

Fleur stood where she was before the easel and felt turned to ice. She had hoped not to see him for a long, long time after that morning—particularly after that morning. She had felt utterly humiliated.

He had been furious. Every word he had spoken had been like the lash of a whip. She had been forcefully reminded of the fact that he had been an infantry officer with His Grace of Wellington's armies for several years. And she had believed that he spoke the truth.

He had given her this post because he pitied her, not because he desired her.

And her first words to him had been, "I will not be your mistress." Words spoken to the Duke of Ridgeway! Her employer. They did not bear remembering.

He got to his feet and turned to her while Pamela played on.

"You brought her here to paint?" he asked.

"Yes, your grace."

"And have not insisted that she do so?"

"She is very excited about her puppy this afternoon, your grace," she said.

"Was it not agreed yesterday," he asked, "that the puppy was not to interfere with lessons?"

"Yes, your grace." She looked into the dark depths of his eyes and firmly quelled the terror that his height, the breadth of his shoulders, his black hair and hawkish features threatened to turn to panic. And she looked at the disfiguring scar, reminding her of the other marks on his body, which were far worse than just scars. "Sometimes with young children, lesson plans ought not to be rigidly adhered to. We have talked this afternoon about the puppy's teeth and the reason for their small size and impermanence—as with Lady Pamela's. We have talked about the shape of the dog's head and of how it will change as it grows. I have explained how your grooms will train the dog so that eventually it can live in the house. We have—"

"I was not about to dismiss you, ma'am," he said, "though it was a good answer. What was the purpose of the painting lesson?"

"I was going to describe Corinthian columns and pediments," she said, glancing out to the pavilion, "and point out how everything is reversed in a reflection. But your daughter is five years old, your grace. Mainly I planned to allow her to enjoy the fresh air and to experiment with using her paints."

Her chin rose stubbornly. Let him reprimand her if he chose. The child had far too little spontaneity in her life.

"Another good answer," he said. "Do you specialize in them?"

There was no reply to such a question.

"I suppose you have noticed," he said, "that the temple is an exact replica in miniature of the central block of the house?"

"Except for the horseshoe steps," she said, turning to gaze across the lake below them. "Is it the same inside too?"

"Very like," he said, "even to the painting on the inside of the dome. But there is no gallery in the temple. It was built to be picturesque, as was everything else in the park, but it is used as a music pavilion during fêtes and garden parties. And will be used by the orchestra at the ball in three days' time. You have been told that you may attend?"

"Yes, your grace," she said.

He turned to talk to his daughter. "Let's walk down to the water's edge," he said. "The pavilion looks more imposing from there. And the bridge can be seen off in the distance, and something of the cascades. Carry the puppy, Pamela. She will never walk so far."

"But it is time for us to go home," Fleur said.

Dark eyes were turned on her. One lifted eyebrow. "Who says so?" he said.

Fleur felt herself flush. "Mrs. Clement will be expecting us, your grace," she said.

"Nanny?" he said. "Then Nanny will just have to wait, won't she?"

Pamela went clattering down the slope to the lake without taking the path that curved around to it at a less steep gradient. The duke held out a hand to help Fleur down.

And she was in that tunnel again, darkness and cold air rushing at her. All she saw was the hand, the long beautiful fingers that had slid down between her thighs and pushed them wide and that had then opened her firmly, readying her for penetration.

He lowered his hand and turned from her. "Just take it slowly," he said, "unless you are planning to take a swim."

And somehow she brought herself out of the tunnel and forced her legs to move so that she could follow him down the slope to the path below, where the puppy was bounding in circles, happy to be on firmer ground.

Another hour passed before they returned to the house. They strolled by the lake and climbed the bank again at another place. The duke described the various prospects to Fleur in a far more knowledgeable manner than Mrs. Laycock had done. The park had been laid out by William Kent—"No relation," the duke added—for his grace's grandfather, replacing the straight avenues and the large flat parterre gardens that had preceded it.

"I believe my grandmother was outraged," he said. "She was a very proper eighteenth-century lady. She believed that the larger one's formal garden, the greater one's consequence."

He carried the puppy for much of the way, smoothing the soft down over its nose with one finger as it nestled against his chest and fell asleep. And he handed the dog to Fleur before chasing a shrieking Pamela across one wide lawn and wrestling her to the grass, where she lay laughing and flailing her arms and legs.

Both father and daughter looked somewhat rumpled by the time they stepped onto the terrace before the house.

"Will Mama's guests be here soon, Papa?" Lady Pamela asked.

"The day after tomorrow, unless any of them are delayed," he said.

"Will I be able to see the ladies?" she asked.

"Do you want to?"

"May I?" she begged. "Mama will say no, I know she will."

"Perhaps Mama is in the right of it," he said, releasing her hand and reaching for the puppy, which Fleur was carrying. "They will not be ladies you would wish to meet, Pamela."

"But . . ." she said.

"Time to go in," he said, looking up into Fleur's eyes, his own hard as his hand brushed against hers beneath the puppy's stomach, and she snatched it away and took a hasty step backward. "I shall return Tiny to the stables."

"Oh," Fleur said. "We have forgotten the easel and paints. I will have to run back for them."

"I shall send a servant," the duke said impatiently. "Don't trouble yourself, ma'am."

Fleur took Lady Pamela by the hand and led her up to the nursery. The child was tired and incredibly dirty and disheveled, facts which Mrs. Clement did not fail to notice and comment upon.

Fleur stood at the window of her room ten minutes later, her ears ringing from the scathing reprimand she had received. It seemed that her grace was to be told of her terrible insubordination in keeping Lady Pamela from the house more than an hour longer than she had been permitted and in returning her looking like a scarecrow and in such a state of exhaustion that she would doubtless be ill the next day.

Fleur stood close to the window and looked out across the lawns, which gave such a misleading impression of peace. She had thought them peaceful. She had thought them heaven. She had been beginning to relax and to feel more happy than she had felt since early childhood.

Should she leave before she was dismissed?

But where would she go and what would she do? Although she had everything she could possibly need at Willoughby Hall, she had not yet been paid. All the money she had was the few coins that remained from the advance that had been given her to buy some clothes. She did not even have enough with which to return to London.

The thought of London made her shudder. There was only one future facing her there.

She was still almost numb with the nightmare of what had happened. This employment had been given to her by the man who filled all her nightmares with terror. It had been no fortunate chance, after all. He had given her employment because he pitied her—or so he said. She did not know whether to trust him or not.

And suddenly she had found today that all her other terrors had been renewed too. Had there been any pursuit? Was there still? Would she hang if she were caught? Even though it had been an accident? Even though she had been defending herself? Was one hanged regardless of circumstances if one killed another human being? Surely not.

But Matthew had been the only witness. And Matthew was a baron and a justice of the peace. It would be his word against hers. And he had looked up from Hobson's dead body and called her a murderer.

She would hang. They would tie her hands and her feet and place a bag over her head and a rope about her neck.

She turned sharply from the window.

She would not think of it. Or of Daniel, she thought determinedly. She would not. But his gentle smile and his blue eyes and his soft blond hair were there before her anyway, and his tall, slender body dressed in its dark, smart clerical garb.

He had never kissed her. Only her hand, once. She had always wanted him to, but he had refused the only time she had asked him. He wanted her pure on their wedding day, he had told her with that sweet smile.

A kiss would have made her impure? She closed her eyes and dragged at the pins that held her hair primly at the back of her head.

He would be revolted at the knowledge of what she had done. He would look at her sorrowfully. Would he forgive her? Doubtless he would, as Jesus forgave the woman taken in adultery. But she did not want his forgiveness. She wanted his love and his sheltering arms. She wanted peace.

But there could be no peace, although for two weeks she had persuaded herself that there could. She had murdered a man and could never go home. She would hang if she were caught. And she had done what she had done—with his grace, the Duke of Ridgeway. And was now caught in his home rather like a bird in a cage.

She dragged her brush ruthlessly through her snarled hair. No matter how long she remained in this house, no matter how often she saw him, she would never be able to feel anything else but the blackest terror and the most nauseated revulsion whenever she set eyes on him.

No matter how elegantly he might dress, she would always see him as she had seen him in that room at the Bull and Horn—tall and muscled and naked, the triangle of dark hair across his chest and down to his navel, the dreadful purple wounds, the terrifying arousal that had penetrated her and hurt her so searingly and violated her so irrevocably.

Raw manhood exerting its ruthless ascendancy over weakness and poverty and hopelessness.

With her head she knew that it was perhaps unfair to hate him. He had paid well for what she had offered freely. He had shown her kindness both with that meal and with this employment.

But she hated him with a horror and a revulsion that might yet send her fleeing from the house without provisions or plans—just as she had fled from Heron House more than two months before.

She closed her eyes again, the brush fallen still in her hand, and pictured his finger smoothing gently over the puppy's fur. She had to swallow several times to overcome the nausea.

THE DUKE OF RIDGEWAY tapped on the door of the duchess's sitting room the following morning and waited for her personal maid to admit him, curtsy, and leave the room quietly. His wife had sent for him. He rarely entered any of her private apartments without such an invitation.

"Good morning, Sybil," he said. "How are you today?" He crossed the room to take her hands and kiss her. She turned her cheek, as usual.

"Better," she said. "I was a little feverish during the night, but I feel better this morning." She withdrew her hands from his. Small, delicate hands that he had used to like to hold and kiss.

"You must take care of yourself," he said. "I would not want you ill again as you were during the winter."

"I instructed Houghton to pay Miss Hamilton and dismiss her," she said breathlessly, looking at him with her wide blue eyes. "He told me that he must consult you first. What are you going to do about it, Adam?"

"Ask your reason for wanting to dismiss the governess, I suppose," he said. "What has she done or failed to do?"

"I mean about Houghton," she said, tears springing to her eyes. She was wearing a flowing white silk-and-lace robe. Her blond hair was lying loose along her back. She looked, her husband thought dispassionately, quite breathtakingly lovely. And as fragile as the young girl with whom he had left his heart when he went to Belgium. "Are you going to let him get away with speaking to me like that?"

"Houghton is my personal secretary," he said, "answerable to me alone, Sybil. I would release him in a moment if he forgot himself to the extent of taking orders from anyone else in this house without first consulting me."

She flushed. "So your secretary is more important to you than I am," she said. "It was not always so, Adam. You loved me once, or so I believed. It seems I was deceived."

"You should know by now," he said, "to come to me personally with all your problems. You would save yourself some humiliation if you would do so. An efficient secretary cannot take orders from two people. What is the problem with Miss Hamilton?"

"You should not need to ask that question," she said, twisting a handkerchief in her hands. "It should be enough that I wish to see her gone. I don't think she is suitable to have the care of my daughter. Please dismiss her, Adam."

"You know," he said with a sigh, "that I do not dismiss even the lowliest of my servants, Sybil, without a very good reason. I don't know if you realize how close members of the servant class live to the edge of poverty. I will not dismiss anyone merely to satisfy a whim."

"A whim!" she said, her eyes widening and filling with tears once more. "I am your wife, Adam."

"Yes." He looked at her steadily. "You are, aren't you?"

She lowered her eyes and sat gracefully on the edge of the daybed. "I am the Duchess of Ridgeway," she said quietly.

"That sounds like a more accurate description of you," he said. His voice held a note of weariness. "Must we always have this sort of conversation, Sybil? Must I always appear to be the tyrant? I'm sorry for my sarcasm. What is the problem with Miss Hamilton?"

"She took Pamela outside yesterday afternoon," she said, "despite the cold wind and the direct sunlight. She nagged at Nanny until Nanny said yes, just for an hour. And she returned more than two hours later. Pamela was dirty and exhausted and is too ill even to rise from her bed this morning, the poor darling. She deliberately disobeyed Nanny, Adam. Even you cannot defend her against that."

"They were with me," he said. "I would not allow them to return to the house when Miss Hamilton would have come."

She looked up at him sharply. "She was with you?" she said, raising her handkerchief to her lips. "For more than two hours?"

"You have the wrong pronoun," he said. "I said *they* were with me—Pamela, Miss Hamilton, and the puppy. If Pamela was dirty, it was because I rolled in the grass with her. If she was tired, it was because I ran and played with her and gave her more than two hours of sunshine and fresh air. Children should be tired after an outing and a romp."

The duchess was very white. "This is intolerable," she said. "I have told you before, Adam, that you are far too rough with Pamela. She is delicate and should be left to my care and Nanny's. And a dog! She can catch goodness only knows what disease from it. Oh, I knew this would happen as soon as you came home. You have no regard for my sensibilities at all. You are so very selfish. I was quite deceived in you."

He looked steadily at her until she lowered her eyes again.

"I will continue to spend as much time with Pamela as I can spare," he said. "She needs a parent's attention more than the coddling of an elderly nurse, Sybil. And she needs activity, both physical and mental. And let me understand you. Does Miss Hamilton take her orders from Nanny?"

"Yes," the duchess said, "of course she does. My darling is just a baby."

"In future," he said, "it will be the other way around. I trust you will inform Nanny of the change. She will pout when you tell her, though you will do so. I will inform Miss Hamilton of the new rule."

Two tears spilled over from the duchess's eyes. "You are a cruel and hard-hearted man," she said. "You will do anything to thwart my will, won't you, Adam? Just because you once did me a kindness, must I be in your debt forevermore?"

He looked down at her tight-lipped. "You know that there has never been any question of any such thing," he said. "And never will be. Only in your imagination, Sybil. Sometimes you almost have me persuaded that I am a tyrant and a villain."

She brushed at her eyes with her handkerchief and twisted it in her lap. "So I am to subject myself to having my daughter taken from my care and from her nurse's care and put into that of your doxy," she said. "Very well, Adam. I am too weak to fight you."

"My doxy?" he said. "Have a care, Sybil. Perhaps I should suggest that you make it unlikely that I would wish for the services of any doxy." The right side of his face smiled fleetingly when she glanced up at him, startled. "No, I didn't think that idea would appeal to you."

"Sometimes I think you will force me to hate you," she said in a low voice that shook from her tears.

"You become tedious," he said.

He watched her as she coughed and sank back against the cushions of the daybed and pressed the handkerchief to her lips.

"I should have insisted that you have that cough looked at by another doctor months ago," he said quietly. "Hartley seems quite unable to cure it. Let me send for a physician from London, Sybil. Let me do something for you. Let there be some kindness between us for a change."

"I think I would like to be alone," she said. "I need to rest."

"I did not plan this," he said wearily. "I did not plan that we would come to bicker and set our wills against each other. I did not foresee that you would come to see me as a tyrant and that sometimes I would be forced into acting like one. I hoped for a good marriage. I did not foresee that we might come to hate each other."

"Sometimes," she said, burying her face in her handkerchief, her voice a thin thread of misery, "I hate you for pretending to be dead and coming back alive. I hate you for driving Thomas away when you knew what we had become to each other. Sometimes I find it hard not to hate you, Adam, though I try not to. You are my husband."

She started coughing again and could not stop.

White-faced, he crossed the room to her, took out his own handkerchief, went down on one knee before her, and held it out to her. But she slapped his hand away.

"Sybil," he said, and rested a hand lightly against the back of her head while she coughed.

But she squirmed away from him, got to her feet, and fled to her dressing room, slamming the door behind her.

The Duke of Ridgeway remained on one knee, his head bowed forward. And he wondered, as he had done dozens of times before, if she had ever loved him. Had she said she did only because she wanted to be his duchess and mistress of one of the most splendid homes in the kingdom? Had all the kisses, all the melting looks and sweet smiles, been artifice?

He had grown up knowing that he would be expected to marry her. And the idea had never disturbed him. But he had not fallen in love with her until he came home from Spain to find her grown up and lovely and fragile, her blue eyes wide with admiration for him. He had fallen deeply in love, painfully in love.

And had it all been completely one-sided? Had her protestations of love been all lies? Or perhaps she too had been bound by the expectations of years. Perhaps she had tried to fall in love with him or at least to develop a regard for him. Perhaps she had tried.

He supposed that she might have felt some regard for him then, when his face was whole, when perhaps he could have been described as a good-looking man. He would never forget the look of deep revulsion on her face when he had caught her up on their first meeting after his return and twirled her about and kissed her.

She had hurt him badly. But he had expected the look to disappear once she had got used to his new appearance. It never had. But by the time of his return, of course, she had been betrothed to Thomas. He had made far too light of that fact at first.

The duke got wearily to his feet and put his handkerchief away in his pocket. If someone had told him that spring of Waterloo and the spring after, when he was coming home, that his love for Sybil would ever die, he would have laughed in derision. A love like his could never die this side of doomsday.

So much for love, he thought with heavy cynicism.

He turned to the door, aware of his wife coughing in her dressing room. There was not the spark of an ember of his love left. Only a certain pity for what she had undoubtedly suffered, and the vague hope of some peace between them. Some hope that he would not always appear to be the villain in their life together.

But it seemed that he was not to be granted even peace.

7

$\mathcal{J}$T WAS PETER HOUGHTON WHO INFORMED FLEUR of the new arrangement later that same morning while she waited in the schoolroom for a pupil who would not come because her nurse insisted that she was ill with exhaustion from her exertions of the day before.

Fleur was a little afraid of Peter Houghton because he undoubtedly knew who she was and what she was. And yet he had treated her with unfailing courtesy in the two days since his return to Willoughby—they both ate with the upper servants at Mrs. Laycock's table. Not by word or gesture had he shown that he felt any distaste at having to consort with her on terms of near-equality. There had been not a whisper or a hint of what she was to any of the other servants.

She was relieved by the new arrangement, not because she wished to have power over Lady Pamela's nurse, but because she wished to feel that she was doing something to earn her salary and keep. She had had the uneasy feeling for the previous weeks that she was there on false pretenses.

The duke himself brought his daughter to the schoolroom that afternoon. Fleur curtsied and did not look directly at him. But, she realized before many minutes had passed, he had no intention of leaving immediately. He settled himself quietly on a chair in one corner of the room and watched.

They worked with the alphabet book for a short while, making a game out of memorizing the letters, each of them thinking of some absurd word that began with the letter in question and then trying to remember each word and its letter in sequence.

"Faradiddle," the duke said when Lady Pamela had puzzled over F for several seconds.

She exploded with sudden laughter.

It was his only contribution to that particular lesson.

They counted up to fifty and back to one again and did some simple sums on paper. They examined a tablecloth that Fleur had found folded in a drawer in her room, and she named each embroidered stitch for Lady Pamela and promised that she could start a handkerchief of her own the next day and learn one of the stitches.

"Can I choose whatever colors I want?" she asked Fleur.

"Any colors you wish," Fleur promised with a smile.

"Red daisies and blue stems?"

"Purple daisies and canary stems if you wish," Fleur said.

"But everyone will laugh."

"Then you must choose whether to pick your own colors and be laughed at or pick the expected colors and not be laughed at," Fleur said. "It is quite simple. The choice will be entirely yours."

Lady Pamela frowned and looked suspiciously at her governess.

They talked about the picture of the pavilion, which had still not been painted, and Fleur lifted down a rather large landscape painting that was on the wall so that her pupil could see how many different colors and shades had been used to create the total effect of sky and grass and trees.

"But the choice is yours, you see," she said. "Your job as an artist is to help the viewer see what you see. And no one can tell you quite what you see. We all see things differently."

"I want you to play the harpsichord for me," Lady Pamela said when the topic was exhausted.

Fleur was very aware of her employer sitting silently in his corner.

"Perhaps you would like to sit on the stool and I shall give you a lesson," she suggested.

But Lady Pamela had already tried to play for herself and had discovered that she could not produce music as Fleur could. She had also learned that even after a lesson or two she had not acquired the magic formula for producing a fluent melody.

"Sit down," she said, "and play for me."

"Please," Fleur said quietly.

But even as she prayed silently for cooperation, she knew that she would not get it.

"Play for me," the child ordered petulantly.

"Please," Fleur said.

"That is silly," Lady Pamela said. "What difference does 'please' make?"

"It makes me feel that I am being asked, not ordered," Fleur said. "It makes me feel good about myself."

"That is silly," the child said.

"Please will you play the harpsichord, Miss Hamilton, while Pamela goes to lie down on her bed?"

Fleur's back stiffened. She had not heard him get up and cross the room.

His daughter threw him an exasperated look. "Please, Miss Hamilton," she said.

Fleur closed her eyes briefly. She would have done anything rather than play. Her hands were clammy. But she sat on the stool without looking around and played Bach, compensating as well as she could for the key that stuck.

"It is your turn now, Lady Pamela," she said when she was finished.

"You are good," his grace said. "Have you seen the instruments in the drawing room and music room?"

Fleur had seen them during the tour with Mrs. Laycock, though she had not had the temerity to touch either one. The pianoforte in the drawing room was better than the one at Heron House, she suspected, lovely as that one had been— Mama's precious treasure. The massive grand pianoforte in the music room she had been able to look at only in awe.

"Yes, your grace," she said. "I saw them on my first day here."

"Come along, Pamela," he said, reaching for his daughter's hand. "We will hear Miss Hamilton in the music room. And we will remember to say 'please.' Won't we?"

"Yes, Papa," she said.

Fleur followed them numbly from the room and along the upper corridor to the far staircase. And yet there was a feeling of excitement too. She was to be allowed to play that pianoforte!

If only she could be alone, she thought as they entered the room next to the library and she approached the instrument and touched its keys reverently. If only he were not there.

"If you please, Miss Hamilton," he said quietly, and he disappeared somewhere behind her back with his daughter.

She played Beethoven. It had been so long. Beethoven was not suited to a harpsichord. She played hesitantly at first, until her fingers accustomed themselves to the smooth ivory of the keys and the flow of the music and until her soul was carried beyond itself and she forgot where she was.

Music had always been her great love, her great escape. Cousin Caroline's barbed tongue, Amelia's caustic comments, the knowledge that she would never see her parents again, the strict discipline and drab routine of her school years—all had ceased to exist when she touched a keyboard.

She bowed her head over her still hands when she was finished.

"May I go and see Tiny now, Papa?" a voice said from behind her, bringing her soul back inside her body again.

"Yes," he said. "Ask a footman to go with you. You might remember to say 'please.' "

"That's silly, Papa," the child said.

Fleur heard the door open and close again.

"You have great talent," the Duke of Ridgeway said. "But you are out of practice."

"Yes, your grace."

"If you are to teach my daughter," he said, "you must play faultlessly yourself. Half an hour a day for her lesson, an hour a day for your practice."

"Where, your grace?" She still had not turned.

"Here, of course," he said.

She rubbed at a key with one finger. "I am not allowed on this floor, your grace," she said.

"Are you not?" he said. "By Nanny's orders?"

"By her grace's," she said.

"Given in person?"

"Yes, your grace."

"You will spend an hour and a half each day in here," he said, "by my express order. I shall explain to her grace."

She could not continue to sit there all day with him standing behind her. She drew a steadying breath, got to her feet, and turned to face him. He was standing quite close, so that for a moment she felt again that terror at his largeness.

"You have had access to a pianoforte for most of your life," he said. It was not a question.

She said nothing.

"You told Houghton that your father died recently in debt," he said.

"Yes."

"Did he?"

She looked up into his eyes.

"Did he die in debt?"

"Yes." She was not sure that any volume had come out with the word.

"And your mother?" he asked.

"She died," she said, "a long time ago."

"And you have no other family?"

She had never been good at lying, though she had done enough of it in the past few months, heaven knew. She thought of Cousin Caroline and Amelia and Matthew and shook her head quickly.

"What are you frightened of?" he asked. "Just of me?"

"I should be with Lady Pamela," she said, raising her chin, firming her voice.

"No, you should not," he said. "My orders take precedence over yours, Miss Hamilton. Pamela is a difficult pupil?"

"She is not used to doing what she does not wish to do, your grace," she said.

"You have my permission to insist," he said. "Provided you do not make of her life a dreary business."

"She is a child," she said. "My greatest delight is in seeing her smile and hearing her laugh."

"Are those skills you can teach, Miss Hamilton?" he asked. "I have never seen or heard you do either."

"I can give her my full attention," she said, "and praise where it is due and encouragement when praise would be inappropriate. And I can give her enough freedom so that she will feel like a child."

He searched her eyes with his so that she felt breathless, and resisted the temptation to panic. She wished she had taken a step back from him when she had first risen from the stool and it would have seemed more natural to do so than to do it now. She felt strangely that she could be scorched by the heat from his body, even though he stood several feet away. His face was too close, as close as it was in all her nightmares, bent over her naked body.

"Your working day is at an end, ma'am," he said. His voice

had changed in tone. It was cold, cynical. "You are dismissed. I shall go and join my daughter in the stables."

"Yes, your grace." She turned to leave.

"Miss Hamilton?"

She half-turned her head.

"I am pleased with what I have seen of your work this afternoon," he said.

She stood still for a moment before leaving the room and closing the door behind her. She drew in deep lungfuls of air before proceeding on her way up to her room.

LORD BROCKLEHURST SENT HIS card up to one of the rooms at the Pulteney Hotel and paced the lobby impatiently.

It was a stroke of raw luck, he knew, despite the fact that the Bow Street Runner had reported the detail to him the day before with puffed chest and important air, as if he had manufactured the whole thing with his superior police skills.

The list of guests for Willoughby Hall had been disappointing. Only two of them he knew even vaguely. There would have been no realistic chance of striking up a close enough friendship with either of them that he could have invited himself along to the house. Besides, all except one couple, with whom he had no acquaintance at all, had left London already.

He would have had to do things the way he did not want to do them. He would have had to go down to Dorsetshire in his capacity as a justice of the peace to arrest Isabella and bring her home for trial. He did not want his hand to be so forced. He did not want all his options to be cut.

Dammit, he did not want to see that lovely neck ringed by a noose.

But only one day after delivering the list and declaring that Lord Thomas Kent was nowhere in Britain, and after having had his bill paid, Snedburg had come bustling back, puffed with importance, to announce that his lordship had that morning set foot on English soil from the deck of an East India Company ship.

"Of course, sir," he had said, "I know from experience that when the nobility disappear from our shores, it is often to take employment with one of the companies. It was a simple, though time-consuming matter, you will understand, to make inquiries. What could have been more fortunate than to discover not only that his lordship had indeed taken himself to India but also that he was bringing himself back again?" He had coughed with self-satisfaction.

Lord Brocklehurst had paid the man more generously than he ought, he felt. Living in town was deuced expensive.

An employee of the hotel bowed in front of him and informed him that Lord Thomas Kent would receive him in his suite. Lord Brocklehurst turned to the staircase.

Lord Thomas Kent was a few years younger than he. The two men had never been very close friends, merely friendly acquaintances who had frequented the same gaming hells and taverns many years before.

Lord Thomas was in his sitting room, dressed in a long brocade dressing gown, when Lord Brocklehurst was admitted by a servant. He had grown more handsome with the passing of early youth, the latter noticed: bronzed, dark-haired, slim, a man of a little above average height.

"Bradshaw," he said, extending his right hand, his teeth very white against his sun-browned face. "I hardly recognized you from the title on your card. Your father passed on, did he?"

"Five years ago," Lord Brocklehurst said. "You are looking well, Kent."

"I've never felt better," the other said. "I thought not a soul knew of my return. I thought I would have to do the rounds of all the clubs today and leave my card at every door in Mayfair. This is a pleasant surprise."

"I heard in passing," Lord Brocklehurst said. "Been gone long, have you, Kent?"

"For well over five years," the other said. "Ever since that debacle over the dukedom. I went running with my tail between my legs. Doubtless you heard."

"Yes." Lord Brocklehurst coughed delicately. "A nasty business, Kent. You have my sympathy."

Lord Thomas shrugged. "I am not sure the sedentary life would have suited me after all," he said. "Or the married life. Too confining by half. Are the ladies as lovely as they used to be, Bradshaw? And as willing? I must say I am starved for an English beauty or two—or twenty."

"And just as expensive as they ever were," Lord Brocklehurst said, "if not more so. You are going home?"

"To Willoughby?" The other laughed aloud. "I think that would be the unwisest move of my life, considering some of the things that were said when I left. It can't be a comfortable thing to have someone who once wore your title breathing down your neck, I suppose—and someone who was once betrothed to your wife. Though it might be worth everything just to see the look on Ridgeway's face."

"Old wounds heal fast," Lord Brocklehurst said, "especially within families. He would probably be delighted to see you."

"The prodigal's return and the fatted calf?" Lord Thomas said. "I think not. I'm deuced hungry and hate eating at hotels. Is White's still standing where it used to stand?"

"I'll be delighted to buy you luncheon there," Lord Brocklehurst said.

"Will you?" Lord Thomas laughed again. "The Heron property is good to you, Bradshaw? I can remember the time when neither one of us had a feather to fly with. Luncheon it is, then, and perhaps tonight we can go in search of wine, women, and cards together, though I might be persuaded to dispense with the cards. Let my man pour you a drink while I dress."

Lord Brocklehurst sipped on his drink a few minutes later and stared thoughtfully at the door through which Lord Thomas had disappeared.

• • •

SIXTEEN GUESTS ARRIVED TO STAY at Willoughby Hall, all on the same day. The Duke of Ridgeway stood beside his wife in the great hall to receive them and circulated among them during tea in the saloon late in the afternoon.

They were not quite the crowd he would have chosen to consort with, given the choice, he reflected, but Sybil was happy and looking quite glowingly lovely, and he supposed she was entitled to some happiness. Indeed, he was glad to see her enjoying herself. It seemed to have been beyond his power to give her any enjoyment since their marriage.

And he was getting mortally tired of sharing a dining table with her, one at the head, the other at the foot, making labored conversation across its empty length.

"Good hunting do you have here, Ridgeway?" Sir Ambrose Marvell asked him as they sipped on their tea.

"My gamekeeper tells me that the deer are increasing at an interesting rate," he replied.

"And the fishing?" Mr. Morley Treadwell asked.

It was easy to see already whom Sybil had invited as her *cher ami*—there would have to be someone, of course, as there always was on such occasions. Sir Philip Shaw, he had heard, scarcely needed to keep a home of his own, spending all his time moving about among the homes of his numerous flirts and mistresses. And the current joke had it that one need not assign a guest bedchamber to Shaw—he would cheerfully share with one of the ladies, usually his hostess.

His indolent, almost effeminate manner and graceful person and permanently sleepy eyes were apparently irresistible to the ladies. And Sybil was already sparkling up at him, one slim white hand on his arm. Where the devil had she met him? But of course she sometimes took herself off on visits without him—she never asked, and he never resented not being asked. Most recently she had spent two weeks at her sister's, apparently in company with other select guests.

The duke sighed inwardly. He hoped he was not going to have to go through that ridiculous farce again of playing the icy husband guarding his conjugal rights. It was so very tedious—and not a little humiliating. And of course it forever enhanced her image of him as humorless tyrant. Perhaps he was just that. He was coming almost to believe it himself.

When could he decently escape? he wondered. And where could he escape to? The lessons abovestairs were doubtless finished for the day. He was glad at least that Miss Hamilton had done her practicing early that morning, when he had been able to listen to her at his leisure. He had opened the door between the library and the music room and sat at his desk and listened. But he had made sure that she saw him. He did not wish to give the impression that he was spying on her.

She really did have talent. Music that he had only ever been able to produce with competence she brought alive and warm and flowing. The hour he had spent listening to her had soothed him far more than the ride he had planned.

He had not entered the room at all, or stood in the doorway to watch her. He would have had to be blind not to have noticed the deep revulsion in her eyes whenever she looked at him. But it did not matter. He was not looking for any sort of relationship with her. He merely hoped she would be good for Pamela. And he liked her music.

"Adam, my dear man." The voice was low, the perfume seductive. Lady Victoria Underwood, widow, who had decided during the Season the year before that they were close enough friends that they could drop the cumbersome formality of using titles, smiled up at him from beneath artfully darkened eyelashes. "What a very splendid home you have. Why have you not invited me here before?"

She was leaning slightly toward him. For some reason she had never found his scar repulsive.

"It makes you quite the most attractive man of my acquaintance," she said to him the year before on one of the many nights when she had failed to entice him into her bed.

He often wondered why he had never given in. She was not beautiful, but there was a seductive sexuality about her. Coupling with her would have been a somewhat more sensual experience than the one he had had with Fleur Hamilton.

But he wished he had not had that thought. He had been unconsciously trying to divorce in his mind the Miss Hamilton who wanted to teach and care for Pamela and who made of Mozart and Beethoven haunting experiences of the soul from the thin and pale and lusterless prostitute he had taken with such quick lust in a cheap tavern room a month before.

"I thought you did not like to leave London, Lady Underwood," he said, smiling.

"Victoria," she said, looking down to his lips. "I believe I would accept an invitation to the Hebrides, my dear Adam, if I knew you were to be there."

"I never would be," he said. "It sounds too cold for me."

"But what a delicious excuse," she said, "to huddle under a blanket for warmth—with the right company, of course."

He laughed and used the excuse of a plate of cakes passing at that moment to draw the Mayberrys into the group.

He could stomach the flirtations and the empty chatter when in London. He could even derive some amusement from them, though he preferred evenings of serious and stimulating conversation with his closer friends. But there he could always withdraw to the quiet of his own home when he had had enough. Here he was in his own home.

That was always the trouble with Sybil's confounded parties.

Fortunately the guests did not linger. Almost all of them had had long journeys and welcomed the chance of some time to rest and refresh themselves in the privacy of their own rooms. The duchess, too, flushed and bright-eyed, retired to her own apartments until dinnertime.

The duke wandered out onto the terrace. He wondered if Pamela was visiting her puppy and heard a distant shriek of laughter even as he did so. He turned and strolled in the direction of the stables, wondering idly if Fleur Hamilton would be there too or if Pamela had brought a footman with her as she had the day before. He did not imagine that Nanny would consider a visit to the stables and a puppy consistent with her dignity.

Pamela was sitting on top of the fence around the paddock beside the stables, her legs swinging, while Fleur, inside the paddock, tickled the puppy's stomach with her slippered foot. She was laughing, a look of such carefree beauty on her face that his grace hung back, reluctant to be seen.

A groom—Ned Driscoll—was also laughing, one foot resting on a lower rung of the fence, his arms draped over the top, his cap pulled low over his eyes.

"I think the puppy likes it," Fleur said.

"But then, who wouldn't, miss," Ned said boldly a moment before spotting his master standing quietly behind him. He straightened up hastily, pulled at the brim of his cap, and scuttled off in the direction of the stables.

Fleur did not look up, and continued to tickle the dog with her toes. But the laughter in her face faded. His grace knew with an inward sigh that his presence had been noted.

"Papa." Pamela looked at him petulantly, her laughter of moments before forgotten. "Mama promised that she would call me down for tea. Nanny got me all dressed up, but Mama did not send, and Miss Hamilton would not let me go down unless she did."

The duke looked at Fleur, who was watching the puppy try to eat the grass.

"She was not sent for," she said. "I explained to her that all the guests must be tired and that her grace must have decided to wait for another day. I brought her out here, hoping she would forget her disappointment."

"But she promised, Papa," the child said. "And Miss Hamilton would not let me go. Nanny would have let me."

"I think not," he said. "And doubtless Miss Hamilton is right. Mama must have decided that some other day will be better, Pamela. I will remind her."

"You are horrid," the child shrieked. "You are both horrid. Mama said I could. I am going to tell Mama."

She jumped from the top of the fence to the outside of the paddock, gathered up her skirt, and raced around the corner of the stable block and out of sight.

"I'll catch up to her," Fleur said.

"Let her go," he said. "She will come to no harm, and sometimes it is best to be alone when in the middle of a temper tantrum."

The gate into the paddock was chained shut. Fleur must have entered it over the fence. He saw her flush as she glanced toward the gate. She arranged her skirt carefully as she set a foot on the lower rung of the fence and swung the other leg over. He kept his hands behind him. He knew she would not welcome his help.

But her skirt caught on the rough wood of the rung below and behind her, and she was stuck. He strode toward her, leaned over to release the fabric, took her by the waist, and lifted her to the ground.

He did not remember her sweet fragrance from that first time. But then, of course, she would have had only water with which to wash herself and her hair at that time. The sun made a shining burnished-gold halo of her hair now. And there was soft warm flesh at her small waist.

She shuddered convulsively and pulled blindly away from him. She made a guttural noise in her throat, similar to the one he remembered her making when he had penetrated her body. She lifted a trembling hand across her mouth and kept it there. She closed her eyes.

He could think of nothing to say and could not move.

She opened her eyes and removed the hand. She opened her mouth as if to speak, bit down on her lower lip, and turned her head aside. And she stooped hastily down to scoop up the puppy, which had come scampering through the bottom of the fence.

"I must take her back to her pen," she said.

"Yes."

He stood aside and watched her go, her golden head bent to the puppy, her walk hasty and self-conscious. And he felt a great weight of depression on his spirits.

But why? A governess—a whore turned governess—shuddered and almost vomited at his touch. There was a lady guest at the house—a baronet's widow—who would welcome his touch and even his presence in her bed, a woman who found his disfigurement arousing and who would perhaps not even blanch if he came to her naked and she saw the other, far worse scars.

What was there to be depressed about? Perhaps he should encourage Lady Underwood. Perhaps she would be a balm to his wounded self-esteem. Perhaps he should make her his mistress for the duration of her stay, have his fill of a woman who wanted him.

Except that by doing so he would be accomplishing exactly what he had come home to prevent Sybil from doing, making of Willoughby a place of debauchery, making himself unworthy of the privilege of being the master of it all.

He was still standing against the fence when Fleur came out of the stables, her arms empty. She glanced his way, turned her head sharply, and hurried off in the direction of the house.

Well.

What the devil had he been thinking of to send her here? It was true that at the time he had not been planning to follow so soon after, but even so, he had known that sooner or later he would be returning to Willoughby. He could never stay away for more than a very few months at a time.

Why had he had her sent here? There were numerous other places he could have sent her. Or he could easily have found her a post with one of his acquaintances. In either case he need not have seen her ever again.

Why had he had Houghton send her here?

Of course, it was not too late, he supposed, to have her sent on somewhere else. Sybil would be delighted; Nanny would be triumphant; Pamela would not be heartbroken; Fleur herself would be relieved beyond measure.

And he?

He turned to walk away from the house toward a grove of trees and the artificial ruins of a tower, which his grandfather had been particularly pleased with. He would think about it some other time. He had been home for only three days. It was no time for hasty decisions.

He rather thought that she would in time prove good for Pamela.

Besides, she needed the pianoforte in the music room. He did not have an instrument to match it on any of his other properties.

The thought consoled him.

The gardeners would need to be reminded, he thought, that there was much deadwood to be cleared out from among these trees.

8

PART FROM A STROLL IN THE PARK THE DAY
after their arrival, the guests did not exert themselves
a great deal. All was in preparation for the grand outdoor ball
that evening. It seemed certain that the event would take place
out-of-doors. The long spell of warm, dry weather continued
through the day.

Servants were frantically busy from early morning on,
catering to the needs and wishes of sixteen newly arrived
guests, preparing a grand banquet for them in the evening,
decorating the area about the lake for the festivities, and
preparing the refreshments for those who would attend the
ball.

Lady Pamela was bouncing with eagerness to watch the
proceedings and was convinced that her mama would allow
her to see all the ladies in their evening finery. Fleur was less
convinced. The duchess did not come to see her daughter all
day, and it seemed altogether likely that she would forget her
entirely until the following day.

She would do what she could to give the child some pleasure, she decided. After a morning of easy lessons, which did
not require too much concentration on her pupil's part, she
took her outside, and they made their way to the spot from
which they had been going to paint the pavilion a few days be-

fore. From there they could watch the preparations without getting in the way of busy workmen.

"Oh, the lanterns!" Lady Pamela exclaimed in some awe, gazing at the hundreds of colored lanterns that were being strung in the trees surrounding the lake and on the island and main paths leading from the house. "They will look like magic tonight, Miss Hamilton."

The orchestra had arrived and were resting and refreshing themselves somewhere in the house. Their instruments were being taken across to the island by boat. On a flat lawn to the west of the lake, closest to the house, a large wooden floor was being laid for the dancing. Tables were being set with white cloths on the north side, directly below where Fleur stood with Lady Pamela.

All the gentry from the neighborhood and the town of Wollaston would come for the ball, Mrs. Laycock had told Fleur. And all the servants would be allowed to attend, provided they were not on duty.

There had been some hunt balls at Heron House. Fleur had always enjoyed them. There was something marvelously exciting about dressing up and seeing all one's acquaintances dressed up too, and in seeing a ballroom decorated with flowers and candles and in hearing it filled with music. There was a wonderful exhilaration in dancing.

But she was quite sure that those balls would be nothing to compare in splendor with the ball that was planned for that evening.

She was, of course, only a servant. She had no grand ball gown or jewels to wear. And it was unlikely that anyone would ask her to dance. But of course! She had almost forgotten in the turmoil of the past few days, in her discovery of just who the Duke of Ridgeway was, in her fear that perhaps by some strange chance one of the guests would be someone who knew her—she had almost forgotten Mr. Chamberlain and his hope that she would dance with him.

She hoped he had not forgotten. Oh, she hoped it with all her heart. She looked forward to seeing him again. And she looked forward to the evening just like a child being offered a rare treat.

"Mama will let me come and see the ladies, won't she?" Lady Pamela said wistfully at her side.

"I don't know, sweetheart," Fleur said, squeezing the child's hand and fearing that she did know very well. "Shall we go and see how Tiny is today? She must be feeling lonely. You have not played with her yet."

"Yes," Lady Pamela said, turning reluctantly away from the view below. "I should have asked Papa when he came to sit in the schoolroom with us this morning. He would have said yes, perhaps."

"I will see what I can do," Fleur said.

The servants ate early that evening. Fleur was back upstairs before her charge's bedtime and could see that there was still a light in the nursery. She knocked and went in.

Lady Pamela's eager expression faded. "Oh," she said, "I thought it was Mama."

"Mama is busy, lovey," Mrs. Clement said. "She will come and spend a long time with you tomorrow. You know Mama loves you."

"Perhaps," Fleur said, glancing at the nurse, "if you put on a warm cloak you can come outside with me now to see the lanterns lit. All the ladies and gentlemen are at dinner still."

"Ooh. May I? May I, Nanny?" Lady Pamela turned pleading eyes on her nurse.

"I will keep her out of the way of the guests," Fleur said.

"She will probably catch cold," Mrs. Clement said. "And her grace will doubtless be angry if she sees her daughter out of the nursery after dinner, Miss Hamilton. But I am reminded that his grace has said that you are in charge here. Do as you wish."

The nurse's tone was hostile, but Fleur smiled at her and at Lady Pamela, who had rushed for her cloak.

She did not really need the cloak, Fleur thought as they stepped outside five minutes later. The air was still warm. And unfortunately it was only early dusk, so the lamps would not look at their best even if they were already lit. But she would do the best she could.

They stayed out longer than she had intended so that Lady Pamela did eventually see the lake and its surroundings in all the magic of the darkness and lantern light. And the orchestra were tuning their instruments inside the pavilion, with its doors thrown open so that the music wafted over the water.

Several of the guests who had not been invited to the banquet began to arrive, and the child's eyes grew round at the splendor of the ladies' gowns and the gentlemen's evening coats, and at the jewels that glittered in the many colors of the lanterns.

And finally, when they were already on their way back to the house, the banquet guests were coming along the terrace all together in a group. Fleur drew Lady Pamela into the shade of a tree.

"We will look, sweetheart," she said. "Don't say anything. Perhaps Mama will be upset to see you outside in the dark."

But she need not have worried. The child seemed quite content to be a silent spectator. She watched in wonder as her mother passed on the arm of a gentleman, laughing and sparkling up at him. The duke was farther back in the group, a lady on his arm.

"Ooh," the child said. "Mama is the prettiest lady. Isn't she, Miss Hamilton? She is the prettiest lady of all."

"Yes, she is, indeed," Fleur said. And she felt that she did not lie.

The child was noticeably tired by the time they arrived back at the nursery and was quite content to give herself over to her nurse's fussing.

Fleur hurried to her room to change into her best dress—a plain blue muslin, which she had thought something of an extravagance when spending the money Mr. Houghton had given her in London. Now it seemed very ordinary indeed in comparison with the gowns she had seen outside.

But it did not matter. She was, after all, only a servant. And nothing could quite quench her excitement this evening. She dressed her hair carefully, the knot at the back of her head a little looser than usual, a few strands of hair allowed to fall over her ears and along her neck.

She felt as nervous as a girl must feel at her come-out ball, she was convinced as she hurried down the stairs and across the hall and outdoors. There were light and music and laughter coming from the direction of the lake. Of course, she had never had a come-out ball.

IF THEY COULD HAVE PLANNED the weather as meticulously as all the other details of the evening had been planned, the Duke of Ridgeway thought, they could hardly have done better. Even as the night wore on, there was still a suggestion of warmth in the air, though the basic coolness was, of course, perfect for those who danced every set. And the breeze was only enough to sway the lanterns in the trees and flutter silks attractively and cool heated cheeks without in any way endangering the elaborate coiffures of the ladies.

He had always enjoyed the more elaborate of the entertainments that Willoughby was famous for. And this was no exception. It was true that he had found the conversation of his guests through much of the day somewhat insipid, but then, tonight all his neighbors were present too. And he had always made a point of being friendly with his neighbors.

He danced the opening set with his wife, who was easily the most lovely of all the ladies present, he thought entirely without bias. She had realized, of course, that a gown of sheer white silk and lace would pick up the colors of the lanterns and would sparkle in the breeze. Sybil always dressed for maximum effect.

He danced with some of his guests and some of his neighbors, and talked with several of the men. He allowed Lady Underwood to persuade him, when he had asked her to dance, to row her across to the island instead and stroll past the pavilion and among the trees, as some of the other guests were doing. He resisted her very open hints that he kiss her among the trees.

And he watched his servants dance and help themselves to refreshments and generally enjoy themselves. He made a point of speaking to as many of them as possible.

He stayed away from Fleur Hamilton. She was looking extremely lovely, the simplicity of her dress and hair succeeding only in making all the other ladies look overdressed. Her hair glowed golden in the light of the lanterns.

And if his wife sparkled, then Fleur glowed as she danced with Houghton, with the vicar, with Ned Driscoll, with Chesterton, with Shaw, and with Chamberlain—twice.

He would stay away from her, the duke decided, for if he had learned one thing about her since his return to Willoughby, it was that she feared him and was repulsed by him. And her feelings were understandable. Only he could expose her for what she had been on one brief occasion. And her memories of that occasion and of the part he had played in it must be less than pleasant for her, to say the least.

He strolled to the tables to talk with Duncan Chamberlain during one break in the dancing. They had never been close friends as boys, as Chamberlain was almost ten years his senior. But they had become friends in later years, particularly since his own return from Belgium.

"We all feared that you would not return in time for the festivities," his neighbor said, extending his right hand. "It would not have been the same without you here, Adam."

"Have I ever missed one of my own balls?" the duke asked. "How are you, Duncan? Is Miss Chamberlain here? I have not seen her."

"Oh, yes," the other said. "And has danced every set."

"I thought perhaps you had left her at home with your children," the duke said. "Are they all well?"

"If tearing a nursery to ribbons and wearing a poor nurse to a shadow and murdering our ears every living moment of the day with whoops and shrieks is a sign that they are well," Mr. Chamberlain said, "then I would have to say they are in the best of health, Adam."

The duke grinned. "I remember last year," he said, "that when your other sister took them for a month, you were like the proverbial fish out of water."

His neighbor smiled sheepishly. "Yes, well," he said, "I suppose our ancestors rather missed the Vikings, too, when their raids finally ceased. Where did you find your governess?"

The duke had a flashing image of Fleur standing quietly in the shadows outside the Drury Lane Theater.

"In London," he said. "Houghton hired her. He is worth his weight in gold. I am pleased with her. I think she is good for Pamela."

"I know it," Mr. Chamberlain said. "She brought your daughter visiting when her grace was indisposed, and did not even blanch when I told her the dogs were probably jumping all over the children. Of course, at that moment she had not yet seen the dogs to know that they resemble young horses more than they do their peers."

"She took Pamela?" the duke said. "I am glad."

"And so am I." Mr. Chamberlain grinned. "You can send her anytime, Adam. You don't even have to send Lady Pamela along to chaperone unless you insist."

"Ah," the duke said. "It is like that, is it?"

"Emily says I need a new wife," his neighbor said. "I am not at all sure she is right, and I am certainly not sure I could find any woman saintly enough or insane enough to take on my trio and me into the bargain. But I am considering the idea. It is an interesting one."

"I would not take kindly to losing a good governess," his grace said.

"Ah, but for friendship's sake you would make the sacrifice," his friend said. "Excuse me. The orchestra sounds as if it means business, and I have asked her to dance again."

"For the third time, Duncan?" The duke raised his eyebrows.

"Counting, are you?" his neighbor asked. "This is no London ball, Adam. I think Miss Hamilton's reputation will survive three dances with one partner. And this is to be a waltz."

The duke stayed where he was and helped himself to some food. No lady was noticeably without a partner. He would take a rest.

Fleur Hamilton and Duncan Chamberlain. Duncan was handsome enough— slim still, his dark hair graying only at the temples. They made a good-looking pair. He wondered how she felt about her partner. But she had accepted a third dance with him. And she was smiling up at him with that sparkle that looked so much more genuine than Sybil's.

How would she receive a marriage proposal from Duncan? he wondered. Would she tell him the whole truth? Or find some other way to explain her loss of virginity?

The duke turned away. He regretted more than he could say the fact that he had not questioned her on that night before doing business with her. He should have realized from her appearance and from the quiet way she had solicited—or not solicited—a customer that she was no experienced whore. He certainly should have guessed the truth from the way she had stood in that room, not moving until he had told her what to do, and then removing her clothes quietly and neatly with no attempt to make his temperature rise as she did so.

He might have saved her before her character and future were in shreds.

But he did not stay turned away. He found himself watching them as they danced—no, watching her—and marveling that she could possibly be the same woman as the thin, lusterless whore whose services he had solicited and used only a little more than a month before.

God, he thought. If only he had realized. If only he had not been so thick-skulled. It was no wonder that she shrank from the mere sight of him and shuddered uncontrollably at his touch.

God! He turned away again, in search of a drink.

FLEUR WAS ENJOYING HERSELF IMMENSELY. There was something unutterably romantic about the outdoors at night, colored lanterns swaying in the trees and reflecting off dark water, beautifully dressed people talking and laughing gaily, music setting toes to tapping and hips to swaying.

She had decided earlier that she was going to enjoy the ball, and she was doing so. Life had been such a nightmare for six weeks, and still and for always the threat would hang over her head that it could be so again, and even worse. But for now she had been given this precious gift of peace—perhaps not forever, perhaps for only a week or a day. But she would not think of forever. She would think only of this night.

She had hoped to dance—Mr. Chamberlain had, after all, more or less asked her in advance. But she had not expected to dance every set of the evening, and with a variety of partners. Even some of the visiting guests danced with her and learned that she was the governess of the house.

Mr. Chamberlain danced with her four times in all, and he talked to her whenever the figures of the dance did not separate them. His conversation was light, amusing, as befitted the occasion. He raised her hand to his lips after the fourth time,

told her with a smile that he must restrain himself from dancing with her again and depriving all the other gentlemen of
the loveliest lady of all—words spoken with a wink—and led
her a little away from the dancing area to where the Duke of
Ridgeway was standing and talking with an older lady.

Fleur wished he had taken her anywhere else. The one
blight on the evening, the one detail that had threatened all
night to ruin her joy, was the constant presence of his grace.
She had not once looked at him, and yet she had found that at
every moment she knew where he was and with whom he
danced or talked.

He looked somewhat different from all the other gentlemen, dressed in black evening clothes and snowy white linen
that sparkled in the lantern light. And of course his height and
his coloring emphasized the darkness that was him.

He looked quite splendid, Fleur supposed, if one saw only
the right side of his face and not the terrifying scar of the left
side. Though why a scar acquired in battle when fighting for
one's country should terrify her, she did not know. Perhaps
even with the disfigurement he would look splendid to someone who had not watched him walk into the shadows of the
Drury Lane Theater, tall and dark and menacing in his evening
cloak and hat, to ask if she was looking for a night's employment.

She tried not to cling too tightly to Mr. Chamberlain's arm.
She tried to keep her smile intact.

"Mrs. Kendall," Mr. Chamberlain said, "have you met Miss
Hamilton, Adam's governess? Or Lady Pamela's governess, I
suppose I should say."

Fleur smiled at Mrs. Kendall as the introductions were
made.

"A splendid evening, Adam," Mr. Chamberlain said. "I don't
know when one of the Willoughby balls has been better. Ah, a
waltz. Ma'am?" He bowed and held out a hand for Mrs.
Kendall's.

They were gone almost before Fleur's mind could register dismay.

"Miss Hamilton?" The duke's dark eyes were glittering down into hers, she saw when she looked up at him. "Would you care to waltz?"

She stared at him, at his hand outstretched for hers, long-fingered, beautiful. And the nightmare was back. Not even this night was to be hers.

She watched as his hand closed upon itself.

"Let's take a stroll instead," he said quietly, and he clasped his hands at his back, turned onto the path that followed the shore of the lake, and waited for her to fall into step beside him.

"You have been enjoying the evening?" he asked. He was following the south shore, the one less frequented, more heavily wooded than the other, though a string of lanterns extended its entire length.

"Yes, thank you, your grace," she said.

"Willoughby has always been famous for its grand entertainments," he said. "And I have always been proud of that reputation. When one has been granted the privilege of inheriting all this, it seems only right to share it with others to some small degree, does it not?"

No one else was walking on this particular path. The wider paths and more open lawns on the north and west sides were crowded with guests. Fleur felt far more terrified than she had felt when walking beside him away from the Drury Lane Theater. Then she had not been terrified at all, only resigned to what must be.

"You dance well," he said. "I have watched you a few times. You have had practice?"

"A little, your grace," she said.

"But you have never been to London for a Season, have you?" he said. "I have never seen you there."

Only on one occasion, Fleur thought, when she had very obviously not been a part of the social whirl of the Season.

"No, your grace," she said.

She was aware of his eyes on her as they walked, and she had to concentrate every effort of will on setting one foot before the other. If she was forced to scream, would she be heard? The sounds of merriment coming from the dancing area and the refreshment tables were loud across the water.

"Where did you learn to dance?" he asked.

"At school," she said. "We had a French dancing master. The girls used to laugh at him because he liked to wave his arms about, a handkerchief always in one hand. And he was more dainty on his feet than any of us." She smiled at the memories. "But he could dance! I have always loved to dance. I have always loved to express music, whether with my fingers on a keyboard or with my feet on a dance floor."

"You do both well," he said.

"Sometimes . . ." She was looking across the water to the back of the pavilion and to the shimmering reflections of hundreds of lanterns. "Sometimes I think that without music, life would have no sweetness or beauty at all."

The waltz music coming from the pavilion was part of the night and the beauty and the hope. She had forgotten her fear, forgotten her companion for the moment.

"Let's dance here," he said quietly, and she was brought jolting back to reality as she spun to face him. He had stopped walking. His left hand was extended to take hers. His face was in darkness, the row of lanterns behind him.

Her right arm felt like a leaden weight as she lifted it and placed her hand in his. She swallowed as she watched and felt his fingers close about it and she felt her heart thump painfully against her ribs and her eardrums. He set his other hand behind her waist, firm and warm. She lifted her left hand to his shoulder, broad and firmly muscled as she remembered it.

She closed her eyes as they danced, slowly at first. And she felt the rhythm of the music and gave herself up to it. The man she danced with led well. He was one with the music and took her into the flow of it and whirled her about, his hand firm at her waist so that at one moment the tips of her breasts brushed against his coat. She would not remember until it was over with whom she danced, who had become a part of the music with her.

But they had walked for several minutes before dancing. There was not a great deal of the music left. It ended finally and far too soon.

"You have music in your very soul, I believe, Fleur Hamilton," a deep and quiet voice said.

And she was aware again of the hand clasping her own and the other spread at her back. She was aware again of the broad shoulder beneath her other hand and of the warmth and smell of him. She opened her eyes and took a step backward, dropping her arms to her sides.

"It is quicker to go back than to walk all about the lake," he said. "Shall we return? Are you hungry?"

"No," she said. "Thank you, your grace."

"I understand that you took Pamela to visit the Chamberlains," he said. "That was kind of you. She sees so little of other children."

"I believe she enjoyed the outing, your grace," she said.

"I'm sure she did," he said. "You have danced with Chamberlain a number of times tonight. I believe he is taken with you."

Fleur turned icy cold. But he did not need to warn her. She was quite capable of doing that for herself.

"He has been kind," she said, "as have several other gentlemen, your grace."

"Kind," he said. "Yes. Miss Chamberlain is at the punch bowl, I see. Would you care to join her?"

"Yes," she said. "Thank you."

A minute later, when she stood beside Emily Chamberlain and the duke had wandered away, she found herself forced to smile at the footman behind the punch bowl and assure him that she was not thirsty, though indeed she was. Her hands, she feared, were shaking too badly to reach out for a glass.

"Is it not a glorious evening, Miss Hamilton?" her companion said. "I am so glad that the weather has held for the occasion."

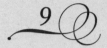

THE DUKE OF RIDGEWAY HAD MADE SOMETHING of a habit since his return home of spending part of his mornings in the schoolroom, quietly observing the lessons there. Very often he would take Pamela afterward to the stables to play with her puppy before luncheon. Fleur had forced herself to accept the situation.

There were no classes the morning after the ball, Lady Pamela having had a late night. In the afternoon, Fleur took the child along the upper corridor before going into the schoolroom, showing her the paintings, pointing out a few important details. On the whole, though, she just hoped that Lady Pamela would absorb the beauty and perfection of the paintings without being burdened with too much technical detail, and want to try harder at her own. She had an eye for form and color, though a natural impatience of temperament always made her rush too much when she painted.

The duke appeared at the top of the staircase and walked toward them before they were finished. Fleur sighed inwardly. She had hoped to avoid seeing him at all that day—her grace and most of the guests, she knew, had gone outside strolling in the park. She hated to remember her encounter with him the night before—her terror as she walked with him along the deserted path, her feeling of nausea when she had been forced to touch him and allow him to touch her, the strange and unexpected magic of waltzing with him on the path, her eyes tightly closed, shutting out the knowledge that it was with him she danced.

Try as she would all through the night, it had been that dance she had remembered of all the magical moments of the evening—until she had drifted off to sleep and he had been bending over her and hurting her and telling her that she did it because she enjoyed it.

Lady Pamela smiled and took his hand and lifted her face for his kiss.

"Timothy Chamberlain's birthday is next week, Papa," she said, "I have been invited, with Miss Hamilton. A letter came this morning. Will Mama let me go? Will you come too?"

"That sounds like a rare treat," he said, as Fleur turned away and entered the schoolroom. "I am not sure I'll be able to come, Pamela, as we have guests here to entertain. I'll see what I can do."

He sat quietly through the afternoon lessons until Fleur dismissed Lady Pamela early.

The duke stood up. "You are going to Nanny in the nursery?" he asked.

"She is going to wash my hair," the child said, pulling a face. "I would rather visit Tiny with you, Papa."

"We already did so just before luncheon," he said. "If Nanny says your hair needs washing, I don't doubt that it does. Off you go."

She went, dragging her feet.

Fleur busied herself putting books away and tidying them on the shelf. She had thought that he would go with his daughter, as he usually did.

"The paintings upstairs are limited in number and scope," he said. "You should show Pamela the paintings downstairs if you believe she is interested."

Fleur said nothing.

"Have you seen the long gallery?" he asked.

"Yes, with Mrs. Laycock, your grace," she said.

"Ah, with Mrs. Laycock," he said. "She is always the first to admit that she is not very knowledgeable about the works of art at Willoughby. Her talents run to more practical matters. The portraits in the gallery would give you material for a whole series of history lessons. And a child is never too young to learn about her family. Are you free?"

Fleur could only turn from the bookshelf, which she could no longer pretend was still untidy.

"We will go there now," he said. "I shall introduce you to my ancestors."

She walked beside him in silence along the corridor, down the stairs, and through the great hall, past immobile footmen, except for the one who sprang forward at his nod, and through the doors into the long wing that was the gallery. It was flooded with afternoon sunlight.

"I love this room," he said, pausing just beyond the doorway. "Even if there were not a single canvas here, I think I would love it."

She followed his glance up to the ceiling with its intricately carved circles of plasterwork leaves and fruit.

"It is a good room to use during persistently rainy weather," he said. "One can get at least some exercise promenading here. We used to spend hours in here as children, my brother and I. I believe there are still skipping ropes and spinning tops and games of spillikins and checkers in the lower cupboards. My wife and Nanny have always preferred to keep Pamela on the upper floor. Perhaps you will enjoy bringing her here occasionally."

They walked to the far end of the gallery, and he spent the whole of the next hour describing the paintings, naming their painters, and giving her some history of each painted ancestor. He spoke with knowledge and pride and some humor.

"There is something," he said, "some warmth, some security, perhaps, in knowing that one is descended from such a line. There is something about being able to call oneself the eighth duke instead of the first. My nose was in existence even with the fourth duke, you see? So I certainly cannot blame my mother."

But the fourth duke wore a long and curling wig.

His grace was looking at her. She could feel his eyes on her and she had to will herself through careful and steady breathing not to stiffen.

"What about your family?" he asked. "Does it have a long history?"

Her parents. Her grandparents, whom she had never known. A few old portraits at Heron House, whom no one seemed able to identify with any certainty. She had grown up with a sense of rootlessness, with a hunger for knowing. Surely, she had thought, if only Mama and Papa had realized how early they would leave her, they would have taught her young, told her something about themselves, about their childhood, about their own parents and grandparents. Or perhaps they had but she had been too young or too inattentive, not knowing that the time would come when she would be hungry for such knowledge.

"Where are you from?" he asked quietly. "Who was your father? Who are you?"

"Fleur Hamilton," she said, wishing they would move on to the next portrait. But Hamilton had been her grandmother's name, had it not? How did she know that? Someone must have told her once upon a time. "Your daughter's governess, your grace." And once your whore, of course.

"Did you have an unhappy childhood?" he asked, his eyes still on her. "Was your father unkind to you?"

"No!" Her eyes blazed at him for a moment. "I was very happy until they died when I was eight."

"Your mother and father together?"

"Yes." And she bit her lip. She had never been a good liar. Her father was supposed to have died in debt quite recently.

They moved on finally and he resumed his description of the portraits. She had scarcely noticed his own at the end of the line when she was with Mrs. Laycock. Perhaps the house-keeper had been talking of something else at the time.

Would she have known him even then, before his return, if she had looked closely enough? Would she have had prior warning? She looked closely now. A slim young man, very young, dressed in riding clothes, a riding crop in one hand, a spaniel at his side. A young and handsome and carefree man with proud, uplifted head and an unmarred face.

No, she would not have known.

For some reason that she could not begin to explain to herself, she felt like crying.

"My pre-Waterloo days," he said. "When I thought the world my oyster with a priceless pearl within. I suppose we all believe that when we are very young. Did you?"

"No," she said. And yet there had been Daniel and her love for him and his for her and the prospect of an endless future in which she would be wanted, in which she would feel needed. "Oh, perhaps once, a long time ago." Was it only a few months? Not a lifetime ago?

"You had a late night and have had a busy afternoon," he said abruptly. "You will want to return to your room to rest for a while."

He opened the door and allowed her to precede him into the great hall. But they arrived there at the exact moment when the front doors were being opened to admit a large number of the guests returning from their walk.

Fleur would have stepped back into the gallery, but his grace was in the doorway directly behind her.

"Ah, Ridgeway," the voice of Sir Philip Shaw said, "and the delectable Miss Hamilton."

"Ridgeway, you dark horse," a jovial, florid-faced gentleman said. "While the rest of us have been baking in the sun, you have been entertaining the governess indoors, where it is cool."

"Sometimes," Sir Hector Chesterton said, "I almost wish I had some daughters of my own."

"May I present Miss Fleur Hamilton to those of you who did not make her acquaintance last evening?" his grace said, a hand at the small of her back. "Miss Hamilton is Pamela's governess."

"You are dismissed, Miss Hamilton. Tea in the saloon immediately, Jarvis." The light, sweet voice was that of the duchess.

Fleur turned and fled without more ado and half-ran up the stairs and along the corridor to her room. How unspeakably embarrassing!

She stood at her open window, enjoying the breeze, unwilling to lie down despite her tiredness. Sleep would only bring the nightmares again.

Once he had been young and handsome and carefree. Once he had thought the world to be his oyster, life a priceless pearl. In his pre-Waterloo days, as he had described them. And yet he had spoken sadly, as if those dreams had proved to be empty, worthless ones. What could possibly make the Duke of Ridgeway less than satisfied with life? she wondered. He had everything.

She still felt like crying, she realized suddenly. Her throat and her chest were aching with a nameless something that made her feel indescribably sad.

"CONFOUND IT," THE DUKE of Ridgeway said, "I am not going to a royal banquet, Sidney."

"I'll be finished in a twinkling if you will just keep your chin from clacking," his valet said, putting the finishing touches to the folds of his master's neckcloth. "You do have guests for dinner, after all, sir."

"Damn your impudence," his grace said. "Are you finished now?"

"And thankful to be, sir," Sidney said. "I'll take myself far away from your temper as soon as I have tidied up in here."

"You wouldn't have to be anywhere near it at all," the duke said sharply, "if that shell had just bounced three inches closer to you at Waterloo."

"That I wouldn't, sir," his valet agreed, turning away to tidy scattered garments and brushes. "But then, neither would you have had to dress for your guests if your shell had bounced half an inch closer to you."

Sidney wisely ignored his master's retort. His sensibilities had grown immune to far worse blasphemies and obscenities during his years with the British army.

His grace gazed irritably at his reflection and at the skillfully knotted neckcloth that he was about to display for the admiration of his wife's guests. He hated to be a dandy at any time and in any place. But in his own home! And for two nights in a row. Last night's ball had been enough formality to last him a month.

He had neglected the guests during the day. Most of them had not been up before noon, and he had made an excuse about business keeping him at home during the afternoon rather than join them on their walk. Confound it, he had a right to some privacy.

But they were his guests.

Of course, he owed something to Pamela too. She was a child and entitled to his time and company. He had been giving her both while Sybil was preoccupied with entertaining her guests and enjoying herself. At least, that was what he had told himself earlier.

He was going to have to stay away from her more often. Or else he was going to have to take her out more—it was high time she learned to ride, though she had always shown a reluctance to do so.

What he was really going to have to do was stay away from the schoolroom. If he was strictly honest with himself, it was not just—or even mainly—Pamela who was drawing him there, or to the library at the crack of dawn each morning lest he be too late and miss her.

Sidney had commented only that morning, as the duke rose from bed, yawning after the late night, that he must be touched in the upper works to rise so early. Perhaps Sidney was right.

And he had woken up suddenly in the night and caught himself in the act of dreaming about waltzing on a deserted path with a woman whose eyes were tightly closed and whose fire-gold hair was loose and spread like a silken curtain over his arm.

It would not do. It just would not do. He should have had Houghton send her elsewhere. It had been madness to have her sent to Willoughby.

The door of his dressing room opened suddenly, without warning, and the duchess stood there, one hand still on it, looking lovely in pale pink lace and considerably younger than her twenty-six years.

"Oh," she said sweetly, "are you still busy? Is it possible for Sidney to leave?"

The valet looked to his master with raised eyebrows, and the duke nodded.

"If you please, Sidney," he said, rising to his feet. "What may I do for you, Sybil?"

She waited for the door to close. "I have never been so humiliated in my life," she said, looking at him with large hurt eyes. "Adam, how can you do this to me, and in front of our guests, too?"

He looked steadily at her. "I gather you are referring to the incident with Miss Hamilton," he said.

"Why did you bring her here?" she asked, clasping her slim white hands together at her bosom. "Was it to hurt me beyond endurance? I have never complained about your long absences in London, Adam. And I have always known why you must go there. I have borne the humiliation without reproach. But must I now endure having one of your doxies in this very house? And in close communication with my daughter? You ask too much of me. I cannot bear it."

"It is a shame you have no audience beyond me," he said, his eyes fixed on her. "Your words are very affecting, Sybil. One might almost believe that you cared. We were coming from the long gallery into the great hall. Does it not seem peculiar to you that we would have chosen such a very public setting for a clandestine rendezvous?"

"It pleases you to use sarcasm," she said, "and to walk roughshod over my feelings. I suppose it will please you to lie too. Do you deny that you are having an affair with Miss Hamilton?"

"Yes," he said. "But you have already labeled me a liar, Sybil, so your question was rather pointless, was it not? Would it be so surprising if I did take a mistress?"

"It is what I have learned to expect of you and to accept," she said. "But though your love for me is dead, Adam, I thought there would have been some remnants of respect left for the fact that I am your wife."

"Wife." He laughed softly and took two steps toward her. "I would not need a mistress if I had a wife, Sybil. Perhaps you would like to protect your interests more actively."

He set one hand beneath her chin and kissed her lips. But she turned her head sharply to one side.

"Don't," she said. "Don't, please."

"I didn't think that idea would have much appeal to you," he said. "Don't worry, Sybil. I have never forced you and am un-likely to start doing so now."

"I feel unwell," she said. "I still have not recovered fully from that chill."

"Yes," he said, "I can see that you are right about that. And you have lost weight, have you not? Did your visit have any other purpose?"

"No," she said, her light, sweet voice shaking. "But I know you are lying, Adam. I know you have been with Pamela's governess. No matter how much you deny it, I know it is true."

He had a sudden and unwelcome mental image of blood—on Fleur's thighs and on the sheet where she had lain.

"It seems," he said quietly, looking steadily at his wife, "that we are both ready to go to the drawing room to make ourselves agreeable to our guests. Shall we go together?" He extended an arm for her hand.

She laid a hand on his sleeve without gripping his arm at all, and walked beside him in silence. A small and fragile and beautiful woman who looked as innocent as a girl.

It was difficult sometimes, his grace thought, to accept the fact that this was his present and his future, the marriage he had dreamed of as a young man. Except that all the dreams were dead and there could never now be any others to take their place.

Just perhaps unwary dreams at night.

He thought again of Fleur, of his first sight of her standing quietly in the shadows outside the Drury Lane Theater, and of his unexpected need for her. The need to spend a night sheltered in the arms and body of a woman who would accept him without question. The need to sleep with his head pillowed on a woman's breast. The need for some peace. The need to soothe his loneliness.

And he thought again of the blood and of her hand, which had been shaking so badly after he had violated her that he had had to hold it while putting the wet cloth in it. And of her hunger and the self-discipline that had held her back from wolfing down the food set before her. And of her humiliation when he had set the coins in her hand, payment for services rendered.

He paused outside the doors into the drawing room while a footman opened them, and entered with his wife on his arm. He smiled and was aware of her bright glances for those of their guests already assembled there.

FLEUR PRACTICED IN THE MUSIC room in perfect privacy the following morning. The door between it and the library remained closed.

And she found herself more self-conscious than on any other morning. Was he there? Was he lurking behind the closed door, listening? Was he about to fling it open at any moment to criticize some error in her playing or to tell her that she was no longer welcome to use that room? Or was he not there at all? Was she indeed as alone as she seemed?

She could not concentrate on the pieces she was learning. She could not lose herself in the music she already knew and could play with her eyes closed. Her fingers were stiff and un-cooperative.

She smiled at herself without amusement as she left the room five minutes before her hour was at an end. Could she relax more, knowing that he was close, than she could when he was absent—this dark, hawkish man who terrified her more than anyone she had ever known, even including Matthew, and whose physical closeness always made her want to turn and run in panic?

All morning as she taught Lady Pamela a variety of lessons, she listened for the sound of a firm tread outside the door and of the doorknob turning.

But they were left in peace. And peaceful the morning seemed, Lady Pamela unusually quiet and docile, until she suddenly snatched up the scissors without warning while they both embroidered and cut first the silk thread with which she had been sewing and then the handkerchief itself with deliberate and vicious slices.

Fleur looked up in amazement, her own needle suspended in the air. She was in the middle of telling a story.

"She said I could go down," Lady Pamela said. "She said! And he said some other time. He said he would remind her. He said it ages ago. I'll never be let to go down. And I don't care. I don't want to go down."

Fleur set her work quietly to one side and got to her feet.

"And now you will tell them that I have been bad," the child said, making one more cut with the scissors, "and they will come to the nursery and scold me. Mama will cry because I have been bad. But I don't care. I don't care!"

Fleur took the scissors and the ruined handkerchief from the little hands and stooped down in front of the child.

"And it's all your fault," Lady Pamela said. "Mama said I was to go down, and you would not let me. I hate you, and I am going to tell Mama to send you away. I am going to tell Papa."

Fleur gathered the child into her arms and held her tightly. But Lady Pamela flailed at her with one free arm and kicked at her with both feet. She broke into loud shrieks as Fleur scooped her up into her arms and sat in the window seat with her, cradling her, rocking her, crooning to her

The door opened and Mrs. Clement came bustling in.

"What have you been doing to the poor child?" she said to Fleur, her eyes glinting. "What is it, poor lovey?"

She reached out her arms to take Lady Pamela. But the child shrieked louder and clung to Fleur, her face hidden against her bosom. Mrs. Clement disappeared again.

Lady Pamela was crying quietly when the door opened again several minutes later. The Duke of Ridgeway closed it quietly behind him and stood looking for a few moments. Fleur had one cheek resting against the top of the child's head. She did not look up.

"What is happening?" he asked, advancing across the room. "Pamela?"

But she continued to cry quietly in Fleur's arms.

"Miss Hamilton?"

She raised her head to look at him. "Broken promises," she said quietly.

He stood there for a while longer and then slumped down onto the window seat beside them, half-turned to them, one of his knees brushing against Fleur's. He reached out to run one finger along his daughter's bare arm as it circled Fleur's neck.

And Fleur looked at him to find him staring back bleakly, his scar starkly noticeable in the light from the window on his weary face. It was once a remarkably handsome face, she thought, remembering his portrait, despite the blackness of hair and eyes and the prominence of his nose—perhaps because of those features. But it still was handsome, the scar somehow enhancing rather than detracting from the strength of his features.

If she had not met him under such terrifying circumstances, if she could but rid her nightmares of the image of that face bent over her while he did painful, humiliating things to her body, perhaps she would always have seen him as handsome.

He shifted his gaze to his daughter. "What can I do, Pamela?" he asked her. "What can I do to set things right?"

It felt as if he were talking to her, Fleur thought with an inward shudder.

"Nothing," the child said, pausing for a moment in her crying. "Go away!"

"Mama promised that you could meet the ladies someday, didn't she?" he said. "And I promised to talk to her and remind her. But I have not done it yet. I'm sorry, Pamela. Will you forgive me?"

"No!" she said against Fleur's bosom.

He sighed and laid his hand over the back of her head. "Will you give me a chance to put it right?" he asked. "There is to be a picnic at the ruins this afternoon. Shall I arrange for you to come too?"

"No," she said. "I want to stay with Miss Hamilton and learn French. She is to teach me this afternoon."

"Please, Pamela?" he said. "If we persuade Miss Hamilton to postpone the lesson until tomorrow?"

Fleur kissed the child's hot temple. "We will learn French tomorrow, shall we?" she said. "It is such a lovely day for a picnic. I expect the ladies will all be dressed in their muslins and have pretty bonnets and parasols."

"And there are to be lobster patties, so I have heard," the duke said. "Will you come, Pamela?"

"If Miss Hamilton comes too," Lady Pamela said unexpectedly.

Fleur's eyes locked with the duke's.

"But Mama and Papa will want you all to themselves," she said.

"Miss Hamilton will be glad of a free afternoon," he said at the same moment. "She does not have many."

"Then I won't go," the child said petulantly.

He raised his eyebrows and Fleur closed her eyes.

"Do you like lobster patties, Miss Hamilton?" he asked quietly.

"They always were my favorite picnic fare," she said.

Lady Pamela jumped down from her lap and pushed untidy strands of hair away from her flushed and puffed face.

"I am going to find Nanny," she said. "I am going to tell her to put my pink dress on me and my straw bonnet."

"Ask her, Pamela," his grace said. "It is better than telling."

He got to his feet as his daughter whisked herself from the room, and looked down at Fleur. "I'm sorry," he said, "that you had to cope with that alone. Nanny sent Houghton running for me with the news that Pamela was screaming and you half-throttling her. I have been greatly at fault in hoping that she would forget her desire to meet the ladies."

Fleur said nothing but gathered up the ruined remains of the handkerchief.

"I will make the arrangements for this afternoon," he said. "If it is any consolation to you, Miss Hamilton, I would say that your pupil is becoming attached to you."

But she did not want to go on the picnic, she thought in some alarm as he left the schoolroom. She would do almost anything to get out of going—except break a promise to Lady Pamela. And so she was stuck with having to go.

She looked back with considerable nostalgia to the first two weeks of her life at Willoughby, when she had been happy despite the disapproval of the duchess and Mrs. Clement.

How she wished that the Duke of Ridgeway had not turned out to be who he was. But of course, she had realized before now, she would not have her post at all if he had not. She would be in London, living in her bare little room, a seasoned whore by now.

She supposed that, after all, she owed him some gratitude.

And if it were true that Lady Pamela was developing something of an attachment to her—though she was not at all convinced that it was so—then it was equally true that she was developing an attachment to the child. Petulant and stubborn as she could be, Lady Pamela had very real feelings and needs. And she needed Fleur, however little she might admit it. It was good to be needed.

It seemed that she had to prepare for a picnic that afternoon.

10

"THERE IT IS," THE DARK-HAIRED, HANDSOME GEN-tleman said to his companion, leaning close to the carriage window as it crossed the bridge and left the lime grove behind and the house came into sight "Impressive, wouldn't you say?"

The fair-haired gentleman traveling with him followed his gaze. "Very," he said. "I can see why it is so frequently admired. And it was all yours for a few months, Kent."

"An amusing experience," Lord Thomas Kent said, "suddenly to be everyone's property just because I was the owner of it all. Almost as if the property owned me instead of the other way around. I thought never to see it again."

"You can be sure," Lord Brocklehurst said, "that when your brother told you never to return he spoke in the heat of the moment. He will receive you with open arms."

Lord Thomas looked amused. "I wonder," he said. "But I am not sorry you persuaded me into coming, Bradshaw. It will be priceless to see their faces—Ridgeway's, all the servants'. And it will be interesting to see my sister-in-law once more. They were not married when I left, you know."

"Magnificent!" Lord Brocklehurst said as the carriage drew to a halt and he gazed up at massive Corinthian columns and the great pediment, which hid the dome from that vantage point. "Quite magnificent. It was good of you to persuade me to accompany you here."

Lord Thomas laughed. "Since it was you who talked me into returning," he said, "it seemed only right that you be witness to the touching reunion."

The look on the butler's face as he came out onto the horseshoe steps to greet the unexpected visitors must have been everything Lord Thomas could have wished for. His wooden butler's expression deserted him for the whole of three seconds as he watched his grace's younger brother descend from the carriage and look up at him with a grin.

"Jarvis!" he said. "So you did get the promotion after all. Are you going to stand there and gawk, or are you going to send someone down to carry our trunks into the house? Is my brother close at hand?"

Jarvis had himself under control. He bowed stiffly from the waist. "His grace is at the ruins with her grace and their guests, my lord," he said. "I shall have the carriage and your bags seen to if you would care to come inside."

"I certainly have no intention of standing outside here until permitted to enter by his august grace," Lord Thomas said with a laugh, turning back to Lord Brocklehurst and ushering him up the steps. "Drinks in the saloon, if you please, Jarvis. What the devil are they doing at the ruins?"

"They are picnicking, as I understand, my lord," Jarvis said, directing the guests with a bow into the saloon.

"How long have they been gone?" Lord Thomas asked, looking about him. "Nothing has changed, I see."

"About one hour, my lord," the butler said.

"An hour?" Lord Thomas frowned. "I'll have time to do the honors and show off all the state rooms to you, then, Bradshaw—after we have refreshed ourselves with a drink and a change of clothes, that is. Have my old room made up for me, Jarvis, and have the housekeeper prepare another room for Lord Brocklehurst. Is it still Mrs. Laycock?"

Jarvis bowed.

"Take yourself off, then," Lord Thomas said. "The drinks first, though.

"So," he said, "we are to kick our heels here for a few hours and feel the suspense mount. I wonder if Ridgeway would be choking on his chicken bone and his wine if he knew I was standing in the middle of his saloon at this very moment." He laughed.

"I am glad to be here, anyway," Lord Brocklehurst said. "I have wanted to visit Willoughby Hall for some time now."

THE DUKE OF RIDGEWAY watched his daughter leave the group with her governess and make for the stables and her puppy. And he wished that he could go with them, take the dog out into the paddock, and romp with it and with them for half an hour.

But he had Lady Underwood on his arm, and the Grantshams were engaging them in conversation.

The picnic, he thought, had gone well enough. Sybil had been alarmed at his announcement that Pamela was to be taken, and had looked defiant when he had reminded her of a broken promise to allow the child to come down to see the ladies on the day of their arrival.

But she would not have to worry about having to look after her daughter, he had told her. Her governess would do that—at Pamela's own request.

Pamela had been in the highest of good spirits and had been made much of by all the ladies and by a few of the gentlemen too. She had grown flushed and loud by the time they had reached the ruins, but Fleur had taken her quietly by the hand, whispered something in her ear, and taken her to see the inside of the tower—Sir Ambrose Marvell had followed them there.

Fleur herself had succeeded in staying in the background the whole of the afternoon and had assisted in the serving of the picnic food at his wife's request. She had made no objection at being treated like a menial servant. Indeed, he had thought, she was probably glad of something to do.

And so they were home, and if he were fortunate he would have a few quiet hours to himself before dinner—unless Lady Underwood contrived to keep him in her company, that was. They made a rather noisy entry into the hall. Jarvis was waiting for him there and bowing before him.

"You have visitors in the saloon, your grace," he said.

The duke sighed inwardly. Who would be calling at this hour of the afternoon? He hoped it was no one who would linger. He turned to make his excuses to Lady Underwood and strode toward the saloon.

"Visitors?" he heard his wife say in her light, pleasant voice. She had been in the best of spirits all afternoon, Shaw dancing attendance on her every movement.

The duke stopped inside the doorway of the saloon and clasped his hands at his back. Strangely, he did not feel particularly surprised, he thought, taking in the bronzed good looks of his brother, his fashionable clothes, his smile. He had surely always known that Thomas would come back.

"You look as if a feather could knock you backward, Adam," Lord Thomas Kent said. "Have you no welcome for me?"

"Thomas." The duke extended his hand and strode toward his half-brother. "Welcome home."

Lord Thomas was smiling, but his eyes moved beyond the duke's shoulder as he took his hand.

"Thomas." The word was whispered, but it filled the saloon.

Lord Thomas' grasp loosened on his grace's hand and his gaze fixed on the figure in the doorway. "Sybil," he said, and his eyes and his smile softened. He moved toward her, both hands outstretched. "How beautiful you look."

"Thomas," she whispered again, and her small white hands disappeared into his bronze grasp.

"Sybil," he said quietly. "I have come home." Then he

turned his head, smiling. "Do you know Bradshaw?" he asked his brother. "Matthew Bradshaw, Lord Brocklehurst, of Heron House in Wiltshire? He was the first friend to call on me after my return from India. And he helped persuade me that I should come all the way home. I have brought him with me for a few weeks."

His grace shook hands with Lord Brocklehurst. "You are welcome," he said. "I am pleased to make your acquaintance, Brocklehurst."

"India?" the duchess was saying, her large blue eyes fixed on her brother-in-law, her hands still clasped in his. "You have been in India, Thomas?"

"Yes," he said, "with the East India Company. I came back to see if jolly old England was still in the same place. So you are the Duchess of Ridgeway after all, Sybil?" He squeezed her hands before releasing them.

"In India," she said. "All this time?" And she began to cough.

"I'll escort you to your room, Sybil," his grace said, taking in her pallor and the spots of color high on her cheeks. "The afternoon's outing has been exhausting for you."

Surprisingly, she took his arm without argument and went with him after he had directed his half-brother to entertain their guest until dinner.

She said nothing as he led her along the hallways to her sitting room and rang the bell for her maid. She just held her shoulders back and stared blankly ahead of her, occasionally coughing.

"Armitage," she said when her maid came into the room, "I will want you to undress me and brush out my hair. I wish to lie down."

She sounded like a tired and bewildered child.

The Duke of Ridgeway, closing her door quietly behind him as he left, could not remember a time when he had felt more furiously angry.

• • •

LORD THOMAS KENT WAS WHISTLING. It felt good to be back. Even though he had left vowing never to return just as vehemently as his brother had ordered him never to do so, it was, after all, Willoughby, his childhood home, his father's home. And all his own for many months when Adam had been reported dead in action.

Yes, it felt good. And it had been worth all to see Adam's face. Good breeding had provided him with an almost adequate mask, of course. Brocklehurst had probably not even realized that the greeting the duke had afforded his brother was less than cordial. But Adam had been white-hot with rage. Lord Thomas knew his brother well enough to have detected that without even looking for it.

It was not nearly time to go down to dinner. He still wore his silk evening shirt open at the neck. His man was brushing his velvet coat, and paused in his task to answer the tap on the door.

"You may leave, Winthrop," Lord Thomas said, smiling at his visitor. "I shall ring when I want you to return."

The man bowed and left the room.

"Well, Sybil," Lord Thomas said softly, still smiling.

"Thomas," she said, fragile and lovely in pale blue silk, her hair loose down her back. "You came home."

"As you see," he said.

"You had the courage to come back," she said, "though he drove you away."

He smiled at her.

"Oh, Thomas," she said, "you have come back."

He turned his hands so that his palms faced toward her, and she uttered a little cry and hurtled across the distance between them and into his arms.

"Did you think I would go away from you forever?" he said against her hair.

"Yes," she said. "I thought you must stay away since he had

ordered you to do so. I thought you would never be able to come back. Thomas," she wailed, looking up at him with horrified and tear-filled eyes, "I married him."

"I know, love. Hush," he said. "Hush." And he found her mouth with his own, ravishing it with his tongue while he wrapped his arms about her small and pliant body. "Ah, you are so beautiful. More lovely than ever, Sybil. How could I have stayed away from you forever?"

"I have not known how to live without you," she said, her voice high-pitched with emotion. "Thomas, I have been half-dead without you. You went to India? I had no idea. I did not know where you were or even if you were still alive. And I don't think he knew either, and if he had, he would not have told me. Why didn't you write? Oh, why didn't you give me some sign?"

"It would not have done," he said. "You know it, Sybil. It was kinder to let you think me gone forever. Dead even. Have you been half-dead without me?" He framed her face with his hands and gazed into her large blue eyes. "But you married him after all, Sybil. I did not expect it of you. I thought you would have remained faithful to my memory. I thought you would have refused him, anyway, of all people."

"I had no choice," she said, "with you gone. Oh, Thomas." She hid her face against him, pressed herself even closer to him. "You were gone. I had no choice. I thought I would die. I wished to die. But he came day after day to beg me. And I did not care anymore with you gone. I married him. I hated him, but I married him."

"Hush," he said. "Hush. I am back now, love." He kissed her again lightly, then more deeply. "Back where I belong, and everything will work out, you will see. Is it time for dinner yet?"

"Not for a while," she said. "There is time."

"Is there?"

He stood back from her and smiled. And she comprehended him, bit at her lip, and reached up trembling hands to the buttons of his shirt. He gazed into her eyes, his own serious, as he slid the blue silk from her shoulders and down her arms and cupped her naked breasts in his hands. "How does Adam treat you?"

"He doesn't." She looked at him in distress. "Thomas, don't talk about him. Please don't. I ought not to be here. I should go. I just wanted to talk with you privately."

He laughed softly. "There is more than one way of talking," he said. "And I have been starved for you, Sybil. Don't leave me now. He won't be looking for you?"

"No, he won't," she said. "Thomas. It isn't wrong, is it?" She buried her face against his shoulder as he lifted her into his arms. "I only ever loved you. You do believe that, don't you?"

"And I only ever loved you," he said, laying her down on the bed and stripping away her clothes. "Why do you think I came home?"

"For me?" she said. "You came because of me?"

"Mm," he said, lying down on top of her and moving against her soft flesh. "God, you're beautiful, Sybil. How could you ever have thought I would not come back to you?"

Beyond the surging of his desire he thought of the unlocked doors of his dressing room and bedchamber and wondered with a certain amusement what would happen if his brother walked into either room.

"Ah," he said against her mouth as he plunged into her. Yes, indeed, it really was very good to be home again.

THE DUKE OF RIDGEWAY had not talked with his brother beyond an exchange of the merest pleasantries. As the gentlemen joined the ladies in the drawing room after dinner, he noticed that his wife was even more happy and animated than she had been since the arrival of her guests, and his jaw set in anger again.

He had been going to visit his brother's room before dinner, but he had stopped himself at the last moment. Years of having to take responsibility for the well-being of others and his years as an officer had taught him that when possible it was better to let anger cool before taking action.

He would wait until the next day, he had decided, before confronting Thomas and demanding an explanation, and before he decided what he must do, if anything.

"I have sent for Pamela," the duchess was telling Mrs. Grantsham and Lady Mayberry, her voice eager, her face bright. She included her husband in her smile when she realized that he was within earshot. "She should be here at any moment."

"For Pamela?" he said with a frown. "Won't she be in bed, Sybil? And very tired after this afternoon?"

"I sent a message to Nanny earlier to keep her up and get her ready," the duchess said. "I wish her to meet her uncle. How could I deprive my darling of the pleasure of sharing in his return?" She smiled dazzlingly at the duke.

Of course! He clamped his teeth hard together and stood very still.

"You must instruct Nanny to take her back to bed after five minutes, then," he said.

"Ah," she said, "but it is Miss Hamilton who is to bring her down, Adam."

What was she up to? The duke frowned.

He had not long to wait. Pamela, all dressed up in frills and bows, her hair styled in dozens of ringlets, her cheeks flushed, and her eyes sparkling with excitement and tiredness, was brought into the room by Fleur, who curtsied and stood quietly inside the door.

The duchess took her daughter by the hand while the ladies fussed over her as they had that afternoon.

"You wanted to see all the ladies dressed for the evening, darling," the duchess said, stooping down and smiling at her. "Well, here they are. What do you think?"

Lady Pamela beamed up at her, and the duchess hugged her.

"There is someone I want you to meet," she said. "Someone you have not met before, though I have told you a great deal about him, and I daresay Papa has too. A very important gentleman." She led Pamela to an ironically smiling Lord Thomas Kent. "This is your uncle Thomas, darling. Make your curtsy to him."

Lady Pamela did as she was bidden and looked curiously up into the face of her uncle, who so much resembled her father except that his features were more openly handsome and carefree.

"So you are Pamela," he said, one finger holding up her raised chin. "You do not have much of your mama in you, do you? You are all your father."

The duke turned away, unable to watch. And his eyes focused on Fleur, who was still standing just inside the door. But she no longer did so quietly and impassively. Her face was so pale that her lips looked blue. He was on the point of crossing hastily to her side when her hand—shaking quite as badly as it had during that first night—reached blindly for the knob of the door, found it, and turned it clumsily.

And she was gone, leaving the door ajar behind her.

He was left staring at the spot where she had stood. But this was not the first time she had been in company with their guests. She had been at the ball two nights before and at the picnic that afternoon. Why the sudden attack of nerves? Was it Thomas' presence? Had she met him before? In London, perhaps?

Had Thomas been another of her customers? He knew he had been her first, but he had often wondered if he had been her last too. There had, after all, been a lapse of five days between his encounter with her and Houghton's hiring her as Pamela's governess.

By some bizarre coincidence, had Thomas had her too? He felt a wild rage at the thought.

Or was it Brocklehurst, perhaps? He also was someone she had not seen until that evening. Was he the one who had been her customer and the sight of whom had sent her all to pieces?

He closed his eyes briefly.

"But where is Miss Hamilton?" the duchess was asking brightly. "Did she not realize she was to wait for Pamela?"

"I gave her permission to leave," the duke said. "I told her that I would take Pamela back to the nursery myself."

The duchess looked at him reproachfully. "But I was planning to present my daughter's governess to Thomas," she said, "and to Lord Brocklehurst, of course. Well." She shrugged. "Another time. To bed, then, darling, with Papa."

She turned back to Lord Thomas as Lady Pamela set her hand in her father's and left the room with him.

"She was the one," her grace said very quietly, "Adam's doxy. I wanted you to see her, Thomas, and know the humiliation he has subjected me to."

"Not any longer," he said, raising her hand to his lips. "I will not let him hurt you any longer, Sybil."

FLEUR HAD THOUGHT HER day was over. Mrs. Laycock was tired after a few busy days and had not invited the governess, as she often did, to spend the evening in her sitting room. Fleur sighed when Mrs. Clement summoned her to the nursery to inform her, tight-lipped, that her grace had requested she escort Lady Pamela to the drawing room after dinner.

"But will that not be after Lady Pamela's bedtime?" she asked.

"Lord Thomas Kent is home," Mrs. Clement said. "Her grace wishes Lady Pamela to meet her uncle."

Fleur thought that Lord Thomas Kent could just as easily have been brought to the nursery the following morning, but she said nothing. She returned to her room to put on her best dress and brush and coil her hair again.

She was not comfortable as she led her pupil into the drawing room later. Lord Thomas Kent had once been Matthew's friend. He could not possibly know her, of course. But his presence at Willoughby was a strong reminder of that constant threat to her security and happiness. She stood inside the door, her eyes lowered, and hoped that no one would feel it necessary to take notice of her. She hoped that Lady Pamela would not be kept long. The child was very excited and very tired.

She raised her eyes as the duchess led her daughter across the room, and looked at Lord Thomas Kent. He was the duke's half-brother, she knew. But anyone could have mistaken them for full brothers. They were remarkably alike except that Lord Thomas was not quite as tall or his face quite so hawkish and severe in its expression. He smiled and was very handsome.

She glanced at the duke to note the contrast between the two and found him watching his brother talk to Lady Pamela with that dark expression that was so characteristic of him. She shivered. How could two men look so much alike and yet so very different?

And her eyes strayed beyond his grace's shoulder to another gentleman, shorter too than the duke, fair-haired, inclined to stockiness. He was looking very directly at her, a gleam of—what?—pleasure? amusement? triumph? in his eyes.

She looked down hastily at the carpet between her feet and felt her heart and every pulse pump the blood painfully through her body. The room about her, the loud buzz of voices and laughter, the reason she was there—all fled from her consciousness, and she was aware only of a strawberry-red rose in the pattern of the carpet. It had a dark green stem and brown thorns.

There was no air in the room. Her hands felt thick and vibrating, as if the blood could not force its way through them. She was losing control of her hands. There was no air to breathe.

There was a door next to her. She reached out a hand to turn the knob, could not find it, bumped her knuckles against it, grasped it, could not control it, and then blessedly jerked the door open.

She fled along the hallway, hesitated when she reached the staircase, fled into the great hall, wrenched open one of the front doors without so much as glancing at the footmen, and fled down the horseshoe steps.

Fresh air. And darkness. And space.

She ran.

She was among the lime trees when pain and breathlessness forced her to stop. She grasped a tree trunk with both hands as the breath sobbed into her lungs, and she doubled up against the pain in her side.

God. Oh, please, dear God, let it not be so. Please, God.

Matthew. He had found her. He had come to take her away.

She stumbled slowly on. When had he come? Why had she not been summoned and arrested immediately? Why had everyone in the drawing room not turned to stare accusingly at her when she brought Lady Pamela in? What sort of a waiting game was he playing?

She leaned against another tree trunk, her cheek against its rough bark, and hugged it with her arms.

What would happen? Would he take her back alone, or would there be someone else to guard her? Would she be bound? Chained? She had no idea how such things were done. How long would she be in prison before being brought to trial? How long would she be in prison after the trial before . . . ?

Oh, please, dear God. Please, dear God.

There was no point in running any farther. He had tracked her this far. There would be no further escape. There was no point in running.

She stood where she was for a long time before pushing wearily away from the tree and making her slow way back to the bridge. And she stood leaning against the parapet, looking sightlessly down at the moonlit cascades, and listening without hearing to the rushing and splashing of water.

She knew for several minutes that there was someone coming, though she did not turn her head to look. Matthew. It would be Matthew. Expecting that she would fight him again? Try to run again? She wondered that he was coming alone. He had not been alone the last time. She had killed his companion then.

Or perhaps he had seen from her face in the drawing room that there was no fight left in her. She was tired of fighting, tired of running. Tired of living.

He stopped at the end of the bridge.

"What is it?" he asked her.

It was not Matthew after all. It was *him*. The thought crossed her mind that under almost any other circumstances she would have been terrified, as she had been two nights before—alone with him like this in the night, far from the house. But there was no point in feeling terror. Only the one inevitable end could hold terror for her any longer.

"Nothing," she said. "I wanted some air."

"And abandoned Pamela in the drawing room?" he said.

She turned her head to look at him. "I'm sorry," she said. "I did not think."

"What is it?" he asked again. "Was it my brother? Do you know him?"

"No," she said.

"Lord Brocklehurst, then?"

"No."

He walked slowly along the bridge toward her. "Was either of them a customer of yours?" he asked.

"No!" Her eyes widened in horror.

"I am the only man to be feared in that particular way, then, am I?" he asked.

She turned away to look down into the foaming water.

"Was it me, then?" he said. "Am I the one you were afraid

of? Were you afraid that I would maneuver just such a meeting as this? Were you afraid of a repeat of two nights ago?"

"I was not afraid," she said. "I was just weary and faint. I needed air."

He leaned an elbow on the parapet beside her and stood looking at her. "You are such a mystery," he said softly. "I do not know you at all, Miss Hamilton, do I?"

Her chest was tight with pain. "You don't need to know me, your grace," she said, and could hear her voice shaking. "I was your whore and now I am your daughter's governess. You do not need to know me in either capacity. I merely exist to provide a service to you."

"I wish you could know that I am not your enemy," he said. "I think you need a friend."

"Men do not make friends with their whores and servants," she said.

"If you are a whore," he said, "I am an adulterer. We are equal sinners. But you at least had good reason for doing what you did. For one night you were a whore. Don't let it blight your whole life. You survived. That is what matters."

"Yes," she said bitterly, "survival is everything."

She felt his fingertips resting lightly against the back of her hand on the parapet. Revulsion sizzled up her arm and into her throat. Her first impulse was to snatch away her hand and back away from him. But she was so alone, so much without hope, so utterly in the grip of despair.

She kept her hand where it was, though she knew that it was trembling beneath his fingers. She wished it were anyone but him. She wished she could take the two steps that separated them and lay her body against his, her head against his broad chest. Oh, she wished it and despised her weakness. She had always stood alone, ever since the death of her parents and her realization that she was not wanted by the strangers who had come to live in their home. She had always been proudly independent and had never allowed self-pity to destroy any chance of happiness that she might have.

She wanted Daniel. She closed her eyes.

His fingers slid across her hand and curled beneath hers. He held her hand in a warm clasp—with those long fingers that had touched her and held her. She could not prevent her deep shudder, and yet she did not pull away. She leaned against the parapet and kept her eyes closed as she had when they had waltzed together.

And he lifted her hand until she felt his lips, warm and still, against the back of it.

God. Oh, dear God.

After a few moments he turned her hand and held her palm, first against his mouth and then against his cheek—the unscarred cheek.

"I know that I am the last person in the world to be able to comfort you," he said. "I know that what I did to you and my appearance make me deeply revolting to you. But if it ever comes to that, Fleur, if there is ever no one else to whom you can turn, then come to me. Will you?"

"I can stand alone," she said. "I always have."

"Have you?" he said. "Ever since the death of your parents when you were eight?"

She was silent. And aching with the sound of her name, the first time anyone had called her Fleur since her parents.

"Come back to the house," he said. "You are cold."

"Yes," she said.

And she allowed him to draw her hand through his arm and lead her slowly and silently on the long walk back. And she wished and wished he were someone different. She longed to lay her head against the broad shoulder beside it, to turn into his arms, to beg him not to leave her alone that night— her last night of freedom. If only he were Daniel.

And she thought with bleak humor of how Daniel would

react to such an invitation. He would be shocked and hurt and sorrowful.

The duke stopped when they reached the upper terrace, at the foot of the horseshoe steps.

"I meant what I said," he said, one hand over hers as it rested on his arm. "I was angry at my own weakness that night, Fleur, and I used you crudely and cruelly. I have much to atone for. I would like to do you a kindness."

"You already have," she said. "You fed me and paid me more than I had earned, and you gave me this post."

He said no more, but only searched her eyes with his for a long silent moment in the darkness until she felt terror welling in her again.

But she remembered the greater terror facing her inside the house and drew herself free of his grace in order to climb the steps unassisted. She hoped she would not be chained, she thought, and began to run. She hoped she would not be carried or dragged from this house the next day in chains. And she hoped . . .

She opened one of the doors herself without waiting for the duke to come up beside her. And she fled across the great hall and through the archway to the staircase as if all the hounds of hell were in pursuit of her.

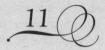

11

THE DUKE OF RIDGEWAY WATCHED HER GO, HIS face impassive for the benefit of the footmen who stood in the hall.

Was it he from whom she fled? And yet, though he had felt her shudder when he touched her, she had fought her revulsion and mastered it just as she had when they had danced. Had she feared that he would suggest taking her to her room or to his?

But no, she must know that he had not had seduction on his mind, that he was deeply concerned about her.

What was the unknown terror that had sent her fleeing first from the house and then back into it?

He felt so very responsible for her, as he did for all his servants and all those under his care. But more than that with her. He was the one responsible for changing her life irrevocably, and that in a manner designed to fill her forever with horror.

He had not kissed her or held her or fondled her. He had merely seated himself and ordered her to remove her clothes, and had watched her every movement. And he had ordered her to lie down while he undressed in front of her. While the candle still burned in the wall sconce, he had pulled her into the position he wanted, the position in which he could demonstrate his mastery over her and all women, and then he had demonstrated that mastery without subtlety or gentleness.

And yet he had taken her to that inn wanting to soothe himself with feminine compassion and warmth. Her very silence and self-possession had inflamed him, angered him. He had wanted her to reach out to him as no one had reached out for more years than he could recall, and she had looked at him with steady acceptance of what she must do to earn her living.

He cursed softly and turned from the hall to rejoin his wife and their guests in the drawing room. And he found himself looking curiously at Lord Brocklehurst, who was conversing quietly and amiably with a small group. The duke joined that group.

"Yes, she is sleeping," he assured Lady Mayberry, who asked about Pamela.

An hour passed before he found himself almost alone with Lord Brocklehurst and uncertain whether he or the other had maneuvered it so.

"You have a fine daughter, your grace," Lord Brocklehurst said with a smile.

"Yes, indeed," the duke replied. "She is very precious to my wife and me."

"The prospect of marriage is appealing when one thinks of acquiring a family of such pretty children," the other said.

"Yes, indeed," the duke said. "You are betrothed?"

"Oh, no, no, not yet," Lord Brocklehurst said with a laugh. "Of course, it must be a worry to have children and the responsibility of giving them all that is the best. How does one choose a worthy governess or tutor, for example? Your governess seems like a quiet young lady. She has been with you long?"

"Quite recently acquired, actually," the duke said. "We are well satisfied with her work."

"It must be time-consuming to check the references of such

an employee," Lord Brocklehurst said, "to make sure that one is not being deceived in any way."

"Perhaps," his grace said. "I employ a secretary for such a purpose. You know Miss Hamilton?"

"Oh, no, no," the other said, "though the name is familiar. And the face too, a little, now that you mention it. I believe I know her family. Perhaps I met her once."

"Ah," the duke said, "Miss Dobbin is to play the pianoforte, I see. I shall draw nearer. Excuse me, Brocklehurst?"

So, he thought, crossing the room to stand behind Miss Dobbin's stool, it was definitely Brocklehurst. And the man was being as secretive about the whole connection as Fleur had been.

Or was he overreacting? Had she merely been embarrassed and distressed to see a man who might recognize her and see her in the lowly position of governess?

Who was she? Who and what had she been? At first he had not been particularly curious about her. Her story had seemed plausible enough. But she had lied to him about her parents. If her father had died in debt, it had certainly not happened recently. But something had happened recently.

And why did the not knowing matter to him? Had he ever wondered about Houghton's past or that of any of his other servants? Fleur Hamilton's past was her own business.

But why had she lied about her father? Why had she lied about not knowing Brocklehurst? Equally intriguing, why had he lied about his acquaintance with her?

His wife, he saw without looking, was paying court to both Shaw and Thomas.

FLEUR WAS IN THE music room early the following morning, playing Beethoven—not at all well. She had not tried any of the new music that morning, but had only tried to steady herself, lose herself in the old. But the magic had deserted her. She stumbled, played mischords, forgot her place.

She would have banged her hands in frustration across the keyboard if the door to the library had not opened earlier as it usually did, but as it had not the morning before, to reveal briefly the figure of his grace.

She had not slept at all. Though she must have done, she reflected, or there would not be the remembered nightmares—the dead face and staring eyes of Hobson, the discomfort of traveling in a coach with her wrists bound in rusty chains at her back, the trapdoor and the knowledge that below it was emptiness and a waiting coffin, the scarred hawkish face above her and the long-fingered hands beneath her buttocks to hold her steady, Matthew with a strawberry-red rose across his dead face, blood running from the puncture made by a thorn.

Yes, she must have slept.

How long would it be? How much longer did she have?

Was she playing Beethoven or Mozart?

She heard the door from the hallway open, though it happened very quietly and the door was behind her. She took her hands from the keyboard and folded them in her lap. She knew who it was. She did not have to look around.

"Ah, Isabella," a familiar voice said. "No, I beg your pardon. Fleur, is it not?"

She got up from the stool and turned to face him. He was smiling, as Matthew so often was. She placed a finger over her lips and pointed in the direction of the open door into the library. He nodded his comprehension. And she led the way from the room.

"There are lawns at the back of the house," she said. "I believe it has stopped raining."

It seemed appropriate that the long spell of warm, sunny weather had broken sometime during the night. The clouds were heavy and low and the grass glistening with the drizzle that had fallen on it, she had seen in a glance from the window of her room earlier.

And it seemed strange now to hear her own voice and to note that it sounded just as it usually did.

"A few questions revealed to me your morning habits," he said.

"Yes," she said. "They are no secret."

She took him to a back entrance, avoiding the great hall. She did not go for a cloak, though it was chilly outside. But she scarcely noticed.

"I will come quietly," she said, walking on ahead of him past the kitchen gardens to the lawns beyond, leaving him to catch up and fall into step beside her. "I don't know if you brought assistance. I don't know if you plan to put fetters on me. I don't know what the law is. But you will not need them. I will come quietly."

Even the clouds were beautiful. Even the wet grass soaking its moisture into her shoes felt wonderful. And she remembered her first sight of Willoughby and her first weeks there. She remembered her buoyant feeling of hope and happiness. She remembered the visit to the Chamberlains and their return visit. She remembered walking this very lawn with Mr. Chamberlain, the children rushing on ahead with a ball. She remembered playing with the puppy in the paddock. And she remembered waltzing on a lantern-lit path.

"Murder is a hanging offense, Isabella," he said.

"I know." Her pace unconsciously quickened. "I also know, as do you, Matthew, that I am no murderer. What happened was an accident caused when I acted in my own defense. But of course that will be an irrelevant point when we both speak in court."

"Poor Hobson," he said. "He was merely stepping up behind you to prevent you from tripping over the hearth yourself, Isabella. It was unfortunate that you were in such a temper because I had been forced to admonish you for your own good. He would be alive now."

"Yes," she said, "it sounds convincing even now, Matthew. And I was foolish enough to panic and run—the actions of a guilty person. What is the procedure? Am I to be bound?"

He chuckled. "You seem to have done well enough for yourself," he said, "though you might have come home, Isabella. There was no need to lower yourself to become a governess. His grace seems pleased with your services, though. And so he should be, if he was willing to pay his man to sit at a certain employment agency for four days before he found a suitable candidate."

She looked at him for the first time. He was still smiling.

"You are his mistress?" he said. "You looked high indeed, Isabella."

"I am his daughter's governess," she said. "Or was. I am your prisoner now, I suppose."

"And yet," he said, "it would break my heart to see that lovely neck with a rope about it, Isabella. And perhaps it is true and you misunderstood the situation and thought self-defense necessary. Who am I to judge your motives? Perhaps it was an unfortunate accident after all."

"What are you saying?" She had stopped walking and stood looking directly at him.

"The simple truth," he said. "I want to give you the benefit of the doubt if I possibly can. You know I love you, Isabella."

"I could play this game out to the end," she said. "But I believe I understand you very well, Matthew. You will agree that Hobson's death was an accident if I consent to be your mistress. Am I right?"

He held his arms out to his sides. "Why the harsh tones? Do you see a pistol about me?" he asked. "Chains? Ropes? Do you see a constable or guard lurking at my shoulder? Do you think I have searched for you all this time just in order to see you executed? Do you know me so little, Isabella?"

"Speak plainly with me," she said. "For once in your life, Matthew, speak plainly. If I refuse to be your mistress, what then? Give me a straight answer."

"Isabella," he said, "I am a guest here. I came with an old friend of mine, Lord Thomas Kent, to spend a few weeks on an estate I have always wished to visit. It is quite splendid, is it not? You are a governess here—a happy coincidence. And of course we must speak of that unhappy death, whose mystery still has not been cleared up because you fled immediately after it. But there is no need to say everything that needs to be said between us at this very moment, is there? You are not going anywhere for the next few weeks, and neither am I."

"No," she said. "I did not think you would be persuaded to speak plainly. But I understand you very well for all that. I have, after all, known you for much of my life. I am to live with a threat hanging over my head. You will dangle me like a puppet on a string."

"You have heard, I suppose," he said, "that the Reverend Booth was, ah, disappointed in you? I believe it is the elder Miss Hailsham who is currently the fortunate recipient of his smiles."

Daniel! Fleur lifted her chin.

"When we leave eventually, Isabella," he said, "I think it would be as well to do so without airing our dirty linen, so to speak, before the duke and duchess, wouldn't you agree? And I am quite sure that you would not wish to cause his grace unnecessary disappointment when you leave by raising false hopes in the intervening weeks, would you? You will, of course, be coming home, where you belong."

"Don't worry, Matthew," she said, "there is no affair to put an end to."

He smiled. "He makes a habit of strolling the back lawns in the early morning, then?" he said.

Fleur turned her head sharply to find that indeed his grace was walking toward them.

"Good morning," Lord Brocklehurst called. "I find that your park has as magnificent prospects at the back of the house as before it."

His grace was carrying a cloak over one arm. He shook it out and set it about Fleur's shoulders without a word to her.

"My grandfather hired the best of landscape gardeners," he said. "I trust you had a good sleep, Brocklehurst?"

"Indeed, yes, I thank you," the other said. "And as you must have guessed, your grace, my feeling of last evening was quite correct. Miss Hamilton and I have a slight acquaintance and have been inquiring into the health of each other's relatives."

"Miss Hamilton," his grace said, turning to her, "I will be giving Pamela her first riding lesson this morning directly after breakfast. You will bring her to the stables, if you please. You are dismissed for now."

"Yes, your grace." She curtsied without looking at either him or Matthew and turned to hurry back to the house.

There was to be some reprieve, then. It was not to be quite as bad as she had feared all night, and for two months before that. He was prepared to give her her freedom in exchange for what he had wanted for three years past. Except that in the past she had been able to treat his attentions with scorn. Now he must feel that he had a hold on her.

And who was she to say he did not? It was all very well now, in the relief of knowing that it was not to be today, to tell herself that she would throw his offer in his face when he told her finally that it was time for them to leave. It was well now to imagine herself telling him, her head thrown back, contempt in her eyes, that she would take the noose rather than him.

But would she when the time came?

And it was quite like Matthew, of course. It amazed her that she had not thought of it as a possibility before. He had wanted her badly enough. Was it likely that he would give her up to the gallows any more willingly than he would have given her up to Daniel?

Of course. She was foolish not to have thought of it.

She unbuttoned the cloak absently as she climbed the stairs inside the house. And then she looked down at it with awareness. It was her own cloak. It had been hanging in her wardrobe.

He must have sent a maid upstairs for it. He had brought it out to her and wrapped it about her shoulders.

And he had ordered her to bring Lady Pamela out to the stables to him after breakfast.

There was to be another day, then. Not chains and a long carriage ride and a dark prison cell at the end of it. Not yet, anyway.

Her step lightened and quickened. There was to be another day.

IT WAS STILL TOO EARLY for breakfast when the Duke of Ridgeway came inside with Lord Brocklehurst. There was still time to accomplish one more thing before eating and going back outside with Pamela.

He sent a servant to summon Lord Thomas Kent to the library if he was up. He must talk to his brother. Somehow, he could not take the coward's way out and just say nothing.

He thought grimly of the night before. Unable to sleep himself, he had done something he rarely did. He had gone into his wife's room very late. He had half-expected to find the room empty and the bed unslept in.

But she had been both there and awake. And feverish and coughing. She had watched him listlessly as he approached the bed.

"You are not well?" he had asked, touching his fingers to her cheek and finding it dry and burning. He brought her a cool cloth from the washstand, folded it, and laid it over her forehead.

"It is nothing," she had said, turning her face from him.

He had stood looking down at her for a long silent moment. "Sybil," he had asked quietly, "shall I send him away? Will it be less painful for you if he is gone?"

Her eyes had been open. She had been staring away from him. And he had watched one tear roll diagonally across her cheek and nose and drip onto the sheet. "No," she had said.

Nothing more. Just the one word. He had turned away after a while and left the room.

Her maid had reported to him that morning that her grace had recovered from her fever.

He fully expected that after a journey of a few days his brother would be still asleep. But he came wandering into the library fifteen minutes after being summoned, his customary half-smile on his lips.

"This brings back memories," he said, looking about him. "Many was the time we were summoned here, Adam, for a thrashing." He laughed. "I more than you, I must confess. Is that why I have been summoned here this morning?"

"Why did you return?" the duke asked.

"The fatted calf is supposed to be killed for the prodigal's return," Lord Thomas said with a laugh. "You have not learned your Bible lessons well enough, Adam."

"Why did you return?"

Lord Thomas shrugged. "It is home, I suppose," he said. "When I was in India, England was home. And when I returned to England, then Willoughby was home—even if I am not welcome here. Sometimes it is not a good thing to be just a half-brother."

"You know that has nothing to do with anything," his grace said harshly. "We were scarcely aware of the half-relationship when we were growing up, Thomas. We were simply brothers."

"But at that time one of us was not duke and afraid the other might waste some of his vast substance," the other said.

"And you know that that was never my concern either," the duke said. "I tried to persuade you to stay. I wanted you to stay.

I wanted to share Willoughby with you. You belonged here. You were my brother. But when you insisted on leaving, then I told you you must not return. I meant ever."

"Ever is a long time," Lord Thomas said, strolling to the fireplace and examining the mosaic lion on the overmantel. "It's strange how I could not even picture this room clearly in my mind when I was in India. But it all comes back now. Nothing ever changes at Willoughby, does it?"

"You couldn't leave her in peace, could you?" the duke said.

"In peace?" Lord Thomas turned around with a laugh. "You mean she has been in peace married to you for the past five and a half years? She does not appear to me like a woman living in wedded bliss, Adam. Haven't you seen that? Are you still besotted with her?"

"She had accepted the fact that you were gone," the duke said, "that you would never return."

"Well." His brother sank into a leather chair and draped a leg over one of its arms. "She does not seem unduly unhappy at my return, either, Adam. She is not as niggardly in her welcome as you are."

"And what is she to do when you leave again?" his brother asked.

"Have I said anything about leaving?" Lord Thomas spread his hands. "Perhaps I will stay this time. Perhaps she will not have to do anything."

"It is too late for you to stay," the duke said curtly. "She is married to me."

"Yes." Lord Thomas laughed. "She is, isn't she? Poor Adam. Perhaps I will take her from you."

"No," the duke said. "Never that. I doubt that would serve your purpose at all, Thomas. You will merely take her heart again. You will convince her again that you love her, that for you the sun rises and sets on her. And then, when you tire of the game, you will leave her. She will not guard her heart against such an ending because she will believe in you as she did before and as she has done ever since you left."

"I gather you must have played the gallant and taken all the blame." Lord Thomas was laughing again. "She did not rain blows at my head as I half-expected her to do. You are a fool, Adam."

"I happened to love her most dearly," his brother said quietly. "I would have given my life to save her from pain. I knew she could no longer love me—if she ever had—and so I allowed her to think me the villain. But perhaps she already thought that. I came back alive, after all, and spoiled everything."

"And you also married her," Lord Thomas said. "You were rather fortunate, I suppose, that Pamela was not born with my mother's red hair. You would have been the laughingstock. As it is, I suppose people only smile behind their hands to think that you came home like an impatient stallion to mount her in the hay without even pausing to change out of the clothes you traveled in or to remove your boots."

"Yes, I married her," the duke said. "You would not, so I did. I do not believe I would have been able to see her live through the disgrace even if I had not still loved her at the time. But you did not even have honor enough to stay away. Perhaps I should have insisted that she listen to the truth. She would be better able to guard against you now."

"Well," Lord Thomas said, jumping to his feet again, "you did not because you were ever the Sir Galahad, Adam. You would not have ridden off to war if you had not been. Perhaps I can put a son in your nursery before I leave again—if I leave. Perhaps he too will be fortunate enough not to have red hair. You seem somewhat incapable of begetting your own heirs. Or should I keep my eye on the governess's waistline?"

The duke took two steps forward, and Lord Thomas found himself standing on his toes, his neckcloth and shirtfront in a grasp tight enough to half-choke him.

"I could have you thrown from my property," his grace

said. "There would be many who would call me fool and weakling for not doing so. But you are my brother and this is your home. And I have enough feeling left for Sybil that I would not snatch you from her before you can make some peace between the two of you. But remember one thing, Thomas. She is my wife and Pamela is my daughter, and I will defend what is mine from disgrace and unnecessary pain. And it would be as well for you to learn that my servants, including Pamela's governess, are under my protection, and protect them I will in any manner I deem necessary."

His brother turned his head from side to side when he was released, to loosen his shirt collar, and brushed at his ruined neckcloth a little shakily.

"I came here because I have been away from both Willoughby and England for more than five years," he said. "I was homesick. You should remember what that is like, Adam. I thought you would have forgiven and forgotten. It seems that I was wrong. Perhaps I should take myself off without further delay."

His brother watched him with tight lips and keen eyes.

Lord Thomas laughed. "But I forget," he said. "I brought Bradshaw with me. It would be rag-mannered to drag him away again less than a day after our arrival, would it not? I shall stay for a short while." He sketched his brother a careless bow and left the room.

His grace sank into the chair behind the mahogany desk, rested his elbows on the arms, and steepled his fingers beneath his chin.

He had known, of course, that talking to Thomas would do no good at all. But he had hoped that he could appeal to some sense of honor. Its absence had not been noticeable when they were boys. They had always been reasonably good friends despite a five-year age difference. And the selfish lack of responsibility that had always been their father's complaint against his younger son could have been expected to disappear with the coming of adulthood and maturity. Anyway, it was too late now for his brother to simply turn and leave. Too late for Sybil. She had seen him again, and all the old wounds must be open and raw again.

He was well aware that she had never stopped loving Thomas. She had never had any feelings for her husband or for the occasional lovers she had taken since their marriage. Thomas was the love of her life.

He had not known it or even suspected it during those months when he had returned from Spain and fallen in love with her and become betrothed to her. She had seemed willing enough. More than that, she had seemed eager. She had told him she loved him. She had allowed him to kiss and fondle her.

But he had been the Duke of Ridgeway and had had a repu tation as something of a hero. And her parents had been ambitious for her. She had always been intended for him.

He had not suspected, though she had told him later, on one of the many occasions when she had wanted to hurt him, that even then she had loved Thomas and for as far back as she could remember.

He had known it only when he returned the year after Waterloo, when she had been betrothed to Thomas and horrified to see him. She would have married Thomas even though he was no longer the duke or owner of Willoughby. She had loved him totally.

But Thomas, who would have married her as the Duke of Ridgeway, part of the trophies that he had unexpectedly inherited from his slain brother, no longer wished to do so when he was simply Lord Thomas Kent again.

But he had not told her. He had become her lover and sworn undying love to her. He had impregnated her. And he had left her in a great hurry after she had told him.

He had told his brother that he was going and his reason for doing so. He had not told Sybil.

God help him, the duke thought, closing his eyes and

resting his forehead against his steepled fingers, he had done everything in his power to persuade Thomas to stay. He had himself loved Sybil so dearly that he had been unable to bear the thought of her grief on being abandoned or of the predicament she would be in.

But Thomas had left.

When Sybil had called with her father two days later, he had told both of them only that Thomas had gone. He had given no reason. And when she had accused him of sending his brother away because there was no room for the two of them at Willoughby, he had only shaken his head and put up no other defense at all. He had felt so desperately sorry for her. And so she had come to believe her own suggestion.

One week later he had called on Sybil and offered for her. He had repeated the call for three days until she accepted him—with ashen face and dead eyes.

She had been three months with child when they married.

And he had known even at the time that he had done things all wrongly, that he should have told her the full truth, made her listen, however painful it would have been to her. She was entitled to know the truth. And only the truth would have given their marriage any chance of success. But he had been too hopelessly in love with her at the time, too full of pity for her. He would have died rather than give her unnecessary pain.

And now he had allowed Thomas to come back—into his home and into Sybil's life.

Was he insane?

He pushed his chair back roughly from the desk and got to his feet. It must be breakfasttime. There were guests to entertain and a riding lesson to give and a day to be lived through.

Sitting and brooding would accomplish nothing whatsoever.

12

HIS GRACE WAS LOOKING TIGHT-LIPPED AND impatient, Fleur saw when she led a reluctant Lady Pamela to the stables after breakfast. He was standing with one booted foot on the lower rung of the paddock fence, a riding crop beating rhythmically against his leg. He was bareheaded and looked very dark and forbidding in his black riding coat.

"Ah, there you are at last," he said, lowering his foot to the ground.

Fleur curtsied and released her hold on Lady Pamela's hand. She turned back to the house.

"May I ride with you on Hannibal, Papa?" the child asked.

"Nonsense," he said impatiently. "You will never learn to ride that way, Pamela. You are five years old. It's high time you could ride alone. Where are you going, Miss Hamilton?"

"To the house, your grace," she said, turning back again. "Is there something else you wish me to do?"

He was frowning. "Where is your riding habit?" he asked, eyeing her cloak and the pale green cotton dress beneath.

"I don't possess one, your grace," she said.

His lips thinned. "Boots?"

"No, your grace."

"You will have to manage without, then," he said. "Call at Houghton's office tomorrow morning. He will have made arrangements to send you into Wollaston to be measured for a habit and boots."

There were two horses and a pony, all saddled, trotting around the paddock under a groom's guidance, Fleur saw in a glance over his shoulder. She was to ride too? Suddenly the day of her temporary reprieve seemed like a very glorious new creation. Suddenly it seemed that the sun must have burst through the clouds.

"Don't tell me that you are afraid of horses too," he said, his frown turned to a scowl.

"No, your grace." She could not repress her smile. She turned her face up to the clouds and felt that it must be bathed in sunlight. She would have twirled about if she had been alone. "No, I am not afraid of horses."

"I will ride with you, Miss Hamilton," Lady Pamela announced.

"You will ride alone," her father said firmly. "That pony is too meek and mild to toss you even if it took it into its head to do something so startling. You will ride beside me and I will hold the leading rein. Miss Hamilton will ride at your other side. You will be as safe as you are in your own bed."

Fleur stooped down and took the child's cold hands in hers. "It is the most glorious feeling in the world to ride a horse," she said. "To be high on the back of an animal who can move so much more surely and swiftly than we can. There is no greater sense of freedom and joy."

"But Mama says I could break my neck," Lady Pamela wailed. "I want to stay here with Tiny."

"You can break your neck if you ride recklessly," Fleur said. "That is why Papa is going to be with you to teach you to ride properly. He would not allow you to fall, would he? And I would not, would I?"

Lady Pamela still looked dubious, but she allowed the duke to lift her into his arms and carry her into the paddock and seat her on the little sidesaddle on the pony's back. Fleur signaled the groom to help her onto the back of the sleek brown mare.

The three of them rode slowly across the back lawns for almost half an hour, Lady Pamela closely flanked by the duke on one side and Fleur on the other. Gradually the terror faded from the child's face. She was even flushed with triumph by the time they returned to the stables, and loudly demanded to know whether the groom her father had summoned had seen her.

"That I did, my lady," the groom said, lifting her to the ground. "You will be galloping to hounds before we know it."

"I want a real horse next time," she said, looking up to her father.

"Let Lady Pamela play with her dog for a while, Prewett," the duke said, "and then escort her to the house and have her taken to her nurse." He turned to Fleur and nodded his head curtly. "Let's ride."

Her eyes widened. Not even the fact that he was to be her riding companion could spoil the beauty and unexpected wonder of this particular morning. She had ridden very slowly with a child and her father. Now she was to ride free?

His grace had already turned his horse's head toward the lawns of the park, which stretched for miles to the south of the house.

WAS IT ONLY TWO NIGHTS before that he had resolved to stop seeing her? the Duke of Ridgeway wondered, taking his horse to a canter and hearing the mare increase its pace behind him.

A number of the gentlemen had gone fishing. Most of the ladies were going into Wollaston. He had told Treadwell and Grantsham that he would probably join them in the billiard room after giving his daughter a short riding lesson.

How foolish of him to have expected to see her arrive at the stables in riding habit and boots. When he had hired her, he had given Houghton instructions to provide her with enough money to buy herself some essential garments. Houghton would have seen to it that there was enough money to do just that. There would have been no extra for riding habits or boots.

It was hard to adjust his mind to some of the realities of poverty.

Would he be indulging in this stolen hour, he wondered, if she had not smiled at him? In reality, of course, she had not smiled at him at all, but at the prospect of riding. Clearly she had misunderstood him earlier and assumed that it was her task only to bring Pamela to the stables.

It was the first time he had seen her smile almost directly at him. And it had been a total smile, lighting up her face, making of its beauty a dazzling thing. He could have sworn that all the rays of the sun had been directed at her face when she had lifted it to the sky, even though the clouds had still been low and heavy.

He had been dazzled pure and simple. And if she loved riding so much, he had decided while they had led Pamela slowly about a back lawn between them, then he would take her riding.

He glanced back over his shoulder and saw that she was not at all perturbed by the pace he had set. She was obviously a woman bred to the saddle. He spurred Hannibal into a full gallop.

Sybil hated riding. She preferred to be conveyed from place to place, she always said, in safety.

He usually did his riding alone.

She drew level with him, and he realized in a flash of surprised pleasure that she was racing him. She tossed him that dazzling smile again—and this time it was directly at him that she smiled. He took up the challenge.

They raced recklessly across the smooth miles of the park. Her mare was no match for Hannibal, of course, but sometimes he allowed her to draw level with him and nose ahead before surging into the lead again. She knew his game very well but would not give in to defeat. She was laughing.

He veered off to his left suddenly, heading directly for the ivy-draped wall that divided this southern end of the park from a pasture. Yes, there it was—the gate. It was a dangerous game. He knew it even as he committed both his own horse and hers to it. But he was in the reckless throes of a race.

He eased back on Hannibal's reins as soon as he had cleared the gate and watched the mare soar over with a clear foot to spare, Fleur bent low over its neck. She was no longer laughing as she slowed the mare with expert hands and brought it alongside Hannibal, leaning forward to pat its neck. But her face was glowing with a beauty and an animation that had his breath catching in his throat. She wore no bonnet. Most of the pins that had held her hair back in its usual neat knot seemed to have been shed along the way. Her head seemed surrounded by a golden halo.

"You have gone down to ignominious defeat," he said. "Admit it."

"But you chose my mount," she said, "and deliberately picked one that is lame in three legs. Admit it."

Touché," he said, laughing. "We must call truce. You have a splendid seat. You have ridden to hounds?"

"No," she said. "I always felt too sorry for the fox or the deer. I ride only for pleasure. There is a great deal of open country about Her—" She stopped abruptly. "About the place where I used to live."

"Isabella," he said softly.

Her eyes flew to his face, and he wished instantly that he could recall the word. It was as if a door had closed across her face. The magic, the insane magic of the past half-hour, was gone.

"My name is Fleur," she said.

"Hamilton? Is that questionable too?" He watched her with narrowed eyes.

"My name is Fleur," she said.

"Since you have only a slight acquaintance with Lord Brocklehurst, then," he said, "it is understandable that he misremembered your name."

"Yes," she said.

"And remarkably surprising that he would use it at all—on such slight acquaintance," he said.

Her eyes looked haunted, as they had the night before when he had come upon her at the bridge. And he hated himself and what he was doing to her. Was it any of his business? Even if she had some mysterious past, even if she was living under an assumed name, was it any of his business? She was doing superior work as a governess and seemed to care for Pamela.

But Isabella? He did not want to think of her as anyone else but Fleur.

Their horses were walking slowly along beneath the wall, turning with it as it ran parallel to the lake a mile to the north.

"You know him very well, don't you?" he said.

"Scarcely at all," she said. "I did not even recognize him until he presented himself this morning."

"Has he harassed you in the past?" he asked. "Are you afraid of him?"

"No!"

"You don't need to be," he said. "You are on my property and in my employ and under my protection. If he has harassed you or threatened you, tell me now, Fleur, and he will be gone before nightfall."

"I scarcely know him," she said.

They had reached another gate in the wall. He leaned out from the back of his horse and unclasped it. He closed it behind them again when they were back inside the park, amongst the trees that extended to the lake on its south side.

"Have you seen the follies here?" he asked.

"No," she said.

He pointed them out to her as they rode past, a triumphal

arch leading nowhere, a sylvan grotto that had never housed either nymphs or shepherds, a ruined temple.

"All of them afford a picturesque view of the lake when you stand close to them," he said. "Mr. William Kent had a sure eye for effect."

As they rode slowly back to the house from the lake, he found himself telling her about Spain and about the army's crossing over the Pyrenees into the south of France. She was asking him quiet and intelligent questions. He was not sure how the topic had been introduced.

He was more sorry than he could say that those magic moments had been so brief. He wished he could have curbed his curiosity about her identity and history, or at least put it off until another time.

For that half-hour he had felt happier and more carefree than he had felt for years. And she had looked more beautiful and more desirable than any woman he had ever known, her face glowing, her untidy red-gold hair framing her face and half-loose down her back. And her looks and her smiles had been all for him.

No, he thought as they rode into the stableyard and she hastily summoned a groom to lift her to the ground, it was as well that the morning had developed as it had. The situation had been wrong and dangerous. He was being tempted as he had been tempted even at his first sight of her outside the Drury Lane.

She was Pamela's governess now, his servant. She was under his protection, as he had told her earlier. It was his duty to protect her from lechery, not to lead the attack himself.

"I daresay Pamela has enjoyed her brief holiday," he said.

"Yes," she said. "We must start lessons early this afternoon." She stood uncertainly, watching him.

"I have some matters to discuss with my head groom," he lied. "You may return to the house, Miss Hamilton."

"Yes, your grace." She curtsied and turned to leave.

He watched her go, wondering if life ever offered happiness in more than very small, very brief doses.

THE FRENCH LESSON HAD gone very well, as had the history lesson, or rather the history story. When Fleur took the large globe from its shelf for a geography lesson, Lady Pamela wanted to know where India was.

"My uncle Thomas was there," she said, and she traced with a finger under Fleur's guidance the long sea route that her uncle must have taken in order to come home to England.

"I don't like my uncle Thomas," she said candidly.

"Why not?" Fleur turned the globe so that India was facing them again. "You have met him only once, and you were tired."

"He did not really like me," the child said. "He was laughing at me."

"This is probably because he is not used to little girls," Fleur said. "Some people do not know how to talk to children. They are a little afraid of them."

"He said I do not look like Mama," Lady Pamela said. "He said I was all Papa. I wish I looked like Mama. Everyone loves Mama."

"And you think everyone does not love you because you are dark like your papa?" Fleur asked. "I think you are very wrong. Dark looks can be very handsome. Your many-times-great-grandmother was very dark and very beautiful. She reminded me of you when I saw her portrait downstairs a couple of days ago."

Dark eyes looked at her critically. "You are just saying that," Lady Pamela said.

"Perhaps you should see for yourself, then," Fleur said. "And perhaps you should start to become acquainted with your papa's family. They go back for hundreds of years, long before you or Papa was ever thought of."

Most of the ladies, including the duchess, were still in Wollaston, Fleur knew. His grace had ridden away with several of the gentlemen to view his farms, though the drizzle had started to fall again an hour before. It would surely be safe to take Lady Pamela down to the long gallery, as his grace wished her to do on occasion.

They looked first at the Van Dyck portrait of the dark lady who had once been Duchess of Ridgeway, surrounded by her family, including the duke, and by the family dogs.

"She is lovely," Pamela said, clinging to Fleur's hand. "Do I really look like her?"

"Yes," Fleur said. "I think you will look very like her when you are grown up."

"Why do the men have such funny hair?" the child asked.

They examined the hair and the beards and the clothes of her ancestors to note how very much fashions had changed over the years. Lady Pamela chuckled when Fleur explained to her that men had used to wear wigs, until quite recent years.

"And ladies too," she said. "Your papa's grandmama would have worn a large wig and powdered it until it was white."

They moved along the gallery to look at a Reynolds portrait of a more recent ancestor so that she could prove her point.

It was an informal lesson without plan or any particular object, but the child was definitely interested, Fleur could see. She must bring her down whenever she knew that they would not be disturbed. She would see to it if she could that Lady Pamela would not grow up with such a poor sense of her family past as she herself had.

But the child quickly tired of examining old pictures.

"What is in those cupboards?" she asked, pointing.

"I believe your papa said that there are some old toys and games there that he and your uncle Thomas used to play with on rainy days," she said.

"Like today," Lady Pamela said, and stooped down to open one of the cupboard doors. She pulled out a spinning top and two skipping ropes. She pushed the top back inside. She had one in the nursery. She picked up one of the ropes and uncoiled it from the heavy wooden handles. "What do you do with these?"

Fleur felt a little uneasy. She had been permitted to bring Lady Pamela down to see the paintings, but nothing had been expressly said about allowing her to play there. But it was time to end lessons for the day, and the weather would prevent them from going outside again.

"You skip with them," she said. "You hold one of the handles in each hand and turn the rope over your head. You have to jump over it when it reaches the ground."

"Show me," Lady Pamela demanded, holding out one of the ropes.

"Please," Fleur said automatically.

"Please, silly," the child said.

It took Lady Pamela a while to catch the idea of turning the handles steadily instead of stopping each time she jumped successfully over the rope. But finally she could jump three times in succession before getting the rope tangled about her feet.

"How can you do it so many times?" she asked Fleur petulantly.

Fleur laughed. "Practice," she said. "Just as with the pianoforte." Though that was ridiculous, she thought, laughing again. She had not skipped rope for perhaps fifteen years.

"Charming," a languid voice said from the doorway, so far distant that neither Fleur nor Lady Pamela had heard the doors open. "Two happy children, would you say, Kent? Ah, but no, one of them transforms herself into Miss Hamilton, now that I have my glass to my eye."

Fleur could feel her face flaming. Lord Thomas Kent and Sir Philip Shaw were strolling toward them along the gallery, Sir Philip's quizzing glass to his eye. She rolled up her own skipping rope with hasty fingers.

"I am skipping," Lady Pamela announced.

"So I see." Lord Thomas regarded them both with laughing eyes and winked at Fleur. "How is my favorite niece today? Can you skip the length of the gallery?"

"I don't think so," Lady Pamela said.

He took a coin from his pocket and stooped down in front of her. "This is yours if you can," he said.

Lady Pamela drew a deep breath and went hurtling off along the gallery, tripping over the rope every few steps. Both gentlemen laughed as they watched her go.

"I forgot to tell her that she must do it without once coming to grief," Lord Thomas said, and strolled, laughing, after her.

"What a charming picture you made," Sir Philip said to Fleur. "I am sorry in my heart that I spoke as soon as I did. I have not seen such a trim pair of ankles in a long while."

Fleur stooped down without replying and put her skipping rope back into the cupboard. She had found the gentleman decidedly flirtatious when she had danced with him on the evening of the ball. By the time she stood up, Sir Philip was standing before her, one hand against the wall, regarding her with heavy-lidded eyes.

"Where do you hide away when you are not with the child, my sweet?" he asked. "Upstairs?"

She smiled briefly and willed Lady Pamela to turn and skip back down the gallery again.

"You must be lonely up there all alone," he said, and leaned forward to kiss the side of her neck.

"Don't," she said firmly.

But the hoped-for interruption came in an unhoped-for way. Two ladies had entered the open doors of the gallery, one of them the duchess.

"Ah, darling," she said, stooping down to kiss her daughter as Sir Philip moved off to examine one of the paintings through his glass. "Making friends with Uncle Thomas, are you?"

"See, Mama?" Lady Pamela held up her coin. "I can skip. I will show you."

"Some other time, darling," her grace said, straightening up. "Miss Hamilton, will you please take my daughter upstairs to her nurse, then await me in my sitting room?"

"The dragon is incensed, I fear," Sir Philip muttered without turning from the picture. "She is usually at her worst when she smiles and speaks so sweetly. My most abject apologies, my sweet. I will make it up to you some other time."

Fleur walked half the length of the gallery, her chin up, though her eyes were lowered to the floor. She curtsied, took the skipping rope from Lady Pamela's hands, took one of her hands in hers, and led her from the room.

"But, Mama," the child wailed. "I want to show you."

"Was it a forbidden romp, Sybil?" Lord Thomas' laughing voice was saying before Fleur was beyond earshot. "How shocking."

FLEUR STOOD QUIETLY INSIDE the door of the duchess's sitting room for all of half an hour. For some five minutes of that time she could hear coughing in the adjoining dressing room. Finally the door opened and her grace came in. She crossed to a small escritoire without even glancing Fleur's way and picked up a letter lying there. Fleur stood for another full five minutes while she read it.

The duchess set down the letter and turned to look Fleur slowly up and down. "Slut!" she said sweetly.

Fleur looked at her calmly.

"By whose authority were you in the gallery?" her grace asked.

"By his grace's," Fleur said.

"I beg your pardon?" The voice was soft, the face delicate and surprised.

"By his grace's, your grace."

"And by whose authority was my daughter playing with the toys there?"

"By mine, your grace," Fleur said.

"I see." The duchess picked up a book from a stool and seated herself gracefully on the daybed.

Fleur stood quietly for several more minutes while her grace turned pages.

"Is it your habit," the duchess said, looking up at last, her voice expressing pleasant curiosity, "to allow every man you meet to fondle you?"

"No, your grace."

"Are you not satisfied with the salary you are paid?"

"Yes, thank you, your grace," Fleur said. "I am very satisfied."

"I thought perhaps it was the money," the duchess said. "I can understand that for some servants it must be tempting to augment wages in such a manner. In your case it seems to be merely that you are a slut."

Fleur said nothing.

"I wish you no ill," her grace said. "You are what you are, Miss Hamilton. Perhaps you are unfortunate to have a mistress who has such tender sensibilities. But it distresses me beyond bearing to think of your being close to my daughter and influencing her. I will expect Mr. Houghton to inform me early tomorrow morning that he has been handed your resignation. I regret having to make such a request. You may go."

"Sir Philip Shaw's attentions were unasked-for and unwanted," Fleur said. "I do not believe you have cause to suspect me with anyone else."

The duchess laid aside her book carefully and looked slowly about the room, her eyebrows raised. "I do beg your pardon," she said with a light laugh, "but is there anyone else in this room?"

"I spoke to you, your grace," Fleur said.

"To me?" The duchess looked at her and smiled. "You have

an unfortunate habit of not identifying the person to whom you speak, Miss Hamilton. I did inform you that you are dismissed, did I not?"

But the door from the dressing room opened before Fleur could turn, and Lord Thomas Kent stepped inside.

"Still here, Miss Hamilton?" he said. "You must be fit to drop. Have you not offered her a seat, Sybil? How uncivil of you." His eyes were laughing.

"You are dismissed, Miss Hamilton," her grace said.

"From the room?" Lord Thomas said. "By all means. But not from the house, I hope. My sister-in-law has the most volatile of tempers, Miss Hamilton. But she is not vindictive once she has calmed down. I believe you will still find yourself with employment by the end of the day. You had better move now before you fall down. I believe you must have been standing on that same spot for the better part of an hour."

He smiled at her as she turned and made her way from the room.

Perhaps she should resign, she thought, assuming that she would have any choice in the matter anyway. Perhaps she should leave even before morning. Even before dinner.

But if she left, Matthew would think she was running from him. And he would come after her and fetter her and take her off to prison this time. Her temporary reprieve would prove to be very temporary indeed.

Besides, even if she did get away without being caught, what would she do? She had no money and no references. Her situation would be appallingly familiar, except that this time she would know how it must end.

She shut the door of her room behind her and locked it. And she threw herself facedown across the bed.

She had been so filled with elation just a few hours before. There had been the fresh air and the outdoors and the blessed, blessed freedom. And there had been that ride and her absurd happiness over the mad and dangerous race. Despite the fact that *he* had been her companion, she had been happier than she could remember being for years. Even happier than she had been at the ball. Her happiness with Daniel had been a quieter, less vibrant thing.

Daniel! She must not think of him. The pain of dull hopelessness would be too hard to bear if she allowed herself to think of him.

"THOMAS," THE DUCHESS OF RIDGEWAY said indignantly, "that was intolerable. You quite undermined my authority, and people tend not to take me seriously anyway because I am so small and mild of manner."

"Are you angry with me?" He leaned down and kissed her, sliding his tongue into her mouth and bearing her back and sideways until she was lying along the daybed. "Do you want to fight me? Kick me? Come on, then." He laughed down at her.

"I am serious," she said, lifting a hand to trace the line of his jaw. "I had quite steeled myself to be strict, and you completely spoiled the effect."

"What has the poor girl done?" he asked. "Allowed a bored guest to taste her lips? I gather Shaw is a lusty enough character, Sybil. Doubtless he was the seducer and she the seducee, even if she was enjoying what she was getting. And one can hardly fault his taste. She is a pretty girl." He laughed at the look in her eyes. "Or would be to a man who is not besotted with you, of course."

"Are you?" she asked, twining an arm about his neck.

"Besotted with you?" he said, the laughter dying from his eyes. "You know there has never been anyone but you, Sybil, and never could be." He kissed her long and deeply.

"She is a woman of loose morals," she said. "She really must go. I was shaking with the distress of having to dismiss her, but I did what I knew to be right."

"She is Adam's, you said?" Lord Thomas smiled at her as

he eased her dress off one shoulder. "Let him amuse himself with her, Sybil. I can be persuaded to comfort you. Or are you jealous?"

"Of Adam?" she said, wide-eyed. "And a governess? I hope I think better of myself than to feel jealousy, Thomas. But I do not think it kind of him to conduct his debaucheries here."

"Leave them alone," he said. "And let Shaw have her too if he wants. And Brocklehurst. The two of them were strolling out on the back lawn and looked to be deep in conversation early this morning. Their tête-à-tête was interrupted by Adam." He laughed. "Let Adam be preoccupied with guarding his hot little property. And I will be preoccupied with guarding you."

"Oh, Thomas," she said, throwing both arms about his neck and drawing his head down onto her shoulder, "it is not funny. There is no humor in this at all. What are we going to do?"

"Patience," he said soothingly. "Something will turn up."

"But what?" she said. "I am married to him. That can never change. Oh, why did you not take me with you when you left? I would have gone to the ends of the earth with you. You should have known that. I would not have cared."

"I could not," he said gently. "I could not have taken you out into the uncertainty of my future, Sybil, especially in your delicate condition. I could not do that to you. It would have been too cruel."

"And it was not cruel to leave me as I was?" she asked.

"Hush," he said. "All will work out, you will see. Does anyone ever walk through either of these unlocked doors unbidden?"

"No," she said. "But don't, Thomas. I'm afraid."

"Don't be," he said, getting to his feet and gazing down at her. "We belong together, Sybil, and you know it. I shall lock the doors and then you may feel quite secure."

He lay down beside her on the narrow daybed when his

task was accomplished, and kissed her, drawing up the muslin skirt of her dress with one hand as he did so.

"Thomas," she moaned, her fingers twining in his hair. "Oh, Thomas, it has been so long. I love you so."

He kissed her again without replying.

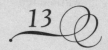

13

*H*IS WIFE WAS BRIGHT-EYED AND APPEARED FEVER-ish, the Duke of Ridgeway saw later that evening, although she was playing the game of charades with all their guests with a great deal of laughter and enthusiasm. The game had become decidedly bawdy as time went on.

The outing to Wollaston and the constant activity of the last several days, including the ball and the excitement over his brother's return, were proving too much for her, though she was not admitting it, perhaps even to herself. But he knew her well enough to know that her fragile health could not take such a hectic pace of living for much longer without breaking down.

He wondered if it was obvious to all their guests that Sybil and Thomas were fonder of each other than one might expect of a sister- and brother-in-law. He supposed that it must be. Certainly Shaw had ceased his marked attentions to her and was directing his gallantries toward Victoria Underwood that evening.

The duke supposed that no one would be particularly scan-dalized even if they had noticed. As he had suspected before he came home from London, his wife's guests were not a group renowned for propriety and restraint. Sidney had in-formed him earlier that a poor chambermaid had been bewildered to find Lady Mayberry in Grantsham's bed that morning and Mrs. Grantsham in Mayberry's.

He watched the scene about him rather grimly. Good breeding dictated that he continue to act the courteous and amiable host despite all. He could not possibly do what he dearly wished to do and get to his feet to make the public announcement that the gathering would be at an end the next morning.

The thought afforded him the only glimmering of amusement he had felt all evening.

Sometimes—just sometimes—he wished that he had not been born to a privileged and decadent class. But he wondered if any class was totally different if one just knew the truth. Perhaps people were people wherever one looked.

The duchess, flushed and laughing, sat down on a love seat. "You always were wonderfully clever at charades, Thomas," she said, smiling up at him until he seated himself beside her. "I am very glad I was of your team. Now we need something quiet and soothing to calm us down."

"I could think of something without even trying," Sir Hector Chesterton said.

Her grace reached out to tap him sharply on the arm with her fan. "I said quiet and soothing, you naughty man," she said. "Who can sing? Walter?"

"No breath, I do assure you, Sybil," that gentleman said. "Let one of the ladies play us a sonata."

"Not I," Mrs. Runstable said. "I am quite hagged."

"I make it a practice," Lady Mayberry said, "to be out of practice whenever I am from home."

Laughter greeted her words.

"It seems that my suggestion was not such a foolish one after all," Sir Hector said, seating himself on the arm of the chair occupied by Mrs. Runstable.

"Music is the soul of love," the duchess said, smiling and wafting one delicate arm in the air. "Give me music, do."

"How I wish I could sing," Lord Thomas said, taking her hand and carrying it to his lips.

"I know of someone who can play like an angel," Lord Brocklehurst said, "and who is not at all hagged from playing charades all night."

His grace felt an uncomfortable premonition and shifted in his chair as Sir Philip Shaw yawned delicately behind a hand.

"And who is this paragon of endless energy?" he asked.

"Miss Hamilton, the governess," Lord Brocklehurst said.

"Ah." Sir Philip fixed him with a languid gaze. "So you have a prior acquaintance with the damsel, do you, Brocklehurst, you lucky devil? And even succeeded in discovering that she plays like an angel? Ah, the pianoforte, I assume you mean? Let us have her down by all means, Sybil."

"It is late," the duke said. "Miss Hamilton is quite possibly in bed."

"Is she, by Jove?" Sir Philip said. "Your suggestion begins to sound more attractive by the minute, Chesterton."

"We do not like to keep our servants busy beyond their working hours," the duchess said.

"But, Sybil, Sybil." Lord Thomas reached for her hand again. "If Miss Hamilton plays like an angel and if it will give Bradshaw pleasure to hear her play, then you really should humor your guest. And if she is in bed, Adam, then you must cancel morning lessons for Pamela and allow her governess to catch up on her sleep. Nothing could be simpler. Bradshaw, pull the bell rope beside you, my dear chap. We will have the governess sent for."

It must be close to midnight, the duke thought as restrained applause greeted his brother's suggestion. Perhaps he should have spoken his protest more firmly. But it was too late. Thomas was giving instructions to Jarvis.

Fifteen minutes passed before the doors opened again to admit Fleur. Such a length of time suggested that she had indeed been in bed.

His grace jumped to his feet even as his brother got to his, and crossed the room to her.

"Miss Hamilton," he said, "my guests have requested that you play the pianoforte for us for perhaps half an hour."

Her face was shuttered, her eyes calm. She looked very much as she had looked in that bedchamber at the Bull and Horn, except that now she was healthy and beautiful. He had not realized then, as he realized now, that she often wore a mask to hide the real and vivid Fleur Hamilton.

And it struck him suddenly that she must think that he had betrayed her, that he had given her access to the instrument in the music room and listened to her each morning just so that he might use her talents for such an occasion as this.

"Will you, please?" he asked her.

"We have been told that you play like an angel," Sir Philip Shaw said.

But they were not my words, his grace told her with eyes that hardened against the cool expression in hers. It was just such an expression that had angered him on that first occasion and had changed the course of his encounter with her.

"She is shy," Lord Thomas said, bowing to her. "Miss Hamilton, would you please do us the honor?"

His grace held out a hand for hers, but her eyes had shifted to his brother, and she stepped past him and across the room to the pianoforte without looking back to him.

She seated herself on the stool, very straight-backed, and looked coolly at Lord Thomas.

"Is there any music in particular that you wish for, my lord?" she asked.

He continued to smile at her. "Something quiet and soothing, Miss Hamilton, if you please," he said.

"A lullaby, no less," Sir Philip said. "Something that will put us in the mood for, ah, sleep, Miss Hamilton."

The duke stood where he was, just inside the doorway, and watched her. She sat looking down at her hands clasped in her lap for a few moments, perfectly calm, perfectly self-possessed. And then she began to play Beethoven's Moonlight Sonata. She had no music.

She played faultlessly, very well even. If something of the magic of her morning performances was missing, probably only he would know it.

And if he continued to stand where he was, he thought as a buzz of quiet conversation spread around him again, then he was going to draw attention to himself. He moved to sit beside one of the ladies who was listening to the music and watched Brocklehurst move around to stand behind the music stool.

Did she play like an angel? If she did not, she certainly looked like one. The unadorned simplicity of her pale blue dress, the same one she had worn to the ball, the plain smoothness of her red-gold hair, the calm beauty of her face—all set her apart from any of the other ladies present. Yes, she looked like an angel.

Who was she? Isabella? Last name unknown? "Her—," she had begun to call her former home. Brocklehurst lived at Heron House in Wiltshire.

He would get to his feet when the music had ended and escort her to the door. She could return to her bed and to sleep.

But his brother spoke before he could do so.

"Bravo, Miss Hamilton," he said. "You have a superior touch, indeed. You have some acquaintance with Lord Brocklehurst? I am sure I speak for the whole gathering when I say that you may be excused now with our thanks. Indeed, both of you are excused. Bradshaw?"

Lord Brocklehurst bowed as she half-turned on the stool.

"I had hoped that I might take a stroll with Miss Hamilton in the long gallery," he said. "With your permission, your grace?" He turned his bow on the duchess.

"You have my permission, Miss Hamilton," her grace said with a smile, "and you may for the present forget about the task I set you for tomorrow morning."

His grace resumed his seat and watched her leave as calmly as she had entered, Lord Brocklehurst a few paces behind her. She afforded him only a brief expressionless glance as she passed him.

"Well, I am for bed," Sir Philip said with a yawn. "May I escort you to your door, Victoria?"

"I think everyone is ready for bed," the duchess said. "I never felt more tired in my life."

The duke rose to offer her his arm. And he wondered if it had been a trick as deliberate on her part as on his brother's, to bring Fleur to the drawing room at a shamefully late hour and then to snare her into a tête-à-tête meeting with Brocklehurst.

"You are feverish again," he said to his wife, a hand over one of hers when they paused a few minutes later outside her dressing room. "You need rest, Sybil. Why don't you stay in bed until noon tomorrow? I will see to the entertainment of our guests."

"I will be better by morning," she said. "I am just tired. And how can I miss a single hour with my guests? Life is so dull when they are not here. You are either away altogether or about your own business somewhere all day."

"It need not have been that way," he said. "We might have made a marriage of it, Sybil. We might at least have shown each other some kindness."

"No, it need not have been this way," she said, looking up at him, her eyes bright and feverish. "I might have been happy. *He* would not have neglected me, Adam. He would not have left me for months at a time and then resented my inviting guests here to relieve my boredom and loneliness. But then, I would not have needed guests with him. I would have been neither bored nor lonely." The color was high in her cheeks.

He opened the door for her.

"I will send for the doctor in the morning if your fever persists," he said, "and for a physician from London if we get no more satisfaction than we did in the winter when you were so ill."

"I don't need anyone but Dr. Hartley," she said petulantly. "Why did you send Thomas away, Adam? I will never forgive you, you know. And I am glad he has come back. Glad!"

She whisked herself inside the room and closed the door hastily. He could hear her coughing behind it.

He turned back with a sigh to the daytime apartments.

FLEUR HAD NOT AT FIRST been sorry to be woken up. The face bent over her, the body that was causing her such tearing pain and such eternal humiliation, was Daniel's. His handsome, pleasant features were distorted by raw carnal lust so that she hardly recognized them. But she knew they were Daniel's.

He had been calling her whore while hurting and hurting her.

The maid who had been sent to her room told her, wide-eyed, that she was to dress immediately and present herself to the company in the drawing room.

He had told everyone, she thought, as she dressed herself hastily and with trembling hands. He had decided to tell everyone, and now he was going to confront her with her crime in front of the whole gathering, for the amusement of all.

Her day of reprieve was at an end. And she was indeed his puppet on a string. And would be for the rest of her life.

She felt weary to the marrow of her bones by the time a footman opened the doors into the drawing room and she stepped alone inside to be confronted with light and sound and the sight of a large number of people. But she would not show it. If it was the last thing she was ever to do, she would carry this off with dignity. Neither Matthew nor anyone else would have the satisfaction of seeing her grovel or beg or break down and cry.

And then his grace was standing before her informing her very briefly that the reason she had been called from her bed at midnight was that he wished to display her talents before his guests. She was now to pay for the privilege she had been granted of practicing alone each day in the music room.

Or so she interpreted the few words he did speak.

She looked into his harsh and shuttered face, she looked at the disfiguring scar, and she hated him. Not only did she feel a fear of him and a physical shrinking from him. She hated him. She hated the fact that he could grant what seemed like free favors and then demand payment for them purely for his own pleasure. She hated him for claiming to care for and protect his servants while using them as slaves to cater to his whims.

She remembered their ride, the exhilaration of their race, the splendid sight of him galloping alongside her on his black stallion, surging ahead of her, leaping over the gate in the wall, laughing at her as she came after. She remembered her own laughter, her own happiness, her own strange forgetfulness, just as it had happened when she had waltzed with him.

And she hated him.

She spoke only to Lord Thomas Kent, who always smiled at her with open friendliness, and who had spoken up on her behalf that afternoon in the duchess's sitting room. She would play for him since he had asked and since she did not have any real choice anyway.

His grace stood at the door for a while and then sat down. He had betrayed her. She had played her whole heart out in his hearing morning after morning and he had never disturbed her. He had always given the impression that he listened but respected her need to be alone with her soul. And yet now he had brought her here to play like a performing monkey for people who had had too much to drink and who had no real interest in music anyway.

Something special about those mornings, something she had not thought of or identified before, died. She was very aware of him sitting next to Miss Woodward, quiet, still, dark, and morose. Listening to her. Watching his performing slave.

She hated him. And she was surprised by the force of her hatred. She had only feared him before.

She had not noticed Matthew come up behind her. Amazingly, she had not noticed. But he was there. She felt his presence as soon as she had finished playing and his grace got to his feet.

But her only friend suddenly became her greatest enemy. Lord Thomas Kent, completely misunderstanding the situation, thinking to do her a kindness, was hinting that she be allowed to escape from the drawing room with her acquaintance, Matthew.

And her grace was agreeing with him and rescinding her command of that afternoon that Fleur hand her resignation to Mr. Houghton the next morning.

And so she had been maneuvered into something that was inevitable anyway. But she could have wished that it were not quite so late at night, that she did not feel quite so weary and hopeless. She could have wished for time.

But time had run out.

Two footmen were lighting some of the candles in their wall sconces the length of the long gallery.

"Take my arm, Isabella," Matthew said. "If we are to stroll, let us do it in a civilized manner."

The footmen closed the doors behind them when they left.

"Why is it that you succeed in looking beautiful even when dressed so plainly?" he asked.

She slid her arm from his. "What do you want, Matthew?" she asked. "If we are not to leave immediately, if you are not to drag me off to prison, what do you want? Do you want me to lie with you here at Willoughby, become your mistress here? I will not."

He sighed. "You make me appear so very uncivilized, Isabella," he said. "Those were your suggestions, not mine."

"Tell me, then," she said, "and stop playing games with me."

"I want you," he said. "I have for a long, long time. Is that so reprehensible?"

"And for a long, long time I have told you that I am not interested in your protestations," she said. "If you had loved me, as you always claimed to do, Matthew, you would have respected my feelings. You would not have interfered between me and Daniel."

"Daniel Booth," he said scornfully. "A smiling, gentle maid. He could not have made you happy, Isabella."

"Perhaps not," she said. "But the choice should have been mine. Why did you arrange things so?"

"So?" He raised his eyebrows in inquiry.

"Your mother and Amelia going away to London," she said impatiently, "and leaving me alone with you. It was so very improper, and they must have known it, and would have done something about it too if they had had any feeling for me whatsoever. And then refusing to let me go to Daniel's sister to stay when she asked me, and refusing to let me marry Daniel by special license. You planned it so, didn't you? So that with no options open to me and no reputation left, I would have no choice but to become your mistress. So that you would have the chance to overpower me even if I refused."

He stopped and took her hands in his even though she tried to pull them away.

"It was more than time for Amelia to go to town for her come-out," he said. "And of course my mother wished to go with her. It would have seemed cruel to send you with them, Isabella. The three of you could never agree."

"It is hard to agree or disagree with someone when you are almost totally ignored from the age of eight," she said bitterly, "except when you are being criticized and scorned."

"However it was," he said, "I thought it kinder to keep you at home where you belonged, Isabella. And it was never my idea to be your guardian, you know. It was your father's will and my father's death that did that—until your marriage or until the age of twenty-five. I did not make those terms."

"Until my marriage!" she said. "I could have been married to Daniel. You could have been free of such a burdensome responsibility."

"It was not burdensome," he said. "But I could not in all conscience consent to your marrying such a milksop, Isabella."

"It was better to make me your mistress," she said.

"You are the only one who has ever used that word," he said.

She laughed. "I suppose you wanted to marry me," she said.

"Wrong tense," he said, holding her hands more tightly. "You are a lady. Isabella, daughter of a baron. How can you suggest that I was out to ruin you?"

She laughed again. "Strange that you never thought to mention the honorable nature of your intentions before," she said. "How delighted your mother would be, Matthew. And I suppose the seduction that evening was to put the stamp of your possession on me before the ceremony."

"Seduction?" he said.

"I was leaving the house," she said, "despite the lateness of the hour and the coldness of the evening. My trunk was in the gig. Miriam was waiting for me at the rectory. But you would not let me leave and berated me for my disobedience. And you were not about to send me to my room, Matthew. You were about to take me to yours. Or perhaps not even that. Hobson was to hold me, wasn't he, right there in the library, while you raped me."

He released one of her hands in order to pass a hand over his forehead. "What strange notions you have, Isabella," he said. "You were screaming at me and fighting like a demented creature because I would not allow you to elope with a man I had refused quite lawfully to allow you to marry. Hobson stepped up behind you to prevent you from tripping over the hearthstone and hurting yourself. And you turned and lashed out at him too and caught him off-balance. It was a crime of passion pure and simple."

"Yes," she said, "I suppose a judge would see it that way—once you had explained it to him."

"It is a pity that the jewels made it seem all rather premeditated," he said. "Though doubtless I was your intended victim."

"The jewels?" She had gone very still.

"Those too costly for my mother to take to London," he said. "They were found in your trunk after you had run away in a panic."

She stared at him. "Found by someone other than you, I gather," she said at last.

"By your maid," he said.

She smiled at him.

"But it must all have been done impulsively," he said. "It must have been hard for you, Isabella, to lose your parents at a young age, to see my father and us come to the house and take over the property and possessions that you had grown to believe were yours. But they can be yours again, and your children's."

"Our children's," she said. "Are you really serious about marrying me, then, Matthew?"

"I love you," he said. "You cannot imagine how I have suffered in the last two and a half months, Isabella, not knowing if I would ever see you again. You must marry me."

"*Must* being the key word, I take it," she said.

"I would never have forced you," he said. "You must know that you were wrong about that."

"My answer is no," she said.

"You will change your mind," he said.

"No, I will not." She smiled at him. "When you leave here, you will leave alone, Matthew."

He raised his hands and set them loosely about her neck.

He lifted them to her chin, tightened them slightly, and jerked upward.

"I have heard that very skilled hangmen can do their job in such a way that death is instantaneous and painless," he said. "Unfortunately, not all are skilled."

Her smile faded. "Thank you," she said. "I have finally had my answer. I marry you, then, Matthew, or I hang. How long do I have to decide?"

But he had no chance to answer. The doors at the end of the long gallery opened to admit the Duke of Ridgeway.

"You are still here," he said. "It is easy to lose track of time amid so many paintings, is it not? But my daughter's governess needs her sleep, Brocklehurst. Perhaps you can continue the viewing some other time. You may return to your room, Miss Hamilton."

But Matthew walked along the gallery with her so that all three of them soon stood in the doorway. And the duke looked assessingly at Matthew and held out his arm to her.

"I will escort you upstairs," he said.

She placed her hand on his arm and did not look back to see what Matthew did. She removed her hand as soon as they had passed through the archway to the staircase. She ascended the stairs as close to the inside wall as possible.

He did not turn back at the top of the stairs as she had expected, but walked along the corridor to her room. And he set his hand on the doorknob. She watched it, the long-fingered, beautiful hand that she so feared.

"I'm sorry, Miss Hamilton," he said quietly.

"Sorry?" She raised her eyes to his face, dark, harsh, and angular in the dim light of the hallway.

"For all this," he said. "For getting you from your bed. For allowing you to be made into a pawn. I will not let it happen again."

She would not lower her eyes from his.

"Did he hurt you?" he asked. "Or harass you in any way?"

"He is not the one who hurt me," she said.

He opened his mouth as if to say something, and closed it again. He looked at her with set lips and tightly clenched jaw. And she wondered, too weary to feel instant terror, if he would open the door soon, usher her inside, and order her to remove her clothes again.

And she wondered if she would obey.

"I'm sorry," he said again, and she watched in horror and fascination as his eyes dropped to her lips and his head drew closer.

He opened the door suddenly and motioned her inside.

"No!" She stood where she was and shook her head slowly from side to side. "No. Please, no. Ah, please, no."

"My God!" He stepped into the doorway and took both her shoulders in a bruising grip. "What do you think of me? Did you think I intended to come inside with you? Did you imagine that I could apologize to you in one breath and seduce you with the next?"

She bit down on her lip and stared at him.

"Fleur." His hands gentled. "Fleur, I did not take you against your will that one time. I would never take you against your will. And I would never again take you with your will, either. I am a married man who has had one lapse in fidelity in five and a half years of marriage. I will not have you afraid for your safety with me."

She was drawing blood from the inside of her upper lip.

He looked into her face, into her tense, horror-filled eyes, made an impatient sound, and drew her into his arms. He held her hard against him until she stopped shuddering and sagged forward. And she turned her head and set it against his steadily beating heart, and closed her eyes.

"You must not fear for your safety with me." His voice was low against her ear. Those fingers were stroking lightly over the back of her neck. "You are the very last person on this earth whom I would want to hurt, Fleur. My God, tell me you no longer believe what you just believed."

"I don't." She pushed wearily away from him. Had the day really been quite as long as it had seemed?

"Well, then." He released his hold on her and took a step to one side, looking down at her uncertainly. "Good night."

"Good night, your grace."

She stepped inside her room and closed the door. She set her forehead against it and took several deep, steadying breaths. She had nothing to fear. He had been alone with her and could have taken her with ease. He could have muffled her screams so that even Mrs. Clement would not have heard. He had not taken her.

He would never do so against her will, he had said, or even with her will.

She had nothing to fear. Yet she could feel his arms straining her against his hard-muscled body. And she could feel his fingers against the back of her neck. She could hear his heart beating, and she could feel herself sagging against him, surrendering to his warmth and his strength. To the illusion of comfort.

She thought very deliberately about who he was and what he had done to her—about his powerful male body and his scars. About his hands.

And she felt fear. Fear because when he had finally touched her, she had forgotten her repulsion—as she had when she had waltzed with him and when she had ridden with him.

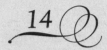

14

*H*IS MASTER WAS IN A BAD MOOD AGAIN, PETER Houghton noticed as he entered his office the following morning—five minutes late, as ill fortune would have it. The duke was standing looking out of the window, his bearing military, one hand drumming a tattoo on the sill.

It must be true, then, what was being said belowstairs about her grace and Lord Thomas, though everyone knew that all was not right with his grace's marriage anyway. And then, of course, there was that report about the duke's ladybird strolling in the long gallery with Lord Brocklehurst after midnight the night before.

Though Houghton had wondered since his return to Willoughby Hall if the governess was after all his master's ladybird. He liked the woman, despite a predisposition not to do so. She was always quietly courteous belowstairs and did not put on airs at Mrs. Laycock's table, even though every word and gesture marked her as a lady born and bred.

"Where the devil have you been?" his grace said, confirming his secretary's suspicions.

"Helping Mrs. Laycock with a small problem in balancing her housekeeping books, your grace," he said.

"How would you welcome a holiday?" the duke asked.

Houghton looked at him suspiciously. Was he about to be

handed a permanent holiday? For being five minutes late at his desk?

"You are to go into Wiltshire for me," the duke said. "To Heron House. I am not sure quite where it is. You will, no doubt, find out."

"To Lord Brocklehurst's, your grace?" His secretary frowned.

"The same," his grace said. "I want whatever you can find out about an Isabella who lived there until quite recently."

"Isabella?" Houghton looked inquiringly. "Last name, your grace?"

"Unknown," the duke said. "And you are to be invisible and mute while finding the answers. Do you understand?"

"Just Isabella, your grace?" Houghton said. "Do you have no other description?"

"Let us say she looks remarkably like Miss Hamilton," his grace said.

Peter Houghton stared at him.

"I can rely on your discretion, Houghton?" his grace asked. "You are going on a long-overdue and well-earned holiday?"

"To visit my cousin Tom," his secretary said, his face impassive, "and his wife, whom I have not yet met. And their new son, to whom I am to be godfather."

"I don't need a family history," the duke said curtly. "You had better leave today, Houghton, or you may miss the christening."

"I am much obliged to you, your grace," Houghton said as his master turned to stride from the room. "I will not forget this favor you have done me."

"You will see about that other matter before you leave?" the duke said, looking back from the doorway. "I gave instructions that she was to go into Wollaston this morning."

"It will be taken care of, your grace," Houghton said briskly.

Well, he thought, the master must be far more discreet than her grace. There had not been a whisper of a scandal belowstairs about his relationship with the governess—the London whore. Though of course there had been the grooms' claim that the two of them had gone riding alone together for a whole hour the morning before—a claim that seemed to be borne out by the fact that he had been instructed to see that the governess was fitted out for a riding habit and boots.

So she was his ladybird after all. And his grace must be smitten indeed if he was about to pry into the poor girl's past. She was living under a false name, was she?

But then, one could hardly blame his grace when the duchess was doing nothing to hide her preference for Lord Thomas.

THE MORNING WAS WET. There was not even the chance of a brief stroll outside after her music practice, Fleur found with regret. And no chance that there would be another riding lesson for Lady Pamela.

But the regret she felt over that fact was tempered by memories of her ride the morning before and the way it had developed. And memories of the night before and of the terror that had led her to make a most embarrassing assumption. And the memory of his arms about her and his heart beating against her ear and the smell of his cologne.

She was glad after all that it was raining.

As she watched Lady Pamela print rows of letters and later told her a story from history while they both embroidered, she began to hope that perhaps his grace would not come to the schoolroom that morning. And she listened for him, every sound startling her.

They were examining the globe again when he came. But instead of taking a seat in one corner as he usually did after kissing his daughter and bidding them both a good morning, he stayed on his feet and handed Fleur a letter.

"It came this morning," he said, "together with one for me in the same hand. You have my permission, Miss Hamilton, to accept the invitation. And I do believe Houghton is waiting belowstairs in his office for you. Have you forgotten your errand for this morning?"

Fleur had not. But she had thought it very likely that he had forgotten, and had not liked to mention the matter to Mr. Houghton at breakfast.

"I will have a carriage brought around for you in half an hour's time," he said. "Pamela, you and I will play with Tiny for a while until it is time for me to join some of the gentlemen. This afternoon you may come with Mama and me to the rectory. Some of our guests wish to see the church. You may play with the children while we do so."

"Ye-es." Lady Pamela jumped up and down on the spot.

"Come along, then," he said, reaching out a hand for hers. "Good day to you, Miss Hamilton."

Mr. Chamberlain was inviting her to join him and his sister and Sir Cecil Hayward for dinner and a visit to the theater in Wollaston that evening. A traveling company of players was to appear there.

She folded the paper and lifted it to her mouth. And she felt an enormous regret for the life that might have been hers at Willoughby. She had work that she was beginning to find quite pleasant, enough social life to keep her active and interested, and the friendship of an attractive gentleman to make her feel like a woman.

She could never have taken that relationship beyond friendship, of course. She had known that and accepted it. She had not asked for much—merely life as it had been for the first two weeks after her arrival.

If only the Duke of Ridgeway had stayed away from home. And if only Matthew had not tracked her there.

The carriage was to be waiting for her in half an hour's time, his grace had said. She hurried to her room to get ready and to pen an acceptance of her invitation.

Peter Houghton gave her a letter to present at Wollaston so

that the bills for her riding clothes could be sent to the house. He also paid her her first month's salary, though she had not been there for quite a month, explaining that he was to leave within the hour for the christening of his cousin's son and might not be back for a week or more.

Fleur enjoyed the next few hours. After her experiences of just a couple of months ago, it was a delightful feeling to be dressed respectably, to ride in a smart carriage, to be treated with deference because the carriage bore the crest of the Duke of Ridgeway, to have a little money to spend on silk stockings, which strictly speaking she did not need, to choose rich velvet fabric for a riding habit and soft leather for boots.

And returning to Willoughby Hall felt like coming home again, she thought later, despite the rain and the heavy clouds. The carriage rumbled over the bridge and she turned her eyes to the house and felt a great churning of love for it. And a great sadness that it would not be her home for much longer.

She smiled at the coachman as he helped her down from the carriage, and would have hurried through the doors to the servants' quarters beneath the horseshoe steps if someone had not hailed her by name. Matthew was hurrying from the direction of the stables.

"I came upstairs after luncheon to visit you," he said as the carriage drew away again. "The child's nurse told me you had gone into Wollaston. Alone, Isabella? Why did you not let me know? I would have come with you."

She stood in the rain and looked at him.

"I shall be leaving on this infernal visit to a Norman church soon," he said. "But I must see you this evening. Where? Your room? Or downstairs somewhere?"

"I have other plans for this evening," she said.

"What?" He frowned at her. Water was falling in a steady stream from the brim of his hat.

"I have been invited out to dinner and the theater," she said. "By neighbors."

"Who is he?" he asked. "You had better not encourage him, Isabella. I would not like it at all."

"Can you not conceive of a relationship of pure friendliness, Matthew?" she asked. Cold water was finding its way in a trickle down her back inside her cloak.

"Not where you are concerned," he said. "Not with your looks, Isabella. We will stay here for a few weeks. But I expect a good portion of your free time. And I do not expect to have to deal with opposition. And that includes the duke. I hope he did not stay with you last night. For your sake I hope it."

"I am wet and cold through to the bone, Matthew," she said. "I am going indoors, if you will excuse me."

He sketched her a bow and turned to run up the marble steps.

Fleur shivered as she let herself in through the servants' doors. Yes, there was always that—the ultimate choice that she was going to have to make: either to marry Matthew, if indeed he did mean marriage, or to stand trial for murder and theft when the only witness was Matthew himself.

MR. CHAMBERLAIN'S CARRIAGE CAME for Fleur early in the evening. She looked down in some regret at her blue muslin dress and wished that she had had something else to wear. But she would not let anything spoil her evening. She was going to enjoy herself, she had decided earlier, especially after her talk with Matthew. If she had not had this invitation to honor, she would have been forced to spend the evening with him. Of course, there were tomorrow evening and the evening after that, but she would think of that when the time came.

Sir Cecil Hayward, a gentleman Fleur remembered seeing at the ball, appeared to have no conversation but what related to horses and hounds and hunting. But both Miss Chamberlain and her brother were lively conversationalists, and Fleur found herself very well entertained during dinner.

She had never in her life attended the theater, a fact that amused Mr. Chamberlain.

"You have never been near a theater, Miss Hamilton?" he said. "Amazing! How would the Shakespeares of our world survive if people were all like you?"

"But I did not say I had stayed away out of inclination, sir," she said, laughing—and remembering a time when she had indeed been near a theater.

"This will be like taking the children out, Emily," he said, smiling at his sister. "I suppose we can expect Miss Hamilton to be all agog and jumping up and down in her excitement."

"I promise at least," Fleur said, "not to shriek and squeal, sir."

"Ah, then," he said, "I suppose we can proceed on our way. You are willing to dispense with the port for tonight, Hayward?"

The theater was far smaller than Fleur had expected, the relationship between audience and players far more intimate. The audience hissed a singer who sang slightly off-key, whistled every time one actress with a particularly fine bosom appeared on the stage, cheered the villain, jeered the hero when he was abject with unrequited love, and applauded and catcalled through the final love scene.

Fleur loved every moment of it, action and audience both.

"Philistines all," Mr. Chamberlain said into her ear. "They came here not to be entertained, but to entertain themselves. Of course, it must be admitted that there are more skilled actors somewhere in this country. I hope this experience will not give you a permanent disgust of the theater, Miss Hamilton."

"Absolutely not," she said. "It has been a lovely evening."

Miss Chamberlain apparently did not agree. The heat and constant noise of the theater had given her a headache. And so after letting down Sir Cecil at his home close to Wollaston, the carriage took Miss Chamberlain home before proceeding to Willoughby Hall. Mr. Chamberlain insisted on accompanying Fleur there at such a late hour.

"Adam was not annoyed at my taking you from the house for a whole evening?" he asked.

"He told me that I might accept the invitation," she said.

"Some people seem to think that their employees are their personal possessions and are not entitled to any free time," he said, "let alone—heaven forbid—some social life. I might have known, of course, that Adam would be more enlightened. I have never known anyone who has succeeded in luring away any of his servants, though I have known those who have tried. Apparently he treats them more like family than employees."

"He is always kind," Fleur said.

"There was universal rejoicing in this part of the world when he came home so unexpectedly a year after being reported dead," he said. "Thomas was probably the only one who was disappointed to find that he was no longer duke."

"And yet," Fleur said, "he is a very pleasant gentleman."

"Oh, yes," he said, smiling at her in the darkness of the carriage. "Granted. You are coming to Timmy's birthday party?"

They conversed easily for a while before lapsing into a comfortable silence.

Mr. Chamberlain turned to her as his carriage crossed the bridge at the end of the lime grove. "I will kick myself for a coward and an imbecile and a slowtop if I do not at least try to kiss you before this carriage stops," he said. "May I, Miss Hamilton?"

What could one say to such a request? No, she supposed, if one disliked the gentleman. She did not dislike Mr. Chamberlain.

"I see that my audacity has silenced you," he said. "And I suppose it is difficult to say a polite 'Yes, sir,' to such a question. I hope it would not be so hard to say 'No, sir,' if that is what you wish to say."

She saw him smile in the darkness before setting one arm

about her shoulders, lifting her chin with his free hand, and lowering his mouth to hers.

It was warm, firm, pleasant. He did not prolong the embrace.

"I wait meekly for a stinging slap on the cheek," he said, withdrawing his arm and hand and sitting upright again. "None? I hope I have not offended you. Have I?"

"No," she said.

"I shall look forward to seeing you in a few days' time," he said. "Perhaps we will even be able to exchange a few words above the shrieking of the children. Birthdays always cause more noise than any two other occasions combined. Have you noticed?"

He waited for his coachman to put down the steps before descending to the wet terrace in order to hand her out. He escorted her up the steps to the main doors, rapped on them, and bowed over her hand, raising it to his lips, before turning to leave.

"Thank you for your company, Miss Hamilton," he said. "I have enjoyed the evening more than I can say."

"So have I," she said. "Good night, sir."

She looked about her as the door closed, half-expecting Matthew or the duke to step out of the shadows. But there was no one except the lone footman who had opened the door.

She ran up the stairs and along to her room. She undressed quickly and climbed into bed, pulling the blankets up about her ears.

She would think only of the evening. At least for one night she would go to sleep happy. She thought about Mr. Chamberlain and his friendly humor. And about his kiss. And she wished that life could have started a little less than a month ago. She wished that there were no Matthew and no Hobson's body lying under the ground somewhere close to Heron House. She wished there had been no London, no necessity of remaining alive there. No Duke of Ridgeway. She even wished in some strange way that there had been no Daniel.

She wished there had been only Willoughby Hall and Mr. Chamberlain.

She thought again of his kiss, which she must not allow to be repeated. And of his attentions, which she must not encourage.

And she remembered warm strong arms tight about her, and a strong-muscled chest against her cheek, and a strongly beating heart against her ear. And she thought of waltzing with a partner who twirled her about with a firm hand at her waist and whose cologne had been a part of the beauty of the night.

She burrowed her head farther beneath the blankets.

THE FOLLOWING DAY CONTINUED WET. The duke rode out in the afternoon with two of his more hardy guests to call upon some of his tenants. When they returned, too late for tea, it was to discover that the entertainment for the evening had been arranged already. Everyone was tired of charades, Lady Underwood informed him, meeting him in the great hall. They were going to dance in the drawing room.

"Indeed?" he said. "And who is to play for us? Miss Dobbin?"

"She is quite willing to do so," Lady Underwood said, "but Walter insists that she be free to dance at least some of the time. Have you noticed that he is quite smitten with her, Adam? And have you noticed that I am less than smitten with Philip but have to make do with him in order to avoid dreadful boredom, you annoying man?"

"Well," he said with a smile, "you will have dancing to entertain you for this evening, it seems. Who is to play when Miss Dobbin is dancing?"

"Oh, the governess," she said. "It is all arranged."

"Is it?" he said. "At whose suggestion, pray?"

"Matthew's, of course," she said. "He claims to have a slight acquaintance with her. I believe it is considerably more than slight, but only time will prove me right or wrong on that. Anyway, she is to play. Do tell me you will waltz every waltz with me, Adam. You do it so divinely."

"I will be honored to dance the first with you," he said. "Pardon me, ma'am, I must change out of these wet clothes."

Did Fleur know how her evening had been organized? he wondered. Had she been consulted? Had she been told or asked? And did she think him responsible again for making use of her talents? He winced at the possibility. She was employed as Pamela's governess, not as entertainer for his guests.

He wondered if anyone had thought of such details as having the furniture moved back in the drawing room and the carpet rolled up and music brought from the music room. He would wager no one had.

FLEUR HAD BEEN LOOKING FORWARD to a quiet evening with her embroidery in Mrs. Laycock's sitting room. But just after lessons had finished in the afternoon she had been handed a hastily scrawled note from her grace, summoning her to play the pianoforte for a dance in the evening.

She was not unduly upset. She had been half-expecting some summons from Matthew, and while this might well be it, at least she would be in the drawing room in company with all the guests. She would not be alone with him.

A line of footmen was still busy rolling the carpet when she arrived in the drawing room. She walked back to the hall to wait until the room was ready for her. And she looked about her at the magnificence of it all.

She looked up to the dome, shadowed in the gathering dusk, and at some of the gilded carvings on the walls between the columns. Winged cherubs blew into slender pipes, their cheeks puffed. Violins were crossed with flutes.

"It was designed to be a place for music," the duke said at her shoulder. "The gallery was made to be used by an orchestra. Unfortunately we have not had a grand concert or ball here for more than a year."

Fleur turned toward him. His face was caught by the shadows of the hall, his eyes blacker, his nose more aquiline, his scar more noticeable than in the light. He was standing close to her, his hands clasped behind him. And she felt breathless and very aware that a solid Corinthian column was at her back.

"You have consented to play for us this evening?" he said.

"Yes, your grace."

"Tell me," he said, "were you asked?"

"Her grace sent me a note," she said.

He grimaced. "I promised this would not happen again, did I not?" he said. "I was from home this afternoon. Miss Hamilton, will you do us the honor of playing? You are quite at liberty to refuse. This is not part of your duties as governess."

"I will be pleased to, your grace," she said.

He treats his employees more like family than servants, Mr. Chamberlain had said of the duke the night before. Her grace had summoned. He had asked.

"You may wish to dance when you are not playing," he said. "I am sure there will be several gentlemen who will be pleased if you do."

"No," she said. "Thank you, but no, your grace."

"And yet," he said, "you appeared to enjoy dancing during the ball a few evenings ago."

"That was quite different," she said.

"Allow me to escort you to the drawing room," he said. He did not offer her his arm.

The drawing room looked somehow larger and more magnificent with the carpet rolled up and the white-and-gold chairs, upholstered in painted silk, moved back against the walls. The pianoforte too had been moved into one corner.

It was one of the most beautiful rooms in the house, Fleur thought, looking about her, unself-conscious because none of the guests were yet present. The walls were a pale blue, the coved ceiling blue, white, and gold. Great sheets of mirror made the room seem larger than it was and multiplied the effect of the crystal chandelier.

"The paintings are from Europe," his grace said, seeing her interest, "though I have tried to gather works of our own artists in some of the other rooms. These are by Philipp Hackert and Angelica Kauffmann. Would you like to look through the music?"

She settled herself at the pianoforte and looked through the pile that someone must have been assigned to bring from the music room. All of it was music suitable for dancing. Many of the pieces were waltz tunes.

During the next two hours she grew increasingly more relaxed in the task she had taken on. Except for Sir Philip Shaw, who came up to the pianoforte and kissed her hand on his arrival in the drawing room, everyone else took remarkably little notice of her, calling to her only when they wanted a particular tune or type of dance. The waltz was an overwhelming favorite. Miss Dobbin appeared to have forgotten that she was to play for part of the evening, and Fleur willed her to continue to forget.

But the time inevitably came when she looked up between dances to find that Matthew was leading Miss Dobbin her way.

"Miss Hamilton," she said, "how well you play. I am wishing now that I had played first so that I would not have to follow you."

Fleur protested that she really did not have to play at all, but Miss Dobbin insisted that dancing was not her favorite activity and she had done enough of it during the ball and the last couple of hours to last her for the next month.

"Besides, Miss Hamilton," Matthew said with a bow, "how

am I to dance with you if you are to sit at the pianoforte all night?"

"I am not here to dance, my lord," she said, "but to provide accompaniment."

"Ah, but you will dance," he said, smiling at her. "Please, ma'am? Because it is I who ask?"

What would he do if she refused? Fleur wondered. Turn to the company and denounce her in a loud voice? Expose her as a murderer and a jewel thief? She thought not. He would embarrass himself by such an exhibition, and that would not serve his purpose at all.

But of course it was an academic question. The truth was that she would not put it to the test, and Matthew must know her well enough to know that she would not.

"A waltz, if you please, Miss Dobbin?" he asked, holding out a hand for Fleur's.

Matthew waltzed tolerably well. But of course she could not give herself up to an enjoyment of the dance. She was a servant in this house, and her cheeks burned at the impropriety of her dancing with the company in the drawing room despite the permission his grace had granted her earlier. She looked about nervously to see how the duchess was reacting at sight of her, but her grace was absent from the room.

And of course she could not forget the last time she had waltzed—on the deserted path south of the lake, her eyes firmly closed. His grace was dancing with Lady Underwood, she could see out of the corner of her eye.

The music drew to an end, but Fleur was given no chance to seat herself behind the pianoforte, as she had planned. Sir Philip Shaw was bowing over her hand.

"Ah, but Miss Hamilton is faint from her exertions at the pianoforte," Matthew said with a smile. "I was about to take her into the hall, Shaw, for some air."

"What a lucky devil you are, Brocklehurst," Sir Philip said, looking Fleur up and down with lazy eyes. "I don't suppose I can remind you of a prior acquaintance too, Miss Hamilton, can I?"

Fleur set her hand on Matthew's arm and lifted her chin.

He took her into the hall and up to the high gallery beneath the dome. He must have found out the staircase during the daytime hours. She had never been up there before.

They seemed much higher up than the gallery had looked from below. And yet the dome still seemed to soar high above. But they were not there to sightsee.

He held her against the inner wall with his body and kissed her: her face, her throat, her breasts through the fabric of her dress. He fondled her breasts with his hands, pushed one knee between her legs. He opened his mouth over hers, prodded at her closed lips with his tongue.

She stood quiet and passive.

"You have never given me a chance, Isabella," he said. "You have disliked me just because my mother and my sister have always treated you rather shabbily, and perhaps because my father was too lazy to intervene. And because I did not notice you when you were a girl. But I was never openly unkind to you. Was I?"

"Not until recent years," she said quietly.

"When have I been unkind?" he asked. "Oh, I suppose you will throw Booth in my teeth again. I was doing you a kindness if you only knew it, Isabella. He is not the man for you."

"And you are?"

"Yes," he said, "and I am. I love you, Isabella. I worship you. And I could teach you to love me if you would give me the chance, if you would not close your mind to me."

"Perhaps I could have liked you," she said, "and respected you too if you had shown me some respect, Matthew. But you have always been like this, grabbing me and protesting your love for me. In the past, of course, I was always free to fight you. Now I am no longer free. I cannot create a scene in this house by screaming, as I would like to do. I am a servant and you are a guest. And I cannot demand that you leave me alone. I have no particular wish to hang. But if you loved me, you would not play this cruel game with me. And you would not force on me attentions that you know to be unwelcome."

"It is because you will not give me a chance," he said.

But he looked behind him at that moment and covered her mouth loosely with his hand. There was the sound of footsteps below, and both of them could see his grace crossing the hall slowly, looking about him. It seemed that he was down there many minutes before he walked on to the long gallery and through the doors.

"Looking for you?" Lord Brocklehurst asked, turning back to Fleur and removing his hand. "He is something of a watchdog for you, is he not, Isabella? Rather strange for a duke with a lowly governess, wouldn't you say? Do you grant him what you deny me? Have a care if you do. If I find it to be true, you will hang by the neck until you are dead. You have my promise on it."

"Words of love indeed," she said.

He kissed her fiercely, cutting the inner flesh of her mouth against her teeth.

"Words of a jealous and frustrated lover," he said. "I love you, Isabella."

She would have gone to her room when he finally brought her down from the gallery. Her mouth felt swollen, her hair disheveled. She felt dirty. But he had a hand on her elbow. And she had agreed to play at a dance for the evening, however long the evening lasted.

She was relieved to find on her return to the drawing room that Mr. Walter Penny hailed her with some eagerness. He wished to dance with a reluctant Miss Dobbin.

Fleur seated herself at the pianoforte and resumed her playing. She wondered just how late it was. It felt as if dawn must surely be lighting the windows. But it was not.

15

THE DANCING HAD BEEN A GOOD IDEA, THE DUKE of Ridgeway thought. Most of the guests appeared to be enjoying themselves, and it was certainly preferable to another evening of charades. The music was lively. Miss Dobbin was competent and Fleur Hamilton good. And the latter had not seemed to resent at all being asked to play.

It would have been a good evening if everyone had stayed in the drawing room to enjoy the dancing and one another's company. But as always seemed to happen during balls and dances, however informal, couples inevitably disappeared.

He would not worry his head over Mayberry's having withdrawn with Mrs. Grantsham, though it angered him that people could behave with such impropriety in other people's homes and under the knowing eyes of other people's servants. But he would worry about Sybil and Thomas, and about Fleur and Brocklehurst too.

Sybil and Thomas had been gone for half an hour. And he was torn between the desire to stay in the drawing room to talk and smile with his guests and dance with the ladies and his need to pursue them and bring them back before gossip settled irrevocably about them.

But perhaps that had already happened. They were certainly making no great secret of their preference for each other. And was that his chief concern—gossip? Was he willing to watch all the signs of the resumption of an affair between his wife and his brother provided they were discreet?

And then Fleur Hamilton left the room with Brocklehurst, and his mental battle was intensified. He had promised her that she was safe on his property and under his protection. But was she being harassed? She had been smiling when she left the room, and there had been no evidence that she was being coerced. Perhaps she was glorying in the chance of mingling with the company, dancing with one of them, being singled out for even more marked attention.

But there had been her terror the first evening she had set eyes on Brocklehurst. There was the fact that both of them claimed only a slight acquaintance, and yet he had called her Isabella. There was the fact that he was the owner of Heron House and she had lived at a place called "Her—."

He watched the gentlemen take their partners for a quadrille, made sure that no lady who appeared eager to dance was without a partner, and slipped from the room.

There was no one in the great hall. The footmen had been withdrawn for the night. And yet he heard voices as he entered it. From behind one of the pillars? From the arches leading to the staircases? He strolled about quietly, but there was no one to be seen. And the voices had ceased. Perhaps he had imagined them. The doors into the salon and the long gallery were closed.

But of course, he thought at last, standing in the middle of the hall and resisting the urge to look up. The old hiding place, which he and Thomas had used countless times as boys, lying flat to observe new arrivals, snickering over the conversations of the footmen when they had thought themselves alone, making owl noises in an attempt to frighten the same footmen.

It would be Thomas and Sybil. Should he look up? Call to them? Climb the stairs to confront them? Give them time to come down of their own accord and return to the dancing?

The confrontation would have to be made. But he would prefer to postpone it to a time when he did not have to return to entertain the guests immediately after.

And what of Fleur Hamilton and Brocklehurst? They had been in the long gallery the last time they had been together— that night with its ghastly aftermath. He crossed the hall to the gallery, opened the door, and stepped inside.

One set of candles halfway along the long gallery was lit. The room was almost in darkness, heavy shadows spreading outward from the central source of light.

They were at the far end, in close embrace. They had not heard him come in. And he had to make the instant decision of whether to leave as quietly as he had come or make his presence known. She was not struggling. Perhaps she would resent his intrusion on a romantic moment. Or perhaps she needed him.

He walked slowly along the gallery, making no attempt to hide in the shadows or dull the sound of his footsteps. And when he was a little more than halfway along, they broke apart and turned to look at him.

Sybil and Thomas.

The duchess turned sharply away to stare out of a window into darkness. Lord Thomas met his brother's eyes in the near-darkness and smiled.

"I was seized with the urge to renew my acquaintance with our ancestors," he said. "But alas, this is not quite the time of day to come picture-gazing. I shall have to do it again in the daylight."

"Yes," the duke said. "I will be wanting a word with you in the morning, too, Thomas. But not now. Now there are ladies in the drawing room who would appreciate your offer to partner them in a dance. Sybil and I will see you there shortly."

Lord Thomas turned to look at the back of the duchess's head. "Do you wish to return with me, Sybil?" he asked. "Or with Adam?"

"She will return with me," his grace said quietly.

The duchess said nothing.

Lord Thomas shrugged. "Oh, well," he said, "I know that when you drop your voice that low, Adam, fisticuffs are not far in the future if I argue. And we must not present bloody noses to your guests, must we?" He touched the duchess on one shoulder. "You will be all right, Sybil?"

Again she said nothing. He shrugged once more and made his way alone along the gallery.

The duke waited a long time, until he heard the door close finally as his brother left.

"Well, Sybil," he said quietly.

She turned to him. The faint light from the candles was gleaming off her blond hair. Her face was shadowed. "Well, Adam," she said, her sweet voice shaking a little. "What are you going to do about it?"

"What do you want me to do about it?" he asked. "How far has it gone? I suppose you love him again—but then, you never stopped, did you? Are you lovers?"

She laughed shortly. "Would you divorce me if I said yes?" she asked. "Would you, Adam? It would make a wonderful scandal, wouldn't it?" Her voice was shaking almost out of control.

"No," he said. "I would never divorce you, Sybil. I think you know that. But you made me certain promises when we married. You owe it to both of us and to Pamela and all those dependent on us to keep those promises, I believe. Thomas is irrevocably in your past. You made it irrevocable when you married me."

"What choice did I have?" she cried passionately. "What choice did I have? I would have been ruined forever, and you had sent him away never to return. And you kept coming and urging me to accept your protection before Papa discovered the truth. I had no choice at all. You are an evil man, Adam."

"Perhaps," he said. "But you have not been exactly the ideal mate either, Sybil. We must just make the best of what we have done with our lives."

"Do you blame me," she said, looking at him with deep revulsion, "for not wanting you to touch me? They would have been kinder to you, those people, if they had left you to die. You are only half a man."

"We had better return to our guests," he said.

"And you talk about my keeping my promises," she said, her voice petulant as it frequently was during their arguments. "Can you honestly tell me that you have kept yours, Adam? Can you tell me that you have never been unfaithful to me?"

He looked at her without answering.

"Do you think," she said, "that I do not know the reason for your frequent journeys to London? Do you think I do not know why you suddenly decided this time that Pamela needed a governess? Don't talk to me of marriage vows. If I have given in to my love for Thomas, it is because I have been driven to it by your debaucheries and your cruelty." She felt about her for a handkerchief and finally took the one he held out to her.

"Now, that," he said, "is a good deal of nonsense, as you are very well aware. Dry your eyes, Sybil, and blow your nose. We have been away from our guests for long enough."

She turned in silence and began to walk along the gallery. When they reached the doors, he opened them, took the handkerchief from her hand, and drew her arm through his. Distasteful and hypocritical as it might seem, he thought, looking down at her beautiful face, the blue eyes lowered, and at her silver-blond hair, there were appearances to consider.

And she, of course, realized it too. She sparkled again as soon as they stepped inside the drawing room. Almost everyone was dancing. Fleur Hamilton was playing the pianoforte.

FLEUR WAS THE LAST to leave the drawing room. The dancers had all drifted away to bed, and a few servants had come in to roll out the carpet and set the room to rights again. She sorted through the music and decided to return it to the music room before going to bed herself.

It was very late. She felt tired. But she did not want to go to bed. She preferred her thoughts when she was somewhat in control of them. She did not want the nightmares that so frequently disturbed her sleep.

She set the branch of candles she had brought with her on top of the pianoforte in the music room and put the music away neatly. And she reached out a hand for the candles again.

But the pianoforte, so much larger and more mellow in tone than the one in the drawing room, drew her like a magnet. She ran her fingers lightly over the keys, not depressing them. And she played a scale, slowly and softly. She seated herself on the stool.

She played Bach, a crisp, fast sonata, her eyes closed. She played rather loudly. Perhaps if she concentrated hard enough, played briskly enough, she could drown out her thoughts.

Perhaps she could drown out Matthew.

But inevitably the music came to an end. She must open her eyes and go upstairs to her bed and accept whatever the remainder of the night had to offer her. She sighed. Last evening with Mr. Chamberlain seemed such a long time in the past already.

"I wish I had enough command of the keyboard to be able to work out my frustrations in that manner," a voice said from behind her.

The Duke of Ridgeway! Fleur leapt to her feet.

"I didn't mean to alarm you," he said. "I couldn't resist coming a little closer when I heard the music."

"I'm sorry, your grace," Fleur said. "I brought the music back. I could not stop myself from playing just one piece."

"After playing all evening?" he said with a smile. "I must thank you for that, Miss Hamilton. I am very grateful."

"It was my pleasure, your grace," she said.

He walked a few steps closer to her. "It was you up in the gallery?" he asked. "You and Brocklehurst?"

She felt herself turn cold. "Yes, your grace."

"Did you go with him freely?" he asked. "Did he force you?"

"No, your grace." She watched his dark eyes. Was she about to be dismissed?

"And this." He indicated her slightly swollen upper lip. "It is cut on the inside?"

She did not answer him.

"It was with your consent?" he asked.

"Yes." She cleared her throat when no sound came out. "Yes, your grace."

His lips thinned as he looked up to meet her eyes. And he passed a hand over his eyes and shook his head. "Come into the library with me," he said, "for a nightcap."

He moved toward the library door without looking back to see if she followed. But he did look back when he opened the door, his eyebrows raised. Fleur crossed the room and preceded him into the library, where candles had been lighted.

He poured her some sherry, and brandy for himself. He indicated the comfortable leather chair at one side of the fireplace and handed her her glass before taking the chair at the other side.

"Here's to good health, Fleur Hamilton," he said, raising his glass to her, "and to happiness. An elusive something, that last, is it not?" He drank some of his brandy.

Fleur sipped her sherry and did not answer. He was sprawled on his chair, relaxed, comfortable, informal. She sat straight and tense on her own.

"Tell me about yourself," he said. "Oh, nothing that will uncover the mystery in which you like to shroud yourself. Who taught you to play?"

"My mother," she said, "when I was very young. My guardian hired a music teacher for his own children and me after that. And at school."

"At school," he said. "Where did you go? No, you will not wish to answer that, I suppose. How long were you there?"

"For five years," she said. "It was Broadridge School. I told Mr. Houghton."

He nodded. "A long time," he said. "Did you like it, apart from the music and dancing lessons?"

"I believe I had a good education there," she said. "But discipline was strict and humorless. There was very little warmth of feeling there."

"But your guardian continued to send you?" he said. "Was there much warmth of feeling at home?"

She looked down into the sherry in her glass. "We were a wonderfully happy family while my parents were alive," she said. "Nothing could appear very warm with them gone. I was too young. I daresay I was difficult to manage."

"You were the orphan spurned, I take it," he said. "Did they not try to marry you off young?"

Fleur thought of the two gentlemen farmers, both over fifty, who had offered for her before she reached even her nineteenth birthday, and of Cousin Caroline's fury when she refused both.

"Yes," she said.

"But you resisted. I suspect you are made of stern stuff, Miss Hamilton," he said. "Stubborn to a fault. Is that how you were described by your guardian and his family?"

"Sometimes," she said.

"Frequently, I would imagine," he said. "Have you never met anyone you wished to marry?"

"No," she said hastily. And she thought about how Daniel had been in her nightmares lately, his image fading in and out with the duke's.

"And did he wish to marry you too?" he asked.

She looked up at him sharply and down into her glass again.

"He was ineligible?" he asked.

"No," she said dully.

"It was spite, then?" he said. "You were not allowed to marry him? Do you have a dowry?"

"Yes."

"But you have no control over it until you marry or reach a certain age, I suppose," he said. "And your guardian decided to cut up nasty. Why did you run away, Fleur? Would your beau not elope with you? Was the money more important to him than you were?"

"No!" she said, looking up at him fiercely. "My fortune was of no interest to Daniel at all."

"Daniel," he said quietly.

She swirled the dark liquid in her glass. She did not think she would be able to raise it to her lips.

"Did you love him?" he asked. "*Do* you love him?"

"No," she said. "That is all a long, long time in the past." Like something from another lifetime altogether.

He downed the brandy that remained in his glass and got to his feet. "Drink up," he said, his hand stretched out for her glass. "It's time for bed."

She took one more sip and handed him the half-empty glass. He set it with his own on a table beside her chair and offered her his hand. She looked at it, at the long, well-manicured, beautiful fingers, and set her own resolutely within it. She watched his fingers close about hers. And she got to her feet.

He did not move. "You won't confide in me?" he asked. "You won't let me help you? It was not of your own free will, was it? This was not consented to, was it?" He ran one finger lightly along her upper lip.

She grabbed for his wrist and gripped it.

"There is nothing to confide," she said. "There is no mystery."

"And yet," he said, "you preferred your life as it had become in London to the one you left behind? And your Daniel would not come after you to rescue you?"

"He did not know I was leaving," she said, still gripping his wrist. "He did not know where I went."

"If I loved you, Fleur," he said, "and knew that you loved me, I would turn heaven and earth upside down to find you if you disappeared."

Her eyes followed his scar up from his chin to his mouth, up his cheek to his eye. And she looked into his eyes.

"No," she said. "No one loves that much. It is a myth. Love can be pleasant and gentle. It can be selfish and cruel. But it is not the all-consuming passion of poetry. Love cannot move mountains, nor would it wish to do so. I don't blame Daniel. Love is not like that."

"And yet," he said, and his dark eyes burned into hers, "if I loved you, Fleur, I would move mountains with my bare hands if they kept me from you."

She laughed a little uncertainly. "If," she said. "Make-believe is a children's game. It is very easy to live with ifs. But real life is different."

She knew he was going to kiss her several moments before his lips touched hers. She supposed afterward that she could have avoided it. He did not imprison her with his arms or back her against a wall. But she did nothing to avoid it. She was rigid with shock, her hand gripping his wrist like a vise. And there was a certain fascination, too, in seeing that dark harsh face, not hovering above her as in her nightmares, but bending close to her own face until she was forced to close her eyes.

And his kiss was so startlingly different from either Matthew's or Mr. Chamberlain's that she did not for the moment think of springing away. There was none of the grinding of lips and teeth that there had been earlier up in the gallery, none of the firm pressure of the night before, but a light and gentle warmth, a living movement over her own lips. And a parting of the lips so that her own were enclosed in moist, brandy-flavored warmth.

He was only the third man ever to have kissed her. Strange,

when he had done that other to her more than a month before. But there had been no kisses to accompany that.

And then she panicked and bent her head back away from him.

She caught sight of the expression on his face before one of his arms came about her and the other behind her head to press it to the folds of his neckcloth. He had looked lost, pained. And it was there in his voice when he spoke.

"Don't spurn me, Fleur," he said. "Please. Just for these few moments don't spurn me. Don't be frightened of me."

And yet every part of her body rested against him and remembered—remembered the sight of him, male and powerful enough to crush the life out of her with his hands, the terrible purple scars of the wounds down his left side and leg. And remembered the feel of him, his hands, his thumbs, his knees holding her legs apart. And the feel of him plunging into her, tearing at her, and the repeated thrust and withdrawal until he was done and there had seemed to be nothing of herself left.

But there was the kindness of the inflated payment and this job, the concern for her well-being, the surprising warmth and gentleness of his kiss, the vulnerability on his face and in his voice. And her terrible loneliness.

And it was difficult to take that memory and this present reality and combine them in her mind. It was difficult to believe that he was the same man. It was difficult to feel with her body the revulsion that her mind instructed her to feel.

She made herself relax against him, feel his body against hers without shrinking. And it was not, after all, hard to do.

"Just for these moments only," he murmured. He was rubbing his cheek lightly across the top of her head.

She did not consciously lift her head. But she must have done so because she was gazing into his eyes again and angling her head for his kiss. And his warm lips were gentle on hers again and moving over them, and the tip of his tongue was moving lightly over her lips until she parted them and opened her mouth, granting him what Matthew had demanded earlier and not been given.

His tongue moved against hers, circled it, explored the soft flesh inside her mouth, the sensitive flesh at the roof.

She heard herself whimper, and stilled both body and mind to the knowledge of what she was doing and with whom. She would not let her nightmares intrude into this waking moment. And it was but for a moment. Just for this moment only. His shoulders were broad and firm beneath her arms, his hair thick and silky between her fingers.

His mouth moved from hers at last to kiss her cheeks, her eyes, her temples. And he wrapped both arms about her, held her arched in to him, and set his cheek against the top of her head.

"God!" he whispered. "Oh, my God." His arms tightened like iron bands about her. "My good God."

She felt the breath shudder into him, and he released her.

They stood looking at each other.

"Fleur," he said. He lifted a hand, and she saw it and knew again to whom it belonged and what it had done to her. She trembled as he cupped one of her cheeks with it. "I wish I could say I am sorry. God, how I wish it. Tomorrow I will apologize to you. Tonight I can't feel sorry, God help me. Go to bed. Go. I cannot escort you tonight. I would not be able to stop at your door."

She went, hurrying to the door, fumbling with the knob, running along the hallway, pounding up the stairs, and racing along the corridor to her room as if she thought he was in pursuit of her after all.

But it was not from him she fled. The person from whom she ran was inside the room with her despite her speed and despite the fact that she had locked the door with hasty, trembling fingers.

What had she done? What had she allowed to happen? Her

breasts were taut and tender. She was throbbing where he had given her such pain on a previous occasion. She could taste his brandy. Her body was in a turmoil of feeling. And her mind was telling her quite dispassionately who he was and exactly how he had made her into a whore and how much money he had put into her palm afterward. He was a man who paid women for sexual favors. He had paid her.

He had been unfaithful to his wife only once, he had told her at one time. She had been almost inclined to believe him. She was almost inclined now to believe that she really had seen that vulnerability in his face and heard it in his voice. She wanted to deceive herself. She did not want to see their encounter as the sordid thing that it had really been.

She had allowed a married man, her employer, to take incredible liberties with her person. And the encounter had not been all one-sided. She had wanted him too.

It was from herself she had fled. But she had brought herself right inside her room, behind its locked door.

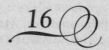

16

THE DUKE OF RIDGEWAY HAD NO IDEA IF FLEUR had gone to the music room the next morning for her early practice. He was out for a long and reckless gallop on Hannibal.

He did seriously consider not returning to the house again. There were numerous things to be done on his own land that he had somewhat neglected for the sake of the entertainment of his guests. There were crops to check on and newborn livestock to be viewed. And of course there were always tenants and laborers to talk to, to convince that he was interested in their well-being and concerned about their complaints.

Or he could ride beyond his lands. He could spend the morning with Chamberlain. He had scarcely spoken with his friend since his return from London. Visiting guests had a tendency to cut one off from one's neighbors and usual habits.

But he resisted both temptations. There were two matters of particular importance to be dealt with at home—two equally unpleasant matters.

He came in limping and barking at his valet to get him some decent clothes so that he would not have to go to breakfast smelling like a horse.

"I just hope you didn't punish poor Hannibal as much as you have punished yourself," Sidney said, "or you will have some unhappy grooms to glare at you next time you go to the stables. I'll help you out of the horsy clothes, sir, and give you a brisk rubbing before I worry about the other clothes. Lie down."

"Keep your infernal impudence to yourself," his grace said. "I have no time for rubdowns."

"If you walk around in that pain all day," Sidney said, unperturbed, "you'll be barking at all the servants, not only at me, sir, and they'll all blame me for it, too, as they always do. Lie down."

"Confound it," the duke said, "I always treat my servants with courtesy."

Sidney gave him a speaking glance and his grace lay down. He groaned as his man set firm hands against his aching side. And he rubbed at his left eye.

"There," Sidney said, so much as if he were talking to soothe a child that the duke smiled despite himself. "It will feel better in a minute. Tight as a coiled spring you are, sir."

Fleur was not in the schoolroom. She was not in the nursery either, as the duke found when he went in there. But Pamela was up and brightened at the unexpected treat of having him with her as she ate her breakfast. She fed the crusts of her toast to the puppy, who sat on the floor beside her, panting and looking hopeful. The day before, the dog had been pronounced house-safe at last and allowed indoors—under certain strict conditions.

"I thought we agreed that Tiny was not to eat food from the table," he said. "She has her own special food, does she not?"

"But I don't give her any of my good food, Papa," his daughter protested. She lowered her voice. "Nanny was furious this morning. Tiny wet the bed."

The duke closed his eyes briefly. "I thought it was also agreed that Tiny not sleep on the bed, but beside it or under it," he said.

"But, Papa," she said, "she was crying and pulling at the blankets with her little teeth. It would have been cruel to make her stay down."

"One word of complaint from Nanny to your mama," he said, "and Tiny will be back in the stables. You realize that, don't you?"

"Nanny won't complain," she said. "I wiped the wet spot with my own handkerchief. And I admired Nanny's new cap."

The duke closed his eyes again. But Mrs. Clement was bustling over from the other side of the room.

"I wish to have a word with Miss Hamilton before morning classes begin, Nanny," he said, getting to his feet. "You will keep Pamela here until she is sent for?"

"Certainly, your grace," she said, curtsying. "We had a little accident with the dog last night. Did Lady Pamela tell you?"

"Yes, she did," he said. "And I believe we have decided that it will not happen again."

Fleur was still not in the schoolroom. He twirled the globe with agitated fingers and picked out a tune with one finger on the harpsichord. He looked at a painting of one of the follies that Pamela had made and one that Fleur herself must have painted. She was talented as a painter too, he thought, picking it up.

He set it down again when the door opened behind him, and wished that he had rehearsed some speech. He deliberately had not done so. He hated rehearsed speeches. They only tended to tongue-tie him completely. He turned to look at her.

Her lip still looked a little swollen. Shadows beneath her eyes suggested that she had not slept well. But she was prettily clothed in her green dress, and her hair was in its usual neat coil at her neck. She stood very straight, tall and slender, with pleasing feminine curves. She was easily the most beautiful woman he had ever known.

It was hard to remember the first impression he had had of her—a thin whore with lusterless hair, pale skin, heavy shadows below her eyes, and dry, cracked lips. And that limp and crumpled blue silk dress. It was hard to realize that she was the same person.

"Miss Hamilton," he said, "I owe you an apology."

"No," she said, staying where she was, just inside the door. "It is unnecessary."

"Why?" he asked.

"You told me last night," she said, "that you were not sorry. You told me that you would apologize to me today. They would be empty words, your grace."

He looked at her and knew that she was right. He was not sorry. At least, in one way he was not sorry. Those moments had given him another brief taste of happiness, like the minutes of their wild ride together. And he knew that, however wrong, he would live on the memory of that embrace for a long time.

"I am sorry," he said, "for the disrespect I showed you, Miss Hamilton, and for the distress I must have caused you. And I am sorry for dishonoring my wife and my marriage. I beg that you will accept my apology."

Her chin was high, her face very calm. She looked as she had looked when he had sat down and ordered her to remove her clothes. And she had removed them with quiet dignity, folding them neatly and laying them beside her.

Fleur!

He closed his eyes briefly. "Will you?"

She hesitated. "Yes, your grace," she said.

Adam, he wanted to tell her. *My name is Adam.* He wanted to hear her say it.

"I will not keep you, then," he said, striding across the room toward her. "I will have Pamela sent to you."

She stood to one side, away from the door. "Thank you, your grace," she said.

Her eyes strayed downward. He was still limping, he realized. He closed the door of the schoolroom quietly behind him. That damned Sidney! Was he losing his touch? The pain in his side and leg was like a gnawing toothache. He made an effort to control his pain as he called at the nursery and bent to kiss his daughter, and as he went downstairs to keep another appointment.

Lord Thomas Kent was already in the library, sitting with a drink in his hand despite the early hour, one booted ankle crossed over the other knee.

"That was another thing Papa used to do," he said with a grin, holding up his glass in a salute as his brother entered the room. "Do you remember, Adam? He would have us summoned here and then keep us waiting for perhaps an hour. We dared not stand anywhere but directly in front of his desk, and we dared not move a muscle or speak to each other because we never knew the exact moment when the door would come crashing open. It was almost worse than the thrashing we knew very well would come at the end of it, wasn't it?" He laughed.

The duke went to sit behind the very desk before which he and Thomas had quailed as children.

"Tell me," Lord Thomas said, "are you going to bend me over the desk, Adam? And are you going to use a cane?"

"She is in love with you," his grace said, looking at the desktop. "She always has been. She bore your child, Thomas. And must you now come back to play games with her and with me?"

"Ah," his brother said, raising his glass to his eye. "This is not to be chastisement, is it, but a serious talking-to. How dreary. And do you still dote on her, Adam?"

"I married her," the duke said. "She is my wife. I owe her my care and protection."

Lord Thomas laughed. "She hates you," he said. "You know that, don't you?"

"Are you sleeping with her?" his grace asked, looking very directly at his brother.

"With my brother's wife?" Lord Thomas raised his eyebrows. "You surely cannot believe me capable of such perfidy and, ah, poor taste, can you, Adam?"

"Are you?"

His brother shrugged.

"Are you in love with her?"

"A foolish question," Lord Thomas said, getting to his feet and examining the mosaic above the mantel. "How can I be in love with my brother's wife?"

"If you are," the duke said, "perhaps I can begin to forgive you. Perhaps you made as much of a mistake in fleeing more than five years ago as I made in not insisting that Sybil listen to the truth. We all act hastily at times and must live forever after with the consequences. But then, nothing is written in stone either."

His brother turned in surprise and grinned at him. "Are you offering to exchange bedchambers with me for the duration of my stay?" he said. "Very sporting of you, I must say, Adam."

"If you truly love her as she loves you," the duke said, ignoring his brother's tone, "then something must be arranged."

"You are considering a divorce?" Lord Thomas continued to grin. "Imagine the scandal, Adam. Could you live with it?"

"There can be no question of divorce," his grace said. "I would not do that to Sybil." He paused and drew a deep breath. "There may be the possibility of an annulment. I would have to make inquiries."

His brother came across the room to set both hands on the desk and lean across it. He looked closely at the duke. "An annulment?" he said. "There is only one really viable ground for an annulment, is there not?"

"Yes," the duke said.

"Am I to understand . . . ?" The grin was back on Lord Thomas' face. "Am I to understand that in more than five years you have never enjoyed Sybil's favors, Adam?" He laughed. "It's true, isn't it? Good Lord. Did you play the part of noble lover to the end as she pined for me? Or did she reject you? You weren't unwise enough to display your wounds to her, were you?" He laughed again.

"Do you love her?" the duke asked.

"I have always had a soft spot for Sybil," Lord Thomas said. "She is lovelier than almost any other woman I have clapped eyes on."

"That is not what I asked," his brother said. "Would you marry her if you had the chance to do so?"

Lord Thomas stood up and looked down at his brother assessingly. "You would do that for her sake?" he said. "Or would it be for your own?"

"I would do it," the duke said, "or at least inquire into the possibility of doing it, if I were convinced that Sybil would have the happiness that you and I between us have deprived her of."

"And Pamela?" Lord Thomas said. "If there were an annulment, the world would know that Pamela is not your child."

His grace spread his hands palm-down on the desk and looked down at them. "Yes," he said. "Could I have your answer?"

"This is sudden." Lord Thomas strolled back to the fireplace and resumed his examination of the mosaic lion. "I will need some time to consider."

"Of course," his grace said. "Take it. But as long as you are in this house under present circumstances, Thomas, Sybil is my wife and I will punish any disrespect shown her."

"Bent over the desk with the cane on the backside after all?" Lord Thomas said. "Have you perfected the art of swishing it in the air before bringing it down on target, Adam? That used to make me almost lose control of my bladder."

"I will expect your answer within the next week," the duke said. "If it is no, I will expect you to leave immediately—and forever."

"I take it I am dismissed," Lord Thomas said, turning to look in some amusement at his brother again. "Very well, Adam, I will take myself from your presence. I believe I am being awaited for a fishing trip anyway."

The duke continued to stare at his hands after the door had

closed behind his brother. And he was being seduced by his own bluff, he thought a few minutes later.

In his imagination he was living through the events that his words to his brother had seemed to make possible—a speedy annulment, Sybil gone, himself free. Free to explore his attraction to Fleur. He closed his eyes and clenched his hands on the desk.

It had been bluff, pure and simple. Never in a million years would Thomas agree to marry Sybil. Had he thought for one moment that Thomas would, his grace thought, then of course he would not even have made the mad suggestion that he had just made. For though such an arrangement would undoubtedly be as satisfactory to Sybil as it would be to himself, there was Pamela to consider. And Pamela must always come first, before her mother's happiness and before his own. She was an innocent and defenseless child.

No, he knew Thomas well enough. He had always liked him when they were boys, when his younger brother's mischievous ways and cheerful lack of principle had brought consequences no more drastic than a thrashing or a serious talking-to. But Thomas had never grown up. He had never passed beyond the irresponsibility of youth. In his one year as supposed Duke of Ridgeway he had put severe strains on Willoughby's considerable resources so that it might well be ruined by now had he continued to be its owner.

Thomas, he firmly believed, was incapable of deep feeling. Doubtless he would have married Sybil had he remained duke, and perhaps it would have been a reasonably successful marriage, but he would never have loved her as she loved him. Had he loved her, even to some small degree, he could not have abandoned her when he knew her to be with child.

The duke knew that Thomas would continue to harass him and amuse himself with Sybil for as long as it pleased him to do so. And that might be a very long time. The only way to frighten him off was by making it seem possible that he could be stuck with his toy for a lifetime.

Thomas would be gone by the time the week was out. The duke was quite sure of it. So sure that he had risked Pamela's future on a bluff.

But, God, it was a sweet, seductive idea. He got to his feet and glanced toward the fireplace and the chair beside it where Fleur had sat the night before. It was just there they had stood.

She had stopped shaking at his bidding. And she had lifted her face for his kiss and opened her mouth to it. Her arms had come up about his neck and her fingers had played in his hair.

For a few minutes, at least, she had forgotten her fear of him. She had wanted him, as he had wanted her. As he wanted her.

Guilt gnawed at him. He had been outraged at the impropriety of the embrace Sybil and Thomas had been sharing in the long gallery. And yet he had engaged in his own not two hours later with the governess.

Fleur. She was coming to dominate his thoughts by day and haunt his dreams by night. He was coming to live for the moments when he could see her, listen to her music, listen to her voice, see her eyes on his. She was beginning to give light and meaning to his days.

In her he was beginning to glimpse the precious pearl that he had once expected of life.

It was a hard life he had dedicated himself to—a life of celibacy for the past six years, with the single exception of that one brief, dispassionate encounter in London.

With Fleur. With a thin, pale whore who had turned out to be a virgin, who had quietly obeyed his every command and had suffered his penetration of her body with only that small guttural sound and the biting down on her lips. Even such a sordid scene she had played out with dignity. She had been a victim who had sunk to the depths but refused to allow her spirit to be broken.

And he must never hold her again. Never kiss her again. For

last night had been a moment for one time only, something that he had not planned. Now that he knew it possible, he would have to guard against its ever happening again. For though his marriage was a heavy burden on him, it was nevertheless a contract he had entered into freely and one he would remain faithful to as far as human frailty would allow.

He might yet have to move Fleur to another post somewhere else, he thought. He was not sure that it would be possible to live in a house with the woman he desired almost more than anything else in life and with his wife, whom he had once loved and with whom he had never lain.

She had cringed from him on their wedding night, screamed at him to get out of her bedchamber. He had told her about his wounds, and of course the disfigurement of his face was there for all to see. He had left her and made no attempt to go to her again until after the birth of Pamela. He had tried to make a friend of her.

But of course, she had believed him the villain who had sent her lover away and then forced her into marriage with himself. What a foolish hope it had been that he could bring her to love him.

The same thing had happened when he went to her two months after Pamela's birth—the same hysteria and look of deep revulsion. He had talked to her about it the following day and she had told him in her usual breathless, sweet manner, tears swimming in her large blue eyes, that if he ever again tried to touch her she would return to her father's house.

It was probably at that moment that his love for her had begun to die a rapid death. He had seen finally, and had admitted the truth of what he had seen, the cold selfishness that was hidden only just behind the angelic exterior.

All that was left after his love had died was a deep pity for her. For clearly her love for Thomas had been a monumental passion that she could not kill, even if she had tried. And of course, she had not accepted the truth, and believed that only his own cruelty had separated her from the man who loved her as dearly as she loved him.

The duke sighed and turned to the door. At last, he thought, he could proceed with the day he had planned. At last he could put his own problems behind him for a short while and concentrate on listening to other people's.

It was only when he was striding toward the stables that he realized he had not eaten breakfast.

And it was only much later that he realized that calling on Duncan Chamberlain was not the thing to have done if he was seeking forgetfulness. For Duncan had asked him how he would feel about losing his governess if she could be persuaded to accept a marriage offer, and he had been forced to smile at his friend and shake his hand and assure him that the whole thing was entirely a matter between him and Miss Hamilton.

He wondered how Chamberlain would feel if he knew how perilously close he had been to having a fist planted right between his eyes.

PETER HOUGHTON ARRIVED BACK from his holiday three days later and regaled Mrs. Laycock, Jarvis, Fleur, and the other upper servants, as they sat at luncheon, with stories of the christening.

"A headful of curls at the age of two months?" Jarvis said, interrupting the speaker. "Is that not unusual, Mr. Houghton?"

"Yes, indeed," Houghton said. "My cousin's wife says that it runs in her family."

"Teeth?" Mrs. Laycock said with a frown a minute later. "At the age of two months, Mr. Houghton?"

"Yes," Houghton said. "Unusual, is it not, ma'am?"

"What was the christening robe like, Mr. Houghton?" Miss Armitage, the duchess's personal maid, asked.

The duke's secretary decided that it would be advisable to cut short his luncheon despite the fact that his grace was from home. There must be a great amount of work piled up on his desk, he mumbled, regretting the lost dessert.

The duke had been from home most of the day. He had taken the gentlemen guests on a ride about some of his farms during the morning after giving his daughter another riding lesson, and he had taken her visiting to the rectory after an early luncheon.

It was late afternoon by the time they returned, and Pamela ran upstairs ahead of him, eager to tell Fleur about the rocking horse at the rectory, which had been broken during her last visit. It was interesting to note, the duke thought, removing his hat and his gloves in the hall and handing them to a footman, that it was her governess, not her nurse, who was to be the recipient of Pamela's confidences.

"Mr. Houghton has returned, your grace," Jarvis informed him, bowing stiffly from the waist.

"Good," his grace said briskly. "Is he in his office?"

"I believe so, your grace."

The duke turned in that direction.

"Well," he said, standing in the doorway, "you took your time about returning."

"Christenings and babies and relatives all wanting to entertain me. You can imagine how it was, your grace," Houghton said.

The duke stepped inside and closed the door. "It is just you and I, Houghton," he said. "And I have enough of charades during the evenings. Well?"

"The lady in question is Miss Isabella Fleur Bradshaw, your grace," his secretary said, "daughter of a former Lord Brocklehurst, now deceased, along with his wife, Miss Bradshaw's mother."

"He was succeeded by the present Lord Brocklehurst?" his grace asked.

"By his father, your grace. His lordship died five years ago, leaving a wife, a son, and a daughter to mourn him."

"And their relationship to Miss Ham . . . to Miss Bradshaw's father?"

"The late baron was his first cousin, your grace," Houghton said.

"The late and the present Lords Brocklehurst were and are her guardians?" his grace asked with narrowed eyes. "What are the terms of guardianship? She must be past her twenty-first birthday."

"Such information is not easy to come by when one is pretending to just idle curiosity, your grace," his secretary said stiffly.

"But I am quite sure you came by it anyway," his grace said. "Yes, I know it must have been difficult, Houghton. I fully appreciate your talents without your drawing my attention to them. Why do you think I employ you? Because I like your looks?"

Peter Houghton coughed. "She will come into her dowry and her mother's fortune when she is twenty-five, your grace," he said, "or when she marries, provided her guardian approves her choice. If he does not, then she must wait until her thirtieth birthday before inheriting."

"And her present age?" the duke asked.

"Twenty-three, your grace."

The duke looked at his secretary consideringly. "All right, Houghton," he said, "those are the facts, and you must be commended for discovering them. Now tell me all the rest. All of it. I can tell from the look on your face that you are fair to bursting with it. Out with it, without waiting to be prompted."

"You may not like it, your grace," Houghton said.

"I will be the judge of that."

"And it may reflect on my judgment in hiring her," Houghton said. "Though," he added with a cough, "we are talking about Miss Bradshaw, are we not, your grace, and not about Miss Hamilton."

"Houghton." His grace's eyes had narrowed dangerously.

"If you would prefer to tell your story with my hand at your windpipe, it is all the same to me. But you might be more comfortable as you are."

"Yes, your grace," Houghton said, coughing again. But hands at windpipes would be mild in comparison with what might happen after the duke had heard all about his ladybird, he reflected, beginning to speak.

There was only one particular thought in the duke's mind. He was glad her name really was Fleur, he thought. It would be difficult to have to start thinking of her as Isabella. She did not look like an Isabella.

He stood at the window, his back to the room, listening. He did not interrupt often.

"Do you have a single source for all these details?" he asked at one point.

"A servant from Heron House, your grace," Houghton said, "a gentleman who liked to frequent the taproom at the inn where I put up, and the curate and his sister. Particularly the sister. I gather she was a friend of Miss Bradshaw's. The brother was more reticent."

"She had a friend, then," the duke said more to himself than to his secretary.

"The gentleman's name?" he asked later. "The taproom gentleman, that is?"

"Mr. Tweedsmuir, your grace."

"First name?"

"Horace, your grace."

"Ah," the duke said. "Did you encounter any gentleman whose first name was Daniel?"

"Yes, your grace."

"Well?" His grace turned impatiently to look at his secretary.

"The curate, your grace," Houghton said. "The Reverend Daniel Booth."

"Curate," the duke said. "He is a young man, then?"

"Yes, your grace," the secretary said. "And a younger son of Sir Richard Booth of Hampshire."

"The detail of your research is admirable," his grace said. "Is there anything you have missed?"

"No, your grace," Houghton said after a reflective pause. "I believe I have recalled everything. Do you wish me to see to the dismissing of Miss Hamilton?"

"Miss Hamilton?" The duke's brows drew together. "What the devil does all this have to do with Miss Hamilton?"

Peter Houghton shuffled through the papers on his desk with nervous hands. "Nothing, your grace," he said.

"Then your question was a strange non sequitur," his grace said. "Have I left enough work on your desk to amuse you for the rest of the afternoon, Houghton?"

"Yes, indeed, your grace," his secretary said. "It will all be attended to before I leave here."

"I would not burn the midnight oil if I were you," his grace said, opening the door into the hallway. "You will doubtless wish for a free evening in which to entertain Mrs. Laycock and a select few others with an account of the christening at which you were recently godfather."

Peter Houghton watched him go. He was not going to dismiss his ladybird after all he had just heard? His grace must be badly smitten indeed.

And what the deuce was Brocklehurst doing at the house if not to arrest her? Houghton shook his head and turned his attention to the mounds of papers on his desk.

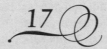

17

*F*LEUR LOOKED FORWARD TO TIMOTHY CHAMBER-
lain's birthday for a variety of reasons. Lady Pamela was
excited about it, and it was always a pleasure to see the child
happy. Lady Pamela had hoped that her mother would accompany her, but her grace, of course, was too busy with her
guests to devote a whole afternoon to her daughter. The child
still hoped that her father would come. Fleur did not share the
hope.

It would be good to spend a whole afternoon away from
Willoughby, she thought. Away from *him*. Not that she had
seen much of him since the morning of his apology. He had
not sat in the schoolroom at all. He had appeared only briefly
at the library door in the mornings when she was practicing in
the music room. She had been required to accompany him
when he gave Lady Pamela another riding lesson on a morning
when it was not raining, but there was no ride afterward.
Apart from that, she had not seen him.

But there was always the chance that she would. Despite
herself, and although she always hoped he would not come,
she listened for his footsteps outside the schoolroom.

And she dreamed of him. But the dreams were no longer the
old nightmare. They were new, for in these dreams he kissed
her deeply, as he had done in reality, and she kissed him back,

as she had done then, and she ran her palms over the strong muscles of his shoulders and undid the buttons of his waistcoat and shirt in order to touch the dark hair that she knew to be beyond them. In her dream she wanted him as she had had him once upon a time, but with tenderness, with his body on hers as well as in, and his mouth on hers.

She always woke in a sweat and burrowed farther beneath the bedcovers. And she always squirmed with shame.

She looked forward to an afternoon away, in the company of children and in that of the safe and amusing Mr. Chamberlain. And she hoped and hoped that the Duke of Ridgeway would not be there, and felt guilt at the thought because his presence would mean the world to Lady Pamela. It would mean that he cared enough to want to share her pleasures.

And she looked forward to the afternoon because it would mean several hours free of Matthew. He had meant what he said when he had told her that he expected a great deal of her spare time. If she walked outside in the mornings or the early evenings, he was there with her. Once when she took Lady Pamela to the bridge to paint, he appeared there and made himself agreeable to both of them for a whole hour. And on the afternoon before the birthday, on the day when Mr. Houghton came home from his holiday and his grace was from home with his daughter, he invited her—with the duchess's approval—on a walk to the lake that several of the guests were to make.

"Matthew," she said in an agony when she had been summoned to the hall and found him waiting there, "I cannot go walking with her grace and some of her guests. I am a servant here."

"But everyone knows that you are also a gentlewoman," he said, "and an acquaintance of mine. And I am a guest here, Isabella, and therefore to be humored. Look, it is a glorious day for a change, and you have a free afternoon. What better way to spend it than in a walk to the lake?"

She had no choice, of course. She returned to her room for a bonnet. And she wondered, as they walked a little behind the other couples, where it would all end, when Matthew would put an end to this whole charade.

"For how much longer are you planning to be here?" she asked him.

"For how long are *we* going to be here?" he asked. "I don't know, Isabella. I am in no hurry, and I thought you might prefer to get to know me again here where there are other people than at home, where there would be just you and I. You seemed to think a few months ago that there was something improper about that, though we are second cousins."

He had a point there, she thought.

"I would like to announce our betrothal here before we leave," he said.

"No!" she said sharply. "Not that, Matthew."

Most of the couples showed no inclination to remain together once they arrived at the lake. Lord Thomas Kent and the duchess got into one of the boats to row across to the island; Sir Philip Shaw and Lady Underwood walked off along the path that followed the north shore; Miss Dobbin and Mr. Penny climbed the bank and disappeared among the trees.

Lord Brocklehurst drew Fleur to the south side of the lake and among the denser trees there to one of the follies she had once ridden past with his grace. It was in the shape of a temple with a semicircular seat inside, looking down on the lake.

"Let's sit," he said.

Fleur sat.

But she turned her head aside sharply when he would have kissed her.

"Give me a chance, Isabella," he said. "You are so beautiful." He touched the hair at her neck with light fingers. "And I mean nothing dishonorable. Heron House was your father's. Your mother was the baroness. You could have it all back for yourself.

I would send my mother and Amelia to live elsewhere if you do not wish to live with them. Give me a chance."

"Matthew," she said, turning her head to look at him, "can you not understand? I do not love you. I do not feel the sort of regard for you that would make me a suitable wife for you. Can we not just go back and tell the truth of what happened and remain second cousins at some distance from each other? Can you not let me learn to respect you even if I cannot love you?"

"Love can grow," he said. "Give me a chance."

She shook her head.

He placed his hands loosely about her neck, as he had done once before, tightened them a little beneath her chin, and jerked upward. And he lowered his mouth to hers.

She waited for him to finish before getting to her feet and stepping outside the temple to look down at the lake. And for the first time there was an anger in her to equal the terror, a total weariness with being a puppet on a string, with being quite out of control of her own life.

"I won't marry you, Matthew," she said, "or be your mistress. And I will not spend any more time with you here at Willoughby Hall. You must do what you will, but that is my decision."

And she closed her eyes and remembered his hands at her throat, the tightening, the upward jerk. Her breath came faster.

If it ever comes to that, he had said to her once—his grace, that was—*if there is ever no one else to whom you can turn, then come to me. Will you?*

There was a yearning in her to do just that—to tell him all, to feel those strong arms about her once more, to hear that steadily beating heart beneath her ear again, to unload all her burdens onto someone else.

And then she would watch his look of disdain, revulsion, condemnation. And she would be alone again, as she had always been alone ever since the death of her parents. The idea that there was someone who might care and help was an illusion. She had known that she could not go to Daniel; she knew now that she could not go to the Duke of Ridgeway. She was old enough, she had lived long enough to know that.

Matthew's hands closed on her shoulders from behind. "You will change your mind," he said. "We will give it a few more days, Isabella."

She bit her lip instead of replying as she had been about to do. Would she? Change her mind? The alternative was so very appalling.

"We should return to the house," he said. "You need to do some thinking, don't you?"

When they entered the great hall from the horseshoe steps sometime later, his grace happened to be crossing it. He looked at her and at Matthew tight-lipped.

"Miss Hamilton?" he said. "I thought you were upstairs with my daughter."

"I have been walking with Lord Brocklehurst, your grace," she said.

He nodded curtly. "She was eager to talk to you," he said. "You had better go up without delay."

"Yes, your grace," she said, curtsying. She fled from the hall and up to the nursery, her cheeks burning from the look of cold disapproval on his face. And she wondered if Matthew would explain to him that the invitation had come from him with her grace's permission.

She looked forward so much to the following day and a whole afternoon away from Willoughby.

MASTER TIMOTHY CHAMBERLAIN WAS celebrating his seventh birthday with his brother and sister, Lady Pamela Kent from Willoughby Hall, and five other children from the neighborhood, including the vicar's two.

It was entirely a blessing for their sanity, Mr. Chamberlain told Fleur when she arrived with her charge, that the weather had decided to cooperate. They would move outside once Timmy had shown the children the nursery, which they had all seen before, and the large bag of colored wooden building bricks that was his birthday present.

Miss Chamberlain greeted Fleur with a smile. "You would not guess from listening to him, would you, Miss Hamilton," she said, "that the idea for a party was all Duncan's? He revels in such occasions."

Mr. Chamberlain grimaced as Fleur laughed. It had not taken her longer than her first day of acquaintance with him to realize that he quite doted on his children.

She was feeling wonderfully happy. She and Lady Pamela had left almost immediately after luncheon and would not return until almost dinnertime. And his grace had not come.

"Timothy had bricks. I am going to get Papa to buy me some," Lady Pamela announced to Fleur in a shriek when the children came hurtling downstairs with demands to be taken outside.

They played hide-and-seek and chasing and ball in the large grounds behind the house, and Mr. Chamberlain organized races of various kinds until several of the children were stretched out on the grass, panting, while the others shrieked more loudly than ever.

Miss Chamberlain formed them all into a large circle to play some singing games—"to quieten them down," she explained to Fleur, who had helped with the races. "Duncan always fails to realize that tiring children does not necessarily quieten them, but frequently has just the opposite effect."

"Well," Mr. Chamberlain said, ignoring the outstretched hand of a small girl with a hair bow almost as large as her head and pinching her cheek instead, "dancing and chanting in a circle is quite beneath my dignity, I am afraid. Miss Hamilton and I are going to leave you to it, Emily. We will all have tea after this. Ma'am?" He held out an arm for Fleur's.

"There are limits to the depths to which I will sink," he said, strolling with her toward the rose arbor at the side of the house. " 'Ring around the rosy' is definitely below that limit."

"I do believe your son is having a wonderful time," she said.

"Yes," he agreed. "One is seven only once, I suppose. Tomorrow he will be his normal boisterous self again. The hysteria will have passed."

Fleur chuckled.

They were inside the arbor, surrounded by the heady smell of roses. He released her arm, cupped her face with his hands, and kissed her briefly and warmly on the lips.

"I have missed you," he said.

She smiled.

"If you were not a governess," he said, "and did not have daily duties to perform, I would probably have haunted Willoughby Hall in the days since our theater visit." He touched her lips with his thumbs.

She looked into his eyes and knew with regret that there were limits for her too beyond which she dare not go.

"Don't," she said as he drew breath to speak again. She lowered her eyes to his chin. "Please, don't."

"What I am about to say is not welcome to you?" he asked.

She hesitated. "I cannot," she said.

"Because of inclination?" he said. "It is something about me? Or my children?"

She shook her head and bit her lip.

"There is some obstacle?" he asked.

Her eyes dropped to his neckcloth. Yes. There were the charges of theft and murder hanging over her head. There was the loss of her virginity. There was the profession she had sampled briefly before becoming a governess.

She nodded.

"Insurmountable?" he asked.

"Yes." She looked up into his eyes again and knew a great sadness of regret. "Quite insurmountable, sir."

"Well, then." He smiled, lowered his hands to her arms, and

leaned forward to kiss her firmly once more. He patted her arms. "Enough of that. This arbor was my wife's pride and joy. Did Emily tell you that? I love to sit here to read—when the children are safely indoors at their lessons or games, that is. Shall we wander indoors for tea?"

"Yes. Thank you," Fleur said.

All her delight in the afternoon was gone. She had not realized that he was quite so close to a declaration, but she had sensed it coming there in the rose arbor. And she felt that she had hurt him and feared that despite what she had said, he would think that it was some lack in himself that had made her draw back from him.

It was almost no surprise when they came from the arbor onto the back lawn again to see the Duke of Ridgeway, his daughter sitting up on one of his shoulders, talking with Miss Chamberlain.

"Ah," he said, turning and smiling and looking at them both with keen eyes. "Duncan? Miss Hamilton?"

"I might have known you would be wise enough to avoid the games and clever enough to arrive just in time for tea," Mr. Chamberlain said. He extended his right hand. "Welcome to Timmy's birthday party, Adam."

"I won second in the girls' race, Papa," Lady Pamela was shrieking, "and we would have won the three-legged race if William had not fallen down."

Fleur turned away with Miss Chamberlain to shepherd the children back to the house for tea.

THE DUKE OF RIDGEWAY rode back to Willoughby Hall sometime later, one arm about his daughter, who rode before him, and listened with half an ear to her excited chatter. He wished that Fleur were riding beside them, but pushed the thought from his mind. It was as well that she was returning home in his carriage.

She really was good for Pamela. He always had been capable of arousing these moods of childhood excitement in her and he had always tried, when he was at home, to take her to visit other children as often as possible. But of course he was away from home for long stretches and always felt guilty about abandoning her. He could not possibly love her more if she really were his, he thought.

Fleur was giving Pamela extended opportunities to be a child. Sybil and Mrs. Clement between them overprotected her. And on the rare occasion when Sybil did take her out, it was to visit adults so that she might sit quietly and Sybil might be complimented on her well-behaved daughter.

Fleur was good for her. She should have children of her own.

Pamela was tracing the line of his scar with one soft finger and singing under her breath. "How did it miss your eye, Papa?" she asked.

"Someone must have been looking after me," he said.

"God?"

"Yes, God."

"Did it hurt?"

"Yes, I suppose it must have," he said. "I don't remember much."

She resumed her quiet singing as she ran her finger along the scar again.

He was feeling guilty. Duncan had spoken very briefly with him as he was leaving.

"It seems you are not in imminent danger of losing your governess after all, Adam," he had said.

His grace had been looking ever since his arrival for some sign of what had happened. They had been alone together somewhere just before his arrival, but their expressions and behavior had given nothing away during tea.

"You changed your mind?" he had asked.

His friend had grimaced. "Rejected," he had said.

Duncan Chamberlain was his friend. He wished for his

happiness. Four years before, he had lost a wife of whom he had been very fond. Fleur would be the perfect second wife for him and stepmother for his children. He should have been sorry to hear that she had rejected Duncan.

But he was feeling guilty. He had felt a surge of elation. And then more guilt. Had she felt forced to refuse because of what he had done to her and made her into? Of course she would have felt forced.

But there was that other, too. He must talk with her. He would have done it that morning, but had not wanted to risk doing anything to spoil the day Pamela had been so looking forward to. He must talk with her the next day.

"Did you kill anyone, Papa?" Pamela asked.

"In the wars?" he said. "Yes, I'm afraid so. But I'm not proud of it. I cannot help thinking that those men had mamas and perhaps wives and children. War is a terrible thing, Pamela."

She nestled her head against his chest. "I'm glad no one killed you, Papa," she said.

He hugged her to him with one arm.

The carriage was drawing to a halt on the terrace as he and Pamela walked from the stables.

"Miss Hamilton," he called as she was about to disappear through the servants' doors.

She stopped and looked at him inquiringly.

"Attend me in the library immediately after breakfast to-morrow if you will," he said.

She turned a shade paler. Perhaps she had heard that he had a tendency to conduct any unpleasant business in the library.

"Yes, your grace." She curtsied and continued on her way.

Perhaps he should have said nothing, he thought, staring at the closed servants' doors. Perhaps he should have just summoned her when he was ready for her. Probably she would worry all night about what she had done wrong.

"Tiny will be sad," Pamela said, tugging on his hand. "She has been without me all afternoon."

"Let's go and see how happy she is to see you, then," he said, smiling down at her.

THE DUCHESS HAD TAKEN to her bed in the middle of the afternoon after a prolonged coughing spell, with chest pains and a fever. She blamed the ride she had taken that morning with several of her guests. She did not ride very often, considering it a dangerous and generally unhealthy activity.

Lord Thomas Kent let himself into her bedchamber an hour before dinner and dismissed her maid. He sat on the side of the bed and took her grace's hand in his.

"How are you, Sybil?" he asked.

"Oh, better," she said, smiling at him. "I am just too lazy to get up. I will come to the drawing room after dinner."

He raised her hand to his lips. "So beautiful and so delicate," he said. "You do not look one day older than when we were betrothed. Will you look as young the next time I see you, I wonder."

Her eyes flew to his face. "The next time?" she said. "You are not going away, Thomas? Oh, no. This is where you belong. You can't go away again."

"I have promised Adam," he said, kissing her hand again and smiling gently at her.

"Promised Adam?" She gripped his hand. "What have you promised?"

"That I will leave within the week," he said. "I cannot really blame him, Sybil. It is not like the last time. You are, after all, his wife."

"His wife!" she said scornfully, sitting up and looking directly into his eyes. "I am his wife in name only, Thomas. I have never let him touch me. I swear I have not. I am yours. Only yours."

"But in the eyes of the law you are his," he said. "And there is Pamela to consider. She must never know the truth. It would be too hard for her to bear. I have been ordered to leave, Sybil, and leave I must. In all conscience, I must leave."

"No!" she cried, gripping his hand even harder. She turned her head aside to cough. "Or if you must go, take me with you. I'll leave him, Thomas. I cannot be away from you ever again. I'll come with you."

He drew her against him and kissed her lips. "I can't take you," he whispered against her ear. "I would not expose you to that sort of scandal, Sybil. And you could not leave Pamela without either of her parents. We must be brave."

She wrapped her arms about his neck. "I don't care," she said. "I care only about you, Thomas. Nothing else matters to me. I am going to come with you."

"Hush," he said, rocking her in his arms. "Hush, now."

And as she quietened down he kissed her again and fondled her breasts through the satin of her nightgown.

"Thomas," she moaned, sinking back against her pillows. "I love you."

"And I you," he said, slipping the satin down over her shoulders and lowering his head to kiss her throat.

He straightened up when a tap at the door was succeeded by its opening.

The Duke of Ridgeway closed the door quietly behind his back. "You are feeling better?" he asked, his eyes on his wife. "I just heard from Armitage that you have been ill again this afternoon."

"Yes, thank you," she said curtly, turning her head away from him.

"You will wish to dress for dinner, Thomas," he said. "You are in danger of being late."

His brother smiled at him and left the room without a word.

"I have sent for Dr. Hartley to call on you tomorrow morning," his grace said. "I can send for him to come immediately if you wish."

"I have no need of a doctor," she said, her face still averted.

"You must see him anyway," he said. "Perhaps he can give you some new medicine that will cure you of that troublesome cough once and for all."

She turned her head suddenly to look at him. "I hate you, Adam," she said vehemently. "How I hate you!"

"For caring about your health?" he said.

"For not caring about me at all," she said. "For ordering Thomas to leave again. You know we love each other. You know we always have. I hate you for ruining our lives."

"He told you that I have ordered him to leave?" he asked.

"Do you deny it?" Her voice was sharp.

He looked at her for a long time, at the woman whom he had loved so passionately once upon a time and whom he could now only pity.

"I suppose that is what my words to him amounted to," he said.

She turned her head away from him again. "I am going with him," she said. "I am leaving you, Adam."

"I doubt that he will take you," he said quietly.

"You know him well," she said. "You know that he would not hurt me for worlds. But he will take me when I have finally convinced him that I will be far more miserable here with respectability and you."

"I doubt that he will take you," he repeated. "I think perhaps this time you will have to face the truth, Sybil. I am sorry. I shall make your excuses to our guests for this evening. I shall come to see how you are later."

"Don't," she said. "I don't want to see you, Adam, not tonight or ever."

He pulled the bell rope next to the bed and waited in silence until the duchess's maid appeared.

"Her grace will need you, Armitage," he said, and left the room.

18

$\mathscr{F}$LEUR STEPPED INSIDE THE LIBRARY WHEN A footman opened the doors for her without either knocking or announcing her. The man closed the doors quietly behind her.

His grace was writing at the desk, though he put his pen down immediately after she came in, blotted carefully what he had written, and got to his feet. He looked at her with that piercing dark gaze that she always found so disconcerting.

She stood very still, her chin held high, her shoulders back. And she wondered, as she had wondered all through a disturbed night, if he was merely going to reprimand her for some unknown offense—but then, why the formal summons to the library?—or dismiss her or try to seduce her again. Or perhaps there was nothing momentous about the occasion at all. She waited.

"The Honorable Miss Isabella Fleur Bradshaw," he said very quietly, "of Heron House in Wiltshire."

Matthew had taken her seriously two days before after all, then. He had told everything. She raised her chin a notch higher.

"Jewel thief and murderer," he said, "or so the suspicion goes. Every suspected criminal is innocent, of course, until proved guilty."

Her eyes did not waver from his.

"Are you?" he asked. "A thief and a murderer, I mean?"

"No, your grace."

"Neither?"

"No, your grace."

"And yet your cousin's most costly jewels were found in the trunk that you were to have taken with you had you succeeded in leaving as planned."

"Yes, your grace."

"And there was a death."

"Yes, your grace."

"You fled," he said, "when your cousin caught you in the act of committing the murder—to London, with nothing but the clothes you were wearing. A blue silk evening gown and gray cloak. And in London you hid and survived in any way you could."

"Yes, your grace."

"But you did not steal there?" he said. "Or even beg?"

"No."

"You sold only what was yours to sell."

"Yes."

He came around the desk and crossed the room to stand a few feet in front of her.

"Will you tell me your story?" he asked. "We might be here all day if I have to ask questions and have monosyllables for answer."

She continued to stare at him.

"Why not?" he asked.

"I will not be believed," she said. "When all this is told in a court of law, Lord Brocklehurst will tell the version he has told you, and he will be believed, as you believe him. He is a man and a baron. I am a woman and a governess—and a whore. It is not worth my while to waste my breath."

"I have learned nothing from Brocklehurst," he said. "All I know, I have learned independently. I heard him call you

Isabella. You yourself called your former home 'Her—.' I sent Houghton to Heron House to find out what he could about an Isabella."

"Why?" The word was whispered.

He shrugged. "Because your past has always been shrouded in mystery," he said. "Because I knew, unfortunately too late, that only extreme circumstances could have forced you into becoming what you became in London in my company. Because I saw the terror in your face when you first set eyes on Brocklehurst in my drawing room. Because both of you clearly lied about the degree of your acquaintance. Because I care."

"Perhaps it is as well," she said. "You have tried to make a liar and a thief and a murderer into your mistress."

"Is that what you believe of me, Fleur?" he asked.

"Yes," she said.

"Even though I sent you to bed rather than accompany you to your room that night for fear I would not be able to let you go?" he said. "Even though I have not come near you since, except to apologize?" He passed a hand over his brow and sighed. "Come and sit down."

"No," she said.

"Fleur," he said, "will you turn around and open the door?"

She looked at him warily and did so.

"Close it again," he said. "What did you see?"

"The footman who let me in here," she said.

"Do you know him?" he asked.

"Yes," she said. "He is Jeremy."

"Do you know him well? Do you like him?"

"He is always friendly and courteous," she said.

"He is to stand there," he said, "until you emerge or until he is summoned or until I send him away. If you were to scream, he would rush in here to your rescue. Come and sit down."

She preceded him straight-backed to two upright chairs

close to the window and sat down on one. She folded her hands in her lap.

"The man who died was your cousin's valet?" he said, taking the other chair. But he did not wait for her answer. "Did you have anything at all to do with his death?"

"Yes," she said. "I killed him."

"But you do not call yourself a murderer," he said. "Why not?"

"He was a great strong man," she said. "He was going to hold me while Matthew ravished me. I pushed him as he came up behind me. He must have been off-balance, as we were very close to the hearth. He fell and hit his head."

"And died?"

"Yes," she said. "He died instantly."

"Had your cousin expressed his intent?" he asked.

"He said that before I left the house again no other man would ever want me," she said. "I believe I was screaming and fighting. I saw him nod to Hobson."

"His valet?"

"Yes. And then he came up behind me." She caught sight of her hands, which were twisting in her lap. She stilled them.

"Brocklehurst's mother and sister had left for London?" he asked. "Why did they leave you without a chaperone?"

"They do not care for me," she said.

"You were going to the rectory," he said, "to stay with Miss Booth. Why did you leave it until the evening?"

"You are well-informed," she said. "You appear to know everything."

"Houghton is a good man," he said. "But it is the whys that still puzzle me."

"Matthew was expecting guests," she said. "They would have played cards and got drunk. I could have slipped away unnoticed. But they did not come. It was the day his mother and sister left. I suppose he planned a night alone with me."

"But you tried to leave anyway?" he said.

"Yes," she said. "He caught me. I think he knew and was waiting for me."

"You did not steal the jewels?" he asked.

"No," she said. "I knew nothing of them until he mentioned them to me here."

"And so you fled," he said, "with only the clothes you were wearing. No money?"

"A little in my cloak pocket," she said. "Very little."

"Why did you not go to the Reverend Daniel Booth?" he asked.

She looked at him and bit her lip. "Daniel?" she said. "They would have come for me there immediately. Besides, he would not have harbored a killer."

"Not even if he loved her?" he said.

She swallowed.

"How long did it take you to get to London?" he asked.

"About a week, I think," she said. "Perhaps longer."

He got to his feet and stood looking out through the window for several minutes, his back to her.

"I would guess that Brocklehurst is prepared to make a trade," he said. "Your body in exchange for your life. Am I right?"

"Yes," she said.

"What is your decision?" he asked. "Have you decided?"

"It is easy to be heroic in one's imagination," she said. "I am not so sure I will be a hero when it comes to the point. I told him two days ago that I would not marry him or be his mistress or have anything more to do with him, and yet when he gave me a few more days to make a final decision, I did not have the courage to repeat what I had just said."

"And yet," he said, turning to look at her over his shoulder, "you are capable of great courage, Fleur. I have seen proof of it, if you will remember—in a certain inn room in London."

She felt herself flush.

"You might have asked for my help, you know," he said. "I

would have given it. And even if I had said no, I could hardly have done worse to you than what I did. But you had the pride and courage—and foolishness—to sell what was yours rather than beg."

She lowered her eyes from his.

"It is not always like that, you know," he said quietly. "When coupled with love, it can be a beautiful experience, Fleur—for the woman as well as the man. Don't be afraid of all men as I know you are afraid of me."

She realized she was biting on her lower lip again only when she tasted blood.

"Now," he said, "what are we going to do about your situation? It is not as hopeless as you seem to think. There are several defenses that can be made."

She laughed.

"Will you allow me to help you?" he asked.

"There were no witnesses," she said, "except Matthew and me. And my maid was the one who discovered the jewels in my trunk. There is no defense except the truth, your grace, and the truth will sound lamentably false when set against the word of Baron Brocklehurst."

He bent down suddenly and took both her hands in his. She had not realized how cold hers were until they were enveloped in the warmth of his.

"You are not going to hang, Fleur," he said, "or languish in prison. I promise you that. You have been living with that terror for weeks, haven't you? Why did you not come to me sooner? But of course, I am the last person you would come to, am I not? For today and perhaps tomorrow I want you to stay with Pamela during lesson times and with Mrs. Laycock at other times. If Brocklehurst tries to speak with you, it is my order as your employer that you keep away from him. Understood?"

"You cannot help me," she said.

He stooped down on his haunches and looked up into her

face. His hold on her hands tightened. "I can," he said, "and I will, though I know that you do not trust me. Do you really believe that I brought you here to be my mistress?"

"It does not matter," she said. She was looking at his hands holding hers. And feeling that she should pull away from them. And wanting to grip them as they gripped hers. And wanting to lean her head forward until her forehead rested on his shoulder. And wanting to trust him and forget about everything else.

She looked up and saw the dark, harsh, scarred face that had hovered over her in her nightmares for weeks and that had more latterly kissed her in her dreams and made her yearn for tenderness and love. She bit her lip again as his face swam before her vision.

"It does matter," he said. "Fleur, it has never been my intention to make you my mistress. What has happened here between us has happened unexpectedly and against my wishes. I am a married man and cannot establish any relationship at all with you. And if I were not married, it would certainly not be as my mistress that I would want you."

She drew blood from her lip again as he raised first one hand and then the other to his lips, his own eyes never leaving hers. And he released one of her hands in order to brush away a tear that had spilled over onto her cheek.

"I will do this for you," he said, "perhaps to atone in some small way for the harm I have done you. And then I will send you away, Fleur. If you must wait for your fortune, I will find you a good position in a home I never visit. I will set you free and never come after you. Perhaps in time you will believe me and trust me."

He released her hands and she covered her face with them, taking deep breaths to steady herself.

"I will have Jeremy escort you upstairs," he said, straightening up. "Rest in your room for this morning. I shall leave orders that you are not to be disturbed—by anyone. I shall take Pamela."

She got to her feet. "That will be unnecessary, your grace," she said. "I have lessons planned."

"Nevertheless," he said, "you will do as I say."

She straightened her shoulders, lifted her chin, and turned to the door. "It will be unnecessary to send Jeremy with me," she said. "I can find my own way, thank you."

He smiled fleetingly. "As you wish," he said.

And so she made her way upstairs alone and into her room. And she stood at the window staring out at the back lawn, deserted at that hour of the morning.

THE DUKE FULLY INTENDED to talk with Lord Brocklehurst without further delay, but a series of events conspired to frustrate his plans.

The doctor was with her grace, Jarvis told him when summoned to the library. His wife and her doctor must come first, then, his grace decided, dismissing the butler with the instruction to bring Dr. Hartley to him before he left.

A bad chill during the winter had left her grace with a weakness in the chest, the man gave as his opinion when he appeared in the library sometime later. Her health had always been delicate. It probably always would be.

"I would recommend a quieter life and less of the outdoors, your grace," he said. "Perhaps a month or two at Bath partaking of the waters would effect a significant improvement in her grace's health."

"She coughs constantly," the duke said. "She suffers from frequent fevers. She has lost weight. It is all the result of a severe chill that just did not go away?"

The doctor shrugged expressively. "There are certain ladies who have delicate constitutions, your grace," he said. "Unfortunately, your wife is one of them."

His grace dismissed the man and stood looking out through the window for a while. He should, he supposed, have insisted on sending for a more learned physician from London. But Sybil had always been adamant in her refusal to hear of any such thing.

He drummed his fingers on the windowsill and turned away. She had refused to admit him the night before. This time he did not wait after tapping at the door of her bedchamber. He let himself in, as he had early the evening before, when he had caught his brother almost in the act of making love to her.

He looked at her grace's maid, who curtsied and withdrew to the dressing room.

"Good morning, Sybil," he said. "Are you feeling any better?"

She had turned her head aside on the pillow at his entrance. She did not answer him.

He walked a little closer. "The fever still?" he asked, laying the backs of his fingers gently against one of her cheeks. "The doctor suggested Bath and a course of the waters. Would you like me to take you there?"

"I want nothing of you," she said. "I am leaving with Thomas."

"Shall I bring Pamela down for a few minutes?" he asked. "I am sure she is longing to tell you about Timothy Chamberlain's birthday party yesterday."

"I am too ill," she said.

"Are you?" He smoothed back her silver-blond hair from her face. "I shall entertain our guests for today, then. You must lie quietly here and not worry. The doctor has given you some new medicine? Perhaps you will feel better by tomorrow."

She said nothing, and he crossed the room to the door. But he paused with his hand on the knob and looked broodingly at her for a long moment.

"Would you like me to send Thomas?" he asked.

She neither turned her head toward him nor answered. He let himself quietly out of the room.

The ladies were on their way into Wollaston with Sir Hector

Chesterton and Lord Brocklehurst. His grace joined some of the gentlemen for billiards. Lord Mayberry, Mr. Treadwell, and Lord Thomas Kent had gone fishing.

After luncheon, when the duke suggested a ride and picnic at the ruins, most of the guests accepted with delight. Lord Brocklehurst, though, with Sir Hector, expressed his intention of remaining at the house, since he had been invited to call upon Sir Cecil Hayward later in the afternoon, whom they had met in Wollaston that morning.

Before leaving for the stables, his grace assigned the footman Jeremy to patrol the upper corridor outside the schoolroom and to escort Miss Hamilton and Lady Pamela wherever they might choose to go during the afternoon.

And he found himself half an hour later in the midst of an encounter that he had planned to postpone until the following day.

"It seems that you and I are doomed to ride together, Adam, since everyone else is paired off," Lord Thomas Kent said. "Perhaps it is as well. I shall probably be leaving tomorrow or the next day."

"Alone?" his grace asked.

His brother looked across at him and smiled. "I cannot think you were serious in the suggestion you made the other day," he said.

"I would not have made it if I had thought for one moment that you would take it seriously," the duke said, his eyes directed forward to where Sir Philip Shaw was flirting quite openly with Lady Underwood.

"There," Lord Thomas said. "You see what I mean? Of course I could not take it seriously, Adam. How could I take Sybil away, knowing what scandal she would be facing? She has lived a sheltered life and can have no conception of what would be in store for her. And of course, women are incurable romantics. They are never prepared for cold reality."

"I think you left her with a large dose of cold reality the last time," the duke said.

Lord Thomas shrugged. "Besides," he said, "she is unwell. I would not be at all surprised to find that she is consumptive."

His grace's lips tightened.

"And the child, of course, must be my primary concern," Lord Thomas said. "How could I take her from you and from this home, Adam? And how could I take Sybil and not the child? Sybil's heart would be broken."

The duke still said nothing.

"Yes," his brother said. "Of course I will leave alone. I really have no choice in the matter if I want to do the decent thing, do I?"

His grace turned his head and looked at him coldly.

"It is just rather a shame that we both fell in love with the same woman, that is all," Lord Thomas said. "We had a good relationship until Sybil entered the picture."

"Perhaps it is a shame that we both did *not* fall in love with her," his grace said. "I could have lived with her loss, knowing she was happy with you, Thomas. I would have recovered because I loved her. What you have succeeded in doing is destroying all her happiness and all my love. Yes, we did have a good relationship—once."

Lord Thomas continued to smile.

"I left a message that you were to go to her when you returned from fishing this morning," his grace said. "Did you go?"

"She is ill," Lord Thomas said. "I am sure she needed to be quiet."

"Yes," the duke said. "It seems hardly worth the effort of visiting her if she is not well enough to be bedded, I suppose."

His brother shrugged.

"I hope she finally realizes the truth about you," his grace said, "though she will not hear it from my lips. Perhaps after all the pain she will finally be free of you and be able to make something meaningful of her life. Hindsight is easy. I can see now that I should have insisted that she listen at the start."

Lord Thomas shrugged once more and spurred his horse ahead to ride beside Miss Woodward and Sir Ambrose Marvell.

Just before dinner that evening a note was delivered to the duke to explain that Lord Brocklehurst and Sir Hector Chesterton were to extend their visit with Sir Cecil Hayward to include dinner and an evening of cards.

And so one rather unpleasant day was almost behind him, his grace thought, though the main order of business would have to be postponed until the following morning. He left a message with Lord Brocklehurst's valet that his grace would be pleased if his lordship would join him for an early-morning ride the next day.

IT WAS VERY LATE. She should have been in bed long before, Fleur knew, especially since she would have to be up even before daylight. But she did not believe she would sleep anyway. She counted her money once more and cursed herself again for buying those silk stockings when they had been a pure extravagance.

She was not sure she had enough. She was not at all sure. But if there was just enough for the ticket, she would not worry about food. She could go without food for a few days. She had done it before.

She could, of course, try to borrow a small sum from Ned Driscoll. But she would probably never see him again to repay the debt, and perhaps she would never have the money with which to do so.

Besides, Ned was already making a sacrifice for her. He had agreed to take her in the gig before dawn into Wollaston to catch the stage. He had been very unwilling to do so, and she was quite sure that if she had offered him money—if she had had money to offer—he would have refused quite adamantly.

But she had had only her persuasive powers and her knowledge that he had a soft spot for her.

Perhaps he would be dismissed for helping her. But she could not think of that. She could not take yet one more burden on her mind. There was no other way of getting to Wollaston on time beyond stealing a horse. She had never stolen anything.

She looked again at the small bundle of clothing that she had tied inside her old gray cloak and wondered if taking the clothes she had bought with his grace's money in London was theft. But the thought of putting on the old silk dress and gray cloak made her shudder.

She was leaving Willoughby Hall. That much she had decided in the course of the day. She had felt rather like a bear chained to a post all day long—indeed, she had felt much the same for almost three months. She could take no more. If she stayed even one day longer she would lose a part of herself, of her innermost being, and when all was said and done, that was all that was left to her.

She was going to the only place she could go and maintain her pride and integrity. She was going home—to Heron House. By doing so, of course, she was only going to certain destruction. But there were some things worse, she had discovered in the course of three months, than the prospect of facing charges that she could not defend herself against. There were some things worse than the fear of the ultimate punishment.

If she were hanged, she would lose her life. If she remained as she was, she would lose herself.

He could help her, he had said. He would help her. As Matthew had done? He would save her from imprisonment and death in exchange for certain favors? He had denied it vehemently and she had believed him—almost.

But how could she believe him? How could he help her? And why would he wish to do so? To him she was only a whore whom he had pitied—perhaps. Or a whore he hoped to entice into a more lasting relationship.

She wanted to believe him. She wanted to trust him. But how could she? She had been alone for so long. Even Daniel, who was gentle and godly, would not have been able to help her in her predicament. He would have had a crisis of conscience if she had asked for his help after admitting to him that she had killed Hobson—even though it had been in self-defense.

She wanted so badly to believe him. She sat on the edge of her bed and closed her eyes. And she realized what had been happening to her over the past weeks. He had been turning—so gradually that she had scarcely noticed the transition—from her nightmare into her dream.

Because she had come to know him as a man worthy of respect, liking, and perhaps even . . . ? No. No.

Because he had planned it that way? Gradual seduction by patient steps, more skilled than Matthew?

She dropped her head forward until her chin rested on her chest. She did not know what to believe, but she did know that she must go away from him as much as she must go away for other reasons. He was a married man and perhaps an evil man.

She had an image of him standing in Mr. Chamberlain's garden, talking with Miss Chamberlain, Lady Pamela sitting up on his shoulder shrieking excitedly into his ear.

She had been his prisoner all day. Jeremy had been outside the library that morning and outside the schoolroom all afternoon. He had escorted her downstairs for dinner and back to her room after she had sat with Mrs. Laycock for a couple of hours.

Had she been his prisoner? Or had he been merely protecting her? Jeremy had told her that Matthew had come upstairs during the afternoon and had been very annoyed to be told that Miss Hamilton had been ordered by his grace to work with her pupil all afternoon without interruption.

But she had felt like a prisoner. Like a prey to both of them. Like a chained bear to their hounds.

She had to leave. She had to go home. Matthew would follow her there, of course, and they would play out the last scene of the drama that had begun almost three months before.

There was no mystery about the conclusion of that drama, of course. But she would no longer avoid it. She had to go back and somehow come to terms with what she had done and with what the consequences were to be.

Better to go back freely than to be taken back in fetters. And better to go back alone and independent than as Matthew's bride or mistress, her integrity forever gone.

She finally blew out the candle and lay down fully clothed on top of the covers of her bed. She stared up into the darkness.

19

$\mathcal{J}$T WAS RAINING AGAIN THE FOLLOWING MORN-
ing. That long warm, dry spell seemed to have deserted
them for good, the Duke of Ridgeway thought as he stood at
the library window looking out. It seemed that they must face
a more typical British summer than the spring had been.

Perhaps it was just as well that it rained. He had been able to
plan his talk with Lord Brocklehurst more carefully than he
would have done if the sun had shone. He strode restlessly to
the desk, gazed down at the unfinished letter lying on its sur-
face, and put it away in a drawer. There was no point in trying
to concentrate on writing.

She had not come down to practice in the music room that
morning. Just on the day when more than ever he needed the
soothing balm of music, she had not come.

And perhaps that was as well too. He was going to send her
away soon. In fact, that was the main topic of the letter he was
writing to the dowager Countess of Hamm, an old friend of his
father's. Once he had had his talk with Brocklehurst, he was
going to make other arrangements for her—unless by some
miracle her fortune could be released to her.

His left hand rubbed absently at an aching hip. He was
going to have to learn to live without her music. And without

the daily sight of her. He was going to have to find someone else who would be as good for Pamela as she was.

His hand opened and closed at his side. Perhaps Sybil would not object to his taking Pamela to London with him for a few weeks or months. He could not leave her again for another long spell—he had decided that at this last homecoming. But how would he be able to stand the loneliness and the constant aggravations of life at Willoughby?

Especially now that *she* had been there.

Several of the guests had expressed their intention the evening before of leaving within the next few days.

There was a tap at the door and Jeremy opened it to admit Lord Brocklehurst.

"I'm sorry about the ride," the duke said after the two of them had exchanged morning greetings. "Have a seat. Can I offer you a drink?" He glanced toward the half-open door leading to the music room.

"I have just had breakfast," Lord Brocklehurst said, sinking into the chair Fleur had occupied a few evenings before and waving a dismissive hand at the offer of a drink. "Devilish weather, Ridgeway. The ladies will be climbing the walls out of boredom. They love to stroll."

"They must do so in the gallery," his grace said. "I understand you are planning to deprive me of my governess, Brocklehurst."

The other's eyes became wary. He laughed. "Miss Hamilton is a very attractive lady," he said.

"It is my understanding that the two of you have an unofficial betrothal," the duke said. "You are a fortunate man."

Lord Brocklehurst was silent for a moment. "She has told you this?" he asked.

The duke took the chair opposite his companion's and smiled. "I hope I have not got her into trouble with you by speaking up," he said. "But I am sure she has not been announcing the news to everyone. She probably thought that as her employer I should be given some notice of her leaving. She will be going with you, I believe?"

Lord Brocklehurst relaxed back in his chair and returned the duke's smile. "I am not at all annoyed at her telling you," he said. "I wished to announce our betrothal officially here, but she has been reluctant. The fact that she is a servant has made her shy."

"Ah," the duke said, resting his elbows on the arms of the chair and steepling his fingers, "it is true, then. Congratulations are in order. When are the nuptials to be?"

"Thank you," Lord Brocklehurst said. "As soon as possible after we leave here. I hope you will not be too greatly inconvenienced, Ridgeway."

The duke shrugged. "Miss Bradshaw has given me a week's notice," he said.

The other nodded, and then his glance sharpened. "She has told you that she has been living here under an assumed name?" he said.

The duke inclined his head. "If the wedding is to be immediate," he said, "you must have decided not to press charges. Of course, when the charges are theft and murder, the decision is not a justice's to make. What you must have decided is that the death was not a murder and the removal of the jewels not a theft. Am I right?"

"What has Isabella been saying to you?" Lord Brocklehurst was sitting up in his chair and gripping the arms.

"Nothing at all," his grace said, crossing one booted leg over the other. "Not even anything about marrying you. I have another source of information."

Lord Brocklehurst was frowning. "What is going on here, pray?" he asked.

"It seems that I have employed a governess who is not who she claims to be," the duke said, "and who may or may not be a murderer and who may or may not be a thief. My daughter's safety and well-being are at stake. I wish to find out some facts from you, Brocklehurst, if I may. I need your assistance."

The other sat back in his chair again. "Perhaps I could have that drink after all," he said.

The duke got to his feet and crossed the room. "Is Miss Bradshaw a thief?" he asked.

"I don't know where you got your information," Lord Brocklehurst said, "but you probably know that some of my mother's jewels were found in a trunk that Isabella was about to take from the house. They were the more costly jewels, which my mother had not taken to London with her."

"Inside the trunk," the duke said. "How did she steal them? If they were so costly, were they not kept very carefully under lock and key? To whom did your mother entrust the key when she left?"

"To me, of course," the other said. "But Isabella has lived in the house all her life. She must have known where the jewels were kept. It is altogether possible that she had a key."

"There was more than one, then?"

Lord Brocklehurst shrugged.

"Was Miss Bradshaw with her trunk until the moment of discovery?" his grace asked.

"The trunk was opened and the jewels discovered after she had run away," Lord Brocklehurst said.

"And where was the trunk while she was speaking with you and after she ran away, before someone decided to open it?" the duke asked.

"It was in the gig she planned to take, and then taken back to her room," the other said.

"I see." His grace handed him his drink and took his seat again. He had not poured a glass for himself. "How many people would have had access to that trunk after Miss Bradshaw last saw it? Was it locked, by the way?"

Lord Brocklehurst was frowning again. "This sounds remarkably like an interrogation, Ridgeway," he said.

"My servants must be above reproach," his grace said, "my daughter's governess, in particular. Is there any possibility that the jewels might have been planted on her?"

"But who would have a motive for doing such a thing?" Lord Brocklehurst asked.

The duke rubbed his chin. "I see your point," he said. "But Miss Bradshaw herself had a motive, of course. You had refused to allow her to marry the local curate, I believe, and she was not to come into her fortune for at least another two years. She was eloping presumably without a penny to her name."

"Your source is well-informed," Lord Brocklehurst said.

"Yes," his grace agreed. "My sources usually are if I pay them any heed. Tell me about that death. Was it murder?"

"She was threatening to kill me," Lord Brocklehurst said. "She was beside herself with anger. Both my valet and I were concerned for her. He tried to prevent her from hurting herself, but she pushed him and killed him. He would not have fallen alone. I believe her action constitutes murder."

"There is no chance that she misunderstood?" his grace asked. "She was, I believe, alone in the house with you, apart from the servants. In that particular room she was alone with two men. Could she have believed that you meant her mischief?"

Lord Brocklehurst laughed. "Isabella has lived as one of my family since she was a child," he said. "She is like a daughter to my mother, like a sister to me. Except that she has come to mean more than a sister could. She has been aware of my regard for her for a long time and aware of my hope that she would be my bride. There was no chance of a misunderstanding. Unfortunately I am her guardian and had been forced on that day to the painful task of thwarting her will when it would have led her to unhappiness."

"I see," the duke said. "If she threatened to kill you, then, it would seem that the killing was premeditated, even though in the event she killed the wrong man. Yes, murder it is. You are quite right. A capital offense. Miss Bradshaw, it seems, is destined to hang."

Lord Brocklehurst took a sip of his drink and said nothing.

"You came here, presumably, to take her away to prison where she belongs," his grace said. "But one thing puzzles me. If she is a murderer and therefore a dangerous criminal, why did you not apprehend her as soon as you arrived, or at least take me aside to warn me of what a desperate fugitive I was harboring?"

Lord Brocklehurst set his drink down carefully on the table beside him. "I came as your brother's guest," he said. "There were other guests in residence. Naturally, Ridgeway, I did not wish to alarm everyone. I was hoping to take her away without any fuss or scandal at all."

"And in the meantime," his grace said, "she might have murdered my daughter and killed us all in our beds."

"I do not believe she is deranged," Lord Brocklehurst said.

"Only backed into a corner," his grace said, "knowing that you have found her and are merely biding your time. From my experience of hunting, Brocklehurst, I would have to say that a cornered animal is the most dangerous animal. Of course, you must really believe what you say. You must consider Miss Bradshaw a great deal less than dangerous if you are prepared to marry her despite all. Despite the fact that she threatened your life and then killed your valet."

"I have never had any intention of marrying her," Lord Brocklehurst said. "At least not since she has revealed herself for what she is."

The duke frowned. "Pardon me," he said. "Did I mishear you a few minutes ago?"

"I did not quite know what you knew or had discovered," Lord Brocklehurst said. "I thought it wise to agree with what you said until I knew what exactly you were trying to say to me. But how could I seriously consider marriage with a woman who would steal from my own mother and kill my man because she was in a passion with me?"

"How could you, indeed?" the duke said. "But do you not think a judge would consider the events of the past days and your admission of a few minutes ago rather strange, Brocklehurst? Do you not think that he might believe you have been offering Miss Bradshaw a deal—a change in your testimony in exchange for her favors?"

Lord Brocklehurst was on his feet. "That is a damnable suggestion, Ridgeway," he said. "When I tell the facts as they were, no judge or jury would hesitate to convict her."

"You will watch the hanging, of course," his grace said. "Will you enjoy watching the noose being slipped over her head and tightened beneath her ear? Will you enjoy seeing her take the final drop?"

Lord Brocklehurst's hands were in fists at his sides. "I loved her," he said. "I suppose I still do. Unfortunately, justice must be done."

"Oh, I hope so," the duke said, his eyes narrowing. "I shall certainly be testifying at the trial, Brocklehurst."

"I understand she is your mistress," the other said. "Once that fact has been established, I don't believe your testimony would be worth a great deal. So your concern is not, after all, for your daughter, Ridgeway, but for your personal comfort. I might have known it. And for her sake you are prepared to make up lies about my intentions toward her."

"Houghton," his grace said, scarcely raising his voice, "would you fetch me a brandy, my dear fellow? I am too lazy to get to my feet again."

Lord Brocklehurst merely stared as the duke's secretary appeared through the half-open door into the music room and proceeded to pour a drink for his employer.

"You made notes, I trust?" his grace said, taking his drink. "Though your memory is quite excellent even without."

"It is all written down, your grace," Peter Houghton said.

"Thank you," the duke said. "I shall not detain you, Houghton. You will wish to return to your chair."

His secretary disappeared from the room again.

"The rain makes for a thoroughly gloomy day," his grace said. "But in one way it has been a blessing in disguise. I do not know where I would have hidden a witness if we had taken that ride, Brocklehurst. Now, tampering with justice is, I believe, an offense. And that, of course, is an overly courteous way of saying that I know it is an offense. What are we going to do about it?"

"We?" Lord Brocklehurst seemed finally to have pulled himself together. "What are *we* going to do about it? Isabella is a murderer. I am taking her back for trial."

"Yes," the duke said, "I tend to agree that there is a case against her. She pushed a man and he died. It would appear to be murder. And jewels were found in her trunk. I think that indeed she must be taken back for trial, Brocklehurst. Not by you alone. I shall see that she is suitably accompanied. And I shall myself attend the trial. I shall ask to testify if I deem it necessary to do so."

"So you would tamper with justice too?" Lord Brocklehurst said, sneering for the first time. "You are trying to blackmail me, Ridgeway?"

"Not at all," his grace said. "I wish you to tell the absolute truth of what happened. But if the absolute truth is that Miss Bradshaw stole your mother's jewels and deliberately killed your valet, then I believe a judge and jury would be most interested in hearing the details of your coming here as a guest and spending some time socially with the woman you came to arrest. They would doubtless be interested to know that you planned to marry her 'as soon as possible.' I believe those were your exact words. Am I right, Houghton?"

There was a short pause. "Yes, your grace," Peter Houghton's voice said from the other side of the door to the music room.

"Miss Bradshaw will probably still hang," his grace said. "But nasty things might happen to you too, Brocklehurst. I am not sure what. I am not as knowledgeable about the law as I suppose I should be as a justice of the peace. Houghton could doubtless discover what your punishment is likely to be. He is quite invaluable as a, ah, source. Would you like him to find out for you?"

Lord Brocklehurst pursed his lips.

"Of course," the duke said, "the judge and jury might well acquit Miss Bradshaw on the assumption that the testimony of the only witness to the murder is thoroughly untrustworthy. Perhaps you would take the fall alone—an unfortunate choice of words. I am not at all sure that the penalty for your crime is death. Indeed, I would guess that it is not. Transportation, maybe? But then, I am only guessing. We will leave it to Houghton to find out."

"I shall be gone from here within the hour," Lord Brocklehurst said stiffly. "I shall not trouble you with my presence any further, Ridgeway."

"Without Miss Bradshaw?" his grace said. "Shall I see that she is brought to trial? Indeed, I believe I must. She has been accused of two capital crimes. For her own peace of mind she must be convicted or cleared. Or you must make some public statement explaining the error of your earlier accusations. You were, of course, distraught over her disobedience and the accidental death of your valet. One is prone to exaggerate under such circumstances. People will applaud your courage in making yourself look a little ridiculous in order to set matters straight."

"The statement will be made," Lord Brocklehurst said through his teeth.

"Splendid," his grace said, getting to his feet finally. He had not touched one drop of his brandy. "I shall look for an official notice of your statement within the next week or two. You are recording all this too, are you, Houghton?"

"Yes, your grace," the voice beyond the door said.

"After Miss Bradshaw's name has been cleared," his grace said, "I shall communicate with you again, Brocklehurst, to see what can be arranged for her comfort until her twenty-fifth birthday. But I need not detain you with a discussion of that point now. Good day to you. Have a pleasant journey. Do you go to Heron House?"

"I have not decided and do not feel it necessary to share my plans with you anyway, Ridgeway," Lord Brocklehurst said, making for the door.

"Ah, quite so," his grace said. He stood beside the chair and watched the other leave.

His shoulders visibly sagged when the door closed.

"Come in here, Houghton," he said. "Have you ever known a more slimy fellow?"

Peter Houghton, closing the music room door behind him as he entered the library, did not seem to think it necessary to reply.

"I was in fear and trembling," his grace said, "that he would see the obvious route out of all his difficulties. It was glaring him in the face so dazzlingly for a whole minute that I am amazed it did not blind him. You saw it too, I presume? Indeed, doubtless you saw it before I did."

"He might have explained that all his attempts to get Miss Hamil . . . er, Miss Bradshaw to marry him were a ruse to get her to go quietly to avoid scandal in the house," Houghton said. "Yes, your grace, I kept my eyes closed for all of half a minute waiting for him to see it. He will curse himself when he looks back and realizes how he could have wriggled out of your trap."

"Knowing you, Houghton," the duke said, "I would guess that the notes you made are beautifully written and meticulously organized. But go over them, if you please. I don't believe we will ever need them, but I want them to be ready if we do."

"Yes, your grace," Peter Houghton said.

"In the meanwhile," his grace said, smiling, "I believe I shall go upstairs to relieve a lady's mind of the heavy burden that has weighed it down for all of three months."

Peter Houghton did not reply as his master left the room, a spring actually in his step. Neither did he smile with amusement or sneer with scorn. He shook his head rather sadly. It was worse than he had thought. She was not his grace's ladybird after all. She was his love.

But his grace was an honorable man.

Houghton felt a deep pity for his employer.

FLEUR HAD JUST ENOUGH money to reach the market town twenty miles from Heron House. Twenty miles seemed a very long way still to go, especially with the weather chilly and unsettled. And a bundle that seemed heavier by the minute and an empty stomach did nothing to improve the prospect of a long walk.

But there was no alternative. She set out to walk the twenty miles. She was fortunate enough to be taken up by a farmer in an uncomfortable and foul-smelling cart for three or four miles. And all of seven miles from home she was recognized by another farmer driving a wagon and was taken right to the door of Heron House. She could only thank him most gratefully and hope that he was not expecting payment.

But then, she thought with a rueful smile as he turned his horses' heads and made off without delay, perhaps his payment would be in the excitement of being the one to break the news in the village that she was home.

The servants clearly did not know quite what to do when she was admitted to the house. She took a deep breath and decided to take the initiative.

"I am fatigued, Chapman," she told the butler, as if she had just come in from an afternoon's walk. "Have hot water for a bath sent to my room, if you please, and send Annie up to me."

"Yes, Miss Bradshaw," the butler said, looking at her rather as if she had two heads, Fleur thought. He spoke again as she turned away to climb the stairs. "Annie is not with us any longer, Miss Isabella."

"She is gone?" she said, turning back to him. "Lord Brocklehurst dismissed her?"

"She had an offer of a place in Norfolk at the house where her sister works, Miss Isabella," he said. "She was sorry to leave."

"Send me one of the other maids, then," Fleur said.

She had been looking forward to seeing Annie again, she thought, climbing the remaining stairs to her room and looking about at all the familiar objects—a part of her identity for so many years. It was almost a surprise to find that nothing had been removed from her room. Even the clothes that had been packed away in her trunk were back there. She need not have brought her new clothes from Willoughby Hall after all.

And she had wanted to talk with Annie, who had apparently been the one to discover the jewels in her trunk. Had the maid been alone when she found them? Had she gone running to Matthew with the news? Had Annie believed her guilty?

She would probably never be able to fill in those blanks in her knowledge now. Annie had gone to Norfolk. Fleur could not recall any mention of a sister in service there. It was probable that Matthew had dismissed her because she was Fleur's maid and no longer needed in the house.

It was strange to be back, to find everything so normal except that Cousin Caroline and Amelia and Matthew were from home. She had fled for her very life just three months before. And she supposed that soon she would be in fear of her life again. Someone would do something as soon as the shock of seeing her just walk back into her home had worn off. Someone would send for Matthew or do something else to detain her.

Matthew himself would doubtless come, once she was missed from Willoughby Hall. Indeed, perhaps he was not far behind her. Perhaps she would not have even the night to herself.

But she was in the only place she could be.

She bathed and washed her hair when water was brought, and put on one of her own dresses. She felt almost herself again as she brushed and styled her hair without the services of the maid who had been sent up to her.

She would not think of Matthew coming. She had a few things to do before he came. And she would not think at all of the recent past. She would not think of Lady Pamela and their days together. She would not think of the magnificent home she had come to think of almost as hers.

And she would not think of *him*. No, she would not.

But she thought of his dark hair and strong, harsh features, of the cruel scar that slashed across the left side of his face. She thought of his hands with their long, well-manicured fingers—hands that she had so feared because they had touched her impersonally and intimately and had held her steady for the infliction of pain and degradation. But the same hands had held hers warmly and cupped her face and wiped away her tears.

She would not think of him. Or if she must, she would remember him telling her to remove her clothes and sitting down to watch the show. Or bent over her, watching as he took her virginity. Or telling her that she was a whore and was enjoying what he did to her—but had he really said either of those things? Or had they been merely part of her nightmares?

She would not think of him. Or if she must, she would remember that he was a married man, that he had a beautiful wife and a daughter whom he dearly loved.

She would not think of him.

"Come in," she called when someone knocked on the door of her dressing room.

It was a maid to inform her that she had visitors belowstairs.

Well, she thought, getting to her feet and squaring her shoulders. It seemed that she was not to have even that one night of peace. It was beginning already. Perhaps coming home had been the most foolish thing she had done in her life.

But she had had to come. She had had no choice short of losing herself.

The butler opened the door into the visitors' salon for her and she stepped inside.

"Isabella!" Miriam Booth, small, rather plump, fair heavy hair in its usual rather untidy knot on top of her head, hurried toward her, both hands outstretched. "Oh, Isabella, my dear, we just heard that you were home."

Tears blurred Fleur's vision as she was enfolded in her friend's arms—but not before she had seen Daniel standing quietly before the fireplace, tall and blond and handsome in his black clerical garb.

"Miriam," she said, her voice quite breaking out of control. "Oh, how I have missed you."

20

THE DUKE OF RIDGEWAY KISSED HIS DAUGHTER and the puppy too when it was lifted up to him.

"No classes this morning, Pamela?" he asked. "Is it a holiday because it is raining, perhaps?"

She chuckled. "I am going to tell Miss Hamilton to take me down to the long gallery to skip with the ropes again," she said, "and to look at the dark lady in the picture who is like me."

"Try asking," his grace suggested. "You are more likely to get what you want."

"Miss Hamilton must have had a very late night," Mrs. Clement said disapprovingly. "She has not appeared from her room yet this morning, your grace."

He frowned. "And no one had been to wake her?" he asked.

"I tapped on her door half an hour ago, your grace," she said. "But it is not my job to wake the governess."

"Do so now as a favor to me, if you will, Nanny," he said. "Pamela, is Tiny supposed to be dragging that blanket across the floor?"

His daughter chuckled again. "Nanny said she could because it is old," she said. "Look, Papa." And she pulled at one end of the blanket while the puppy tugged and strained at the other, growling with excitement. Lady Pamela giggled.

Mrs. Clement came bustling back into the nursery a couple

of minutes later. "Miss Hamilton is not in her room, your grace," she said. "And the bed is made up, though I know no maid has been in there this morning."

The duke glanced at the window and the rain beyond. "She must have been delayed belowstairs," he said.

There was consternation in the kitchen a few minutes later when the duke himself strode in from the direction of the servants' stairs. Mrs. Laycock, he was informed, was busy with the household accounts in the office beside her sitting room.

"But Miss Hamilton was not down for breakfast this morning, your grace," she said in answer to his question. She had stood on his entrance. "I assumed she was eating in the nursery with Lady Pamela. She does so sometimes."

"Come with me, Mrs. Laycock, if you will," the duke said, and led the way up the servants' stairs to the *piano nobile* and on up to the nursery floor.

He knocked at Fleur's door before opening it and stepping inside.

"No chambermaid has been in here this morning?" he asked.

"I very much doubt it, your grace," the housekeeper said.

There were no combs on the dressing table. No hairpins or perfumes or any of the paraphernalia that always cluttered his wife's dressing room. He crossed the room to the wardrobe and opened the door. There was a new jade-green velvet riding habit hanging inside, and a faded and crumpled blue silk gown. He touched the latter briefly.

"She has gone," he said.

"Gone, your grace?" Mrs. Laycock opened a drawer of the dressing table. It was empty. "Where would she have gone? And why?"

"Foolish woman," the duke said, closing the door of the wardrobe and standing facing it. "Where has she gone? That is a good question. And how did she leave here? By foot? It would take her almost all night to reach Wollaston."

"But why would she leave?" Mrs. Laycock was frowning in thought. "She seemed happy here, your grace, and is very well liked."

"Go back downstairs, Mrs. Laycock, if you please," his grace said. "Find out what you can from the servants. Anything at all. I shall go to the stables to question the grooms."

"Yes, your grace." She looked at him strangely and left the room.

None of the grooms knew anything. The foolish woman must have walked, the duke thought. And he wondered when during the night the rain had started. And he wondered where she was going. To London to lose herself again? It might be harder to find her this time. She would doubtless stay away from employment agencies—and from fashionable theaters too.

And he wondered if Houghton had paid her at all yet.

"Driscoll," he said, turning to one of the youngest of his grooms, "ride down to the lodge, if you please. I want to know if and when Miss Hamilton passed the gates."

"Yes, your grace," the groom said, but he hovered where he was instead of rushing into immediate action.

The duke looked steadily at him.

"May I speak with you, your grace?"

The duke strode out into the stableyard, heedless of the rain. Ned Driscoll followed him.

"I took Miss Hamilton into Wollaston this morning before first light, your grace, in the gig," he said. He added irrelevantly, "She got wet."

"For what purpose?" his grace asked.

The groom was twisting his cap nervously in his hands. "To catch the stage, your grace," he said.

The duke looked at him steadily. "On whose orders did you take the gig?" he asked.

Ned Driscoll did not answer.

"Why did you lie to me a few minutes ago?" the duke asked. Again there was no answer.

"One or more of the other grooms must have known that you were gone," the duke said.

"Yes, your grace."

"So he or they lied too."

Ned Driscoll was watching his cap turning in his hands.

"You must have expected to be found out," the duke said. "You must expect dismissal."

"Yes, your grace."

"Did she pay you?"

"No, your grace." The groom's tone was indignant.

The duke looked at his young groom, standing with feet firmly planted on the cobbles of the stableyard, his eyes downcast, his cap turning and turning in his hands, his wet hair plastered to his head, his shirt clinging to his shoulders and chest. He remembered a certain morning when the same groom had stood outside the paddock laughing at Fleur and openly admiring her as she tickled the puppy with one toe.

"I will want my traveling carriage ready before the doors in one hour's time," he said. "You may inform Shipley to be ready to take the ribbons. You will accompany him. We will probably be away for several days. You will need to pack a bag."

"Yes, your grace." Ned Driscoll looked up at him with wary eyes. His cap had fallen from his hands.

"If we have lost her beyond trace," his grace said coldly before turning away, "I shall beat you to a pulp on the road, Driscoll, and tie you upright to the box beside Shipley for the return journey."

His wife had got up that morning and appeared to be feeling considerably better, the duke thought with some relief as he strode back to the house. He would feel guilty about leaving her if she were still indisposed. She was in the morning room, playing cards.

"Sybil, a word with you, if you please?" he said after standing behind her chair until the hand that was being played had been finished.

"Jessica will sit in for you," Mr. Penny said. "Jessica?"

The duke led his wife from the room and in the direction of her sitting room.

"I have to leave for a few days," he said, "on unexpected business. Are you feeling well enough to entertain alone?"

"If you will remember," she said, "I invited my guests when you were from home and not expected back, Adam. I have learned to be alone and not expect help from you."

"I hope to be back within a week," he said.

"Don't hurry," she said. "The guests are all leaving soon. Indeed, Lord Brocklehurst has been called away and must leave today. I shall probably be gone myself by the time you return, Adam. I shall be leaving with Thomas."

He opened the door into her sitting room and followed her inside.

"When I return," he said, "I shall take you and Pamela to Bath for a few weeks. The waters and the change of air will do you good, and Pamela will enjoy something different. Perhaps we can start again, Sybil, and make something at least workable of our marriage."

"I am going to be happy," she said. "Before you return, Adam, I am going to be happy and I am going to stay so for the rest of my life."

"Sybil." He took her by the shoulders and looked down into her upturned face—lovely, fragile, and youthful. "I wish I could save you from pain. I wish I could go back and do everything very differently. He will not take you with him."

She smiled at him. "We will see," she said.

He squeezed her shoulders and left the room. He should not be going, perhaps. He should send Houghton after Fleur and remain with his wife. She was going to need someone within the next few days.

But he was the very last person she would need. When Thomas left, she would hate him with a renewed intensity. He would probably never be able to establish anything resembling peace between them.

He took the stairs two at a time to say good-bye to Pamela and assure her that he would not be gone for long. Even so, he left her in tears after she had pounded his chest with her fists and told him she hated him and did not care if he went away forever.

"I want Miss Hamilton," she said petulantly.

And he could not even assure her that he would bring Fleur back with him. Whatever happened, he would not be able to do that.

He left Willoughby before Lord Brocklehurst.

At the stagecoach stop in Wollaston he discovered that Fleur had taken a ticket to a market town in Wiltshire—probably not far from Heron House, he guessed. At least she had not gone to London.

But in all the guesses he had made over the past few hours, he had clung most firmly to the conviction that it would be to Heron House that she would have gone. If he had found no trace of her he would have gambled on going there. She had fled once—with terrible consequences. She would not do so again. Not Fleur. He believed that he was beginning to understand her quite well.

The foolish woman.

Did she still trust him so little? Did she still believe that his intention was to make her his mistress? Did she not realize what superhuman control he had had to impose on himself that night in the library to send her to bed alone? When he had wanted her so badly and when he had known that she would have been easily seducible?

He could have had her that night. He could have had that memory.

He turned his attention to the rain and mist and clouds beyond the window. Before the carriage traveled even one mile farther, he must be clear in his mind about why he was making this journey. He was doing so in order to inform an innocent young woman that she could stop living with nightmares, that she was free. He was going in order to arrange some interim future for her until she came into her fortune and could live independently.

He was going because she was, or had been, his employee, his dependent, and he cared for all his servants.

He was not going because he loved her.

Although he did.

"WHERE HAVE YOU BEEN? We have been so very worried about you. But how wonderful to see you again." Miriam Booth set her hands on her friend's shoulders and stood back from her.

Fleur laughed shakily and drew a handkerchief from a pocket to blow her nose. "I was frightened and foolish," she said. "But it feels good to be back."

She glanced across the room to the silent figure of the Reverend Daniel Booth.

"Why did you not come to me, Isabella?" he asked.

"I was frightened," she said. "I had killed Hobson."

"But it was an accident, surely," he said. "You did not mean to kill him, did you?"

"Of course she did not mean to kill him," Miriam said, putting a protective arm about her taller friend's shoulders. "That was always the most ridiculous idea I have ever heard. It was an accident. They were trying to stop you from coming to stay with me, weren't they, Isabella?"

"Yes," Fleur said. She closed her eyes briefly and opened them to look at the Reverend Booth.

"But by fleeing, you made yourself look guilty of murder," he said. "I wish you had come to me."

"You would have helped me?" she asked.

"It is my job to help people in trouble," he said gravely. "In your case, Isabella, it would have been more than my job."

"Oh," she said. "I did not know. I thought you would have called me murderer and turned me over to Matthew."

"The only sin you are guilty of, I believe, is uncontrolled passion," the Reverend Booth said. "That is not quite murder."

"Uncontrolled passion!" Miriam said scornfully. "What was she supposed to do, Daniel? It was most improper of Lord Brocklehurst to expect Isabella to stay in the house alone with him. If he had tried to detain me under such circumstances, I would probably have taken an ax to both him and his valet."

"Miriam!" her brother said reproachfully.

"I did not steal any jewels," Fleur said. "I did not even know I was accused of such a thing until Matthew told me so a couple of weeks ago. Do you believe me, Daniel?" She took a few steps toward him.

"Of course I believe you if you say so," he said gently.

"Well, I believe you even without your saying so," Miriam said hotly. "The very idea! You have seen Lord Brocklehurst, Isabella? And escaped from him again?"

"It is a long story," Fleur said. She covered her face loosely with her hands. "Oh, how good it is to be with friends again and not have to hide the truth. I had to come back to see where it all happened again, to try to fill in some gaps of memory, to ask a few questions."

Miriam patted her reassuringly on the back. "We will help you in any way we can," she said. "We have been longing to do just that. Haven't we, Daniel?"

"I'll tell you everything," Fleur said. She looked up again at the Reverend Booth. "Will you do something for me first?"

"What is it?" he asked.

"I have to go back into the library," she said. "I have to see where it happened. I am afraid to go in alone."

Miriam's arm came about her shoulders again. But the Reverend Booth had moved. He was beside her, his arm extended for hers. She slipped her own gratefully through it and looked up into his unsmiling face.

"You are to be greatly commended for your willingness to face your past," he said. "Lean on me, Isabella. I will help you."

The library was, of course, just the library, as it had always been. Nothing was different. There was no blood on the hearth, no signs of a struggle, no ghosts lingering behind the curtains or among the books. Just the library, a room of which she had always been fond.

It was there she had stood, she thought, abandoning the arms of both her friends, forgetting their very presence, a few feet in front of the fire, facing Matthew in anger and accusing him of being a gothic guardian who had done everything but lock her up in order to curtail her freedom.

And Matthew had been telling her that she would not demean herself by living with Miriam Booth and that she would not marry Daniel Booth by special license or elopement or any other means. She would not be leaving the house. She would be staying there, where she belonged.

Through her fury she had gradually seen and understood the look on his face. And she had understood what he meant when he said that no other man would ever want her by the time she next left the house.

Matthew had been troublesome for a few years and she had come thoroughly to dislike him for his unwanted attentions. But she had never been afraid of him. She had never been afraid for her virtue.

But the circumstances, she supposed, had inflamed him. Apart from the servants, he had her alone in the house. She had seen in his face that he had meant to have her—that night and in that very room.

And she had understood that it was no momentary decision on his part. It was unlike him to have his valet with him in a downstairs room. She had wondered why Hobson was there, pretending to be busy with something at the far side of the room. But she had understood finally.

And fear had mingled with her fury. She had seen the look

Matthew had directed at Hobson and had felt rather than heard the man come up behind her. She had known exactly what was about to happen to her.

She still could not recall the rest, even staring as she was at the place where it had all happened. Just someone screaming and flailing her arms. And Hobson lying on the floor, his head sliding from the corner of the hearth, his face ashen, his eyes staring upward. And Matthew leaning over him, kneeling beside him. And looking up at her.

"I hope you are satisfied, Isabella," he had said in a queer, tight voice. "You have murdered him."

And panicked flight. And the small measure of reason somewhere at the back of her mind that told her she could not go to Daniel or Miriam or to anyone she knew—because she was a fugitive from the law, a murderer who would be hanged if caught.

"It was not reason but the devil who counseled you so, Isabella," Daniel's quiet voice said from behind her, and she realized that she had spoken all her memories out loud.

"Oh, Isabella," Miriam said, her voice full of distress. "How you have suffered. And what a villain Lord Brocklehurst is. I always thought him guilty only of being a tyrant. He is the one who deserves to hang. No, Daniel, I mean it. Every word of it. And then he put the jewels in Isabella's trunk just in case the murder charge was not quite enough."

The Reverend Booth offered his arm and they returned to the salon. Fleur wished he were not quite so proper in his behavior. She needed badly to be held in his arms, to rest her head on his shoulder. But it was a pointless thought anyway. Even if he did not believe her guilty of murder and theft, there was that other thing now to set her forever apart from him.

There was no point in loving Daniel any longer.

She told them everything, omitting only the way she had met the Duke of Ridgeway and the real reason for Peter Houghton's being at Miss Fleming's employment agency.

"So I came home," she said when she had come to the end of her story. "I suppose Matthew will be here tomorrow, or perhaps even later tonight. I suppose I will be in prison somewhere by this time tomorrow."

"Nonsense," Miriam said briskly. "But you must come to the rectory for tonight, Isabella. You will be safer there."

Fleur shook her head. "No," she said. "I am staying here. But I will come tomorrow morning. I want to see Hobson's grave. I must see it. Was his funeral well-attended, Daniel?"

"It was not held here," he said. "His body was sent away to the town where he was born."

Fleur frowned. "But where?" she said. "Oh, I must find out. I must see his grave. I don't think I will quite be able to accept the reality of it all until I do. I did not mean him harm, you know. I was terrified, and I suppose I wanted to hurt him so that I could get away. But I never wanted him dead." She closed her eyes. "Can you find out where he was taken, Daniel?"

"I don't know how," he said. "I think it best if you stay away from there anyway, Isabella. If he has family members there and they see you and find out who you are, they will suffer greatly."

She looked down at the hands in her lap.

Miriam patted them briskly. "Enough for tonight," she said. "You must be exhausted, poor Isabella. And if you will not come to the rectory, then we will come back here as soon as possible in the morning to help you face Lord Brocklehurst when he arrives."

The Reverend Booth got to his feet. "That sounds like the best plan," he said, "if you are sure you will not come with us. Sleep well, and try not to worry. I will speak myself in court if I must, and give you a good character." He lifted one of her hands to his lips. "Good night, Isabella."

"Good night, Daniel," she said.

Miriam kissed her and hugged her.

For the first night in a long while, Fleur slept soundly, undisturbed by either dreams or nightmares.

THE DUKE OF RIDGEWAY put up at the village inn for the night. He could have journeyed on to Heron House, but it would have been close to midnight by the time he arrived there, and he decided to wait until the morning. She was in no great danger. He knew he was ahead of Lord Brocklehurst, even if that gentleman had decided to return to his home.

Besides, he did not think that Brocklehurst would try anything too foolish as far as Fleur Hamilton was concerned. Fleur Bradshaw. Isabella Fleur Bradshaw.

Fleur.

It was almost the middle of the next morning when his carriage took him along the winding, wooded driveway to the neat Palladian mansion that was Heron House. It was flanked by an orangery and greenhouses at the one side, stables at the other. There were colorful formal gardens set out before it. The sun was trying to break through the clouds as the carriage drew to a stop before the marble steps leading to the main doors.

"Miss Bradshaw, if you please," he told the butler, handing him his hat and cane.

"Miss Bradshaw is in London with Lady Brocklehurst, I'm afraid, sir," the butler said, inclining his head.

"Miss Isabella Bradshaw," his grace said.

"And who may I say is calling?" the man asked.

"You may not," the duke said curtly. "Show me to the room where she is, please."

Something in the duke's manner caused the man to turn and lead the way to his left along a tiled hallway to a room at the front of the house. She must have heard his approach, then, the duke thought. She must have seen his arrival.

He walked past the butler into a square room that was obviously a morning room. Sunlight was slanting through its long windows. The clouds must have parted finally, he thought irrelevantly.

She was standing in front of a chair from which she must have just risen, across the room from the door. She stood very straight, her chin high, her hands clasped loosely before her. She was wearing a pretty sprigged-muslin dress. Her hair was styled in soft curls and ringlets.

She looked more beautiful than he had ever seen her, his grace thought, even as his eyes took in the pallor of her face, the firm set of her jaw.

And then her expression changed and the tension almost visibly disappeared from her face and body.

"I thought you were Matthew," she said. "I thought that was Matthew's carriage. I thought he had come."

He took one step toward her, thinking that she was about to faint. But instead she moaned and hurtled across the room and straight into the arms he reached out for her.

"Oh, I thought you were Matthew," she said as his arms closed about her softness and his nostrils were filled with the sweet fragrance of her hair. "I thought you were Matthew."

"No," he murmured against her ear. "It's just me, love. He is not going to hurt you anymore. No one is going to hurt you anymore."

She looked up at him, her eyes dazed, and her fingertips touched the scar along his cheek. "I thought I would never see you again," she whispered.

He swallowed as he watched her eyes fill with tears.

"I am here," he said. "Can you not feel my arms about you? I have you safe, love."

And he lowered his head and opened his mouth over hers.

And heard her moan again.

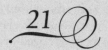

21

IT HAD BEEN A FRUSTRATING MORNING. FLEUR had woken up with renewed energy and hope after a good night's sleep. The rain had stopped, although the sun was still covered with clouds. And she remembered the visit of the evening before and smiled at the knowledge that she still had friends.

But there must be so little time, she told herself as she went downstairs for an early breakfast. Matthew would surely be home at any time. He must guess that she would have returned to Heron House rather than to London. Or would he? Perhaps it would seem to him that she had fled again, hoping never to be found. London would be the obvious destination if that were the case. Perhaps he would pursue her there.

Unless he had the sense to call at the stagecoach office, of course, to find out where her ticket had taken her.

Annie was gone. That was an annoyance. There were all sorts of questions concerning the jewels that she would have liked to ask her former maid. But there was no time to brood on regrets.

"Chapman," she asked the butler at breakfast, "where was Hobson's body taken for burial?" She flushed at the necessity of speaking so openly on a topic that must have the servants' quarters abuzz.

"I don't rightly know, Miss Isabella," he said.

"Then will you send me someone who does," she said.

"I'm not sure that anyone knows," he said.

Chapman had never been the most garrulous of souls.

"Someone must have taken him there," she said. "And perhaps someone went to attend the funeral. One of his friends? Lord Brocklehurst himself?"

"His lordship, yes, miss," he said. "Flynn drove the carriage. He is with his lordship now."

"The body would have gone separately," she said. "By wagon, I suppose. Who drove that?"

"Yardley, miss," the butler said.

"Then send Yardley to me, if you please," Fleur said.

"He is gone, Miss Isabella," he said. "Into Yorkshire, I believe it was. He took a new position there."

"I see," she said. "I suppose if I were to ask to speak with the person who laid out Hobson's body and placed it in the coffin, that person would also be gone."

"Yardley did those things, miss," he said, "with his lordship. His lordship was quite broken up over what had happened."

Fleur set her napkin on the table. She had lost her appetite.

In the stables it was the same story. No one knew where Hobson had been taken for burial. Yardley had taken him. And Flynn had taken his lordship the following day. No one remembered Hobson's ever saying where he came from.

Finally she went back to the house and into the morning room, which had always been her favorite. Cousin Caroline had never liked it because the direct sunlight gave her the headache, she claimed. And Amelia was rarely up in the mornings. So it had always seemed like her own room, Fleur thought, wandering to the window and looking out at the neat squares of flowers and low clipped hedges of the formal gardens.

There seemed to be nothing she could find out. What was more frustrating, she did not know what there was to find out.

She knew almost the whole of it. She had killed Hobson—accidentally. Matthew had had his body taken back to his own home for burial. Matthew had also planted Cousin Caroline's jewels in her trunk and made sure that someone else discovered them there. Even if she could talk with Annie, there was really nothing she could do to prove that she had not put them there herself.

Perhaps she was foolish after all not to have fled to London when she had had the chance. The servants had a way of looking at her as if they rather expected to glance down and find that she was swinging an ax from one hand. When Matthew came, it would all begin. Or rather, it would all come to an end. And despite Daniel's and Miriam's protestations of the night before, she doubted that anyone or anything could save her. She was quite unable to prove her innocence.

But, no. She could not do any more running. She was where she had to be.

The quiet resignation of the thought did not last more than a moment. A carriage had appeared through the trees of the driveway in the distance—a carriage approaching the house.

Her hands turned cold suddenly and she could feel her heart pounding painfully against her ribs and in her ears. Her face turned cold. There was a dull buzzing in her ears.

She turned from the window and sat down on the edge of a chair, her hands clasped tightly in her lap, her back straight. She concentrated on not fainting.

And she concentrated on calming herself. She had five minutes at the longest. He must find her quite calm. He must not find her cringing and pleading.

And she must not—even if he were still prepared to offer it—accept any sort of proposal from him. She must not. *Please, God*, she prayed silently, *give me the strength not to lose my integrity or myself. Please, God.*

She did not get up again or look out of the window even when the sounds of horses and carriage wheels drew close.

She straightened her shoulders, lifted her chin, and concentrated on breathing slowly and deeply.

She rose to her feet when the door opened and he stepped past Chapman and into the room.

It took her a few moments to realize that he was not Matthew. At first her eyes would not relay the message to her brain. And then she felt all the breath shudder out of her.

"I thought you were Matthew," she said. "I thought that was Matthew's carriage. I thought he had come."

But he was not Matthew. He was everything that Matthew was not. He was safety and comfort and warmth. He was home. He was everything in the world that was hope and sunshine. He took a step toward her and opened his arms to her, and she was in those arms without ever knowing how the distance between them had closed.

"Oh, I thought you were Matthew," she said, feeling his arms close warmly about her, feeling the powerful muscles of his thighs against hers, the broad firmness of his chest against her breasts. Smelling that cologne fragrance that was peculiarly his. "I thought you were Matthew."

His breath was warm against her ear. "No," he said. "It's just me, love."

She touched his shoulders, felt strength and firmness there as he murmured comforting words. And she looked up into the dark, harsh face that she had thought never to see again, that she had been trying not to think of at all. She reached up a hand to touch his scar, so familiar to her eyes.

"I thought I would never see you again," she said. The wonder of it was there to her sight, in her fingertips, in her body, in her nostrils. The wonder of it. Not yet in her brain. Only in her senses. And deeper than her senses. His face blurred before her eyes.

"I am here," he said.

She watched his mouth as he spoke, listened to the deep tone of his voice, looked up into his dark eyes, and closed her own.

And she was suddenly safe and beyond safety. Enveloped in warmth and strength. She opened her mouth for more of it. And felt an ache of longing spiral down into her throat and into her breasts and stab down into her womb and between her thighs.

She kept her eyes closed and threw back her head as his mouth moved from hers and trailed warm kisses along her throat. He held back her shoulders with strong hands.

"You are safe, my love," he said against her ear. "No one is ever going to hurt you again."

My love. *My love.* He was the Duke of Ridgeway. At Heron House. He had come after her all the way from Willoughby Hall.

She pushed away from him, turned her back on him, crossed the room to one of the windows. There was a silence.

"I'm sorry." His voice came from across the room. He had not come up behind her, as she had half-expected. "I did not mean for that to happen."

"What did you mean to happen?" she asked. "What are you doing here? I did not steal anything from your house except perhaps the clothes I bought in London with your money. You may have them if you wish."

"Fleur," he said quietly.

"My name is Isabella," she said. "Isabella Bradshaw. Only my parents ever called me the other. You are not my father."

"Why did you run away?" he asked. "Did you not trust me?"

"No," she said, turning to look at him. He was her customer of the Bull and Horn Inn, she told herself deliberately. She looked down to his hands, which she had always so feared. "Why should I have trusted you? And I did not run away. I stopped running. I came home. This is where I was born, you know. In this very house. This is where I belong."

"Yes," he said. "I see you in your own proper milieu at last. You are waiting for your cousin to come home? You are waiting for the worst?"

"That is not your concern," she said. "Why did you come? I will not go back with you."

"No," he said. "I will not take you back, Fleur. You do not belong in my daughter's schoolroom and I will not take you into any of my homes ever again."

She turned away to a side table and began to rearrange the flowers in a bowl that stood there. She quelled the quite unreasonable twinge of hurt.

"Or try to establish you in any other home, if that is your fear," he said. "I came to set you free, Fleur."

"I have never been in thrall to you," she said. "For all the money you have given me, I have rendered suitable services. The clothes you may take with you when you leave. I do not need to be set free. I have never been bound to you."

He took a step toward her, but there was another tap on the door, and she froze as it opened.

"The Reverend and Miss Booth are here to speak with you, Miss Isabella," the butler said, his eyes going briefly to the duke.

"Show them in, please," she said, feeling a great surging of relief. And she hurried across the room to hug Miriam and to smile at Daniel.

The duke had strolled across to stand at the window she had earlier vacated.

"Miriam, Daniel," she said, "may I present his grace, the Duke of Ridgeway? My friends Miriam Booth and the Reverend Daniel Booth, your grace."

The men both bowed. Miriam curtsied. They all exchanged curious glances.

"His grace has come to assure himself that I arrived home safely," Fleur said. "Now that he has done so, he is about to leave."

"He is about to do no such thing," his grace said, clasping his hands behind him. "There was no grand reunion a moment ago. Do I take it that the three of you have met before, since Miss Bradshaw's return?"

"We were here last evening," the Reverend Booth said, stepping forward. "Miss Bradshaw is among those who care for her again, your grace. We will look after her. You need have no further concern about her."

The duke inclined his head. "You will be pleased for her sake, then," he said, "to know that Lord Brocklehurst will be making a public statement within the next few days to the effect that the death of his valet was accidental, with no question of murder at all, and that the whole alarm over the misplacement of certain jewels was a false alarm. There was, in fact, no theft at all."

Fleur's hands were in the tight clasp of her smiling friend.

"If the statement is not made," the duke continued, "though I believe there is no realistic chance that it will not be, then there will be a trial in which Miss Bradshaw will most certainly be acquitted and numerous serious grounds for bringing Lord Brocklehurst himself to trial will arise."

Miriam's arms were about Fleur, and she was laughing. "I knew it," she said. "I knew the whole thing was quite ridiculous. Isabella, my dear, you are like a block of ice."

"I hope you are not raising Miss Bradshaw's hopes without good cause, your grace," the Reverend Booth said.

"I would not do anything so cruel," the duke said. Fleur looked at him. "I had a long talk with Brocklehurst and got enough of the truth out of him that he will not wish to pursue the course he was taking, I believe. And there was a witness to our talk, whose presence he was unaware of through most of it."

"Matthew has admitted the truth?" Fleur said.

"To all intents and purposes," his grace said. "I don't believe you have anything more to fear from him, Fl . . . Miss Bradshaw."

She put her hands up over her face and listened to Miriam's bright laughter. She was aware of Daniel crossing the room to shake the duke by the hand.

"What a wonderful morning this is," Miriam was saying. "I felt guilty about closing the school, but now I am very glad I did so." Her voice seemed very far away.

"She needs to sit down," another voice was saying, and strong hands were taking her by the arms and lowering her to a chair. And one of those hands cupped the back of her head and forced it down close to her knees. "It's all over, Fleur. I told you you were safe."

THE DUKE OF RIDGEWAY liked Miriam Booth. She appeared to be just the sort of friend Fleur needed. She was sensible, practical, cheerful, affectionate. Once Fleur had recovered from her partial fainting spell, Miriam took her off to her room for a while, despite her protests.

He was not so sure he liked Daniel Booth. The man was blond and handsome, quiet and gentle. Yes, all the qualities to make women fall in love with him. Combined with his clerical garb, they might well be irresistible to most women, his grace conceded.

And he cared about Fleur. As soon as the women had left the room, he asked detailed and perceptive questions until the whole story was told.

"Such a man ought not to be the social leader of a community," he said. "He ought to be prosecuted. Unfortunately, to do so would be to cause Isabella further stress. One must accept the arrangement you have made as satisfactory, I suppose."

"Those are my conclusions too," his grace said. "Personally I would like to take the man apart limb from limb and bone from bone, but that, again, would not be in Miss Bradshaw's best interests."

The Reverend Booth looked at him with very direct eyes, which seemed to see through to his soul.

"Miss Bradshaw ought not to remain here," the duke said,

"though I am quite sure she is in no danger from her cousin. It would not be appropriate for a lady of her rank to return to my home as my daughter's governess. I plan to find Brocklehurst and persuade him to release a sizable allowance to her until she gains control of all her fortune at the age of twenty-five. Failing that, I shall try to place her with an older lady as a companion."

Again those eyes looked into his soul and saw everything.

"I believe you have done more than an employer is called upon to do for those dependent upon him," the Reverend Booth said. "Isabella has been fortunate. But she is among friends again now. My sister and I have discussed plans for her future. Now that we know she will not be going to trial, we can present those plans to her for her approval."

And one of those plans involved the curate's marrying Fleur, his grace thought. And perhaps she would marry him, too, if she could somehow get past a certain event that had taken place in her life in London. And perhaps it would be the very best thing that could happen to her. She had been going to marry the man before the death of Brocklehurst's valet had changed everything. She probably loved him, and he appeared to care for her.

The duke was not at all sure he liked Daniel Booth.

He should take his leave. There really was no further reason for staying, especially if her friends were willing to help her settle somewhere other than Heron House. He should wait until she reappeared, say a formal good-bye to her, and then begin his journey home.

He could be back at Willoughby less than a week after leaving. Back with Pamela. Back perhaps before Thomas left, in time to offer Sybil some sort of support in the agony she would suffer when he did so. Not that she would allow him near her, of course.

He should go back and try to begin the process of forgetting. It must be done soon. Why defer it?

And yet he accepted an invitation to luncheon and retold his story to an almost silent Fleur and a brightly curious Miss Booth. Fleur looked not nearly as relieved or excited as she should have looked. But of course, the stress of months had only just been lifted from her shoulders. It must be difficult to adjust her mind to the knowledge that it was over, that she was free.

And of course it was not over. The scars would remain for a long time. And one fact would remain with her for a lifetime. He met her eyes across the table as Miriam talked, and saw doubt there and pain. And he wanted to reach out a hand to her and ask her what it was, how he might help her.

But he could not help her. He returned his eyes to his plate. When all the events of the past months had been sorted through, it would be obvious to her that he was the only person who had done her permanent harm. Perhaps the thought had already struck her.

He should take his leave immediately after luncheon.

"So you will take the cottage that used to be Miss Galen's, Isabella?" Miriam Booth was saying. "And help me at the school, as we originally planned? That will be splendid for a while, will it not? Until other arrangements can be made, that is. Perhaps under the circumstances Lord Brocklehurst can be persuaded to consent to . . ." She smiled. "Well, perhaps he will not act quite the tyrant he has always been."

"I will have to think, Miriam," Fleur said. "Yes, I think that would be a good idea. I always did love Miss Galen's cottage. All those roses!"

"Can't you see that Isabella's mind is in a spin, Miriam?" the Reverend Booth asked quietly. "She needs time to think about her future. I have to return to the village. This is my afternoon for visiting the sick. Are you coming with me?"

Miriam pushed her chair back and got to her feet. "Yes," she said. "Unless you would like me to stay with you, Isabella?"

Fleur shook her head and smiled.

The Reverend Booth too got to his feet and looked inquiringly at the duke.

"I will begin my journey home this afternoon, then," his grace said. "Would you care for a stroll in the garden first, Miss Bradshaw?"

"Yes," she said without looking at him.

The Reverend Booth looked full at him, and the duke knew that he did not like the man at all.

"IT WAS GOOD OF YOU to come," Fleur said, "and to do what you have done. Thank you, your grace."

They were strolling side by side in the formal gardens, not touching. They had seen the Reverend Booth and Miriam on their way back to the village.

"You are not happy," he said. "What is it?"

"Of course I am happy," she said. "How could I not be? For several months I have lived with the conviction that I would hang sooner or later. It is not a pleasant prospect. One finds oneself wondering about all the morbid details. And I returned here yesterday to find everyone looking at me as if I were a murderer and a thief. It will be something to have my name cleared."

"Yes," he said, and walked beside her in silence for a while. "What is it?"

She did not answer for a long while. "I came here to try to come to terms with what happened," she said finally, "or perhaps to look for some evidence to prove my innocence. It seems that I do not need that evidence any longer. But there are so many unanswered questions. And I have come up against a brick wall here."

"Explain," he said.

"My maid has gone to other employment," she said. "She is the one who discovered the jewels. I wanted to know where the jewels were. Were they carefully hidden, or were they on top? If I were the thief, I would have to be dreadfully stupid to lay them on top, wouldn't I?"

"Was your trunk locked?" he asked.

"No, of course not," she said. "I was going only as far as the rectory."

"And it was left in an untended gig outside the house?" he asked.

"Yes," she said. "Yes, of course. I would have had to be very foolish to leave costly jewels in just such a way. I would surely have smuggled them out some other way or hidden them on my person. But I don't know what the pieces were or how large they were. Anyway, Annie is gone and I cannot ask her any questions."

"An annoyance," he said. "I will have her found if it is important to you."

"Mr. Houghton?" she said, smiling fleetingly. "No, that is not the main frustration. The worst thing is that I cannot find Hobson."

"The valet?" he said. "He is not six feet beneath the church-yard?"

"He was taken to his own home for burial," she said. "But no one seems to know where that is. The groom who took the coffin there has since gone to Yorkshire, and the coachman who drove Matthew there is still with him. It was Yardley, the man now in Yorkshire, who helped Matthew lay out the body and seal it in the coffin."

"Was it, indeed?" he said.

"Somehow it is important to me to see his grave," she said. "You see, I did not murder him, but I did kill him. Had I not been hysterical and pushed him, he would not have fallen and he would not have died. I killed him. I was the instrument of his death. Somehow I have to learn to live with that on my conscience. I have to come to terms with it. I have to see his grave."

"You cannot shift the burden from your shoulders by

telling yourself that the man brought his fate on himself and that your cousin was also responsible?" he said. "You cannot tell yourself that you were in no way to blame at all?"

"Yes," she said. "With my head I can. But the knowledge that I pushed him and that he died will always be with me. I know it is foolish. I will not detain you, your grace. You must be eager to be on your way and have as much daylight as possible for your journey."

"There must be someone who knows where the valet came from," his grace said. "Did he have friends among the servants? In the village?"

"I don't know," she said.

"Then we must find out," he said. "I must try to emulate my secretary and discover all there is to be discovered. I shall ask around in the village. Will you question the servants again?"

"I have spoken with most of them already," she said. "They know nothing, and it has to be remembered that they are Matthew's servants, not mine. Besides, this is none of your concern, your grace. You wish to be on your way."

"Do I?" he said, stopping on the graveled path and taking both her hands in his. "I want to see you happy, Fleur, and completely free. I can't leave you until I know that you are both."

"But why?" she asked, looking wide-eyed into his eyes.

"You know very well why," he said fiercely, squeezing her hands until they hurt before turning to stride in the direction of the stables.

She ran to catch up to him. "Because of what you did to me?" she said. "But I was standing outside the theater for that very purpose. If it had not been you, it would have been someone else. Perhaps not that night. But the night after."

He stopped suddenly and took her hands once again. "Thank God it was me," he said, his eyes burning into hers. "If it had to be anyone, then thank God it was me." He released her hands. "I shall return early in the morning," he said. "I hope I will be able to bring you some information."

He strode away again, and this time she did not follow. She stood looking after him.

And there was one thought uppermost in her mind. There was to be a reprieve of one day. Tomorrow he would say good-bye and would be gone forever. But not today. Not quite yet.

Tomorrow.

22

*W*E ARE PLEASED TO SEE YOU BACK HOME, MISS, if you will pardon me for saying so." The little maid who had been sent to take Annie's place was hanging up in the wardrobe the muslin day dress Fleur had just removed. Her manner was suddenly confidential. "As Ted Jackson said, you could not be guilty of those things you are supposed to be guilty of if you have come back of your own accord. Not that most of us thought you were guilty anyway, miss."

Fleur came out of a deep reverie. "Thank you, Mollie," she said. "It is kind of you to say so."

Mollie's voice lowered and became even more confidential, though the door of Fleur's dressing room was firmly closed and no other servant probably anywhere near it. "And if you was to ask me, miss," she said, "I would say that Mr. Hobson got no more than he deserved. I never did like him. He always thought he was God's gift to women."

Hobson had been a handsome man in his own way. Mollie could not be described as a pretty girl, by any stretch of the imagination. Fleur guessed that the maid had been spurned by him at some time.

"He expected favors for nothing in return," Mollie said, confirming her suspicions. "But I never would listen to his sweet talk, miss, though he tried it on me more than once."

"Did he?" Fleur had spent another frustrating two hours since the Duke of Ridgeway had left, questioning the servants. She was tired, and she wished she had said nothing to him. By now he would be on his way back to Dorsetshire and she would be able to start thinking about the rest of her life. As it was, he was coming back the next morning, and she was unable even to feel the full elation that his story should have brought her. "Did he ever talk about himself, Mollie?"

"All the time," the girl said. "It was his favorite subject, miss."

The words were spoken with such spite that Fleur smiled despite herself.

"His father made good over at Wroxford," Mollie said, "as a butcher, miss, and that was how Mr. Hobson was able to get such a grand position as gentleman's man. But for all that, he had no cause to put on such airs."

"So that is where he is from?" Fleur said. "Wroxford?"

"Oh!" Mollie's hand came across her mouth with a loud slap. "Mr. Chapman will kill me. He said we was to remember who was paying our wages and say nothing."

"To me?" Fleur said. "You were to say nothing to me?"

"On account of the fact that his lordship will be packing you off to jail as soon as he comes home, miss," Mollie said. "Though I don't think you deserve to go there. And nor do most of the others, miss. Mr. Chapman is going to kill me for sure."

"The butler will hear nothing from my lips, Mollie," Fleur said. "And I do thank you for telling me as much as you have. That is where Hobson is buried, then?"

"I suppose so, miss," Mollie said. "I don't rightly know or care. Wroxford is all of thirty miles away. I would not walk thirty yards to put flowers on his grave. I prefer Ted Jackson to him any day of the year, even if Ted is only an undergardener. Ted treats a girl as if she is special."

Fleur got to her feet and brushed at the skirt of her silk evening dress. She did not really know why she had changed, since she would be dining alone. But it did feel good to be a lady again, to be surrounded by all her own familiar possessions.

"I must go down to dinner," she said. "Thank you, Mollie. I will not need you later. You may have a free evening, unless someone else finds something for you to do belowstairs. Does Ted have a free evening too?" She smiled.

The girl grinned at her in conspiratorial manner. "That he does, miss," she said. She crossed the room ahead of Fleur, but hesitated when her hand was on the doorknob. She looked about the room as if she expected to see the butler and perhaps a few other servants hiding behind the furniture. "I was a particular friend of Annie's, miss. She looked after me, like, when I was new here."

"Yes?" Fleur looked at the girl's flushed cheeks.

"That night," Mollie said, "you had left a pair of gloves in your dressing room, miss. Annie ran down to the gig with them and put them inside your trunk, on top."

"Did she?" Fleur said.

"There was no jewels in there then," the girl continued, "but when Annie opened the trunk later, the jewels was there, on top of the gloves. And just when she opened the trunk, his lordship and Mr. Chapman came into your room without knocking. She told them what I have just told you, miss. The next day she was sent away. She was frightened, and she told me, but she said I had better not say anything. They had given her a lot of money."

"Had they?" Fleur said.

"Mr. Chapman will kill me if he finds out, miss," Mollie said.

"Well, he won't," Fleur said. "I believe that before many days have passed, Mollie, Lord Brocklehurst himself will make clear to everyone that the matter of the jewels was an entire misunderstanding. But even so, I am glad to have had some proof of the matter myself. Thank you. You are the bravest of the servants in this house, and I will not forget it."

Wroxford, she thought as she walked downstairs to dinner. Thirty miles away. And Mollie was right. Thirty yards would be too far to go to see Hobson's grave. Except that she had killed him, and no man, however bad, she believed, deserved death at another's hands. She must at least try to ease her conscience by kneeling at his grave.

Thirty miles. She would not be able to go there and back all within one day.

"BUT WROXFORD MUST BE thirty or thirty-five miles away," the Reverend Booth said. "I cannot at all understand your wish to go there, Isabella. All you will see there is a grave, and perhaps a headstone. Why travel thirty miles for that?"

It was quite early the following morning. Fleur had found herself unable to wait at home for someone to call upon her. She wanted to be on her way. She would not be able to rest or know any final peace of mind until she had been to Wroxford.

"When I ran away," she said, "it was as if I left behind an unfinished story. I have the feeling that nothing is ended despite what his grace said yesterday. And I think I will still have this feeling even after Matthew has made his statement. I was involved in a death and did not stay for the funeral. I think that is one reason for funerals, isn't it—to help those left behind accept the reality of the death."

"You are fortunate enough to have been granted a reprieve," the Reverend Booth said. "Why not put it all behind you, Isabella? Why not start fresh today, forget everything that has gone before?"

"After I have been to Wroxford I will," she said. "I have been thinking, Daniel, and I think Miriam's suggestion is the very best thing for me. I will be happy in Miss Galen's cottage and I will enjoy teaching at Miriam's school. I will begin a new life, but I must go to Wroxford first. I was hoping that you would come with me. Won't you?"

He had been standing behind his desk since his house-keeper had shown her into his study. He came around it now. "Go with you?" he said. "Have you lost all sense of propriety, Isabella? It is not even very proper for you to be here alone with me when Miriam is busy at the school. It would take us two days to go to Wroxford and back."

"Yes," she said. "I thought you would not wish to see me go alone."

"I don't." His tone was exasperated and he grasped her hands and squeezed them. "You must forget this madness. You are about to be released from one scandal. I don't want even the breath of another to smear your character. I want you to be my wife. Perhaps Lord Brocklehurst will consent now to our marrying. If not, then I want to continue with our earlier plan. I will marry you by special license. Will you, Isabella?"

Her eyes were on their clasped hands. "No, Daniel," she said. "That is out of the question now."

"Because of the scandal?" he said. "But that is all over now. It was not so long ago that you were pleased at the idea of marrying me. You told me that you loved me."

"I can't marry you, Daniel," she said. "Too much has happened."

He released her hands and turned away from her in order to shuffle a pile of papers on his desk. "I have been meaning to ask you about the Duke of Ridgeway," he said, "and the strange fact of his following you here after going to extraordinary lengths to clear you of the charges against you. What is it all about, Isabella?"

"He is a kind man who cares for his employees," she said. "I would say he is loved as well as respected by his servants."

"And by you?" he asked. "Do you love as well as respect him?" He had turned again. His blue eyes looked directly into hers.

"Of course not," she said. Her eyes wavered and held on his.

"And what are his feelings for you?" he asked. "He is a married man, is he not?"

"I have told you," Fleur said. "He is a caring employer. He takes his responsibilities seriously."

"He has nothing to do with your reluctance to marry me, then?" he asked.

She shook her head.

"I will say no more on the matter, then," he said a little stiffly. "But I am pleased that you are home and safe, Isabella. And I am pleased that you will be working with Miriam. She needs help and I know she values your friendship, as I do."

"Thank you," she said. She stood looking at him for a long moment. "Daniel, I would like to tell you the full truth."

"It is often as well," he said. "It is good to unburden the conscience."

"When I was in London," she said, "I was starving and I could find no employment at all. The time came when I had been two days without food."

He stood looking gravely at her.

"It seemed to me at the time," she said, "and I believe I was right, that I had three possible ways of surviving. I could beg or I could steal or I could . . ." She swallowed awkwardly. "Or I could offer my body for sale."

He did not help her. They stood in silence for a few moments.

"I sold my body," she said. "Once. I would have done so again and again if I had not been offered the governess's post that took me into Dorsetshire."

"You are a whore," he said very softly.

She covered her lips with one shaking hand and then lowered the hand again. "Present tense?" she said. "Is that something that is always present tense?"

"Isabella." He turned away and leaned both arms on the desk. "There must have been some alternative."

"Thieves in London are very well-trained from infancy," she said. "I don't believe I could have competed. Should I have died, Daniel? Should I have starved to death rather than become a whore?"

"Oh, dear God," he said. "Dear God."

And in the silence that followed, Fleur knew that his words had not been just an exclamation.

He lifted his head at last, though he did not turn around. "Are you sorry?" he asked. "Have you repented, Isabella?"

"Yes and no," she said steadily after a pause. "I am more sorry than I can say that it happened, Daniel, but I am not sorry that I did it. I know that I would do it again if it were my only means of survival. I suppose I am not the stuff that martyrs are made of."

His head dropped again. "But how can you expect God's forgiveness if you do not truly repent?" he said.

"I think perhaps God understands," she said. "If he does not, then I suppose I have a quarrel with him."

He said nothing for a long while.

"So you see," she said, "I cannot marry you or anyone else, Daniel. For though I am not sorry for what I did, I do know that I am a fallen woman, and I am prepared to live with the consequences of that fact. I am going to Wroxford. By the time I return, you will doubtless have decided whether I am worthy to work with Miriam in the school." She crossed the room quietly to the door.

His voice stopped her. "Isabella," he said, "don't go there. It is not fitting, a lady alone."

"But I am no real lady, am I?" she said. "Don't worry about me, Daniel. I will be back within a couple of days."

She let herself quietly out of the room and out of the house. She did not, as she had planned to do, walk along the village street to the school to call upon Miriam and the children. She untethered the horse that she had ridden from the house, mounted unassisted into the sidesaddle, and turned in the direction of home.

And she remembered her love for Daniel as if it were a thing of the distant past. A sweet memory that lingered in the mind but was incapable of being rekindled.

THE DUKE OF RIDGEWAY had left his carriage at the village inn and ridden over to Heron House. He did not have anything of value to report. The landlord of the inn and his customers had all known Hobson. None of them knew where he was from or where he had been taken for burial. One man had declared that he was from London, but a chorus of voices disagreed with some scorn. Hobson, it seemed, had not had a cockney accent.

The talk about the valet had led inevitably to talk about Fleur and her strange and unexpected return. No one, it seemed, believed her to be guilty. Hobson, his grace gathered, had been known as a nasty customer, and Brocklehurst himself was not highly regarded.

The announcement that would soon be made and the dropping of all charges against her would clearly only confirm what people already knew.

He wished he could have found the information Fleur wanted. He would have liked to do that, to know that she could go and see the grave and finally put behind her the nightmare of the past months. He would like to think back on her and know that she was at least at peace with herself and the world.

She was not at home, the butler at Heron House told him. And he did not know if she really was from home or if she had denied him. Either way, there was no real point in pressing the issue, he supposed. He had nothing to tell her and therefore no business seeing her. He should leave without further ado.

"Kindly tell Miss Bradshaw that I was unable to find the

information she wanted," he told the butler, deciding that he would not wait.

He would go to London. That was probably where Brocklehurst had gone. It should be an easy matter to track him down and make sure that he had not delayed in putting everything right. And he would try to see to it that some settlement was made on Fleur until her twenty-fifth birthday. He would also see Brocklehurst's coachman so that he could send back to her details of the location of Hobson's grave.

And then it would be home to Willoughby, Fleur Bradshaw set firmly out of his mind and out of his life. He would devote his energies to being a good father. And perhaps some sort of peaceful relationship could be established with Sybil. He would try, anyway.

His mind was made up. But all his resolutions wavered as he was riding away from the house and met Fleur at a bend in the driveway. She was wearing a black velvet riding habit and hat, a color which looked quite stunning against the vivid red-gold of her hair.

"Oh," she said, "you startled me."

"Good morning, Fleur," he said. "I have just been to call on you. I'm afraid I have no good news, but I hope to be able to send some to you. I am going to London and plan to talk with your cousin's coachman."

"It is Wroxford," she said. "My maid let it slip last night. Apparently all the servants have been instructed to keep their mouths shut around me."

"Wroxford?" he said. "Where is that?"

"About thirty miles away," she said. "Daniel says I am foolish to want to go there, and I suppose he is right. But I must go."

"Yes," he said, "I can understand that." He watched the skill with which she restrained her frisky horse and watched the animation in her face. So vivid and so beautiful—and so unlike the way she had looked when he first saw her. "He and Miss Booth are to go with you?"

"Oh, no," she said. "Miriam has her school. She already took a day off yesterday for me. And Daniel cannot come. It would be improper."

"But he would let you go alone?" he said. "Is not that far more improper?"

"But to be fair," she said, smiling, "he is not *letting* me do anything or stopping me from doing anything. He has no right."

"And you are going?" he said.

"Yes."

Her horse was snorting and tossing its head and pawing the ground, impatient to be on its way.

"Has he had a gallop this morning?" he asked.

"No," she said. "But I was about to give him one."

"Come along, then," he said, and he led the way through the beech trees that lined the driveway to open tree-dotted parkland. He looked back to Fleur, who had followed him. "Perhaps you can keep up this time, since you have had your choice of horse and I do not have Hannibal with me."

She smiled at him and gave her horse the signal it had been waiting for.

He should not have done it, the duke thought. He should not have grabbed for himself this one final half-hour of sheer pleasure with her. And sheer pleasure it was, as it had been the last time they rode together. Fleur Bradshaw, it seemed, came fully alive when on horseback. She laughed across at him as her horse overtook his own, and was smiling when he passed her again as they circled up behind the stables and the house.

He should have said good-bye to her when they were on the driveway, and continued on his way. On his way out of her life.

He should not even have come. He should have sent Houghton. He should not be feeding a forbidden love.

But he would never see her again. Soon he would be gone, and he would not think of her or pine for her. He had a life to get on with and other people whose happiness to look to even if he could not expect any great happiness for himself.

One final half-hour. Surely he could be excused for stealing that much for himself.

Fleur overtook him once more and gradually reduced her horse's speed and turned it in the direction of home.

"That should satisfy you," she said, leaning forward to pat her horse's neck.

The duke dismounted and handed his reins to a waiting groom. He stretched up his arms to lift Fleur to the ground, and waited while the groom led both horses away. His hands were still at her waist.

"You are leaving for Dorsetshire now?" she asked.

"London first," he said. "I have some business to do there before returning home."

"Yes," she said. "Will you give my love to Lady Pamela and tell her that I miss her?"

"Yes," he said. Her hands were on his arms. "Fleur."

She smiled at his neckcloth. "Good-bye," she said. "Thank you for coming."

I love you, he wanted to tell her. *I'll always love you, though I must leave you.*

"I'm coming to Wroxford with you," he said. "If we leave within the hour, we can probably reach there by tonight. To-morrow you can see what you wish to see and we can be back here by tomorrow night. I'll return to the village for my carriage."

"No," she said. She was looking full into his eyes, her own wide and startled. "We could not do that, your grace, you and I alone."

"And you cannot do it alone, either," he said. "There are such people as highwaymen out on our roads. And you must stop for meals and take a room for the night. It is out of the question for you to do those things alone."

She stared at him. Her hands were still on his arms, his at

her waist. "Why?" she almost whispered, leaning toward him. "You have a home and a wife and a daughter to go back to. Why delay on my account?"

"Fleur . . ." he said. But he stopped and broke eye contact with her. He looked over her head to the stables, where the groom who had taken their horses was trying to look engrossed in his task of removing her sidesaddle. "I am coming with you. Go and change and pack a bag. I shall be here in one hour's time or less."

She said nothing else, but watched him as he strode away from her, untethered his horse, and swung himself into the saddle.

"One hour," he said to her as he took his horse past her and turned its head for the driveway.

He had stolen half an hour and convinced himself that it was no serious sin against his responsibilities to his family and dependents.

Now he was stealing two days. He was not so sure he would be able to quiet his conscience this time.

Except that she needed him. For some reason that only she could understand fully, she needed to see the grave of the man she had accidentally killed. That grave was thirty miles away. She needed his escort.

And except that he loved her.

IT WAS A VERY comfortable carriage, Fleur thought, relaxing back against soft green cushions and noticing that the springs made a mockery of the rough roads over which they passed. What a difference from the journey she had made by the stage just a few days before.

And yet she was not relaxed, either. The Duke of Ridgeway sat beside her, both of them silent, just a small space separating their shoulders.

Why had he come? Why was he taking such an interest in

her affairs? And why had she let him come? She might have said no. She might have argued the point more vigorously.

"Why?" she asked, as she had more than an hour before outside the stables. "Why are you here in Wiltshire? Why are you taking me to Wroxford?"

He did not look at her, but out of the window. She thought for a while that he would not answer.

"You know that you did not murder your cousin's valet," he said, "that in large measure you are not responsible for his death. And yet you have to see your involvement with him to its conclusion. You have to make this journey, a thing that very few people except you would understand. I feel something similar with you."

She said nothing more for a while. She understood his answer. It made sense to her.

"I don't understand," she said at last. "I have never understood it, though in your case I find it particularly difficult to understand. The duchess is very beautiful. You have a daughter who thrives on your love and a home that must be one of the loveliest in all England. Why do men like you need women for casual and sordid relations? I don't understand."

He continued to look out of the window. "I can't answer for other men," he said, "only for myself. I will not say much about my marriage, Fleur, because I owe my wife privacy, if not myself. I will only say that it is a difficult and an unhappy marriage and has been from the start. Sometimes it is difficult not to feel certain cravings. But I was faithful to my marriage until that one occasion with you."

Fleur looked at his profile, at the scarred side of his face. Cravings? Did he not have a normal marriage?

"I don't know why it happened on that occasion," he said. "I had not planned it and you did nothing to entice me. You stood still and quiet in the shadows. I could not even see you clearly. Perhaps . . ." He stopped talking, and Fleur thought that he would not continue. But he did after a while. "Perhaps something in me recognized you. I don't know."

"Recognized?" The word came out as a whisper.

"My pearl beyond price," he said quietly.

Fleur watched him swallow.

"And then I was angry," he said, "because having made the decision to be unfaithful, I wanted a night of forgetfulness. I wanted to be able to blame you afterward. But you did nothing, only allowed me to use you. It was a dreadful experience for you, Fleur, and it was quite unpleasant for me. I got what I deserved, I suppose."

"Why did you send Mr. Houghton to find me?" she asked. "Was it just guilt?"

He turned and looked at her for the first time. "For a long time I told myself that that was the reason," he said. "I suppose that with my head I am still telling myself that. Don't probe any further, Fleur."

They stared at each other for a long while before she looked down at her hand, which was lying palm-down on the seat between them. No, she would probe no further. She did not want to know the truth. It was too strange, the fate that had brought them together, and too cruel.

She could feel his eyes on her hand too. And he set his own beside it, that beautiful long-fingered hand that had once terrified her and that still disturbed her and made her feel breathless. Their little fingers almost touched.

They sat like that, still and silent, for a long while before he moved his little finger to stroke lightly over hers. And she spread hers and bent it so that their two fingers twined together.

Their eyes watched their hands. They touched at only the one point. They said nothing.

23

THEY STOPPED FOR A MEAL THAT WAS NEITHER luncheon nor dinner, and continued on their way.

There was a strange ease between them, the Duke of Ridgeway thought. Strange because they had traveled for several hours in near-silence and had eaten their meal without a great deal of conversation. Strange because they were alone together after all that had passed between them. There should have been an awkwardness, an embarrassment, but there was not.

When they resumed their seats in the carriage and it drew out of the innyard onto the open road again, he took her hand in his and rested their clasped hands on the seat between them. She made no resistance. She curled her fingers around his hand.

He wished that they had three hundred miles to travel, not thirty. Or three thousand.

He could feel her eyes on him, but he did not turn his head. He wished, as he had wished at the start of their journey, that he had thought of sitting on the other side of her, his good profile facing her.

"How did it happen?" she asked him quietly.

"This?" he said, indicating his scar with his free hand. "I have very little memory of just what occurred. It was at the

Battle of Waterloo, of course. I was with the infantry. We were in square, holding a cavalry charge at bay. But it was very frightening for some of the younger boys—and for all of us, I suppose—to see cavalry charging at us and to have only bayonets and the other men forming the square as a defense. It is a good defense, almost impregnable, in fact, but it does not feel safe. A few of our men panicked and turned away together. I leapt forward to try to hearten them and make sure that the square was not broken, and got caught on the face by a bayonet."

Fleur grimaced.

"Not even an enemy's," he said, smiling. "Ironic, is it not? I believe I can recall the sharp pain and my hand coming away all red from my face. That is the last I remember. A shell must have hit at that moment and caused the other wounds."

"You were almost a year recovering," she said. "You must have suffered a great deal."

"I believe so," he said. "Mercifully, I seem to have been somewhat out of my head during the worst of it. It was hard, though, to adjust my mind to the knowledge that I would carry around the visible effects of what happened for the rest of my life."

"The wounds still hurt sometimes?" she said.

"Not often." He smiled at her again.

"I have seen you limping," she said.

"When I am tired or under some stress," he said. "That is when Sidney, my man, plays tyrant and orders me to submit myself to a massage. He has a most impertinent tongue and magic hands."

She smiled at him. "Why did you go?" she asked. "If you were a duke, it would have been most unusual for you to be a part of the army, especially as an infantry officer. Did you not have a happy childhood?"

"Quite the contrary," he said. "I was privileged and happy and sheltered. No human being is entitled to enjoy such a life without paying back a little. There were thousands of men fighting for our country who really owed it almost nothing except their birth. And yet to them it was worth fighting for. The least I could do was fight alongside them."

"Tell me about your childhood," she said.

He smiled. "That is a large question," he said. "Do you want to hear about what a good little boy I was or about what a rogue I could be? Unfortunately, I sometimes drove my father to distraction. And the footmen. One poor fellow who lived in terror of ghosts and devils found two in the grand hall. Two named Adam and Thomas, who inhabited the gallery and made strange noises when he was on duty during the evenings. They haunted him for three whole weeks before they were finally caught. I can still feel the walloping I had for that. I believe I had to lie facedown on my bed for at least a couple of hours afterward."

She laughed.

"It was a wonderful childhood," he said. "We were Greek gods among the temples and Vikings on the lake and bear hunters by the cascades. Our father used to spend a great deal of time with us, teaching us to fish and to shoot and ride. My stepmother taught me how to play the pianoforte, though I do not have your talent. And she taught us to dance. There was always a great deal of laughter during those lessons. She used to accuse us both of having two left feet."

"And yet you dance so well now," Fleur said.

"I wish Pamela's childhood could be as happy," he said. "I wish there could have been other children. I always wanted a large family."

He realized what he had said when she looked inquiringly at him.

"I will devote myself to her happiness when I go home," he said. "I'll stay with her. I'll not leave her again."

He closed his eyes and braced one booted foot against the seat opposite. It was late afternoon. The drowsy hour.

He had never voiced that dream before—the dream of sons of his own, and daughters too, running free at Willoughby, their shouts and laughter bringing the place alive again. It was not fair to Pamela that she be so alone.

His children and Fleur's. They would take them riding and picnicking and boating. And fishing too. He would teach Fleur to fish. And she would teach the children to play the pianoforte, and herself play for their entertainment some evenings. And together they would teach their children to dance. They would teach them to waltz.

And he would love her by night. He would sleep with her all night and every night in the large canopied bed that had been his father's before him and that had never held a woman since his father's death. And he would fill her with his seed. He would watch her grow with his children. And he would watch those children being born and watch her giving birth to them.

He had paid his dues for a life of incredible privilege and for a childhood of wonderful security. He would be happy again and happy forever. He would open the oyster shell and find the pearl within.

He opened his eyes and became aware of his surroundings when her head touched his shoulder. She was breathing deeply and evenly. He turned his head very slowly so as not to wake her and rested his cheek against her soft curls. And he breathed in the scent of her. Their hands were still clasped together.

He closed his eyes again.

WROXFORD WAS NOT QUITE a town. It was a large village. Darkness had begun to fall when they arrived there, and the churchyard was quite large. It was altogether possible that they had just missed finding the correct tombstone in the half-light, the Duke of Ridgeway reassured her after they had searched without success. Or perhaps there was no tombstone yet. They should ask at the vicarage.

But the vicar was from home, at the bedside of a sick parishioner, his wife explained. She had no knowledge of such a grave. There were Hobsons in the churchyard, yes, but the last to be buried there must be old Bessie Hobson, all of seven or eight years before. Certainly there had been none buried there in the past six months. There had been only one funeral in that time, and that had certainly not been a Hobson.

"This man was valet to Lord Brocklehurst of Heron House," the duke explained. "His father was a butcher here at one time, I understand."

The vicar's wife nodded. "That would be Mr. Maurice Hobson, sir," she said. "He lives on the hill now." She pointed to the east. "A redbrick house, sir, with roses in the front garden."

"How strange," Fleur said as they turned away, the vicar's wife standing politely on the doorstep to see them on their way. "Mollie was quite sure it was Wroxford, and it seems to be the right place. His father does live here. But he was not buried here? I must speak with Mr. Hobson. It is not too late, is it?"

"I'm afraid so," he said. "We will put up at the inn for tonight and I will call on Mr. Hobson in the morning. Alone, Fleur. I don't think it advisable for you to meet him."

"But I cannot expect you to do that for me," she said.

"I will do it nevertheless," he said, handing her back into his carriage. "And for tonight you are Miss Kent, my sister."

"Yes," she said. "Thank you. But what can it mean? Matthew did not have Daniel bury Hobson because he wanted to bring him home. But this is home, and the burial was not here."

"I am sure there is a perfectly good explanation," he said, taking her hand in his again. "I shall discover what it is tomorrow. Are you hungry? And don't say no. I am, and I hate eating alone."

"A little," she said. She smiled quickly at him. "Oh, not very.

But what can be the meaning of it? Have we come all this way for nothing? Is this business never to have an ending?"

"Tomorrow," he said. "For the rest of this evening you are going to sit and watch me eat, and eat a little yourself, and tell me all about your early childhood. I entertained you this afternoon before we both fell asleep. Now it is your turn."

"There is not much to tell," she said. "My parents died when I was eight. I cannot remember a great deal."

"More than you think, I will wager," he said. "Here we are. I hope this inn offers somewhat better accommodation than the one in your village. And better food too."

They were given small rooms next to each other. There was nothing fancy about either one, but the inn did boast a private parlor, which the duke engaged for the evening. There were about a dozen men in the public taproom.

She should feel embarrassed, Fleur thought. She was alone during the darkness of the evening with the Duke of Ridgeway. They were to sleep in adjoining rooms in a village inn. They had been alone together all day, their hands clasped for most of the time. And she had woken up at some time late in the afternoon with her head on his shoulder.

She had removed it carefully, hoping that he was asleep too and would not know. But he had been quietly looking out of the window. Her hand had still been in his. And he had turned his head to smile at her. She had smiled back a little shamefaced but not nearly as confused as she might have expected to be.

It was almost as if, she thought, when they had left Heron House they had also left behind them the world and normal life and normal propriety. Almost as if they had made a tacit and mutual agreement to live these two days as if they were the only two days left in life.

And in a way they were. By the next night they would be back at Heron House. The morning after, he would leave and she would never see or hear from him again.

Two days seemed very little time.

No, there was no time for embarrassment or awkwardness between them. There was only the rest of that evening and the next day.

They sat a long time over their dinner. And she discovered that he had been quite right. When she started talking about her childhood, she found that she remembered incidents and feelings she had not thought of for years.

"I suppose," she said at last, "that I should be thankful for those eight years. Many children do not have even that long a time of love and security. I have been in the habit of thinking that I had a rather hard lot. It does me good to remember."

"Fleur," he said, his dark eyes smiling at her, "you *have* had a hard lot. But you are a strong person, a survivor. I hope that one day you will find a happiness you have never even dreamed possible."

"I will settle for contentment," she said. And she told him her plans.

"The children will be fortunate," he said. "I know you are a good teacher and care for children, Fleur. And I would guess that Miss Booth is well-liked too. And what about the Reverened Daniel Booth?"

"What about him?" she asked warily.

"You were to marry him," he said. "You loved him, didn't you?"

"I thought I did," she said. "He was kind to me at a time when I did not know much kindness. And he is a handsome man."

"You don't love him now?" he asked.

"I think he is too good for me," she said. "He can see a clear distinction between right and wrong, and he will stick by what he believes to be right no matter what. I can see too many shades of gray. I would not make a good clergyman's wife."

"Has he asked you again?"

"Yes," she said. "I said no." She hesitated. "I told him everything. Except your name."

"Yes," he said, "you would tell him. And he did not repeat his offer?"

"I had already refused," she said.

"He cannot love you, Fleur," he said. "He is not worthy of you. If I were in his place, I would fight for the rest of a lifetime to get you to change your mind. And I would honor you the more for your courage and your honesty."

She repositioned the spoon in her saucer. "A clergyman is not worthy of a whore?" she said. "Are we living in a topsy-turvy world?"

"Did he call you that?" he asked.

"Yes, he did use the word." She took her hands away from the spoon and clasped them in her lap. "It is the simple truth, is it not?"

"It is a good thing he is thirty miles away," he said. "My fists itch to rearrange the features on his face." He slammed his napkin down onto the table and got to his feet. "I could kill him, the sanctimonious fool."

"I should have added," she said, "that he said the word more in horror and pain than in condemnation."

He moved around the table and leaned over her, one hand braced on the table. "Fleur," he said, "don't ever let yourself be dragged down by that label. Promise me you won't."

"I have accepted the fact that I did the only thing it seemed possible to do at the time," she said, looking up into his eyes. "It is in the past. Like your scars with you, it will always be with me and it will always affect my life. But I will not let it destroy me."

"I would double my own scars and live with them," he said, "if only I could remove yours from you, Fleur." His eyes burned down into hers.

"Don't." She reached up one hand and cupped his scarred cheek with her hand. "Don't, please. What happened was not your fault. None of it was. And I think that everything that happens in life happens for a purpose. We become stronger people if we are not destroyed by the troubles of life."

"Fleur." He held her hand against his cheek. "And is there a purpose to this too? To you and me and to the fact that we must never see each other again after tomorrow?"

She bit her lip.

He straightened up and released her hand. "I am going for a walk," he said. "Come. I will see you to your room first. It has been a long and an eventful day. Tomorrow we will find what you have come to see, I promise you."

She preceded him up the stairs and turned the key in the lock of her door. He was standing at quite a distance from her when she looked up.

"Good night, Fleur," he said.

"Good night, your grace."

"Adam," he said. "Say it. I want to hear you say it."

"Adam," she whispered. "Good night, Adam."

And he was gone, his booted feet heavy on the stairs even before she had closed and locked her door behind her.

THE DUKE OF RIDGEWAY walked back from the red house on the hill the following morning, deep in thought. Had Brocklehurst been that obsessed with her? It seemed that he must have been if he had gone to such extraordinary lengths to get her within his power.

And yet he had been content to net her, knowing very well that she neither liked nor respected him and could never love him. There were some strange men in the world.

There was something not at all normal about Brocklehurst.

Unless he had misinterpreted events entirely, the duke thought. But what other possible explanation could there be?

Fleur was in the private parlor at the inn, where he had left her after an early breakfast. He had persuaded her, with some difficulty, to allow him to go alone to Mr. Hobson's house.

"Well?" She stopped moving as he opened the door, and gazed tensely at him.

"It seems that the burial took place at Taunton," he said. "It is about twenty miles from here, forty from Heron House. Mr. Hobson has been there and seen the grave. There is a tombstone there now."

She stared at him. "At Taunton?" she said. "But why?"

"It seems that Hobson was killed close to there," he said, "when he and Brocklehurst were returning from London. Brocklehurst buried him there before traveling on here to break the news to the family."

Fleur stared at him. "I don't understand," she said. "It was at Heron House that he died."

"Of course," the duke said.

"The only reason he was not buried there was that his family was here," she said.

"Yes."

She frowned at him.

"We will go to Taunton and see this thing through," he said. "Are you ready to leave?"

She continued to frown at him. The truth, or what must clearly be the truth, had not yet dawned on her. And perhaps it was as well. Perhaps it was not, after all, the truth. He would say nothing of his suspicions to her.

"Yes," she said.

Fifteen minutes later they were on their way.

"This makes no sense," she said. "Taunton is not even on the direct route to Wroxford."

She reached out her hand for his without even realizing what she was doing, he guessed. He took it in his and rested it on his thigh.

"Relax and enjoy the journey," he said. "We will ask questions when we get to the end of it."

"We will not get home today," she said. "Your journey will be delayed for another day."

"Yes," he said. And he raised her hand to his lips before returning it to his thigh. He looked into her eyes.

"I'm sorry," she said.

"I'm not."

She caught her lower lip between her teeth.

"What shall we talk about today?" he said. "School? Tell me about yours. It was not a happy experience, was it?"

"Oh, in some ways," she said. "I learned to love books while I was there and to love music even more than I had before. I learned to live with my imagination. It can add a wonderful dimension to life."

"Yes," he said. "It can make a dreary life seem bright, can't it?"

They smiled at each other before she talked on.

TAUNTON WAS A VERY small village. There was nothing there beyond the church and a few houses, one shop, and a small tavern. His grace had pointed out a decent posting inn on one main road a few miles back. They would stay the night there, he had said.

But Fleur did not take a great deal of notice. They were close, and she was leaning forward in her seat. Her heart was thumping.

And this time there was no missing it. It was there and new and large and proclaimed its legend for all to see: John Hobson, Beloved son of John and Martha Hobson, 1791–1822. RIP.

God. Oh, God. Fleur stood beside it, turned to stone herself. She had killed him. He had been thirty-one years old. He had been someone's beloved son. Martha Hobson had borne him. John Hobson had watched the son named after him grow up.

They both must have felt pride when he became valet to Lord Brocklehurst of Heron House. They would have boasted of him to their friends. And now he was dead and cold beneath the ground.

She had killed him.

"Oh, God," she said, and she went down on one knee beside the grave and touched the cold headstone.

"Fleur." There was a light hand on her shoulder. "I am going to the vicarage for a moment. I will be back."

But she did not hear him. Hobson was lying in the ground beneath her, that large and powerful and handsome man. He was dead. She had killed him.

She did not know how long she knelt there. Finally two strong hands took her by the arms and helped her to her feet.

"I'll take you back to that inn," he said. "You can rest there."

They were inside the carriage again, without her having any memory of having walked there.

"I didn't know it would be like this," she said. "At first I did not think a great deal about him. I was too concerned about myself. I did not even have many nightmares. And then I thought that perhaps he had deserved what happened, though I was sorry. And in the last week I have known that I must come here, must see his last resting place. But I did not know it would be like this." Her hands were over her face.

"You will be able to lie down and rest soon," he said. His arms were about her. One hand had loosened the strings of her bonnet and tossed it aside. He had her head cradled on his shoulder, his fingers smoothing through her hair. He was murmuring to her.

"I didn't want him to die," she said. "I didn't mean to kill him."

He secured two rooms for them at the posting inn, rooms far larger and better-appointed than those they had occupied the night before. There was a private parlor between them.

"I want you to lie down for an hour," he said, leading her

into one of the bedchambers, taking her by the arms, and seating her on the bed. "We will have a late dinner together. I want you to sleep."

She obeyed the pressure of his hands and lay back against the pillows. He removed her shoes for her. She felt numb, still not quite in touch with reality.

"You will want to remove your dress, perhaps, when I have left," he said.

"Yes."

"I have a few calls to make," he said. "I will be back."

"Yes," she said. It did not occur to her to wonder on whom he would be paying calls in a part of the country that was quite strange to him. She closed her eyes.

And felt his lips touch hers briefly before he left the room.

She must have slept, she thought. It felt as if she had been gone for a very long time, though she was still wearing her dress, she saw, and he was standing over her as he had been when she had closed her eyes. And indeed there was a candle burning in the room, and darkness beyond the windows.

"I thought you would have given me up for lost long ago," he said. "I thought you would have eaten and sent my dinner away cold already. Have you been sleeping all this time?"

She looked at him, dazed. The right side of his mouth was curved into a smile. His dark eyes sparkled down into hers. She was lying on an inn bed, she thought, the Duke of Ridgeway standing over her.

"I have some good news for you," he said. "You had better not stand up until you have heard what it is. Or even sit up, for that matter."

"Good news?" she said.

"You have not killed anyone," he said. "By deliberate intent or by accident or by any other means. You did not kill Hobson. The man is still alive somewhere, doubtless with a great deal of Brocklehurst's money in his pockets."

She stared up at him, at the strange bizarre dream that had just walked into her sleep.

"The only thing that is buried in the cemetery here," he said, "is a coffin filled with stones. It seems that our man was merely stunned by the hearthstone, Fleur. You are quite, quite free, my love—free of the noose and free of your conscience."

24

THEY DINED VERY LATE. THE DUKE HAD NOT expected to be gone quite so long, and Fleur had not expected to sleep so deeply.

"I really did not expect that anything would be done until tomorrow at the earliest," he told her as they sat down to eat in their private parlor. "I reckoned without the curiosity and zeal of Sir Quentin Dowd." Sir Quentin, he had told her, was the local magistrate. "I believe he would have dug up the whole graveyard single-handed if there had been no servants on hand and if I had been unable to show him the exact grave."

"But what made you suspect it? I don't understand." That was a phrase she seemed to have repeated many times in the course of the day, Fleur thought.

"Why would one not wish to have a man buried either in the place where he died and was known or in the place where his family lived?" he said. "Your cousin seemed to have had a choice, and yet chose neither. In fact, he went literally out of his way to have the burial carried out in a strange place, where neither of them was known."

"Someone might have wanted to see the body?" she said.

"I would imagine his family would have insisted on it," he said. "And perhaps a few of the servants at Heron House or Hobson's friends in the neighborhood would have expressed the wish too. Your cousin could not risk that happening. He did not cover his tracks well, of course, and he told conflicting stories to various people. But then, I suppose he did not expect that anyone would be curious enough to do any careful investigating. Eat up."

Fleur looked at her plate, though she could not remember how food had got onto it. "How can I eat?" she asked.

"With your knife and fork," he said. "How does it feel to be free?"

"But where did he go?" she asked. "And why? Why would he let his family think him dead?"

"Undoubtedly for money," he said. "I would guess he is on the Continent somewhere."

"And why would Matthew do it?" She frowned. "It was a diabolical plot. And all so that I would hang? Does he hate me so much?"

"You know the answer to that," he said. "He never had any intention of letting you hang. He wanted you in his power for the rest of your life. He has a strong obsession for you, Fleur."

"But I have always disliked him," she said. "How could he have wanted me, knowing that? And knowing that I would hate him for forcing me into such a thing?"

"For some men it is enough to have power over something they desire," he said. "Sometimes there seems even to be a special thrill about being hated. I don't know if your cousin is one of those men. I would not have said so from my acquaintance with him at Willoughby. He did not seem demonic. But his actions certainly suggest that he is."

"I shall not look forward to his coming back home and living close to me again," she said.

"Fleur." He reached out and touched her hand. "Do you really expect such a thing? Sir Quentin at this very moment is breathing fire and brimstone. Your cousin is in deep trouble, I promise you. I don't believe you will have to fear his coming home for a long time to come."

"Oh," she said. She looked down at her plate again. "I am not hungry."

He got to his feet and rang for a waiter to remove the dishes. They were both silent until the task was completed.

"I keep waiting to wake up," she said. She crossed the room and stood looking down into the empty fireplace. "I was very foolish to run, wasn't I? I should have gone to the rectory as I had planned to do."

"But he would have carried out the same plan," he said, "and perhaps got away with it."

"Yes," she said. "I don't know if anyone else would have guessed the truth. I would not have. Only you. And I would not have met you if I had not run."

He stood a short distance from her, watching her gaze into the fireplace. "I wish you had not had to suffer so much," he said quietly. "I wish you had asked me for help, Fleur. I wish I had thought to ask if you needed my help. I wish it had been different."

"But it was not," she said.

"No."

"Why have you done all this for me?" She turned her head to look at him. "Tell me the truth."

He shook his head slowly.

"I don't think I could have been more terrified of the devil than I was of you," she said, "when it was happening and in my thoughts and nightmares afterward. And when you came home to Willoughby and I realized that the Duke of Ridgeway was you, I thought I would die from the horror of it."

His face was expressionless. "I know," he said.

"I was afraid of your hands more than anything," she said. "They are beautiful hands."

He said nothing.

"When did it all change?" she asked. She turned completely toward him and closed the distance between them. "You will not say the words yourself. But they are the same words as the ones on my lips, aren't they?"

She watched him swallow.

"For the rest of my life I will regret saying them," she said. "But I believe I would regret far more not saying them."

"Fleur," he said, and reached out a staying hand.

"I love you," she said.

"No."

"I love you."

"It is just that we have spent a few days together," he said, "and talked a great deal and got to know each other. It is just that I have been able to help you a little and you are feeling grateful to me."

"I love you," she said.

"Fleur."

She reached up to touch his scar. "I am glad I did not know you before this happened," she said. "I do not believe I would have been able to stand the pain."

"Fleur," he said, taking her wrist in his hand.

"Are you crying?" she said. She lifted both arms and wrapped them about his neck and laid her cheek against his shoulder. "Don't, my love. I did not mean to lay a burden on you. I don't mean to do so. I only want you to know that you are loved and always will be."

"Fleur," he said, his voice husky from his tears, "I have nothing to offer you, my love. I have nothing to give you. My loyalty is given elsewhere. I didn't want this to happen. I don't want it to happen. You will meet someone else. When I am gone you will forget and you will be happy."

She lifted her head and looked into his face. She wiped away one of his tears with one finger. "I am not asking anything in return," she said. "I just want to give you something, Adam. A free gift. My love. Not a burden, but a gift. To take with you when you go, even though we will never see each other again."

He framed her face with his hands and gazed down into it. "I so very nearly did not recognize you," he said. "You were so wretchedly thin, Fleur, and pale. Your lips were dry and cracked, your hair dull and lifeless. But I did know you for all that. I think I would still be in London searching for you if you had not gone to that agency. But it's too late, love. Six years too late."

He lowered his head to kiss her, and heat flared instantly. He lifted his head.

"I have only tonight to offer you," he said. "Tomorrow I will be taking you home and continuing on my way to my own home."

"Yes," she said.

"Only tonight, Fleur."

"Yes."

"We will make it enough."

"Yes."

"We will make it last for all eternity."

"And even beyond that," she said.

"Fleur," he said. "My beloved. It was the love of my life I recognized outside the Drury Lane Theater. You know that, don't you?" His lips were against hers.

"Yes," she said. "Yes."

"I love you. You must know that I have loved you from the first moment I saw you standing in the shadows."

"Yes." She opened her mouth beneath his, touched his lips with her tongue. "Adam. Love me. Take away my fears."

He kissed her deeply, reaching into the heat of her mouth with his tongue, molding her body to his with his hands, waiting for it to surrender fully against his own.

"Are you still afraid?" he asked against her lips.

"Mortally." She kept her eyes closed. "Of the stages that follow this. But I want it all with you, Adam. I want your hands on me, and your body. I want you in me."

He kissed her again and felt her with his hands—the full,

firm breasts already hard-tipped beneath her dress, the small waist and shapely hips, the softly rounded buttocks.

"Fleur." He whispered her name into her mouth. He wanted her with a fierce pain.

"Keep touching me," she whispered. "Give me courage. Your hands are so warm and so strong. Give me courage."

He bent and swung her up into his arms and carried her through the open door into her bedchamber. He set her down on the bed.

And she knew that she was committed, that she could not go back, though she knew equally that he would have stopped at any moment she said the word. She loved him more than life and she wanted more than anything else at that moment for the memory of an ugly coupling to be erased and replaced with a memory of love.

But she was afraid. Mortally afraid. She was afraid of the intense burning look in his dark eyes. She was afraid of his hawkish features and slashing scar. She was afraid of his hands, which covered her breasts and felt their tips with his thumbs and which moved first behind her head to remove the pins from her hair and then behind her back to undo the buttons of her dress. And she was afraid of his body, still hidden beneath his clothing.

"We can make this enough," he said, looking down into her face, his hands stilling at her back. "We can make this much loving enough, Fleur. I will merely hold you for a few minutes longer to give myself the courage to let you go."

"No," she said. "I want all of it, Adam. I want all of you. I want to give you all of me."

He slid the dress off her shoulders, down her arms, down over her hips and her legs. She watched his eyes as her chemise and her undergarments and stockings followed. And she remembered standing naked before him, her clothes in a neat pile on the floor beside her.

"Make me forget," she said. "Adam, make me forget." She reached up her arms to him.

"You are so beautiful," he said, leaning over her to bury his face in her hair. "The most beautiful woman in the world." One hand stroked over a breast. A warm, long-fingered hand.

She reached up to undo the buttons of his waistcoat and shirt.

And he was afraid. She was so very beautiful. He wanted to be perfect for her. He raised himself to a sitting position again.

"I will close the door," he said. The light from two branches of candles was shining through the doorway and slanting across the bed.

"No," she said, reaching for him.

"Fleur," he said, looking down into her eyes, troubled. "I don't want you to see me again. I am very ugly."

"No." She caught him by the arms, pulled him down to her. "I want to see you. I must see you. Please, Adam. I will be afraid in the darkness."

He stood up beside the bed and undressed very deliberately. And he watched her watch him, as he had done on a previous occasion. Except that then he had been angry, daring her to show distaste, while this time he waited for it with a dull certainty that it would happen.

"Adam," she said when he stood naked beside the bed finally, "you are not ugly. Ah, you are not ugly. But I am so glad I did not know you before the wounds. I would not have been able to bear it." She reached out a hand to touch his left side lightly, and ran the hand down his side and thigh. "You are not ugly."

He lay down beside her on the bed, looked into her eyes, smoothed back the silky red-gold hair that he had loosened. And he kissed her again.

She spread one hand over the heavy hairs on his chest and lifted the other to explore the rippling muscles of his arm and shoulder. She moved it down over his chest, around to his back. Her tongue circled his, stroked over it, was stroked in its turn. And she felt his hands move over her, touch her, explore her, arouse her.

And she was no longer afraid. Her breasts were taut and tender to his touch. His hands were sending aching vibrations from them up into her throat. There was a heavy throbbing between her legs.

He had taken her once, briefly and dispassionately. Apart from that one occasion, it was many years since he had had a woman. He wanted to be perfect for her. He needed to bury himself in her and release his seed into her with a few swift thrusts. But he wanted to be perfect for her.

He moved a hand down between her thighs, opened her gently with his fingers, touched her, stroked her lightly. She was hot and wet to his touch. She moaned and twisted against him.

"I won't hurt you," he said, his mouth against hers again. "This time it won't hurt, Fleur. I promise you. Are you still afraid?"

"Yes." Her voice was a sob. "Yes. But come to me, Adam. Come to me."

He lifted himself over her and lowered himself on top of her, his head turned against the side of hers. And terror flared again as his legs came between hers and pushed them wide and his hands came beneath her to lift and tilt her.

And then he was coming into her, warm hard maleness mounting all the way into her. Without any tearing. Without any pain. Only the throbbing and the aching all about him and the waiting for him to put an end to it. She could hear someone moaning.

He drew his hands from beneath her and lifted himself on his forearms and looked down at her. Her eyes looked back into his. Her hair was spread like a flaming halo all about her head.

"I want it to be good for you," he whispered. "I want it to be perfect for you, Fleur. Tell me what to do. Do you want it ended quickly?" He withdrew from her, pushed slowly in again.

She raised her knees, set her feet flat on the bed on either side of him. She closed her eyes and threw her head back. She moaned again. He stroked her slowly and deeply, over and over again.

He lowered his head to brush her lips with his. "I want it to be perfect for you," he said. "Tell me when to come, Fleur. Tell me when you want me to come."

She opened her eyes and looked up into his. And she saw the dark hair, the hawkish face, the scar, the powerful shoulder muscles, the dark chest hair. And she felt his strong thighs pressing her own wide and felt his slow and deep and intimate strokes into the very depths of her. She remembered very deliberately that first encounter with him. And she let it go, let it slip beyond the realm of conscious memory.

"I think the aching will drive me mad," she whispered to him. "And I want it to go on forever."

But when he lowered himself onto her again and brought his arms about her and quickened his rhythm, she raised her knees to hug his hips and knew that forever must be held to a moment. She tilted herself against him, tensed against him, waited for the shattering of sanity.

He felt her come, though she said nothing. And he slid his hands gratefully beneath her again and thrust and held deep inside her several times until he could feel her tension soften and tremble about her central core.

"Now, my love," he said against her ear. "Now. Come with me now."

And he listened to her strange cry as he pushed into her once more and felt his own breath release with a sigh against the side of her face just as his seed had sprung deep inside her.

She shuddered and trembled about him and against him and abandoned herself to the aftermath of love, content to feel his body bear her down into the bed with its relaxation, content to rest her spread thighs against his, content to feel his hands cupping her hips, and to feel him throbbing deep in the part of her that belonged to herself and the man to whom she chose to give it.

She had chosen to give to him. Only him. Him, this once only and forever.

He disengaged his body from hers, lifted himself away from her, brought her over onto her side against him, his arms about her. He drew the bedclothes up about them.

"Fleur." He kissed her warmly, lingeringly. "Have the ghosts been banished?"

"Adam." Her eyes were closed. The fingertips of one hand moved lightly over his face. "You are beautiful. So very beautiful."

She was not sleeping, as he was not. He held her close, one hand smoothing through her hair, and communicated with her beyond the medium of words. They had only the one night. There was no time for talk. Or for sleep.

They lay quietly in each other's arms until it was time to love again.

FLEUR DOZED OFF TO SLEEP at some time just before dawn. The duke cradled her head on his shoulder and rubbed his cheek lightly against the top of her head. He stared upward into the darkness. The candles in the parlor had burned themselves out long before.

It should be possible, he thought, to set her up somewhere in a house of her own, somewhere not too far from Willoughby perhaps, or somewhere close to London. He would be able to visit her for days or weeks at a time. It would become more his home than Willoughby.

They could be married in all but name. There had never been a marriage with Sybil. It was not even a consummated marriage. He could be faithful to Fleur. They could even have a child, perhaps. Or children.

It should be possible. He turned his head to kiss the top of hers. Surely it would be possible to persuade her. She loved him as he loved her. She had told him so and she had spent most of a night showing him so.

A cottage by the sea, perhaps. They could walk along the cliffs together, blown by the wind, looking out across the water. They could stroll along the beach. They could take their children running and playing on the sand.

He rubbed his cheek against her hair again. Pamela would enjoy the beach. He must take her. Willoughby was less than ten miles from the sea. He must take her before the summer was over, perhaps arrange to go with Duncan Chamberlain and his children. Pamela would enjoy the company of other children.

She would never be able to enjoy the company of Fleur's children and his—those mythical children who lived in their mythical cottage in a make-believe world.

He could have ended his marriage to Sybil within a year of its making had he chosen to do so. He had not so chosen. He had committed himself to the vows he had made even though she refused to allow him the rights that would have made a proper marriage of it. He had committed himself because at the time he still felt some leftover love for her. And he had done it because of Pamela. So that Pamela would not be a bastard.

Half a commitment was no commitment at all. Either he belonged to Sybil and Pamela or he belonged to Fleur. There could be no double life. Not for him, anyway.

He tightened his arm about Fleur and continued to stare upward.

"What is it?" she asked, turning more fully against him.

He kissed her unhurriedly.

"I want to tell you something before the morning comes," he said.

"Yes."

The imminence of dawn was like a tangible thing in the room.

"After tomorrow," he said, "I will recommit myself to my marriage. I hope I will have the strength to live with that commitment for the rest of my life, with no more lapses. For Pamela's sake I will hope it."

"Yes," she said. "I know, Adam. You don't have to feel that you owe me anything. We agreed that there was just tonight. And I would not be your mistress even if you wished me to be."

He set a finger over her lips and kissed her forehead. "This is what I want to say," he said. "In one way, Fleur, you will always be my wife, more my wife than Sybil is. And physically I will always remain faithful to you. There will never be any other woman in my bed."

Her lips were still against his finger.

"My marriage is a marriage in name only," he said, "and always has been."

He heard her swallow. "Pamela?" she whispered.

"Is Thomas'," he said. "He abandoned Sybil, leaving her with child. I had recently returned from Belgium and still fancied myself in love with her, or with the person I thought she was."

She let out a ragged breath.

"From the moment of Pamela's birth she has been mine," he said. "I would die for her. If there were any serious question of my annulling my marriage in order to be with you, I would not do so because of Pamela. If the choice were between her and you, Fleur—and perhaps it is—then I would choose her."

She was pressing the top of her head against his chest.

"Yes," she said. "Yes."

"Do you hate me for that?" he asked.

"No." There was a long pause. "That is the very reason I love you, Adam. There is very little room in your life for yourself. It is filled with your concern for the well-being of others. I did not know it or expect it at first, but I have come to see it more and more."

"And yet I have taken this night for myself," he said. "It is a selfishness and a moral wrong, Fleur, or so your curate friend would say." He kissed her briefly. "But I don't want to talk. I want to love you one more time. I wanted you to know, though, that I will remain faithful to you and will always think of you as my wife."

"A piece of eternity," she said, touching his lips with her fingertips. "It has been wonderful beyond words. I would not exchange it for ten years added to my lifespan, Adam. And there is still a little of it left."

She turned onto her back and reached up her arms for him as he rose over her once more.

25

THE SCENERY BEYOND THE CARRIAGE WINDOW grew more familiar as they neared home. They had sat side by side throughout the journey, their shoulders touching, their hands clasped, saying almost nothing.

"There are only a few miles to go?" he asked her.

"Yes."

His hand closed more tightly about hers for a moment.

"You must apply to whoever does Brocklehurst's business for him," he said. "It should be possible to get at least some of your money before your twenty-fifth birthday. You will be able to live in some comfort then."

"Yes," she said.

"I shall have Houghton look into the matter too," he said.

"Thank you."

There was a silence again.

"I cannot come here again, Fleur," he said. "I will not even write."

"No," she said. "I know. Or I to you."

"Will you promise me if you are ever in any need or trouble to write to Houghton?" he said. "Promise me?"

"Only in the very extremest of circumstances," she said. "No, Adam. In all probability, no."

He stroked her fingers with his own. "Fleur," he said. "If you are with child . . ."

"I am not," she said.

"*If* you are," he said, raising her hand to his lips. "If you are, you must let me know. I know your instinct will lead you to keep it from me. But you must let me know. It would be my child too. The only child of my own body I would ever have. I would send you to one of my other homes and care for the both of you."

"I am not with child," she said.

"But you would let me know?"

"Yes," she said.

He lowered their hands again to rest on his thigh.

They were no more than two miles from the village, four from Heron House. Fleur concentrated on breathing quietly and evenly, suppressing the panic that was churning her insides.

"You will move into your cottage immediately?" he said.

"Yes." She focused her mind on her future plans. "I will stay at Heron House tonight for the last time and move to the village tomorrow. I shall start at the school the day after, if Miriam is ready for me. I am going to enjoy it immensely."

"Are you?" he said. "Are you going to teach the children music, Fleur?"

"Singing, yes," she said. "There is no instrument, but it does not matter."

He was smiling at her. "I am glad you have a good friend to be close to you," he said.

"Miriam?" she said. "I have other friends in the village too, Adam. Or acquaintances who will be friends as soon as I am living among them and no longer at the house. Don't worry about me. I will be happy."

"Will you?" He was looking sideways into her face, a mere few inches from his own.

"Yes," she said. "The pain will be intense for a while. I know it and expect it. But it will fade. I don't intend to pine away. I intend to live. I have had my little glimpse of paradise, which is more than many people have in a lifetime. Now I will go back to living."

"Pamela was upset when I left," he said. "I have not always been unselfish where she is concerned. I have left her far too often. I am looking forward to getting back to her."

"Yes," she said, "and so you should be. She is worth living for, Adam."

The carriage rumbled over the wooden bridge that would take them into the village. Fleur closed her eyes and rested her cheek against his shoulder. His hand tightened again over hers.

"Oh, God," she said.

"Courage." His cheek came to rest against the top of her head. "If I had a choice between feeling this pain and not doing so, Fleur, I would choose the pain because without it there would never have been you."

"I am greedy." She took a deep and audible breath. "I want the pain gone and I want you, Adam. I don't know if I am strong enough to do this."

His hold on her hand was painful. "You want me to take you somewhere where we can be together occasionally, then?" he asked.

"Once a year? Twice a year?" Her eyes were still closed. "Heaven to look forward to twice a year?"

"It could be more often if you were close," he said.

"A cozy cottage near Willoughby?" She was smiling. "And your visits to look forward to frequently. And never having to say good-bye. And children perhaps. Yours and mine. Would they be dark or red-haired, do you think?" Her voice disappeared into a thin thread.

"If it is what you want," he said, "I will give you that life."

"No," she said. "We are just talking of dreams, Adam. With a little temptation mixed in. Neither of us would be able to accept it as reality."

The carriage was turning from the main roadway to wind up the long driveway to Heron House.

"When we get there," she said, "don't come into the house with me, Adam. Just drive away."

"Yes," he said.

They said no more, but just sat as they were. She wanted him to take her into his arms and hoped he would not. She would not be able to bear it if he did. She would begin thinking that dreams could be made reality.

One more bend in the driveway and they would be through the gateway and on the straight axis with the house. Two more minutes at the longest.

"I'll not be able to say anything," she whispered. "Just leave."

"I love you," he said. "For all of my life and forever and eternity. I love you, Fleur."

She nodded and turned her head to press her face briefly into his shoulder.

"Yes," she said. "Yes."

Two people were coming down the steps of the house as the carriage drew up before it. Miriam and Daniel, Fleur saw.

"Isabella!" Miriam cried as Ned Driscoll opened the carriage door and let down the steps. "We have just ridden over to see if you were home yet. We expected you yesterday. Oh, good afternoon, your grace." She curtsied hurriedly.

The Reverend Booth reached up a hand to help her down. "Isabella," he said, watching the duke climb out behind her, "did you not take a maid? Why did you not do so?"

"Did you find Hobson's grave?" Miriam asked. "And is your mind now set at rest, Isabella? Word was circulating in the village yesterday that there are no longer any charges against you, that the death was an accident and the supposed theft a misunderstanding. It is all over, the whole ghastly business. Is it not, Daniel?"

"Miss Bradshaw," a quiet voice said from behind Fleur, "I will be taking my leave."

"You are not coming into the house, your grace?" Miriam asked.

Fleur turned, her friends just a couple of steps behind her. She lifted her hands and he took them. He looked deeply into her eyes as he raised one to his lips.

"Good-bye," he said.

Adam. Her lips formed his name, though no sound emerged.

And he was gone—into the carriage to sit on the far side while Ned closed the door, turned to smile and incline his head to her, and vaulted up onto the box with the coachman.

And he was gone, along the driveway, through the gates, and around the first bend.

He was gone.

"Well, he was in a hurry to leave," Miriam said cheerfully. "Isabella, you foolish, independent woman. Why did you not call on me to go with you? You know I would have closed the school for a few days. But by the time Daniel had told me that he had refused to accompany you, you were gone already. And imagine our dismay to discover that you had gone with the Duke of Ridgeway."

"It is done, Miriam," the Reverend Booth said. "There is no point in scolding further. We will come inside with you, if we may, Isabella. It will relieve your mind, no doubt, to tell us all that happened."

"You must be exhausted," Miriam said, stepping forward to take her arm. She smiled up into her face and then turned back sharply to her brother. "Take Isabella's bag inside, will you, Daniel? I want to have a brief word with her before we join you."

She waited until he had disappeared into the house.

"Oh, Isabella," she said quietly, touching her friend's arm, patting it. "Oh, my poor, poor dear."

Fleur stood staring down the driveway as if turned to stone.

• • •

AT LEAST THERE WAS PLENTY with which to keep herself busy. Fleur was thankful for that fact more than for any other in the coming days and weeks. At least there was plenty to do.

She removed all her possessions to the cottage that had been Miss Galen's and arranged and rearranged them to her satisfaction. At first she did everything for herself, including the cooking, since she could not afford to hire a servant. She spent many hours in the small garden, restoring the overgrown hedges and rosebushes to their original neatness and splendor.

And she taught the twenty-two pupils at Miriam's school alongside her friend and discovered the challenge of instructing more than one child at a time.

She kept an eye on an elderly couple who lived next door to her, taking them some cakes when she baked, sitting and listening to their endless stories of the past, including many of her mother and father.

And she had friends to visit and be visited by. There was always Miriam, of course, who spent a great deal of her free time with her and who was cheerfully friendly without ever prying. For undoubtedly she knew. There had been that tact of hers in sending Daniel inside the house after Adam had left, and her simple words of sympathy and understanding. But if she was curious, she never showed it. She never asked questions. She was a true friend.

And there was Daniel too. He did not cast her off despite her confession to him and her improper behavior afterward in going to Wroxford with Adam. And there were several other inhabitants of the village and a few of the neighboring gentry who had held off as long as she was living at Heron House with her relatives but who were only too pleased now to make a friend of her.

Matthew did not come home. Neither did Cousin Caroline and Amelia, even when the London Season came to an end.

Word came to the village that the ladies had traveled north with friends. Rumor had it that Matthew had removed himself to the Continent to avoid some unknown embarrassment. Fleur did not know the truth of any of the stories. And she did not care where any of them were, provided they stayed away. She hated the thought of Cousin Caroline's coming back, and she dreaded that Matthew would come.

She spoke with the steward at Heron House, and he promised to communicate with Lord Brocklehurst's man of business in London concerning her affairs.

She had her answer in an unexpected way. She was sitting in her small parlor one afternoon, sipping on a cup of tea after a tiring day at school and wondering if she had the energy to go outside later to clip a hedge that had grown untidy again. She got to her feet with a sigh when there was a knock at the door. And she stood gaping at Peter Houghton a few moments later, her stomach feeling as if it were performing a complete somersault.

"Miss Bradshaw," he said, making her a polite bow.

"Mr. Houghton?" She stood aside, inviting him to enter.

"I was sent to London to carry out some business for you, ma'am," he said. "It seemed as well to call here on my way back to Willoughby Hall instead of writing you a letter."

"Oh, yes," she said. "Thank you." She would not at all have enjoyed receiving a letter from Willoughby, only to find that it was from the secretary. "Won't you have some tea?"

She sat on the edge of her chair listening to him, drinking in the sight and sound of him, this fragile link with Willoughby and Adam. And remembering the first time she had seen him at Miss Fleming's agency.

Matthew had indeed fled the country. Someone must have tipped him off to the fact that his deception had been uncovered and that awkward, incriminating questions were about to be asked. Mr. Houghton, it seemed, had spoken with Matthew's man of business, had pulled a few strings in high places, and had arranged it that her guardian was now a distant cousin, Matthew's heir, whom she had met only once. And that man, whom Mr. Houghton had also called upon, had been quite uninterested in guarding either the person or the fortune of a twenty-three-year-old female relative he did not even know.

She was to be given a very generous allowance for the following year and a half, after which her dowry and her fortune would be released to her whether she was married or single.

Mr. Houghton coughed. "I believe his exact words were that you could marry the sweep's climbing boy tomorrow for all he cared, ma'am," he said. There was a gleam in his eye for a moment.

She had never known that Mr. Houghton had a sense of humor, Fleur thought, smiling.

He would not stay for dinner or even for a second cup of tea. He wished to cover several more miles before darkness, he said.

Fleur got to her feet and clasped her hands in front of her. He would be gone in a few minutes. Until then she would hold firm. She would not ask a single question about *him*. Not one.

Peter Houghton coughed again, pausing by the outer door before opening it. "His grace could not go himself to London, of course," he said. "He sent me in his stead."

"Yes," Fleur said. "I am grateful to you, sir. And to him."

"He is making plans to take the duchess and Lady Pamela into Italy for the winter," he said.

"Is he?" Wounds that had scarcely begun to film over and knit together were being ripped apart again.

"For her grace's health," Houghton said. "And I believe for his own too. He has not been quite himself."

A sharp-bladed knife was scraping at the wound.

"The climate of Italy should help them both," she said.

He reached for the knob of the door and turned it.

"I was instructed to make a purchase in London, ma'am,"

he said, "and to make sure that it was sent on to you here. It should arrive within the week. I was to inform you that it is more in the way of a contribution to the school than a personal gift."

"What is it?" she asked.

"It should arrive within the week," he repeated.

And he bowed to her again, bade her a good day, and was gone.

She was left with the painful ache of knowing that the one small link with Adam was even then rolling out of the village. And with the knowledge that he loved her enough to have sent his secretary to London on her behalf. And that he was sending her a gift, supposedly for the school.

But really for her.

And with the knowledge that soon—within a few months—he would be gone from England. Not that it mattered. She would never see him again anyway. But Italy! Italy was so very far away.

Sometimes pain could be almost past bearing.

There was plenty to do to keep her busy, but she wished it were possible to keep her mind as effectively occupied as her hands and body.

She could not keep the thoughts of him at bay. And they were painful beyond belief. She would never see him again, never hear from him again. And yet she was to know and to believe for the rest of her life that he loved her. Twenty years later, if she was alive then and knew him to be alive, she was to believe that he loved her. And yet she would never be able to verify the truth of it. She would wonder—she was already wondering—*do you love me still? Do you remember me?*

In some ways, she felt, it would be almost easier to know that he did not love her, that he was happy somewhere else with someone else. At least then she would be able to set about the task of living her own life with a little more determination.

Perhaps. And yet, as she lay in bed at nights reliving those days of travel with him, when they had talked easily to each other and grown to be friends and sometimes sat quietly together in perfect peace and harmony, their hands clasped, she was not sure she would be able to live with the knowledge that he was happy somewhere else, that he had forgotten her. And as she relived that night, when they had told their love over and over again with their bodies, she did not think she would be able to bear knowing that there could ever be another woman for him.

And yet it hurt to know that he was unhappy, trapped in a marriage that was really no marriage at all, undertaken for the sake of a little girl who was not even his.

It hurt to know that the barrier that kept them apart, and would do so for the rest of their lives, was as flimsy and as strong as gossamer.

The culmination of her pain came with two events that happened on the same day, one month after she had moved to her cottage.

She was called from the school early in the afternoon to take delivery of a pianoforte, which had been brought all the way from London. There was a number of curious people in the street, and somehow all the children were out there too, swarming about the large wagon that held the instrument.

"A pianoforte!" Miriam gasped, and clasped her hands to her bosom. "For you, Isabella? Did you order it?"

"It is for the school," Fleur said. "It is a gift."

"A gift? For the school?" Miriam turned wide eyes on her. "But from whom?"

"We must have it carried in," Fleur said.

She did not know where Daniel had come from, but he was there.

"It is too valuable an item for the schoolroom," he said. "We must put it in your cottage, Isabella."

"But it is for the children," she said. "So that I can teach them music."

"Then you must take them one or two at a time to your cottage for their lessons," he said.

"Oh, yes," Miriam agreed. "That will be the best possible idea, Isabella. What a wonderful, wonderful gift." She squeezed her friend's arm but did not repeat her question about the giver.

And so Fleur found herself with a pianoforte in her parlor and a whole box of music. When she was finally alone, having been assured by Miriam that she was no longer needed so close to dismissal time at school, she sat on the stool and touched the keys with shaking fingers.

But she did not play. She lowered the gleaming lid over the keys, pillowed her head on her arms, and cried and cried until she was sore from the crying. They were the first tears she had shed since his leaving.

She could see him in the early mornings opening the connecting door between the library and the music room, standing there deliberately until she saw him so that she would not think that he intended to eavesdrop without her knowledge. She could hear herself playing, lost in the music, but feeling him there in the next room, silently listening.

For so long she had thought that she hated him, that she feared him and was repulsed by him. And she had been afraid—oh, mortally afraid—of the strange, unexpected attraction she had felt to him.

He had sent her this one precious gift, knowing how much music meant to her. But he would never hear her play it. She would never be able to play it for him.

All her tears were spent by the time, later the same evening, she discovered a flow of blood, which told her that she would not bear his child either. She was more than a week late.

It had been foolish, foolish, of course, to have hoped that it was true. She should have been panicking for that week. It would have been disastrous if it had been true.

But the heart cannot always be directed by the head, she was discovering. She felt as bleak and as empty, lying on her bed after she had cleansed herself and put the padding in place, as she had the day he left.

She would not have cared, she told herself. She would not have cared about all the awkwardness and scandal. A great deal of hope could build in eight days. She had begun to believe in her hope.

"Adam," she whispered into the darkness. "Adam, there is too much silence. I can't bear the silence. I can't hear you."

The words sounded ridiculous when she heard them. She turned onto her side and hid her face against the pillow.

SOON AFTER PETER HOUGHTON'S VISIT, Fleur asked Mollie, the maid from Heron House, if she would like to move to the cottage to keep house for her. Mollie was delighted at the chance to be housekeeper and cook as well as maid. But she hinted that Ted Jackson would be unhappy to have her so far away. Before a month had passed, Mr. and Mrs. Ted Jackson were both living at the cottage, and Fleur had a handyman and gardener as well as a housekeeper.

Once she was no longer alone in the house, the Reverend Booth sometimes visited her without his sister. He found her presence relaxing, he would say, watching her at her embroidery. And he liked to listen to her play the pianoforte.

Fleur enjoyed his visits and looked back with some nostalgia to the time when she had believed herself in love with him. If all those events had not happened, she often thought—if Cousin Caroline and Amelia had not left for London, if Matthew had not stopped her from leaving the house, if Hobson had not fallen and she had not fled, thinking she had killed him—how different life might be now. She would have moved to the rectory as planned and lived there with Miriam until Daniel had come with the special license.

They would have been married now for many months.

They would have sat every evening as they often sat now. Perhaps she would be with child.

And she would have been happy. For without the experiences of the previous months, perhaps she would never have seen the narrowness of Daniel's vision. Perhaps she too would have continued to see morality in strict terms of black and white. And she would never have met Adam. She would never have known the passionate, all-consuming love she felt for him.

She would have been happy with the gentle love that Daniel had offered. Sometimes she wished she could erase the past months, go back to the way things had been. But one could never go back, she realized, or truly wish to do so, because once one's experience was enlarged, one could no longer be satisfied with the narrower experience.

Besides, despite all the pain, despite all the despair, she would not wish to have lived her life without knowing Adam. Without loving him.

"You are happy here, Isabella?" the Reverend Booth asked her one evening.

"Yes." She smiled. "I am very fortunate, Daniel. I have this home and the school and friends. And a wonderful feeling of safety and security after all the anxiety of that thing with Matthew."

"You are well-respected and liked," he said. "I thought that perhaps you would find it difficult to settle here after all you had gone through."

She smiled at him and lowered her head to her work again.

"I sometimes wish we could go back to the way things were before that dreadful night," he said, echoing her own thoughts. "But we can't, can we? We can never go back."

"No," she said.

"I thought," he said, "that it would be possible to love only someone I felt to be worthy of my love. I thought I could love other people in a Christian way and forgive them their shortcomings if they repented of them. But I could not picture myself loving or marrying someone who had made a serious error. I was wrong."

She smiled at her work.

"I have been guilty of a terrible pride," he said. "It was as if I believed a woman had to be worthy of me. And yet I am the weakest of mortals, Isabella. I can only look at you and marvel that you have not been embittered or coarsened by your experience. You are far stronger and more independent than you were before, aren't you?"

"I like to think so," she said. "I think I realize more than I did before that my life is in my own hands, that I cannot blame other people for anything that might go wrong with it."

"Will you do me the honor of marrying me?" he asked.

For all the words that had led up to the proposal, she was taken by surprise. She looked up at him, her needle suspended above her embroidery.

"Oh, Daniel," she said. "No. I am so sorry, but no."

"Even though I know of your past?" he said. "Even though I can tell you that it makes no difference to my feelings for you?"

She closed her eyes.

"Daniel," she said. "I can't. Oh, I can't."

"It is as I thought, then," he said, getting to his feet and touching her shoulder. "But you have severed all relations with him, have you not? I would expect no less of you. He is a married man. I am sorry, Isabella. I am truly sorry. I would wish for your happiness. I will pray for you."

He left the house quietly while she stared down at her work.

He did not come alone again for several weeks, though he called sometimes with his sister. And he frequently came to the school.

When he did come alone once more, it was during the afternoon of a day when there was no school. He brought a letter with him.

"I would send it back unopened if I were you," he said to her gravely as he handed it to her. "As your minister, I would advise it, Isabella. You have put up such a strong fight against your weaker self and have come so close to winning the battle. Let me send it back for you. Or destroy it without reading it."

She took the letter from his hands and looked down at the seal of the Duke of Ridgeway and the handwriting that was not Mr. Houghton's. It had been longer than four months—or perhaps four years or four decades or four centuries.

"Thank you, Daniel," she said.

"Be strong," he said. "Don't give in to temptation."

She said nothing, but continued to stare down at the letter. He turned and left without another word.

She hated him. She had not expected ever to feel hatred for him again. But she hated him. He had said that he would never see her again, never write to her. And she had believed him.

She had pined for him, thought she could not live on without one more sight of him or word from him.

And he had written. To open the still-almost-raw wound once again. To force her to begin all over again. And in the future she would never again be able to trust him to keep temptation out of her life.

Daniel was right. She should send the letter back unopened so that he would know that she was stronger than he. Or she should destroy it unread. She should give it to Daniel to send back or destroy.

She went into the parlor and stood it, unopened, against a vase on the pianoforte. And she sat quietly in her favorite chair, her hands in her lap, looking at it.

26

"WELCOME HOME, YOUR GRACE," JARVIS SAID with his characteristic stiff bow.

The Duke of Ridgeway acknowledged his butler's greeting with a nod and handed him his hat and gloves.

"The house seems very quiet," he said. "Where is everyone?"

"All of the guests have left, your grace," the butler said. "Most of them departed two days ago."

"And Lord Thomas?" the duke asked.

"Left yesterday, your grace."

"And where is the duchess?"

"In her apartments, your grace."

The duke moved away from him. "Have Sidney sent to me," he said, "and hot water for a bath."

It was an enormous relief, he thought as he strode along the marbled corridors to his private rooms, to be out of his carriage finally. It had seemed so very empty and so very quiet without her. And there had been little to do all through the journey except think. And remember.

He did not want to do either. He was going to have a brisk bath, change into clean clothes, go up to see Pamela, and then call on Sybil. Thomas had left, then, without her. And he supposed that he would be the villain again, as he had been the last time.

Poor Sybil. He felt genuinely distressed for her, and he knew well how she was feeling—sore, empty, quite unable to convince herself that life could ever again bring any happiness. It was hard sometimes to know with one's heart as one knew with one's head that there would ever be reason to laugh again.

"Where the devil is that water?" he said ungraciously as his valet came through the door of his dressing room.

"Somewhere between the kitchen and here, sir," Sidney said. "You will only tighten the knot of your neckcloth beyond any possibility of loosening it if you jerk on it like that. Let me undo it properly."

"Damn your impudence," his grace said. "How have you managed to live through the past week without me to fuss over like a damned mother hen?"

"Very peacefully, sir," his valet said. "Very peacefully indeed. The side is aching?"

"No, it is not aching," the duke said impatiently. "Ah, at last." He turned to watch two menservants carry in large pails of steaming water.

"I shall rub it down for you anyway after you have bathed, sir," Sidney said. "Sit down and let me tackle that knot or it will be fit only to be sawn through with a knife."

The duke sat down and lifted his chin like an obedient child.

He was eager to bathe and dress and be on his way upstairs. To see Pamela. Yes, very definitely to see Pamela. There was no one else. There would be no more of the old urge to go up there, to sit in the schoolroom and listen to her talk and turn every lesson into an adventure. From now on there would be only Pamela.

And yet he was impatient to be up there even apart from his eagerness to see his daughter. Perhaps he had to prove to himself that Fleur really was gone. In some ways she was fortunate, he thought. She would be living in a place where he had never been. There would be no ghosts. He was going to have to enter the nursery and the schoolroom, the music room, the library, the long gallery—all the places he associated with her.

But he did not want to think. He would not think. He got restlessly to his feet after Sidney had untied the knot in his neckcloth with almost insolent ease, and pulled impatiently at his shirt buttons. One came off in his hand, and he swore and dropped it onto the washstand.

"Someone must have slept on a mattress made of coal lumps last night," Sidney said cheerfully to no one in particular.

"And someone is asking to be tossed out on his ear outside this house," the duke said, discarding his shirt and sitting down again so that his valet could help him remove his Hessian boots.

THE DUCHESS OF RIDGEWAY was in her sitting room. His grace could hear her coughing as he approached. He tapped on the door and waited for her maid to answer it and to curtsy to him and leave the room.

She was standing at the far side of the room, between the slender pillars that supported the entablature. She was dressed in a flowing white nightrobe, her hair loose down her back. She looked as pale as the robe except for the two spots of color high on her cheekbones. She looked thin and gaunt. Surely, the duke thought as he strode toward her, she had lost weight even since he last saw her.

"Sybil," he said, reaching out his hands for hers and bending to kiss her cheek. "How are you?"

Her hands were as cold as ice, her cheek cool.

"Well," she said. "I am well, thank you."

"I heard you coughing," he said. "Is it still bothering you?"

She laughed and withdrew her hands from his.

"You don't look well," he said. "I am going to take you and Pamela to London, where you may consult a physician who knows what he is doing. And then we will go to Bath for a month or two. The change of air and scenery will do us all good."

"I hate you," she said in her light, sweet voice. "I wish there were a stronger word to use because I feel more than hatred for you. But I cannot think of any other way of saying it."

He turned away from her. "He left yesterday?" he asked.

"You know he did," she said. "You ordered him to leave."

He passed a hand across his brow. "I suppose you begged him to take you with him," he said. "Why do you think he refused, Sybil?"

"He has too much regard for my reputation," she said.

"And he would put your reputation before your happiness?" he said. "And his own? Did you find his refusal convincing?"

"I want to be alone," she said, crossing to the daybed and sitting down on it. "I want you to go away. I hoped you would not come back this time. I hoped you would find her charms just too enticing. I wish you would go back to her so that I would never have to see you again."

He sighed and turned to look down at her. "Six years ago," he said, "I would have given my life to save you from pain, Sybil. I think perhaps I gave more than that. I still hate to see you in misery. You are my wife and I am pledged to do all in my power to secure your safety and happiness. I know you are feeling a pain almost too great to be borne. But nothing can be accomplished by looking back. Can we not just go on together and try to make what remains of our lives at least peaceful?"

She laughed again without looking at him.

"A marriage works in two directions," he said. "I am your husband, Sybil. You are pledged, too, to do all in your power to secure my happiness. Would it not give your mind something to focus on, trying to please me? I would not be hard to please. I would be satisfied with a little kindness, a little companionship."

This time she looked at him as she laughed. But the laughter turned to prolonged coughing.

He went down on his knees in front of her, set his hand over the back of her head, offered her his handkerchief. She pushed his hand away.

"On Monday," he said when the coughing finally stopped, "we will leave for London. In three days' time. Instruct Armitage to start packing your trunks."

She laughed again. "You can keep your doctors, Adam," she said. "No doctor can do anything for me. I want nothing to do with them." She unfolded her handkerchief and smiled at him as she revealed the bright red spots of blood on it.

He stared at them, felt the blood drain from his head, and lowered his forehead to rest against her knees.

"You must have known," she said. "If you did not, you must be remarkably stupid. Go away, Adam. I want nothing to do with you or with any of your doctors."

He raised his head and looked into her face. "Sybil," he whispered. "Oh, my poor dear. Why have you not said anything before? Dr. Hartley knows? Why did he not tell me? You should not have been going through this alone."

"Why?" she asked. "Do you plan to die with me, Adam? Or will you just hold my hand through it all? No, thank you. I would prefer to do it alone."

She turned her head away sharply as her face crumpled before his sight.

He was on his feet instantly and drawing her up and into his arms. He held her close to him, rocked her against him, kissed the top of her head.

But she pushed away from him as soon as she had regained some control. "I want to be alone," she said. "I want to die alone. If Thomas is not here to hold me, then I will die alone. No!" She turned sharply as he moved his hand toward her. "You do not have to do the generous thing and send for him.

That is what you were about to offer to do, isn't it? I can read you like a book, Adam."

He said nothing.

"I know he would not come," she said. "He would not come if I were healthy and you offered me with a million pounds. Do you think he would come to help me die?"

"Sybil," he said, reaching out a hand to her.

She laughed more harshly than she had laughed before. "Do you think I do not know the truth?" she said. "Do you think I have not always known it deep down? But it does not make me hate you any the less. I hate you for being so noble and so understanding. I hate you for being always so willing to take the blame. I am glad I have consumption. I am glad I am going to die." She turned her back on him.

"I will not let you go without a fight," he said. "There are treatments that can help your condition. If only you had told me sooner, or the doctor had—I suppose you swore him to secrecy—we could have been doing something already. A warm climate helps, so I have heard. I shall take you somewhere where it is warm. Spain, perhaps, or Italy. We will go there for the winter. By next summer you will have recovered. Sybil, don't give up hope. Don't give up your will to live."

"I want to lie down," she said. "Pull on the bell rope to summon Armitage, Adam. I am tired."

He did so immediately and turned back to her. "I am going to nurse you back to health," he said, "whether you like it or not. And whether you hate me or not, I am going to keep you alive and with me. And with Pamela. Think of her, Sybil. She needs you alive. She worships you."

"Poor little darling," she said. "She will be an orphan indeed when I am gone."

"She will always have me," he said. "Her father. And she will have you too. I will have Houghton work on arrangements for a removal to Italy for the winter."

The maid came into the room at that moment.

"Her grace is unwell and tired," the duke said. "Help her to her bed, if you please, Armitage."

He watched his duchess, fragile and lovely, lean heavily on her maid's arm as they disappeared into the dressing room. He resisted the impulse to scoop her up into his arms and carry her to her bed. He knew that such a gesture would not be appreciated.

TWO DAYS AFTER THE duke's return, Peter Houghton was sent to London to consult with the duke's lawyer and Lord Brockle-hurst's to see what he could arrange for Fleur's comfort. And he was to purchase a pianoforte to send her as a gift to the school. Fleur must have a pianoforte, his grace persuaded himself.

One gift. That would be all. One gift and no more communication ever.

He spent part of the morning of his first day at home taking his daughter and her dog for a long walk. He promised her that in the afternoon they would ride to Mr. Chamberlain's house so that she could play with the children.

"I will ride with you, Papa," she said carelessly.

"Not a bit of it," he said, laughing. "You will ride your own horse, Pamela. I thought you had recovered from your fears."

"But I will not have Miss Hamilton to ride on my other side," she said.

"You do not need any assistance," he said. "You can ride quite well on your own now. I must see about finding you another governess, one who will enjoy going into Italy with us."

"I don't want another governess," she said. "I want Miss Hamilton."

"Well," he said, stooping down to scoop the dog up into his arms to carry through the house and up the stairs, "Miss Hamilton has moved on to another life, Pamela. She is teaching a whole schoolful of children."

"She didn't like me," she said, pouting. "I knew all the time that she didn't like me."

He set a hand on her head and rubbed hard. "You know that is not true, Pamela," he said. "She loved you."

"Then why did she leave?" she asked. "And she did not even say good-bye."

He sighed and was glad of the diversion caused when the dog leapt from his arms at the top of the stairs and raced for the door into the nursery. Pamela giggled and raced after it.

He strode outside to the stables and had his horse saddled. And he rode for the next few hours, completely forgetting about luncheon, cantering up over the back lawns, through the trees, past the ruins, avoiding the park at the front of the house.

He tried to keep his mind focused on his plans for the future. He would take Sybil to London before they left England. They would find out what the most skilled physician had to say about her condition and her chances of recovery. And then they would go to Italy, at least for the winter months, and he would make sure that she soaked up sunshine every single day.

She was twenty-six years old. Far too young to die.

It was strange, he thought, how a person could know something perfectly well in the far recesses of the mind, and yet not know it at all. Had he known or suspected that Sybil had consumption? All the symptoms had been there, glaring him in the face. But no one had said anything. He would have thought that the doctor, at the very least, would have informed him.

Thomas had mentioned that perhaps she was consumptive. But he had denied the possibility.

Perhaps his own denials had been similar to Sybil's. She had known the truth about Thomas all along, she had said the day before. And yet at the same time she had not known, or had denied the knowledge even to her own heart.

She was coughing blood already. That meant that the

disease was in its final phase, did it not? That there was no hope of recovery?

But he would nurse her back to health.

If only, he thought, she were willing to accept his care, his companionship, the affection he was still willing to give her. But she was not.

Sybil had always been her own worst enemy, he thought. Undoubtedly her experience with Thomas, a pregnancy outside wedlock, and the compulsion on her to marry Adam though she did not love him had all been searing indeed. He would not belittle the pain she must have lived through. How could he when he was living through much the same pain himself? But she could have helped herself.

If she had really known deep down that Thomas had cruelly abandoned her, she could have made an effort to make at least something of her marriage. She could have lavished all her love on Pamela, even if not on himself. Since all happiness had been taken from her, she could have concentrated on giving happiness to other people.

But Sybil's character was not a strong one. Had she been given happiness, doubtless she would have remained sweet all her life. But she was a taker, not a giver, and once everything she held dear had been taken from her, there had been nothing left in her life except bitterness and hatred and a desperate reaching out for sensual gratification.

He could only feel deeply sorry for her. And obliged to help her through this new and worst crisis in her life. It would be too sad for her to die so young and without ever having discovered that there was a great deal to give to life.

It was not easy, of course, to turn one's back on the pains of the past and give all one's energies to the present and the future. Not easy at all.

He found himself after all turning his horse's head for the front of the house and cantering over the rolling lawns of the long park. And then galloping, urging Hannibal on to ever faster and faster speed, never quite able to outdistance his thoughts.

He turned almost by instinct to his left after a couple of miles and leapt the gate into the pasture. And he drew up on the reins and patted his horse's neck. And looked back and saw her in memory sailing over the gate after him with a foot to spare. He bent his head forward and closed his eyes.

No, it was not easy. He had had a sleepless night, his arms and his body aching for her. And he remembered again the softness and fragrance of her hair, the smooth silkiness of her skin, the fullness of her breasts, her small waist and flaring hips, her long, slim legs, her hot and eager mouth, her warm and wet and womanly depths.

And he remembered her quiet and sleepy and warm in his arms between lovings, smiling at him in the dim candlelight, words between them quite unnecessary. And holding his hand in the carriage, her shoulder resting just below the level of his.

Fleur. God. Fleur.

If Sybil died, the thought came unbidden, he would be able to marry Fleur.

He shook his head violently and turned his horse for the long walk up through the pasture. He was not going to let her die. She was his wife and ill and unhappy. He was not going to let her die.

He was not going to think of Fleur. He had no right to think of her. He was married to Sybil.

He followed the route he had taken on a previous occasion with Fleur. And yet, after passing through the gate back into the park, he took a different direction until his horse stepped out onto the path on the south side of the lake, opposite the pavilion on the island.

Where he had waltzed with Fleur during the outdoor ball.

Just there. On the path. She had been terrified of him, terrified of his touch. She had closed her eyes very tightly. And then the music and the atmosphere had caught her up in their magic as they had caught him up, and they had waltzed as if they had been made to dance together all their lives.

Beautiful, beautiful Fleur in her plain blue gown and with her glorious fire-gold hair.

He stared at the spot where they had danced. But there was no music, no lanternlight. No Fleur.

Just a sunlit path and the sounds of the breeze in the trees and of birds singing.

He swallowed twice and turned his horse for home.

Sybil had gone into Wollaston that morning. He must go to her to see that she was safely back and none the worse for her outing. It was such a beautiful warm day. Perhaps she would like to take a short walk, leaning on his arm.

And perhaps hell would freeze over too.

THEY WERE TO LEAVE at the end of September, more than three months after Fleur had left Willoughby Hall. The Duke of Ridgeway was thankful to have at least part of the autumn in England. He wandered about his land, sometimes on foot, sometimes on horseback, sometimes alone, sometimes with his daughter and the collie if they were on foot glorying in the changing colors of the leaves and the many-colored carpet underfoot. Pamela liked to walk on the crisp leaves with him, crunching them underfoot.

He knew that he would miss it all during the winter. He was reminded of the long months and years of the campaigns against Bonaparte and his homesickness then as he traveled about with the armies.

But they must leave. Sybil did not want to go, and stubbornly declared that she would not do so. But this was one matter on which he would exert his authority and insist on obedience. If she had no will to live, then he would have the will for her. He would inject his own strength into her and make her well again.

She did not show many outer signs of her illness. With her guests gone, she was restless again and constantly out visiting, sometimes taking Pamela with her, though more often going alone. When she invited guests to the house—he rarely did so for fear of overtiring her—she sparkled and was gay. Duncan Chamberlain looked distinctly uncomfortable one evening when she chose to flirt with him.

But there were times—sometimes whole days together—when a high fever and the coughing kept her confined to her own rooms.

The duke visited her there daily, asking after her health, trying to draw her into conversation. She was not to be drawn.

And she would not go to Italy or see any of his doctors, she declared whenever he raised the subject.

She kept to her rooms the day before that set for their departure. Peter Houghton took her mail there to her late in the morning, including a letter from a friend in London with whom she often corresponded.

It was a cold and blustery day, one that constantly threatened rain. It was high time they were on their way to warmer climes, the duke thought as he left the nursery, where all was excitement and half-packed trunks, and made his way downstairs to pay his daily call on his wife. She had not come to luncheon.

She had gone out before luncheon, her maid told him. Armitage had thought that her grace had gone only for a short walk, but she must have misunderstood the matter. Her grace must have taken the carriage and gone into town.

The duke frowned. He had come from the stables little more than an hour before. No one had said anything about Sybil's taking out a carriage.

And yet it was not the sort of weather in which she would walk. And luncheon had been two hours before.

"Thank you," he said, nodding curtly to his wife's maid.

No carriage had been taken, he discovered five minutes later at the stables. The duchess had not been there.

"But I did see her this morning walking in that direction, your grace," Ned Driscoll said, pointing toward the lake. "But that was hours ago."

"Thank you," the duke said.

It was starting to rain, a cold, driving rain, which quickly chilled the body even through clothing and found a cheerless path down one's neck. The duke walked briskly toward the lake.

One of the boats was out on the water, he saw instantly—overturned and floating without direction. Something dark was caught among the reeds close to the island.

Some minutes later, from the other boat, he disentangled his wife's body from the reeds and lifted her into the boat. He rowed back to shore, beached the boat, lifted her carefully into his arms, and began the walk back to the house.

Even soaking wet, with her clothes saturated, she weighed no more than a feather. One white and fragile hand was resting across her stomach.

His feet felt as if they were made of lead. There was a soreness in his throat and in his chest that impeded his breathing.

He had loved her once—her beauty and her light step and her sweet voice. With all of a young man's ardor he had loved her. And he had married her and vowed to love and cherish her until death. Yet he had been unable to protect her from the sort of despair that had driven her to take her own life.

There were a few grooms outside the stables, watching his approach as if they had sensed that something was wrong. And Jarvis and a footman were somehow out at the top of the horseshoe steps as he carried his burden up them.

"Her grace has met with an accident," he said, surprised at the firmness of his own voice. "Send Armitage and Mrs. Laycock to her room, please, Jarvis."

"She is hurt, your grace?" The butler for once had been surprised out of his stiffness.

"Dead," his grace said, walking past him and into the great hall and past Houghton and his brother's valet standing there, the latter covered with the dust and mud of travel.

He carried his wife into her bedchamber and laid her carefully on her bed, straightening the sprawling limbs, arranging the wet clothing neatly, reaching out to close the dead eyes, touching the beautiful silver-blond hair, now wet and muddy. And he knelt beside the bed, took one of her hands in his, laid it against his cheek, and wept.

Wept for the death of an ardent and immature love that had been unable to bring any comfort or peace to the beloved. And wept for the woman he had taken to wife with such high ideals—the woman who had just killed herself rather than face a final illness with only his arms to comfort her. Wept for his own frailty and infidelity. For his own humanness.

He got to his feet eventually, knowing that Armitage and Mrs. Laycock had been standing behind him for some time. He turned without a word and went through the dressing room into the oval sitting room.

His steps took him to the escritoire, on which was an open letter. He should not read it, some remote part of his mind told him. It was his wife's. But his wife was dead.

And so he bent over it, quite without curiosity. And found out thus, before Houghton and his brother's valet had the chance to speak with him, about Lord Thomas Kent's death in a gaming-hell brawl a few days before.

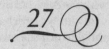

27

SHE KNEW, OF COURSE, THAT SHE WOULD EVEN-tually open the letter. She had known it from the moment Daniel had set it in in her hands. How could she not open it, reach out one more time to touch his life?

And yet she resented it. And hated him. For in four and a half months she had realized that she was not over the pain at all, that it would take many more months of determined living in the present before she would stop longing for him by day and aching for his arms at night.

She got up and made herself a cup of tea, drank it slowly and deliberately, looking at the letter propped against the vase the whole time.

And finally she admitted to herself that the reason for delay was not so much her resentment, her knowledge that to read his message would open all the wounds again, as something else entirely. The reason she delayed was that she knew that it would take only a few minutes to read the letter. And then there would be no more. Once again there would be the emptiness and the silence stretching out to infinity.

She set her cup and saucer aside, reached out for the letter, weighed it in her hands, lifted it to her lips, pressed it against her cheek.

Perhaps it was, after all, she thought, a letter from someone else in the house. From Mrs. Laycock, maybe. The thought set her stomach to churning and her fingers to tearing at the seal in a panic.

Her eyes went straight to the bottom of the page, to the signature. "Adam," he had signed himself in heavy bold handwriting. She bit down on her lower lip and closed her eyes briefly. And sat down in her chair again.

"My dearest Fleur," he had written, "I write to tell you of two bereavements in my family. My brother was killed in a fight in London a little more than a month ago. My wife died of accidental drowning the very day the news of his death reached Willoughby. I have buried them both, side by side, in the family burial ground."

Fleur lowered the letter to her lap. She closed her eyes tightly and set one hand over her mouth. Adam. Oh, poor Adam.

"Tomorrow I am taking Pamela traveling on the Continent," the letter continued. "She has been inconsolable. She adored Sybil. I shall stay away with her for the winter and perhaps for the full year of our mourning.

"When the year is over, I shall come into Wiltshire. I will say no more now. You will understand that the past month has been a distressing one. And I owe her a year of mourning, Fleur, and my brother, too, of course.

"I wanted you to know these things before I leave. And I will add that I meant every word of what I said to you when I was in Wiltshire."

Fleur lowered the letter to her lap again, folded it neatly, and noticed almost dispassionately that her hands were trembling.

She was dead. His wife was dead. He had written that she had died by accident, but she had died on the day word of Lord Thomas' death had come to them. And Lord Thomas was Lady Pamela's father. She had taken her own life, then. She must have thrown herself into the lake.

Oh, poor Adam. Poor Adam. How he would blame himself!

But she was dead. He was free. After the year of his mourning was over, he was going to come into Wiltshire. In eleven months' time. At the end of September.

No, she must not think it. She must not expect it. For eleven months seemed an endless eternity. Anything could happen in that time. One of them could die. He could have a change of heart. He could meet someone else on his travels. He could enjoy traveling so much that he would stay away for years. Lady Pamela could be unwilling for him to come to her.

Anything could happen. Eleven months ago she had not even met him. And yet it seemed that she had known him forever. That meant that she had longer than forever to wait, and then he might not come at the end of it.

She would not think of it, she decided, getting to her feet and propping the letter carefully against the vase again. She would not think of it. If he came at the end of the year, then she would hear what he had to say. If he did not come, then she would not be disappointed because she would not expect him.

And yet that night and for many nights to come she dreamed of him, strange, disturbing dreams in which he reached out to her an expanse of water just wide enough that she could not see him clearly and called to her in words she could not quite hear. And each time she awoke, her arms were empty and the bed beside her cold.

She redoubled her efforts to be a good teacher and gave up many of her spare hours to the instruction of music. And she visited her neighbors—particularly the elderly ones, who depended upon visitors to relieve the tedium of the day—and accepted every invitation she received. Even when Cousin Caroline came home—Amelia was married and living in Lincolnshire—and she knew that they would be at the same entertainment, she went too.

And she clung to her friendship with Miriam as if to a lifeline.

She was right about one thing, she thought whenever she

permitted herself to think consciously about the matter. Eleven months was longer than an eternity.

"WILL WE BE GOING home soon, Papa?" Lady Pamela Kent was sitting on the carriage seat opposite her father, stroking one finger up over the nose and over the top of the head of her dog, whose eyes were closing in ecstasy.

"Soon," he said. "Will you be glad? We have seen many wonders together in the past year, haven't we? Perhaps you will be dull at home."

"I can hardly wait," she said. "Why are we going to see Miss Hamilton, Papa? Is she going to be my governess again?"

"Would you like her to be?" he asked.

"Yes," she said after thinking for a moment. "But I would be afraid she would go away again." She looked up at him with suddenly anxious eyes. "You won't go away, Papa, will you? When we are at home, you won't go back to London and leave me alone?"

The old anxiety. For weeks after her mother's death she had woken screaming almost nightly, terrified that she had been abandoned. The Duke of Ridgeway smiled comfortingly at her. Even before they had set off on their travels he had had to spend almost every moment of every day with her. For a long time he had had to bring her into his bed at night so that his voice and his arms would be there for her when she woke up.

"I will not be going anywhere," he said. "From now on, Pamela, wherever I go, you will go too."

"I wonder if Timothy Chamberlain and the others have grown," she said.

"I daresay they have," he said. "Or maybe it was just the continental air that stretched you out."

She looked at him and giggled.

"What if we do not take Miss Hamilton back to Willoughby

as your governess?" he said. "What if we take her back as your new mama?"

She looked at him blankly. "But I have a mamá," she said.

"Yes." He knew that he should have broached the subject with her long before. But he had never found the right words or the courage. He was not sure that he had found the words yet. "You have a mama, Pamela, and she will always be more dear to you than anyone else in life until you grow up and have a family of your own. But since Mama cannot be with you any longer, wouldn't you like someone else who would do with you some of the things Mama would have done?"

"Miss Hamilton?" she said doubtfully.

"You like her, don't you?" he asked.

She hesitated. "Yes," she said. "But she went away without saying good-bye, Papa."

"That was not her fault," he said. "She would have done so if she could. But she had to run from a wicked man, Pamela, and had no chance to say good-bye to anyone. I believe she loved you."

"But if she is to be my mama," she said, "then she will have to be your wife, Papa. How would you like that?"

He looked at her gravely. "I would like it very well," he said.

"You would not find it a trouble to do that for me?" she asked, turning her head aside and wrinkling her nose as the dog sat up and tried to lick her face.

"No," he said. "It is something I want too, Pamela. You see, I love Miss Hamilton."

She pushed the dog away with uncharacteristic roughness. "But you love *me*!" she said.

"Of course I do." He moved across the carriage to sit beside her, and lifted her onto his lap. "You are my daughter. My first-born and my very own. Nothing will ever change that, Pamela. You will always be the first girl in my life. But we can all love more than one person. You loved Mama and you love me, don't you?"

"Yes," she said doubtfully. "And I love Tiny."

"Well, then," he said. "I love you and I love Miss Hamilton. And if she marries me and we have other children, I will love them too. And you will always be their eldest sister—always someone special."

"Is she going to come with us right away?" she asked. "I am going to show her Tiny. She will be surprised to see how big she has grown, won't she? And I am going to tell her that I was not sick on the boat. Don't you tell, Papa. Let me."

"Agreed," he said, resting his cheek against the top of her head. "I haven't asked her yet, Pamela. Maybe she will say no. Maybe she is quite happy where she is, teaching in her school and living in her little cottage. But I shall ask her." He chuckled. "Don't you ask. Let me."

"Agreed," his daughter said, and wriggled from his lap to worry the dog, who had settled peacefully on the other seat.

The duke sat back against the cushions and watched them. It was very possible that she would say no. Indeed, perhaps she was married already—to her Daniel or to some other gentleman of her neighborhood. He must not allow himself to hope too much.

A year before—or eleven months before, when he had finally pulled himself free of the worst of the nightmare surrounding the double death of his brother and his wife—he had felt confident of her answer though he had felt obliged to stay away from her during the year of his mourning. He had allowed himself only that one brief letter.

But eleven months seemed like an eternity. He and Pamela had traveled for the whole of that time and had seen many places and met many people. It seemed like longer than a year since he had been in England.

He could remember the words she had said to him—how could he ever forget? And he could remember the passionate abandon with which she had given herself to him on that one night before he left her. He had relived that night many times in his imagination. At the time he had believed that her love, like his own, would last for all eternity and even beyond. But now he was less sure.

Her love had not been of such long duration as his own. She had hated him and been repulsed by him—with good reason. It was only in those last days, when they had traveled together in search of Hobson's grave, that she had grown comfortable with him, that they had developed a friendship and become lovers.

It was understandable under the circumstances that they had ended up in each other's arms.

Perhaps for her there was no more to it than that. Genuine as her feelings had been at the time, perhaps they had faded in the days and weeks that had followed his departure. He must be prepared to find her cool and embarrassed by his visit.

He closed his eyes and allowed himself to be lulled by the motion of the carriage. He must not expect that she had thought of him every moment of every day—not consciously, perhaps, but deep down where feelings and meanings are. He must not expect that she had made him part of her dreams, both waking and sleeping. He must not expect that she was like him.

Fleur. He would see her the next day if she had not moved away.

At last. Ah, at last. The more than fifteen months since he had squeezed her hands and said good-bye and jumped into this very carriage to be taken away from her seemed longer than forever. Far longer.

FLEUR WAS TEACHING READING to a group of the youngest children while Miriam was conducting a geography lesson with the others.

But it was doubtful that anyone was learning a great deal, Fleur thought, smiling at one little boy to bring his attention back to the lesson. There was an air of suppressed excitement in the room. It did not take a great deal to excite these children. They were to go on a nature ramble as soon as morning classes were over, taking their luncheon with them. It was the end of September, the last opportunity they would have for such an outing before the weather grew too cold.

She and Miriam were to accompany the children, as well as Daniel, who often came into the school to give a scripture lesson, and Dr. Wetherald, who had been showing a marked preference for Miriam in the past several months, though Miriam declared in her usual cheerful, forthright manner that they were just friends. Fleur had been interested to note, though, that her friend blushed when saying so.

There really was no need of so many adult chaperones, Fleur thought, but it was a treat for them, too, to get out into the fresh air and the countryside for the whole of an afternoon.

A knock on the door destroyed the last vestiges of the children's attention. Fleur smiled and shook her head as the eyes of her group of children, and doubtless their minds too, followed Miriam to the door.

"Is Miss Hamilton here, please?" a polite young voice asked.

Fleur spun around on her chair.

"I am afraid there is no one of that name here, my dear," Miriam said. "Are you . . . ?"

"Pamela!" Fleur was up out of her chair and hurrying across the room, her arms outstretched. "Here I am. Oh, how tall you have grown, and how good it is to see you." She bent down to hug the child and was instantly aware of a tall, dark figure standing some distance behind her, against the crested carriage.

"Papa says the air of the Continent has made me grow," Lady Pamela said. "Tiny is in the carriage, Miss Hamilton. Wait until you see how she has grown. She is not tiny any longer.

And I was not sick coming across in the boat from France, though some of the ladies were."

Fleur was stooped down in front of her. "I am very proud of you," she said. "And are you on your way home?" If her life had depended upon it, she did not believe she could have shifted her gaze to the man standing a few feet away.

"Yes," Lady Pamela said. "I can scarcely wait. But Papa wanted to come here first. I am not to tell why. I got to tell you about not being sick on the boat."

Fleur laughed. And she was aware suddenly of the hum of voices behind her. She straightened up and turned.

"This is Lady Pamela Kent," she said, taking the child by the hand and drawing her into the schoolroom. "She has just come from a year of traveling on the Continent. This is Miss Booth, Pamela, and all the children of the village."

Lady Pamela smiled about her and moved closer to Fleur's side. Miriam was curtsying—to Lady Pamela and beyond her.

"Good morning, your grace," she said. "Children, make your bows and curtsies to his grace, the Duke of Ridgeway, if you please."

And Fleur turned her head jerkily at last and met his eyes.

And she felt instant shock. He was taller than she remembered, his hair blacker, his eyes more piercingly dark, his nose more prominent, his scar more noticeable. All had been softened in memory. She felt an unexpected surging of the old fear.

She curtsied to him. "Your grace," she murmured.

He inclined his head to her and to the room in general. "Good morning," he said. "I hate to interrupt classes, but if I know young people and the way their minds work, I would guess that I am the most popular man in the village at the moment."

Giggles from the girls, shouts of laughter from the boys.

Classes were at an end, it seemed. The girls were openly admiring Lady Pamela's fashionable clothes and she was eyeing them with shy interest. The boys were gazing at the duke in some awe. He was conversing politely with Miriam. And then Dr. Wetherald was there, and Daniel too, and Lady Pamela was gazing pleadingly up at her father.

"May I, Papa?" she was saying. "Oh, please, may I?"

"You are hardly dressed to go rambling," he was saying with a smile.

"But I have other dresses," she said. "I can change. Oh, please, Papa. Please. Miss Hamilton, may I go? Please?"

Miriam was looking very directly at her. It was Miriam, it seemed, who had suggested that Lady Pamela might enjoy joining the school ramble, though his grace must realize that they intended to be gone for several hours.

"Only Papa can say yes to that," Fleur said, smiling at the eager, pretty face of her former pupil. "But I know you would have a great deal of fun."

One minute later Lady Pamela was dashing for the carriage, having been granted the permission she had begged for.

"I am going to bring Tiny," she shrieked. "May I, Miss Hamilton?"

Miriam was laughing. "I will take very good care of her, your grace," she said. "And my brother and Dr. Wetherald will be with me to lend a hand. Three adults will be more than enough. We will not need your presence, Isabella. You had better stay to entertain his grace, since he will have a wait of several hours."

Fleur opened her mouth to speak and closed it again.

It seemed that all the children found it impossible to speak in less than a shriek. The schoolroom sounded very quiet indeed when all of them and the three adults had set off on their way.

"Miss Booth is a kind lady," the Duke of Ridgeway said from behind her shoulder. "Pamela will talk about this treat for weeks to come."

"Yes," she said. "I am glad for her, your grace."

"Your grace?" he said quietly.

She glanced over her shoulder and fixed her eyes on his neckcloth.

"Can we go somewhere else?" he asked. "To your home, maybe?"

"Yes," she said. "It is quite close by."

She locked the school carefully and walked by his side along the street to her cottage. They did not touch or speak a single word.

28

SHE LAID DOWN THE BOOKS SHE HAD BEEN CARRY-
ing and watched him set his hat and gloves on a table. She
turned and led the way into a square and cozy parlor, the
pianoforte in one corner dwarfing the rest of the furniture in
the room.

It was as he had thought, as he had led himself to expect.
She was not really pleased to see him. She was awkward and
embarrassed.

"Won't you have a seat, your gr . . . ?" Her hand was gestur-
ing to a chair. She stopped and flushed.

So very beautiful. His breath had caught in his throat as
soon as he had seen her stooping down to hug Pamela. More
beautiful even than he had remembered. There was a poise
about her, a sense of dignity that was more pronounced than it
had been before.

He was very aware of his own ugliness, of his scar. And he
had to consciously resist the impulse to turn sideways so that
she would not see it.

"I shall ring for some tea," she said, "and for something to
eat. It is luncheontime. Doubtless you have been traveling
since breakfast, have you? You must be hungry."

"I am not," he said quietly. "Are you happy, then? The

school seems to be a merry place. This is a cozy cottage, and larger than I expected."

"Yes." She smiled at him. "I am happy. I am doing what I like doing, and I am surrounded by my friends."

"I am glad," he said. "I had to come to make sure."

"Thank you," she said. "That was good of you. You must be very eager to be home, having been away so long."

"Yes," he said. "Very eager."

And yet, he thought, he had not prepared himself well at all. He had thought he had. He had thought he was prepared for the worst. But his heart was a lead weight in his chest and he could not think of home or the winter ahead or of all the years after that.

Not without Fleur. Willoughby would not be home without her, or the future worth living. Not after a year of hope that he had tried to persuade himself was not hope at all.

She plumped a cushion on a chair quite unnecessarily and sat down, although he had not accepted her invitation to seat himself.

And she searched in her mind for something to say and kept her expression politely bright.

For a whole month—for eleven months—she had persuaded herself that he would not come, that he would forget about her, regret his hasty words of love to her. And yet for the past month she had expected him hourly and told herself and told herself that he would not come.

He was standing in her parlor, his hands behind his back, looking dark and morose, looking as if he wished to be anywhere else on earth but where he was.

He had come out of a sense of duty, because he had said he would come. Adam and his damnable sense of duty! She hated him again, wished him a million miles away.

"You have not been troubled by Brocklehurst or his family?" he asked her stiffly.

"No," she said. "I have heard nothing of Matthew, though

rumor has placed him anywhere from South America to India. Cousin Caroline is here, but I believe she intends to visit her daughter for the winter."

"And the Reverend Booth and his sister are still your friends," he said. "I am glad."

"Yes," she said.

She wished with all her heart that Lady Pamela had not gone on the ramble. She wished that he could leave without further delay. She wished she could start living the rest of her life.

If only he had not allowed Pamela to go with the other children, he thought. If only there were some way he could leave immediately. He could take himself off to the village inn, he supposed, but if he suggested doing so, she would think that she had failed in hospitality.

"Thank you for the pianoforte," she said. "I have not had a chance to thank you before. You intended it to be kept in the schoolroom, of course, but both Miriam and Daniel agreed that it would be safer here."

"You know that it was a gift for you alone," he said.

And he watched broodingly as she flushed and looked down at her clasped hands. Her knuckles were white with tension.

He remembered her hands touching him, moving lightly over the wounds on his side. He remembered her telling him he was beautiful. He remembered her telling him that she loved him. He felt an almost overwhelming sadness. He strolled toward the pianoforte and stood looking down at the keys. He depressed one of them.

"The tone is good?" he asked.

"It is a beautiful instrument," she said. "It is my most prized possession."

He smiled, and he glanced up at the vase standing on the pianoforte and the letter propped against it. He reached out and picked the letter up.

"This is my letter to you," he said.

"Yes." She got to her feet, flushing, and reached out a hand for it.

"Has it been there for almost a year?" he asked.

"Yes." She laughed breathlessly. "It must have been. I am not a very tidy person."

He glanced about him at the neat, uncluttered room. And he felt a quite unreasonable surging of hope.

"Why?" he asked her. "Why do you keep it there?"

She shrugged. "I . . . I don't know," she said foolishly. She could think of no reasonable explanation. How foolish he would think her. How humiliating if he should guess the truth. She smiled, her hand still outstretched for the letter. "I shall put it away."

"Fleur?" he said.

She dropped her hand. She had told him just a little more than a year before that she loved him and always would. Should she be ashamed now that she had spoken the simple truth? Was pride to be guarded at all costs?

"Because it is not only the pianoforte that is my most treasured possession," she said, fixing her eyes on the top button of his waistcoat. "That is too. I keep them together."

"Fleur," he said softly.

"I have nothing else of you," she said. "Just those two things."

She wished she could see that button clearly. She wished that he would not see her with tears in her eyes. But she was not ashamed of loving him. She had said she would and she did.

She watched the blur of white as he tossed the letter aside. She watched his waistcoat come closer. She felt his hands framing her face.

Her jaw was set hard. Her face looked as if made of stone. But there were the tears glistening on her eyelashes. And there were her words. And the letter, propped on top of the pianoforte almost a year after she had received it.

"My love," he said, cupping her face in his hands. If she was to reject him, then so be it. But she would know that he had kept faith with her, that he still loved her more than life and would do so always.

He watched her bite at her upper lip, reach out with trembling hands to touch his waistcoat, withdraw her hands again.

"I love you," he said. "Nothing has changed in the fifteen months since I told you that. And nothing will ever change."

"Oh," she said. She could find no other words and knew that she would not be able to speak them even if she did. She reached out to touch him again and found her hands to be as far beyond her control as her voice was.

But she did not have to find words. Or control. His head bent to hers and his lips touched her own and parted over them, and his hands left her cheeks, one arm to come about her shoulders and the other about her waist. She was drawn against the strength of him, and it did not matter that she was trembling.

Fleur. Soft and warm and feminine, her body arched unashamedly to his, her lips parting beneath his own, her mouth opening to his tongue, her arms coming up about his neck.

Fleur. He allowed himself the full luxury of hope.

"I love you too," she whispered against his mouth. She kept her eyes closed. There could be no more thought to pride. "I have not stopped loving you for even a moment. And the letter is not always against the vase. Only by day. By night it is beneath my pillow."

"On the assumption that the pianoforte is too large to put there?" he said with such unexpected humor that she burst into laughter.

He joined in the laughter and hugged her to him.

"Fleur," he said at last against her ear, "this cannot really be the first time I have laughed in a year, can it? But it feels like it."

She drew her head back and looked fully at him for the first time. "I thought I would never see you again," she said. "When you broke every bone in my hands that morning and jumped into your carriage and drove away, I thought I would never ever see you again."

"Well," he said, smiling at her, "that should be no tragedy. I am not much to look at, am I?"

"I don't know," she said, tilting her head to one side. "Aren't you? To me you are all the world."

"A dark and scarred world," he said.

"A beautiful world," she said. "A face with character. The face I love most in all the world."

He took her quite by surprise suddenly by bending down and scooping her up into his arms and sitting with her on his lap on a sofa.

"Guess what I have in my pocket," he said.

"I don't know." She circled his neck with her arms and smiled at him. "A priceless jewel you bought for me."

"No," he said. "Try again."

"A snuffbox," she said.

"I don't use the stuff," he said. "You are not even close."

"A linen handkerchief," she said.

"My other pocket." He was laughing again, and she with him. "What do I have in my other pocket?"

"I don't know," she said. "How am I supposed to guess?"

"You should know," he said. "What, of all other things, would I be sure to bring with me when I came for you at last?"

She shook her head, her smile fading.

"A special license," he said, suddenly serious too. "A special license, my love, so that I can make you mine without delay once I have got you to say yes."

"Adam," she said, touching his scarred cheek. "Oh, Adam."

"Will you?" he said. "Will you marry me, Fleur? I know I am no prize, and you know some unsavory things about me. But you would have my undivided love and devotion for the rest of a lifetime. And you would be a duchess, if that is any lure, and mistress of Willoughby. Will you, Fleur?"

"Adam," she said, tracing the line of the scar downward from his eye to the corner of his mouth. "Think carefully, do. Think of what you know about me, about what I was, what I am."

"A whore?" he said so that her eyes flew to his in shock and her face flushed painfully. "I am going to tell you something, Fleur, and I want you to listen very carefully. Sybil had consumption. It is very unlikely that she would have survived this year. But she could have had that year or part of it, anyway. She could have had my support and even affection and all of Pamela's love. But she had had one cruel disappointment in life and another lesser one last summer. She lost her will to live. She would not accept the comfort I tried to give her. She almost totally ignored Pamela. And finally, when she had word of Thomas' death—before I did—she took what little remained of her life."

"The poor lady," Fleur said. "I do feel desperately sorry for her, Adam."

"So did I," he said. "But listen to me, Fleur. You were put into a dreadful situation over a year ago. You faced either a noose about your neck or a nightmare of a marriage if you went back home, or starvation if you stayed in hiding. But did you give in to self-pity? No. You fought, doing everything you had to do to survive. You did the ultimate, Fleur. You became a whore. I pity my wife. I honor you more than I can say in words."

She swallowed. "Perhaps because you know you were the only one," she said. "How would you feel if there had been a dozen others? Two dozen? More?"

"Fit to kill," he said. "Before my marriage, Fleur, I slept with more than a dozen women. I could not possibly put a number on them, the women I bedded. How do you feel about that?"

She was silent for a while. "Fit to kill," she said.

"Does it make you stop loving me?" he asked.

"No." She laid a palm against his cheek. "That is in the past,

Adam. I have no control over that and you cannot change it. I don't care about your past."

"And I don't care about yours," he said. "Will you be my duchess, Fleur?"

"Pamela?" she said.

"She seemed a little troubled that I was willing to sacrifice myself by making you my wife just so that I could also make you her mama," he said. "I had to assure her that it was what I wanted too." He smiled.

"She adored her mother," she said.

"Yes, and always will," he said. "We will have to make sure that she never forgets Sybil, Fleur. And we will hope that memory somewhat distorts the truth. We will hope that she remembers Sybil as a constantly attentive mother as well as a beautiful and indulgent one. You will never be her mother, but you can be her stepmother. And I can tell you from experience that it is possible for her to love both. I have faint, flashing images of my mother and have always associated those images with unconditional love. But I was dearly fond of my stepmother, Thomas' mother."

She lowered her head to his shoulder.

"Will you marry me?"

"Yes," she said, and closed her eyes. There were no other words to say. How could one put into words a happiness that filled one so full to the brim that it was almost a pain?

He settled his cheek against the top of her head and closed his eyes. And felt that there was no further need of words for the moment. It was as he remembered it the night they made love. They could communicate more perfectly through the silence than through the imperfection of words.

"I have a confession to make," he said at last. "I dreaded having a letter from you to say you were with child, and yet I looked for that letter and hoped for it. You see how in my selfishness I would have made you suffer?"

"I cried when I knew I was not," she said.

He laughed softly and turned her face up to his with one hand at her chin and kissed her deeply and lingeringly.

"We will have you with child just as soon as can be," he said. "Tonight maybe?"

"Tonight?" She was laughing against his neck.

"On our wedding night," he said. "Is it too soon?"

"Tonight?"

"We can wait if you want," he said. "We can have a planned wedding. We can have it in London if you wish, with half the *ton* in attendance. I daresay even the king would come if we invited him. But I would rather have it today, Fleur. We could spend our first night here in your cottage. Do you have a guest room for Pamela?"

"Yes," she said, touching his lips with one light finger. "I have dreamed of having you here with me, Adam. My arms have been so empty without you and my bed so cold."

"They will not be empty tonight, my love," he said, "and the bed will be warm. And you will not need to dream any longer. It will all be reality."

"I won't need your letter beneath my pillow tonight," she said.

"Or the pianoforte either," he said, and they both laughed and hugged each other.

"Oh, Adam," she said, "I have been so lonely without you. It has seemed such an eternity."

He turned her face up again and they smiled at each other.

"No longer," he said. "No more loneliness, Fleur, for either of us. Only our marriage and our children and Willoughby and growing old together. Only our love forever." He lowered his head and kissed her mouth softly. "And longer than forever."

Return to Dianne Walker
991-242-8136
6-22-13 / 6-24-13

About the Author

*M*ARY BALOGH is the *New York Times* bestselling author of the acclaimed Slightly novels: *Slightly Married, Slightly Wicked, Slightly Scandalous, Slightly Tempted, Slightly Sinful,* and *Slightly Dangerous,* as well as the romances *No Man's Mistress, More Than a Mistress,* and *One Night for Love.* She is also the author of *Simply Unforgettable, Simply Love, Simply Magic,* and *Simply Perfect,* her dazzling quartet of novels set at Miss Martin's School for Girls. A former teacher herself, Balogh grew up in Wales and now lives in Canada.

If you loved

The Secret Pearl,

don't miss

Simply Love,

the breathtaking novel
from *New York Times* bestselling
author Mary Balogh as she continues the
enthralling story of four remarkable
women—friends and teachers at Miss Martin's School
for Girls. At the center of this spellbinding novel is
Anne Jewell, a teacher haunted by a scandalous past . . .
until she meets a man who teaches her
the most important lesson of all:
Nothing is simple when it comes to love . . .

On sale now
Read on for a peek!

MARY
BALOGH

SIMPLY
LOVE

*I*T WAS NOT THAT HE FELT INTIMIDATED, BUT Sydnam Butler was nevertheless moving out of Glandwr House into the thatched, whitewashed cottage that lay in a small clearing among the trees not far from the sea cliffs on one side and the park gates and driveway on the other.

As steward of the estate for the past five years, Sydnam had lived in his own spacious apartments in the main house, and he had always continued to live there even when the owner, the Duke of Bewcastle, was in residence. Bewcastle had always come alone and had never stayed for longer than a few weeks at a time.

But this coming visit was going to be altogether different from what he was accustomed to. This time Bewcastle was bringing his wife with him. Sydnam had never met the Duchess of Bewcastle. He had heard from his brother Kit, Viscount Ravensberg, who lived on the estate adjoining Lindsey Hall, that she was a jolly good sort, who had been known to coax laughter even from such a perennial iceberg as Bewcastle.

Sydnam was somewhat shy with strangers, especially when they were to be sharing a roof with him. And no sooner had he grown accustomed to the idea that the duchess was accompanying Bewcastle on this particular visit than he received another brief letter from his grace's secretary to the effect that all the other Bedwyns were coming too, with their spouses and children, to spend a month or so by the sea.

Sydnam had grown up with the Bedwyns. They had all been playmates together, despite a broad range in their ages—the boisterous Bedwyn boys; the fierce Freyja, who had always refused to be treated as a girl; and Morgan, who though the youngest of them all and female to boot had usually found a way to be included in the frolics; and the Butlers, Kit and Sydnam and their late eldest brother, Jerome. All except Wulfric, now Bewcastle, in fact.

Sydnam was not intimidated by the prospect of their coming to Glandwr, then. He was only a little overwhelmed by it. They were all married now. He had met some of their spouses—Lady Aidan, Lady Rannulf, the Marquess of Hallmere—and he had found them all amiable enough. And they all had children now.

Sydnam was not a recluse. As Bewcastle's steward he had to see all sorts of people on business. There were also neighbors who liked to consult him on farming issues and other matters to do with the land and the community in which they all lived together. And he had a few personal friends—the Welsh minister and the schoolmaster in particular. His acquaintances were almost exclusively male, though. There had been one or two women during the past five years who had indicated a willingnesss to pursue a relationship with him—it was no secret, he supposed, that he was a son of the Earl of Redfield and independently wealthy even though he worked for a living. But he had given them no encouragement. He had always been very well aware that it was his social status and his wealth that had encouraged them to overlook a physical revulsion that none of them had been quite able to hide.

Having to face the bustle of a large gathering at Glandwr was just too much for him when he was accustomed to the vast, empty, quiet house. And so he was moving out and into the cottage, at least until the house was empty again.

He resented the expected intrusion, if the truth were known, even though he knew that he had no right to object to a man's coming to his own home with his own wife and his brothers and sisters—and anyone else he chose to invite, for that matter.

He did not look forward to the summer.

He would stay out of the way as much as he was able. He would try at least to remain out of sight of the children. He did not want to frighten them. The worst feeling in the world was to see fear, revulsion, horror, and panic on the faces of children and to know that it was his own appearance that had caused it.

One month, Bewcastle's secretary had written. Thirty-one days, if that statement was to be taken literally. It seemed like an eternity.

But he would survive it.

He had survived a great deal worse. There had been days—and nights—when he had wished he had not done so. Survived, that was.

But he had.

And in more recent years he had been glad that he had.

ANNE HAD INSISTED UPON TRAVELING the long distance to the Duke of Bewcastle's estate in Wales in the marquess's second carriage with the children and their nurse, despite the fact that at each stop she was urged to join Joshua and Lady Hallmere in theirs. She preferred to think of herself as a servant rather than a guest—and good heavens, the duke and duchess did not even know she was coming!

It was a thought that sometimes brought her close to panic. They would quite possibly have strong objections even if she did hide in the nursery for the whole month.

They arrived late in the afternoon of the third day, turning off the coast road with its scenery that reminded Anne of Cornwall to pass between two large open gates and proceed along a driveway that wound between shrubs and trees and eventually rolling lawns to either side.

"Oh, look, Mama." David, who had been seated quietly beside her while both Daniel and Emily slept on the seat opposite, Emily in the nurse's arms, suddenly plucked at her sleeve and pointed ahead. The side of his face was pressed against the glass.

Anne tipped her head sideways and looked. The house had come into view, and the sight of it did nothing to settle the butterflies that were dancing in her stomach. Glandwr was indeed a vast mansion of gray brick in the Palladian style. It was both impressive and beautiful. And yet, she thought, this was not even the duke's principal seat. He spent only a week or two of each year here, Joshua had said.

How could anyone be *that* wealthy?

"I can hardly *wait*," David said, his eyes huge, his cheeks flushed. "Will the other children be here already?"

He felt none of Anne's misgivings, of course. He felt only excitement over the prospect of having other children—other boys—to play with for a whole month.

Fortunately their actual arrival occured in a flurry of cheerful confusion as the three carriages drew up on the graveled terrace before the main doors and disgorged their passengers and luggage while at the same time a vast number of people spilled out of the house to greet them. Among them Anne recognized the tall, dark figure of Lord Aidan Bedwyn with his military bearing and the dark, lovely Lady Morgan Bedwyn, whose married name she could not recall. She had met them in Cornwall four years ago.

David was swept forward by a newly awakened, bright-cheeked Daniel to be caught up in all the noise and bustle of the greetings—one would have thought that none of them had seen one another for a decade instead of a week or so. Anne abandoned him and hurried inside through a side entrance with the nurse.

She had no wish whatsoever to be mistaken for a guest.

She was not to remain unnoticed, though, she soon discovered. The housekeeper came looking for her after she had been in the nursery for a while, seeing David settled in the large room he was to share with Davy and Alexander and watching him glow with excitement as he met all the children and was absorbed into their midst as if he had been one of them all his life.

He was in safe hands, Anne realized as she followed the housekeeper down to the floor below and into a sizable bedchamber with comfortable furnishings, pretty floral curtains and bed hangings, and a view of the sea in the distance.

It was unmistakably a guest chamber rather than a servant's room, she saw with some dismay. She ought to have clarified her exact status here with Joshua and Lady Hallmere before their arrival. She ought to have made it clear to them that she wanted to be classed with the servants, or at least with the nurses and governesses—if there were any of the latter. But then she had assumed that it did not need to be said.

"I hope I have not put you to a great deal of trouble," she said with an apologetic smile, "arriving unexpectedly like this."

"I was delighted, mum, when Mr. Butler said the duke and duchess were coming with a large party," the housekeeper told her with a pronounced Welsh accent. "We don't see company often enough here. Mr. Butler hired extra help and I had every room in the house prepared just in case. So it's no trouble at all. I'm Mrs. Parry, mum."

"Thank you, Mrs. Parry," Anne said. "What a lovely view."

"It is that," the housekeeper agreed, "though the view from the back rooms is just as grand. You will want to tidy up and maybe rest awhile, mum. I'll send a maid up to unpack your things for you."

"There really is no need," Anne assured her hastily. Heavens, she was not *really* a guest. She was certainly not entitled to the services of a maid. "But the idea of a rest sounds very inviting."

SHE UNPACKED HER MODEST TRUNK and put everything away—she even found that there was a dressing room attached to her bedchamber. She lay down on the bed when she was finished, more because she did not know what else to do than because she was weary.

She would cheerfully cower right here in this room for the next month, given half a chance, she thought. But—sadly—it was too late to wish yet again that she had remained in Bath.

She fell asleep while she was in the middle of worrying.

When she awoke an indeterminate amount of time later, she jumped hastily off the bed and washed her hands and face. If the promised maid should arrive, she would perhaps not be able to avoid going down to dinner. She could not *possibly* do that. She was ravenously hungry, she realized, not having eaten since luncheon at a wayside inn, but being hungry and alone seemed preferable to having to dine with the duke and his family.

Good heavens, did Joshua really expect that she would be *welcomed* into their midst? As a social equal?

She slipped on her outdoor shoes and wrapped a cloak about herself in case the sea air was chilly. She could not avoid mealtimes for a whole month, of course, but perhaps by tomorrow she would feel sufficiently rested and in command of herself to suggest to the housekeeper that other arrangements be made for her accommodation and meals.

She slipped out down the back stairs and through the side door by which she had entered the house earlier. She hurried down the driveway, not sure where she was going exactly, but not really caring as long as it was far enough away to be out of sight of the house. Just past the thatched cottage, before she had to make the decision whether to leave the park entirely or turn back, she noticed a well-worn path to her right that must lead to the sea, which she had been able to see from the window of her bedchamber.

She turned and walked along it and soon found that she was indeed on top of high cliffs with the sea below and coarse grass to either side of the path and some gorse bushes and other wild flowers.

There was something about the sea that had always called to her spirit. Somehow it reminded her of her littleness in the grand scheme of things, and yet strangely that was a soothing rather than a belittling thought. It made her feel a part of something vast, her own little worries and concerns of no great moment after all. When she was close to the sea, she could believe that all was well—and somehow always would be.

She could have lived contentedly in Cornwall for the rest of her life if only . . .

Well, if only.

She would not have lived there all her life anyway. She had been going to marry Henry Arnold, and he lived in Gloucestershire, where she had grown up.

She sat where she was for a long time until she realized that the evening was now well advanced. She was suddenly glad of her cloak. The day had been warm, but dusk was approaching, and the breeze blowing off the sea was fresh and slightly moist. It smelled and tasted salty.

She got to her feet, scrambled back up to the cliff path, and strolled onward, her face lifted to the breeze, alternating her gaze between the beauty of the gradually darkening sky above and the corresponding loveliness of the sea below, which seemed to be absorbing the light from the sky so that it turned silver even as the gray overhead deepened—one of the universe's little mysteries.

It was as she walked onward that she became aware that she was not the only person out taking the evening air. There was a man standing out on a slight promontory ahead of her. He was gazing out to sea, unaware of her presence.

Anne stood quite still, undecided whether to turn back in the hope that he would not see her at all or to hurry past him with a brief greeting and a hope not to be detained.

She did not believe she had seen him before. He was not either Lord Aidan Bedwyn or Lord Alleyne. But he was probably one of the other Bedwyns or their spouses. This was, after all, the duke's land, though it was possible he allowed strangers to wander here beyond the cultivated bounds of the park.

It was still only dusk. There was light by which to see the man. And as she looked Anne found it difficult either to retreat or to advance. She stood and stared instead.

He was not dressed for evening. He wore breeches and top boots, a tight fitting coat and waistcoat, and a white shirt and cravat. He was hatless. He was a tall man, with broad shoulders, slender waist and hips, and powerfully muscled legs. His dark, short hair was ruffled by the breeze.

But it was his face, seen in profile, that held Anne transfixed. With its finely chiseled features it was an extraordinarily handsome face. The word *beautiful* came to mind, inappropriate as it seemed to describe a man. He might have been a poet—or a god.

He might well be, she thought, the most beautiful man she had ever set eyes upon.

She felt a craving to see him full face, but he was obviously still quite unaware of her presence. He looked as if he were in a world of his own, one that held him quite motionless, the gathering gray of the evening sky sharpening his silhouette as she gazed at him.

Something stirred inside her, something that had lain dormant in her for years and years—and something that must *remain* dormant. Good heavens, he was a total stranger, and if her guess was correct he was someone's husband. He was certainly not someone about whom to weave romantic fantasies.

She could not simply retreat, she decided. He would probably see her and think her behavior peculiar, even discourteous. She could only continue on her way and hope that a cheerful *good evening* would take her past him without the necessity of introductions or the embarrassment of having to walk back to the house with him, making labored conversation.

She wished then that she had decided to go back. But it was too late to do that. As she approached closer to the man, keeping to the footpath that would pass behind the promontory on which he stood, he became aware of her and turned rather sharply toward her.

She stopped short, not more than twenty feet from him.

And she stood transfixed again—but with horror this time. The empty right sleeve of his coat was pinned against his side. But it was the right side of his face that caused the horror. Perhaps it was a trick of the evening light, but it seemed to her that there was nothing there, though afterward she did recall seeing a black eye patch.

He was a man with half a face, the extraordinary beautiful left side all the more grotesque because there was no right side to balance it. He was beauty and beast all rolled into one. And all of a sudden his height and those powerful thighs and broad shoulders seemed menacing rather than enticing. And equally suddenly the beauty of the gathering darkness and the peaceful solitude of the scene were filled with danger and the threat of an unknown evil.

She thought he took one step toward her. She did not wait to see if he would take another. She turned and ran, leaving the path and the cliff top behind her, half stumbling over the uneven ground, tugging at her cloak as it snagged against gorse bushes, and feeling the sharp sting of their scratches on her legs.

The trees surrounding the inner park were dark and threatening as she crashed through them, making all sorts of loud noises to reveal where she was. The lawn when she reached it looked dauntingly wide and very open, but she had no alternative but to dash across it and hope that at least she would be within screaming distance of the house before he caught up with her.

But her first panic was receding, and when she glanced quickly and fearfully over her shoulder, she could see that she was alone, that he had not followed her. And with that realization came a return of some rationality.

And deep shame.

Was she a child to believe in monsters?

He was merely a man who must have suffered some fearful accident. He had been out to take the air, as she had. He had been minding his own business, enjoying his own solitude, gazing quietly at the view, perhaps as affected by its loveliness as she had been. He had not said or done anything that was remotely threatening except to take that one step toward her. Probably all he had intended was to bid her a good evening and go on his way.

She felt quite mortified then.

She had run from him because he was maimed. She had judged him a monster purely on the strength of his outward appearance. And yet she had a reputation for tenderness toward the weak and handicapped. When she became a governess, she had deliberately taken a position with a child who was not normal, according to the definition of normality that society had concocted. She had loved Prue Moore dearly. She still did. And she was forever instilling into the girls at school and into David her conviction that every human being was a precious soul worthy of respect and courtesy and love.

Hunger and shame made her feel somewhat light-headed. But she closed her eyes, drew in deep lungfuls of sea air, and then opened her eyes and deliberately returned the way she had just come.

Darkness was definitely falling now, and she was aware that

she ought not to be wandering thus in a strange place. But she had to go back and make amends if she could.

She came to the path she had been following. And there, she thought as she looked about to get her bearings, was surely the promontory. She looked left and right and decided that yes, that was certainly the place where he had been standing.

But he was no longer there.

She could not see him anywhere.

She hung her head and stood where she was for some time. She might have said good evening to him and nodded genially. He probably would have replied in kind. And she might then have walked onward, content with her behavior, and mourned whatever it was that had destroyed his beauty.

But she had recoiled from him, run away in fright and revulsion. How had he felt? Was this how other people treated him too? Poor man. At least all her hurts were inner ones. People—especially men who had looked on her with admiration and interest—sometimes shrank from her when they knew her for what she was, an unwed mother, but at least she could walk along a street or a cliff path without causing anyone to turn in horror and run.

How *could* she have done it? How could she? And now she had been suitably punished for her cowardice in running away from the house. She had been discourteous—worse!— to a fellow human being who had in no way offended or hurt her.

It was suitable punishment, she thought as she drew near to the house and her stomach rumbled with emptiness, that she must go hungry to bed.

She could not get the maimed man out of her mind all night. She kept waking and thinking of him.

Poor man. What must it be like to carry one's pain and one's deformities like that, for all to see? Ah, the loneliness of it!

Poor man.

But such beauty! Such physical perfection to have been so cruelly destroyed!

SYDNAM WATCHED HER GO. For a moment he considered going after her, but he would only increase her panic by doing that.

Besides, he did not feel at all kindly disposed toward her.

Who the devil *was* she? Lady Alleyne Bedwyn perhaps? She was the only one of the Bedwyn wives he had not met. But what had she been doing out here alone? Why was Alleyne not with her? And had no one warned her about the monster who was Bewcastle's steward?

He had been in another world. Or rather he had been in this world, but he had been deeply immersed in the final, breathtaking moments of a dying day, with the sun just dropped behind the western horizon but the night not yet quite descended. It was a scene of grays and silvers and majesty. His right hand had itched to grasp his paintbrush more tightly so that he could reproduce the scene both as he saw it and as he felt it. But he had resisted the urge to flex the fingers of that hand, knowing that as soon as he did so he would have to admit to himself, yet again, that it was a phantom hand he carried at his side, that both it and his right arm were no longer there, just as his right eye was no longer there.

But he had still not come to the moment of that admission. He had still been transported by beauty. He had still been immersed in the illusion of happiness.

And then something—a flutter at the corner of his eye, a footfall, perhaps—had brought awareness crashing back and he had sensed that he was no longer alone.

And when he had turned, there she was.

For that moment before it happened the woman standing on the path had seemed part of the beauty of the evening. She had looked tall and willowy, her cloak flapping in the breeze and revealing a dress of lighter color beneath. She had not been wearing a bonnet. Her hair was fair, perhaps even blond, her face oval and blue-eyed and lovely.

She had looked like beauty personified. For one moment he had thought...

Ah, what was it he had thought?

That she had walked out of the night into his dreams?

It was embarrassing even to consider that that was perhaps what he had thought before he had come jolting back to reality.

But certainly he had taken a step toward her without speaking a word. And she had stood there, apparently waiting for him.

And then he had seen the horror in her eyes. And then she had turned and fled in panic.

What had he expected? That she would smile and open her arms to him?

He gazed after her and was again Sydnam Butler, grotesquely ugly with his right eye gone and the purple scars of the old burns down the side of his face, paralyzing most of the nerves there, and all along his armless side to his knee.

He was Sydnam Butler, who would never paint again, and for whom no woman would ever walk beautiful out of the night.

But he had left self-pity behind long ago, and resented moments such as this when defenses had been lowered and it crept back in like a persistent and unwelcome guest to torment him. He knew that it would take him days to recover his equilibrium, to remind himself that he was now Sydnam Butler, the best and most efficient steward of the several Bewcastle employed to run his various estates—and that was the duke's assessment, not his own.

He did not linger on the promotory. The magic was gone. The silver had gone from the sea to be replaced by a heaving gray, soon to be black. The sky no longer held even the memory of sunset. The breeze had turned chilly. It was time to go home.

He headed off along the path, in the direction from which the woman had come. After a few steps he realized that he was limping again and made a determined effort not to.

He was more glad than ever that he had moved out of the house and into the cottage. He liked it there. He might even stay after Bewcastle and all the others had returned home. A cottage, with a cook, a housekeeper, and a valet, was all a single man needed for his comfort.

Belatedly it struck him that there had been nothing grand about either the woman's cloak or the dress beneath it, and her hair had not been dressed elaborately. She must be just one of the servants who had come with the visitors.

It was a relief to realize that she was only a servant. There was less of a chance that he would see her again. Whenever she had any free time from now on, he did not doubt that she would stay far away from the cliffs and the beach, where she might encounter the monster of Glandwr again.

For an unguarded moment he had yearned toward her with his whole body and soul.

He thought resentfully that she would probably haunt his dreams for several nights to come.

If only he knew exactly how long Bewcastle intended to stay, he thought as he let himself into the cottage and closed the door gratefully behind him, he could begin counting down the days, like a child waiting for some longed-for treat.